THIS
SAVAGE
SONG

this Savage Song

A MONSTERS OF VERITY NOVEL

VICTORIA SCHWAB

GREENWILLOW BOOKS
An Imprint of HarperCollinsPublishers

This Savage Song

Copyright © 2016 by Victoria Schwab

The text of this book is set in 12-point Dante MT Regular.

Book design by Paul Zakris

Library of Congress Cataloging-in-Publication Data

Names: Schwab, Victoria, author.

Title: This savage song / Victoria Schwab.

Description: First edition. | New York, NY : Greenwillow Books,
    an imprint of HarperCollins Publishers, [2016] |
    Series: Monsters of Verity ; 1 |

Summary: "As the heirs to opposing sides in a warring city, Kate Harker
    and Augustus Flynn should never have met. A Romeo and Juliet-esque
    fantasy about the difference between good and evil and the blurry gray
    area in between"—Provided by publisher.

Identifiers: LCCN 2016005221 | ISBN 9780062380852 (trade ed.)
    —ISBN 9780062380869 (pbk. ed.)

Subjects: | CYAC: Good and evil—Fiction. | Love—Fiction. | Fantasy.

Classification: LCC PZ7.S39875 Th 2016 | DDC [Fic]—dc23
    LC record available at https://lccn.loc.gov/2016005221

18 19 20 21 PC/LSCC 10 9 8 7 6 5 4

First paperback edition, 2017

 GREENWILLOW BOOKS

To the strange, and the mad, and the monstrous

Plenty of humans are monstrous,
and plenty of monsters know how to play at being human.

—V. A. VALE

PRELUDE

KATE

The night Kate Harker decided to burn down the school chapel, she wasn't angry or drunk. She was desperate.

Burning down the church was really a last resort; she'd already broken a girl's nose, smoked in the dormitories, cheated on her first exam, and verbally harassed three of the nuns. But no matter what she did, St. Agnes Academy kept *forgiving* her. That was the problem with Catholic schools. They saw her as someone to be saved.

But Kate didn't need salvation; she simply needed out.

It was almost midnight when her shoes hit the grass below the dorm window. The witching hour, people used to call it, that dark time when restless spirits reached for freedom. Restless spirits, and teenage girls trapped in boarding schools too far from home.

She made her way down the manicured stone path that ran from the dormitories to the Chapel of the Cross, a bag slung over her shoulder, bottles inside clinking together like spurs in rhythm with her steps. The bottles had all fit, save for one, a vintage wine from Sister Merilee's private store that hung from her fingertips.

Bells began to chime the hour, soft and low, but they were coming from the larger Chapel of the Saints on the other side of campus. That one was never fully unattended—Mother Alice, the school's head-mistress-nun-whatever, slept in a room off the chapel, and even if Kate had wanted to burn down that particular building, she wasn't stupid enough to add murder to arson. Not when the price for violence was so steep.

The doors to the smaller chapel were kept locked at night, but Kate had pocketed a key earlier that day while enduring one of Sister Merilee's lectures on finding grace. She let herself in and set the bag down just inside the door. The chapel was darker than she'd ever seen it, the blue stained glass registering black in the moonlight. A dozen pews separated her from the altar, and for a moment she almost felt bad about setting fire to the quaint little place. But it wasn't the school's only chapel—it wasn't even the nicest—and if the nuns at St. Agnes had preached about anything, it was the importance of sacrifice.

Kate had burned through two boarding schools (metaphorically speaking) in her first year of exile, another one in her second, hoping that would be it. But her father was determined (she had to get it from someone) and kept digging up more options. The fourth, a reform school for troubled teens, had stuck it out for almost a year before giving up the ghost. The fifth, an all-boys academy willing to make an exception in exchange for a healthy endowment, lasted only a few short months, but her father must have had this hellish convent of a prep school on speed dial, a place already reserved, because she'd been packed off without so much as a detour back to V-City.

Six schools in five years.

But this was it. It had to be.

Kate crouched on the wooden floor, unzipped the bag, and got to work.

The night was too quiet in the wake of the bells, the chapel eerily still, and she started humming a hymn as she unpacked the duffel: two bottles of jack and almost a full fifth of vodka, both salvaged from a box of confiscated goods, along with three bottles of house red, a decades-old whiskey from Mother Alice's cabinet, and Sister Merilee's vintage. She lined the contents up on the back pew before crossing to the prayer candles. Beside the three tiers of shallow glass bowls sat a dish of matches, the old-fashioned kind with long wooden stems.

Still humming, Kate returned to the liquor cabinet

on the pew and unscrewed and uncorked the various bottles, anointing the seats, row after row, trying to make the contents last. She saved Mother Alice's whiskey for the wooden podium at the front. A Bible sat open on top, and in a moment of superstition, Kate spared the book, lobbing it out the open front door and onto the grass. When she stepped back inside, the damp, sweet smell of alcohol assaulted her senses. She coughed and spit the acrid taste from her mouth.

At the far end of the chapel, a massive crucifix hung above the altar, and even in the darkened hall, she could feel the statue's gaze on her as she lifted the match.

Forgive me father for I have sinned, she thought, striking it against the doorframe.

"Nothing personal," she added aloud as the match flared to life, sudden and bright. For a long moment Kate watched it burn, fire creeping toward her fingers. And then, just before it got too close, she dropped the match onto the seat of the nearest pew. It caught instantly and spread with an audible *whoosh*, the fire consuming only the alcohol at first, then taking hold of the wood beneath. In moments, the pews were going up, and then the floor, and at last the altar. The fire grew, and grew, and grew, from a flame the size of her nail to a blaze with a life of its own, and Kate stood, mesmerized, watching it dance and climb and consume inch after inch until the heat and the smoke finally forced her out into the cool night.

Run, said a voice in her head—soft, urgent, instinctual—as the chapel burned.

She resisted the urge and instead sank onto a bench a safe distance from the fire, trailing her shoes back and forth through the late summer grass.

If she squinted, she could see the light of the nearest subcity on the horizon: Des Moines. An old-fashioned name, a relic from the time before the reconstruction. There were half a dozen of them, scattered around Verity's periphery—but none had more than a million people, their populations locked in, locked down, and none of them held a candle to the capital. That was the idea. No one wanted to attract the monsters. Or Callum Harker.

She drew out her lighter—a beautiful silver thing Mother Alice had confiscated the first week—and turned it over and over in her hands to keep them steady. When that failed, she drew a cigarette from her shirt pocket—another bounty from the confiscation box—and lit it, watching the small blue flame dance before the massive orange blaze.

She took a drag and closed her eyes.

Where are you, Kate? she asked herself.

It was a game she sometimes played, ever since she learned about the theory of infinite parallels, the idea that a person's path through life wasn't really a line, but a tree, every decision a divergent branch, resulting in a divergent you. She liked the idea that there were a hundred different Kates, living a hundred different lives.

Maybe in one of them, there were no monsters.

Maybe her family was still whole.

Maybe she and her mother had never left home.

Maybe they'd never come back.

Maybe, maybe, maybe—and if there were a hundred lives, a hundred Kates, then *she* was only one of them, and that one was exactly who she was supposed to be. And in the end, it was easier to do what she had to if she could believe that somewhere else, another version of her got to make another choice. Got to live a better—or at least simpler—life. Maybe she was even sparing them. Allowing another Kate to stay sane and safe.

Where are you? she wondered.

Lying in a field. Staring up at stars.

The night is warm. The air is clean.

The grass is cool beneath my back.

There are no monsters in the dark.

How nice, thought Kate as, in front of her, the chapel caved in, sending up a wave of embers.

Sirens wailed in the distance, and she straightened up on the bench.

Here we go.

Within minutes girls came pouring out of the dormitories, and Mother Alice appeared in a robe, pale face painted red by the light of the still-burning church. Kate had the pleasure of hearing the prestigious old nun let out a string of colorful words before the fire trucks pulled up and the sirens drowned out everything.

Even Catholic schools had their limits.

An hour later, Kate was sitting in the rear seat of a local patrol car, courtesy of Des Moines, hands cuffed in her lap. The vehicle barreled through the night, across the dark expanse of land that formed the northeast corner of Verity, away from the safety of the periphery, and toward the capital.

Kate shifted in the seat, trying to get more comfortable as the cruiser sped on. Verity was three days across by car, and she figured they were still a good four hours outside the capital, an hour from the edge of the Waste—but there was no way this local officer was taking a vehicle like this through a place like that. The car didn't have much in the way of reinforcement, only its iron trim and the UVR—ultraviolet-reinforced— high beams tearing crisp lines through the darkness.

The man's knuckles were white on the wheel.

She thought of telling him not to worry, not yet— they were far enough out; the edges of Verity were still relatively safe, because none of the things that went bump in the capital wanted to cross the Waste to get to them, not when there were still plenty of people to eat closer to V-City. But then he shot her a nasty look and she decided to let him stew.

She rolled her head, good ear against the leather seat as she stared out into the dark.

The road ahead looked empty, the night thick, and she studied her reflection in the window. It was strange, how only the obvious parts showed up against the darkened glass—light hair, sharp jaw, dark eyes—not the scar like a drying tear in the corner of her eye, or the one that traced her hairline from temple to jaw.

Back at St. Agnes, the Chapel of the Cross was probably a charred husk by now.

The growing crowd of girls in their pajamas had crossed themselves at the sight of it (Nicole Teak, whose nose Kate had recently broken, flashed a smug grin, as if Kate was getting what she deserved, as if she hadn't *wanted* to get caught), and Mother Alice had said a prayer for her soul as she was escorted off the premises.

Good riddance, St. Agnes.

The cop said something, but the words broke down before they reached her, leaving nothing but muffled sounds.

"What?" she asked, feigning disinterest as she turned her head.

"Almost there," he muttered, still obviously bitter that someone had forced him to drive her this far instead of dropping her in a cell for the night.

They passed a sign—235 miles to V-City. They were getting closer to the Waste, the buffer that ran between the capital and the rest of Verity. A moat, thought Kate, one with its own monsters. There was no clear border, but you could feel the shift, like a shoreline, the ground sloping away, even though it stayed flat. The last towns gave way to barren fields, and the world went from quiet to *empty*.

A few more painfully silent miles—the cop refused to turn on the radio—and then a side road broke the monotony of the main stretch, and the patrol car veered onto it, wheels slipping from asphalt to gravel before grumbling to a stop.

Anticipation flickered dully in Kate's chest as the cop switched on his surrounds, UVR brights that cast an arc of light around the car. They weren't alone; a black transport vehicle idled on the side of the narrow road, the only signs of life its UVR undercarriage, the red of its brake lights, and the low rumble of its engine. The cop's circle of light glanced off the transport's tinted windows and landed on the metal tracery capable of running one hundred thousand volts into anything that got too close. *This* was a vehicle designed to cross the Waste—and whatever waited in it.

Kate smiled, the same smile Nicole had flashed her outside the church—smug, no teeth. Not a happy smile, but a victorious one. The cop got out, opened her door, and hauled her up off the backseat by her elbow. He unlocked the cuffs, grumbling to himself about politics and privilege while Kate rubbed her wrists.

"Free to go?"

He crossed his arms. She took that as a yes, and started toward the transport, then turned back, and held out her hand. "You have something of mine," she said.

He didn't move.

Kate's eyes narrowed. She snapped her fingers and the man shot a look at the rumbling tank of a car behind her before digging the silver lighter from his pocket.

Her fingers curled around the smooth metal and she turned away, but not before she caught the word *bitch* in her good ear. She didn't bother looking back. She climbed into the transport, sank against the leather seat, and listened to the sound of the cop car retreating. Her driver was on the phone. He met her eyes in the rear-view mirror.

"Yeah, I've got her. Yeah, okay. Here." He passed the cell back through the partition, and Kate's pulse quickened as she took it and brought it to her left ear.

"Katherine. Olivia. Harker."

The voice on the line was low thunder, rumbling earth. Not loud, but forceful, the kind of voice that demanded respect, if not outright fear, the kind of voice Kate had been practicing for years, but it still sent an involuntary shiver through her.

"Hello, Father," she said, careful to keep her own voice steady.

"Are you proud of yourself, Katherine?"

She studied her nails. "Quite."

"St. Agnes makes six."

"Hmm?" she murmured, feigning distraction.

"Six schools. In five years."

"Well, the nuns said I could do anything if I put my mind to it. Or was that the teachers back at Wild Prior? I'm starting to lose track—"

"*Enough.*" The word was like a punch to the chest. "You can't keep doing this."

"I know," she said, fighting to be the right Kate, the one she wanted to be around him, the one who *deserved* to be around him. Not the girl lying in the field or the one crying in a car right before it crashed. The one who wasn't afraid of anything. Anyone. Not even him. She couldn't manage that smug smile, but she pictured it, held the image in her head. "I know," she said again. "And I have to imagine these kinds of stunts are getting hard to cover up. And expensive."

"Then why—"

"You know why, Dad," she said, cutting him off. "You know what I want." She listened to him exhale on the other side of the line, and tipped her head back against the leather. The transport's sky roof was open, and she could see the stars dotting the heavy dark.

"I want to come home."

AUGUST

It began with a bang.

August read the words for the fifth time without taking them in. He was sitting at the kitchen counter, rolling an apple in circles with one hand and pinning open a book about the universe with the other. Night had swept in beyond the steel-shuttered windows of the compound, and he could feel the city pulling at him through the walls. He checked his watch, the cuff of his shirt inching up to reveal the lowest of the black tally marks. His sister's voice drifted in from the other room, though the words weren't meant for him, and from the nineteen floors below he could hear the layered noise of voices, the rhythm of boots, the metallic snap of a gun being loaded, and the thousand other fragmented sounds that formed the music of the Flynn compound. He dragged his attention back to the book.

It began with a bang.

The words reminded him of a T. S. Eliot poem, "The Hollow Men." *Not with a bang but a whimper.* Of course, one was talking about the beginning of life and the other about the end, but it still got August thinking: about the universe, about time, about himself. The thoughts fell like dominoes inside his head, one knocking into the next into the next into the—

August's head flicked up an instant before the steel kitchen door slid open, and Henry came in. Henry Flynn, tall and slim, with a surgeon's hands. He was dressed in the task force's standard dark camo, a silver star pinned to his shirt, a star that had been his brother's once and before that his father's and before that his great-uncle's, and on, rolling back fifty years, before the collapse and the reconstruction and the founding of Verity, and probably even before, because a Flynn had *always* been at the beating heart of this city.

"Hi, Dad," said August, trying not to sound like he'd been waiting all night for this.

"August," said Henry, setting an HUV—high-density UV beacon—on the counter. "How's it going?"

August stopped rolling the apple, closed the book, forced himself to sit still, even though a still body was a busy mind—something to do with the potential and kinetic energy, if he had to guess; all he knew was that he was a body in search of motion.

"You okay?" asked Henry when he didn't answer.

August swallowed. He couldn't lie, so why was it so hard to tell the truth?

"I can't keep doing this," he said.

Henry eyed the book. "Astronomy?" he said asked with false lightness. "So take a break."

August looked his father in the eyes. Henry Flynn had kind eyes and a sad mouth, or sad eyes and a kind mouth; he could never keep them straight. Faces had so many features, infinitely divisible, and yet they all added up to single, identifiable expressions like pride, disgust, frustration, fatigue—he was losing his train of thought again. He fought to catch it before it rolled out of reach. "I'm not talking about the book."

"August . . . ," started Henry, because he already knew where this was going. "We're not having this discussion."

"But if you'd just—"

"The task force is *off the table.*"

The steel door slid open again and Emily Flynn walked in with a box of supplies and set them on the counter. She was a fraction taller than her husband, her shoulders broader, with dark skin, a halo of short hair, and a holster on her hip. Emily had a soldier's gait, but she shared Henry's tired eyes and set jaw. "Not this again," she said.

"I'm surrounded by the FTF all the time," protested August. "Whenever I go anywhere, I dress like them. Is it such a step for me to *be* one of them?"

"Yes," said Henry.

"It isn't safe," added Emily as she started unpacking the food. "Is Ilsa in her room? I thought we could—"

But August wouldn't let it go. "Nowhere is *safe*," he cut in. "That's the whole point. Your people are out there risking their lives every day against those *things*, and I'm in here reading about stars, pretending like everything is fine."

Emily shook her head and drew a knife from a slot on the counter. She started chopping vegetables, creating order of chaos, one slice at a time. "The compound is safe, August. At least safer than the streets right now."

"Which is why I should be out there *helping* in the red."

"You do your part," said Henry. "That's—"

"What are you so afraid of?" snapped August.

Emily set the knife down with a click. "Do you even have to ask?"

"You think I'll get hurt?" And then, before she could answer, August was on his feet. In a single, fluid move he took up the knife and drove it down into his hand. Henry flinched, and Emily sucked in a breath, but the blade glanced off August's skin as if it were stone, the tip burying in the chopping block beneath. The kitchen went very quiet.

"You act as though I'm made of glass," he said, letting go of the knife. "But I'm not." He took her hands, the way he'd seen Henry do so many times. "Em," he said, softly. "*Mom*. I'm not fragile. I'm the *opposite* of fragile."

"You're not invincible, either," she said. "Not—"

"I'm not putting you out there," Henry cut in. "If Harker's men catch you—"

"You let Leo lead the entire task force," countered August. "His face is plastered everywhere, and *he* is still alive."

"That's different," said Henry and Emily at the same time.

"How?" he challenged.

Emily brought her hands to August's face, the way she did when he was a child—but that wasn't the right word. He'd never been a child, not really, children didn't come together fully formed in the middle of a crime scene. "We just want to protect you. Leo's been part of the campaign from day one. But that makes him a *constant* target. And the more ground we gain in this city, the more Harker's men will try to exploit our weaknesses and steal our strengths."

"And which am I?" asked August, pulling away. "Your weakness, or your strength?"

Emily's warm brown eyes went wide and flat as the word spilled out. "Both."

It was unfair to ask, but the truth still stung.

"Where is this coming from?" asked Henry, rubbing his eyes. "You don't really want to fight."

He was right, August *didn't* want to fight—not on the streets in the dead of night, and not here with his family—but there was this horrible vibration in his bones, something struggling to get out, a melody getting louder and louder in his head. "No," he said. "But I want to *help*."

"You already do," insisted Henry. "The task force can only treat the symptoms. You and Ilsa and Leo, you treat the disease. That's how it works."

But it's not working! August wanted to shout. The V-City truce had held for only six years—Harker on one side, and Flynn on the other—and it was already fraying. Everyone knew it wouldn't hold. Every night, more death crept across the Seam. There were too many monsters, and not enough good men.

"Please," he said. "I can do more if you let me."

"August . . . ," started Henry.

He held up his hand. "Just promise me you'll think about it." And with that he backed out of the kitchen before his parents were forced to tell him the truth.

◈

August's room was an exercise in entropy and order, a kind of contained chaos. It was small and windowless, close in a way that would have been claustrophobic if it weren't so familiar. Books had long outgrown their shelves and were now stacked in precarious piles on and around his bed, several more open and splayed, pages down, across the sheets. Some people favored a genre or subject; August had little preference, so long as it wasn't fiction—he wanted to learn everything about the world as it was, had been, could be. As someone who had come quite suddenly into being, like the end of a magic trick, he feared the tenuous nature of his existence, feared that at any moment he might simply cease to be again.

The books were stacked by subject: *astronomy, religion, history, philosophy.*

He was homeschooled, which really meant he was *self*-schooled—sometimes Ilsa tried to help, when her mind worked in columns instead of knots, but his brother, Leo, had no patience for books, and Henry and Emily were too busy, so most of the time August was on his own. And most of the time it was okay. Or rather, it *used* to be okay. He wasn't sure when exactly the *insulation* had started to feel like *isolation*, just that it had.

The only other thing in his room besides furniture and books was a violin. It sat in an open case balanced across two stacks of books, and August drifted instinctively toward it, but resisted the urge to take it up and play. Instead he nudged a copy of Plato off his pillow and slumped down onto the tangled sheets.

The room was stuffy, and he pushed up the sleeves of his shirt, revealing the hundreds of black tallies that started at his left wrist and worked their way up, over elbow and shoulder, around collarbone and rib.

Tonight there were four hundred and twelve.

August pushed the dark hair out of his eyes and listened to Henry and Emily Flynn, still in the kitchen, as they talked on in their soft-spoken way, about him, and the city, and the truce.

What would happen if it actually broke? When. Leo always said *when*.

August hadn't been alive to see the territory wars that broke out in the wake of the Phenomenon, had only heard tales of the bloodshed. But he could see the fear in Flynn's eyes whenever the topic came up—which was more and more often. Leo didn't seem worried— he claimed that Henry had *won* the territory war, that whatever happened to cause the truce was their doing, that they could do it again.

"When it comes," Leo would say, "we will be ready."

"No," Flynn would answer, his expression bleak, "no one is ready for that."

Eventually, the voices in the other room faded, and

August was left alone with his thoughts. He closed his eyes, seeking peace, but as soon as the silence settled it was broken, the distant stutter of gunfire echoing against his skull as it always did—the sound invading every quiet moment.

It began with a bang.

He rolled over and dug the music player out from under his pillow, pressing the buds into his ears and hitting play. Classical music flared, loud and bright and wonderful, and he sank back into the melody as numbers wandered through his head.

Twelve. Six. Four.

Twelve years since the Phenomenon, when violence started taking shape, and V-City fell apart.

Six years since the truce that put it back together, not as one city, but two.

And four since the day he woke up in a middle-school cafeteria as it was being cordoned off with crime-scene tape.

"Oh God," someone had said, taking him by the elbow. "Where did you come from?" And then, shouting to someone else, "I've found a boy!" She'd knelt down so she was looking into his face, and he could tell that she was trying to block his view of something. Something terrible. "What's your name, hon?"

August had looked up at her blankly.

"Must be in shock," said a man.

"Get him out of here," said another.

The woman took his hands. "Honey, I want you to close your eyes." That was when he saw past her. To the black sheets, lined up like tallies on the floor.

The first symphony ended in August's ears, and a moment later, the second started up. He could pick out every chord, every note; yet if he focused hard enough, he could still hear his father's murmur, his mother's pacing. Which is why he had no trouble hearing the triple beep of Henry's cell. No trouble hearing him answer it or catching the words when his voice dipped lower, threading with concern.

"When? You're sure? When was she enrolled? No, no, I'm glad you told me. Okay. Yes, I know. I'll handle it."

The call ended, and Henry went silent before speaking again, this time with Leo. August had heard everything but his brother's return. They were talking about *him.*

He sat up, yanking the buds from his ears.

"Give him what he wants," Leo was saying in his low, even way. "You treat him more like a pet than a son, when he's neither. We are soldiers, Flynn. We are holy fire. . . ." August rolled his eyes. He appreciated his brother's vote of confidence, but could do without the righteousness. "And you're smothering him."

That much he agreed with.

Emily joined in. "We're trying to—"

"To protect him?" chided Leo. "When the truce falls apart, this compound will not keep him safe."

"We're not sending him behind enemy lines."

"You've been given an opportunity. I simply suggest you use it. . . ."

"The risk—"

"Is not that great, as long as he's careful. And the advantage—"

August was sick of being talked about as if he weren't there, as if he couldn't *hear*, so he shoved to his feet, upsetting a tower of books on his way past. He was too late—the conversation was over by the time he opened his door. Leo was gone, and his father was reaching out, as if about to knock.

"What's going on?" he asked.

Henry didn't try to hold back the truth. "You were right," he said. "You deserve the chance to help. And I think I've found a way."

August broke into a smile.

"Whatever it is," he said, "I'm in."

MONSTER, MAY I?

1

This was *not* what August had in mind.

The schoolbag sagged open on the bed, spilling supplies—and the uniform was way too tight. Emily claimed that was the style, but August felt like the clothes were trying to strangle him. The Flynn Task Force outfits were flexible, designed for combat, but the Colton Academy uniform was stiff, suffocating. His shirtsleeves came to rest just above his wrist bones, and the lowest of the black tallies on his forearm—now four hundred and eighteen—showed *every time* he crooked his elbow. August growled and tugged the fabric down again. He ran a comb through his hair, which didn't really stop the black curls from falling into his pale eyes, but at least he tried.

He straightened and found his gaze in the mirror, but his expression stared back with a vacancy that made him shudder. On Leo, the expressionless planes of his face registered as confidence. On Ilsa, the evenness read as serenity. But August just looked *lost*. He'd studied Henry and Emily and everyone else he came across, from the FTF cadets to the sinners, tried to memorize the way their features lit up with excitement, twisted with anger or guilt. He spent *hours* in front of the mirror, trying to master the nuances and re-create those faces, while Leo looked on with his flat black stare.

"You're wasting your time," his brother would say.

But Leo was wrong; those hours were going to pay off. August blinked—another natural act that felt unnatural, affected—managed a tiny, thoughtful crease between his brows, and recited the words he'd practiced.

"My name is—Freddie Gallagher." There was a slight hitch before the *F*, as the words scratched his throat. It wasn't a lie, not really—it was a borrowed name, just like *August*. He didn't have one of his own. Henry had chosen the name August and now August chose the name Freddie, and they both belonged to him, just as neither did. That's what he told himself, over and over and over until he believed it, because truth wasn't the same thing as fact. It was personal. He swallowed, tried the second line, the one meant only for him. "I am not a . . ."

But his throat closed up. The words got stuck.

I am not a monster, that's what he wanted to say, but he couldn't. He hadn't found a way to make it true.

"Don't you look handsome," came a voice from the door.

August's gaze traveled up a fraction in the mirror to see his sister, Ilsa, leaning in the doorway, wearing the barest hint of a smile. She was older than August, but she looked like a doll, her long, strawberry-blond hair pulled up in its usual messy nest, and her large blue eyes feverish, as if she hadn't slept (she rarely did).

"Handsome," she said, pushing off the door, "but not happy." Ilsa padded forward into the room, her bare feet moving effortlessly around the books, though she never looked down. "You should be happy, little brother. Isn't this what you wanted?"

Was it? August had always imagined himself in FTF fatigues, guarding the Seam and protecting South City. Like Leo. He heard the troops talk about his brother as if he were a god, keeping the darkness at bay with nothing but the piece of music in his head. Feared. Worshiped. August straightened his collar, which made his sleeves ride up *again*. He tugged them down as Ilsa snaked her arms around his shoulders. He stilled. Leo refused such contact, and August didn't know what to make of it— too often touching was a part of taking—but Ilsa had always been like this, tactile, and he reached up and touched her arm.

Where his skin was marked with short black lines, hers was covered in stars. A whole sky's worth, or so he thought. August had never seen more than a handful of real stars on nights when the grid went down. But he'd heard about places where the city lights didn't reach, where there were so many stars you could see by them, even on a moonless night.

"You're dreaming," said Ilsa in her singsong way. She rested her chin on top of his shoulder, and squinted. "What is that in your eyes?"

"What?"

"That speck. Right there. Is it fear?"

He found her gaze in the mirror. "Maybe," he admitted. He hadn't set foot in a school, not since the day of his catalyst, and nerves rang like bells behind his ribs. But there was something else, too, a strange excitement at the idea of playing normal, and every time he tried to untangle how he felt, he just ended up in knots.

"They're setting you free," said Ilsa. She spun him around and leaned in until her face was barely an inch from his. Mint. She always smelled like mint. "Be happy, little brother." But then the joy fell out of her voice, and her blue eyes darkened, sliding from noon blue to twilight without a blink between. "And be careful."

August managed a ghost of a smile for her. "I'm always careful, Ilsa."

But she didn't seem to hear. She was shaking her head now, a slow, side-to-side motion that didn't stop when it should. Ilsa got tangled up so easily, sometimes for a few moments, sometimes a few days.

"It's okay," he said gently, trying to draw her back.

"The city is such a big place," she said, her voice tight as strings. "It's full of holes. Don't fall in."

Ilsa hadn't left the Flynn compound in six years. Not since the day of the truce. August didn't know the details, not all of them, but he knew his sister stayed inside, no matter what.

"I'll watch my step," he said.

Her fingers tightened on his arms. And then her eyes lightened and she was there again. "Of course you will," she said, all sunshine.

She kissed the top of his head, and he ducked out of her arms and went to his bed, where his violin case sat open, the beautiful instrument waiting inside. August wanted to play—the desire a hollow weight in his chest, like hunger—but he only let himself run his fingers over the wood before snapping the case shut.

He checked his watch as he moved through the dark apartment. 6:15. Even here, twenty stories up, at the top of the Flynn compound, the first morning light was still buried behind the sprawl of buildings to the east.

In the kitchen he found a black lunch bag with a note pinned to the front:

Have a great first day.

I hope you don't mind, I took a bite.

~Em

When August opened the bag, he saw that everything inside, from the sandwich to the candy bar, was already half-eaten. It was a sweet gesture, really. Emily hadn't just packed him a lunch. She'd packed an excuse. If anyone bothered to ask, he could say he'd already eaten.

Only a green apple sat, untouched, in the bottom of the bag.

The kitchen lights came on as he was shoving the lunch sack in his bag, and Henry wandered in, nursing a cup of coffee. He still looked tired. He *always* looked tired.

"August," he said with a yawn.

"Dad. You're up early."

Henry was practically nocturnal. He had a saying— *the monsters hunt at night, and so must we*—but lately his nights had gotten even longer. August tried to imagine what he must have been like, back before the Phenomenon—before violence gave way to the Corsai and the Malchai and the Sunai, before the anarchy, the closed borders, the infighting, the chaos. Before Henry lost his parents, his brothers, his first wife. Before he became the Flynn the city turned to, the only Flynn it *had*. The creator of the FTF, and the only man willing to stand up to a glorified criminal and *fight*.

August had seen photos, but the man in them had

bright eyes and an easy smile. He looked like he belonged in a different world. A different life.

"Big day." Henry yawned again. "I wanted to see you off."

It was the truth, but not the whole truth. "You're worried," observed August.

"Of course I am." Henry clutched his coffee cup. "Do we need to go over the rules again?"

"No," answered August, but Henry kept talking anyway.

"You go straight to Colton. You come straight home. If the route falls through, you call. If security's too tight, you call. If there's any trouble—anything at all—even a bad *feeling*, August—"

"I'll call."

Henry's brow creased, and August straightened. "It's going to be fine." They'd gone through the plan a hundred times in the last week, making sure everything was in order. He checked his watch. Again the tallies showed. Again he covered them. He didn't know why he bothered. "I better get going."

Henry nodded. "I know this isn't what you wanted, and I hope it proves unnecessary, but—"

August frowned. "Do you really think the truce will break?" He tried to picture V-City as it must have been, two halves at war along a bloody center. In North City,

Harker. In South City, Flynn. Those wanting to pay for their safety against those willing to fight for it. Die for it.

Henry rubbed his eyes. "I hope it holds," he said, "for all our sakes." It was a deflection, but August let it go.

"Get some rest, Dad."

Henry smiled grimly and shook his head. "No rest for the wicked," he said, and August knew he wasn't referring to himself.

He headed for the elevators, but someone was already there, his shape silhouetted by the light of the open doors.

"Little brother."

The voice was low and smooth, almost hypnotizing, and a second later the shadow shifted and stepped forward, resolving into a man with broad shoulders and a wiry form, all lean muscle and long bone. The FTF fatigues fit him perfectly, and beneath his rolled sleeves, small black crosses circled both forearms. Above a chiseled jaw, fair hair swept down into eyes as black as pitch. The only imperfection was a small scar running through his left eyebrow—a relic from his first years—but despite the mark, Leo Flynn looked more god than monster.

August felt himself standing taller, trying to mirror his brother's posture before he remembered that it was too rigid for a student. He slouched again, only this time too far, and then couldn't remember what normal looked like. All the while, Leo's black eyes hovered on him, unblinking. Even when he was flesh and blood, he didn't quite pass for human.

"The young Sunai, off to school." There was no uptick in his voice, no question.

"Let me guess," said August, managing a crooked grin, "you wanted to see me off as well? Tell me to have fun?"

Leo cocked his head. He'd never been very good at sarcasm—none of them were, really, but August had picked up scraps from the guys in the FTF.

"Your enjoyment is hardly my concern," said Leo. "But your focus *is*. Not even out the door, August, and you've already forgotten something."

He lobbed an object through the air and August caught it, cringing at the contact. It was a North City medallion, embossed with a *V* on one side and a series of numbers on the other. Made of iron, the medal prickled unpleasantly against his palm. Pure metal repelled monsters: Corsai and Malchai couldn't touch the stuff; Sunai simply didn't like to (all the FTF uniforms were traced with it, but his and Leo's had been woven with an alloy).

"Do I really have to wear this?" he asked. The prolonged contact was already making him nauseous.

"If you want to pass for one of them," said Leo simply. "If you want to get caught and slaughtered, then by all means, leave it off." August swallowed, and slid the pendant over his head. "It's a solid forgery," continued his brother. "It'll pass a cursory inspection by any human eye, but don't be caught north of the Seam after dark. I wouldn't test it against anything that actually comes to heel at Harker's side."

Of course, it wasn't the metal alone that kept the monsters at bay. It was Harker's sigil. His law.

August settled the medallion against his shirt, zipping up the FTF-issued jacket over it. But as he moved to step into the elevator, Leo barred his path. "Have you eaten recently?"

He swallowed, but the words were already rising in his throat. There was a difference between the inability to lie and the *need* to speak the truth, but silent omission was a luxury he didn't have when it came to his brother. When a Sunai asked a question, he commanded an answer. "I'm not hungry."

"August," chided Leo. "You're always hungry."

He flinched. "I'll eat later."

Leo didn't respond, only watched him, black eyes narrowed, and before he could say anything else—or make *August* say anything else—August pushed past him. Or at least, he tried to. He was halfway to the elevator when

Leo's hand snapped out and closed over his. The one holding his violin case.

"Then you don't need this."

August went stiff. In four years, he'd never left the compound without the instrument. The thought made him dizzy.

"What if something happens?" he asked, panic climbing.

A ghost of amusement rippled through Leo's features. "Then you'll just have to get your hands dirty." With that, he pulled the case from August's grip and nudged him into the elevator. August stumbled, then turned back, his hands prickling with the sudden absence of the violin.

"Good-bye, brother," said Leo, punching the button for the lobby.

"Have fun at school," he added as the doors slid shut.

August shoved his hands into his pockets as the elevator plunged twenty floors. The compound was part skyscraper, part base of operations, all fortress. A concrete beast, steel, barbed wire, and Plexiglas, most of it dedicated to barracks housing members of the task force. The vast majority of the FTF's sixty thousand officers were housed in other barracks across the city, but the nearly a thousand stationed at the compound served as camouflage as much as anything. The fewer people coming in and out of the building, the more each one stood out. And if you were Harker, trying to ferret out

Flynn's three Sunai, his secret weapons, you were keeping track of every face. It wasn't so much a problem for Leo, since he *was* the face of the FTF, or Ilsa, since she never left the compound, but Henry was determined to keep August's identity a secret.

On the ground floor, people were already streaming in and out of the building (with the night curfew as it was, days started early), and August moved with them, as if he were one of them, across the concrete lobby and through the guarded doors and onto the street. The morning washed over him, warm and bright and tarnished only by the disk of metal scratching against his skin and the absence of his violin.

Sunlight seeped between the buildings, and August took a deep breath and looked up at the Flynn compound looming overhead. Four years of hardly ever going out, and even then, almost always at night. Now here he was. Outside. Alone. Twenty-four million people in this supercity at last count, and he was only one of them, just another face in the morning commute. For one, dazzling, infinite moment, August felt like he was standing on a precipice, the end of one world and the beginning of another, a whisper and a bang.

And then his watch beeped, dragging him back from the edge, and he set off.

II

The black sedan cut through the city like a knife.

Kate watched as it carved down streets, across bridges, the traffic splitting like flesh as the car sliced its way through North City. Outside, the morning was loud and bright, but from within, it looked like an old movie, all the color leeched out by the tinted windows. Classical music piped through the radio, soft but steady, reinforcing the illusion of calm that most people bought into so willingly. When she asked the driver, a stone-faced man named Marcus, to change the station, and he ignored the request, she put her left earbud in and hit play. Her world became a heavy beat, a rhythm, an angry voice, as she leaned back into the leather bench of the backseat and let the city slide past. From here, it looked almost normal.

V-City was a place Kate knew only in glimpses, snap-shots, time-lapse moments strung together with years of space between each one. She'd been sent away once for her own safety, stolen a second time in the dead of night, and banished a third for her mother's crimes. But she was finally back where she belonged. In her father's city. At her father's side.

And this time, she wasn't going anywhere.

Kate fiddled with her lighter as she studied the tablet propped in her lap, a map of V-City filling the screen. At first glance, it looked like every other supercity—a high-density center trailing off at the edges—but when she tapped the screen with a metallic nail, a new layer of information appeared.

A black line cut across the image from left to right, bisecting the city. The Seam. In reality, it wasn't a straight line, but it was a hard one, carving V-City in two. Stand on the North side, and you were in Callum Harker's territory. Stand on the South side, and you were in Henry Flynn's. Such a simplistic solution to six messy, brutal years of fighting, of sabotage and murder and monsters. Draw a line in the sand. Stay on your half. No wonder it wasn't holding up.

Flynn was an idealist, and it was well and good to talk of justice, to have a "cause," but at the end of the day his people were dying. Flesh and bone versus tooth and claw.

V-City didn't need a moral code. It needed someone

willing to take control. Someone willing to get his hands dirty. It needed Harker. Kate had no pretentions—she knew her father was a bad man—but this city didn't need a good one.

Good and *bad* were weak words. Monsters didn't care about intentions or ideals. The facts were simple. The South was chaos. The North was order. It was an order bought and paid for with blood and fear, but order all the same.

Kate traced her finger along the Seam, over the grayed square that marked the Barren.

Why had her father settled for only half the city? Why did he let Flynn hide behind his wall, just because he had a few strange monsters on a leash?

She chewed her lip, tapped the map again, and a third layer of information appeared.

Three concentric circles—like a bull's-eye—ghosted over the top of the map. It was the risk grid, designed to show the increase in monsters and the need for vigilance as one traveled in toward the center of the city. A band of green formed the outer ring, followed by yellow, and red at the center. Most people didn't pay attention to the zones during the day, but everyone knew the boundaries, the place where the violent red gave way to the vigilant yellow before bleeding into the relative safety of the green. Of course, for those with her father's protection, the risk dropped to almost zero . . . so long as you stayed within the North City limits. Go past the green and you hit the Waste, where North and South didn't matter, because it was every man for himself.

Go far enough and you eventually found safe ground again; out near the borders where monsters were still rare, the population kept low. Out where supercity people weren't welcome in case they brought the darkness with them like a plague. Where a girl might burn down a chapel, or lie in a field of grass beside her mom and learn the summer stars . . .

Somewhere, a horn, and Kate looked up, the house in the country dissolving back into the city streets. She stared past the partition and the driver and the front window, at the silver gargoyle on the hood. The car had originally come with an angel ornament, arms and wings flung back by some invisible wind, but Harker had broken it off and replaced it with the beast, hunched forward, tiny claws curling around the front lip of the grill.

"This is a city of monsters," he'd said, tossing the angel in the trash.

Her father was right about that. But monsters—*real* monsters—didn't look like the stupid little hood ornament. No, real monsters were *much* worse.

III

August tipped his face toward the sun, savoring the late summer morning as he walked, letting his body move and his mind go blissfully still. It was amazing how easy it was to think in straight lines when he was in motion, even without the violin. He made his way down cracked sidewalks, past buildings with boarded windows. Half the structures were burned-out husks, abandoned and gutted, any useful materials scraped out to fortify other buildings. South V-City still looked like a ravaged corpse, but it was rebuilding. FTF were everywhere, standing on rooftops, patrolling the streets, radio signals crackling from the handhelds on their uniforms. At night, they hunted monsters, but during the day, they tried to stop new ones from being made. Crime. That was the cause. Corsai, Malchai, Sunai–they were the effect.

August blended in with the heavy foot traffic as he made his way north, the noise of the city like music around him, full of harmony and dissonance, rhythm and clash. It layered and layered until the melody tipped into discord, the wonder turning to distress, and he had to fight to focus on the path instead of everything in it. The path itself was easy, four blocks straight up Center Ave.

A beeline to the Seam.

August's steps slowed as it came into sight.

The barrier was massive, a three-story barricade cutting east to west through the downtown, warded with stripes of pure metal and studded with cameras. The wall was the result of six years of territory war, each act of violence, each human death, ushering more Corsai and Malchai into the world, all because the Flynns had the city, and Harker wanted it.

Two blocks to the west sat the Barren—a ruined block of scorched earth, a reminder to both sides. It had been a plaza once, a piece of green at the heart of the city, but now there was nothing. Some people said you could see the outlines of the dead still ghosted on the pavement. Most of the FTF said that Henry Flynn had detonated a weapon there on the last day of the territory wars, something bad enough to scrub every sign of life. August didn't believe that—didn't *want* to believe it—but whatever happened that day, the threat of an encore was enough to make Harker call terms, agree to cut V-City in two.

By day, the capital was still unified, at least in theory. Three gates were punched out of the Seam to let people through, but they were monitored by armed men and the ever-watchful red eyes of the moving cameras, and everyone who passed through had to show identification while the scanning cameras verified them as human.

Which was a problem.

August turned down a narrow half-ruined street that ran parallel to the Seam until he reached an office building, its windows replaced by sheets of steel, a pair of FTF flanking the door. The woman at the front desk offered him a short nod as he passed through security and down a separate elevator to the basement. Small dots of neon paint on the wall marked the path and he followed them through a web of dank hallways to a wall. Or what *looked* like a wall. Metal sheeting pushed aside to reveal a tunnel, and August made his way along until he reached a matching false wall on the other end. He slid it open, and stepped out into the cellar of a ground floor apartment.

It was quiet here, and he paused, hating how relieved he felt to be alone again so soon. He gave himself ten seconds, waiting for his heart to slow and his nerves to settle, before he dusted himself off, and climbed the stairs.

Paris was chain-smoking and cooking breakfast.

She didn't even startle when August appeared in the kitchen behind her.

"Morning, doll," she called, her iron medallion dangling dangerously close to her omelet. Allies on the North side were rare, and extremely expensive, and even then they were risky, but Henry and Paris were old friends, and she'd passed Leo's inspection. August looked around. Her apartment was . . . cozy, like pictures he'd seen in magazines from before the Phenomenon. Tile and wood and window glass. "Subway pass is on the table."

"Thanks, Paris," he said, unzipping his FTF jacket and hanging it on a hook by the door. His shirtsleeves had ridden up again, and two rows of black tallies were now showing. He pulled the material down, even though Paris couldn't see the marks. Couldn't see anything, for that matter.

Paris might be blind, but her other senses were sharp. Sharp enough to notice the absence of his violin, the barely audible vibration of its strings within the case. She blew a thoughtful puff of smoke.

"No concert today?" she asked, dripping ash into her eggs.

August's fingers curled the way they always did around the case's handle but found only air. "No," he said, digging the Colton Academy blazer from his bag

and shrugging it on before the hall mirror. He was surprised to see his features crinkle, almost automatically,
into a frown.

"Flynn told me about your music," mumbled Paris, to
herself, and he knew by her tone that when she said *your*,
she meant all three of them. "Always wondered what it
sounds like . . . ."

August buttoned the blazer. "I hope you never know,"
he said, heading for the door. "I'll be back before dark."

"Have a good day at school," she called as it closed
behind him, and unlike Leo, she actually sounded like
she meant it.

August stepped onto the street and breathed a sigh of
relief when he saw the Seam safely at his back. And then
he turned north, and his eyes widened. He'd braced
himself, but the difference between the two sides of
V-City still caught him in the chest. North City wasn't a
bombed-out shell. Whatever scars it had, they'd all been
covered up, painted over. Here the buildings glittered,
all metal, stone, and glass, the streets dotted with slick
cars and people in nice clothes—if Harker had enforcers
on the street, they blended in. A shop window was filled
with fruit so colorful it made August want to try it, even
though he knew it would taste like ash.

Anger flared through him at the sight—the *illusion*—
of this safe, clean city, and the tallies across his skin

prickled in warning, their warmth countered by the sickly cool weight of the medallion against his chest. Focus, focus.

The nearest subway station sat a block away. South City had shut down the subways—it was too dangerous, what with the Corsai flocking to the dark—and boarded up the passages as best they could, even though August knew the FTF still used the tunnels when they had to.

He took the stairs two at a time. He'd read somewhere that V-City had grown up as much as out, that the buildings were actually built on *top* of the old grid, the subways where the original streets used to be. He didn't know if it was true, but the subway station below was as clean as the roads above, buffed white stone and, somewhere underneath the sounds of foot traffic, a strain of classical music. A piano concerto. No signs of struggle or suffering, no remnant of the terrors that came out at night. It was a trick, meant to lure South siders over and remind North siders why they paid the price.

August got to the platform just in time to miss the train. He slumped back against a post to wait for the next one, his attention wandering from a couple kissing farther down the line to a busker playing guitar before it finally settled on a small girl in front of him, clutching a woman's hand. She looked over at him, and August stared back, fascinated by the sight of such a young child. There were so few children in the compound, so few in South City for that matter. The girl broke into a toothy grin, and August found himself smiling back.

And then she starting singing.

"*Monsters, monsters, big and small,*" she sang cheerfully. "*They're gonna come and eat you all.*"

A shiver ran through him.

"*Corsai, Corsai, tooth and claw,*
Shadow and bone will eat you raw.
Malchai, Malchai, sharp and sly,
Smile and bite and drink you dry."

August swallowed hard, knowing what came next.

"*Sunai, Sunai, eyes like coal,*
Sing you a song and steal your soul."

The little girl's smile grew even wider.

"*Monsters, monsters, big and small,*
They're gonna come and eat you all!"

She gave a small, delighted squeal, and August felt ill and took a step away.

When the train pulled into the station, he chose another car.

IIII

Monsters, monsters, big and small . . .

Kate hummed as the car barreled on. She tapped the tablet's screen, closing out of the map and opening a new window, clicking through the folders on her father's private drive—she'd swiped the access codes on her first night home—until she found the ones she was looking for. Harker had surveillance throughout North City, not just on the Seam but on nearly every block of the red zone. Every day the footage was checked and then cleared, save for any "incidents"—those were stored so he could see them and take action, if necessary. These "incidents" would never make the news, of course. They knew better than to put stuff like this on TV. It would disturb the illusion of normalcy, of safety—and that's what the people were paying for.

But Harker had to keep an eye on his monsters. Had to know when new ones showed up, when old ones misbehaved. The culled footage had been filtered into categories. *Monster. Human. Genesis.*

Kate had been working her way through the footage since the moment she arrived, trying to learn everything she could about the *real* monsters of Verity. She tapped *Genesis*, and it brought up two further options. Corsai or Malchai (they'd never caught a Sunai's creation on film). She felt like she was traveling down a rabbit hole as she tapped *Corsai* and the screen filled with video clips, the thumbnails nothing but a blur of shadows. Her fingers hovered for a moment over the grid, and then she tapped a clip, and the footage expanded to fill the screen.

The film had been trimmed, all the fat cut away, leaving only the violent meat of the incident behind. The camera didn't have a good angle, but she could still make out two men at the mouth of an alley, standing beneath a streetlight. It took her a moment to realize she was watching a fight. It started out as nothing, a conversation gone south, a shove into the wall, a clumsy punch. One of the men went down, and the other started kicking him—over, and over, and over—until the man on the ground was not a man, but a twitching tangle of limbs, his face a bloody mess.

The attacker took off, and for several long seconds, the man lay there on the pavement, chest lurching up and down in a broken way. And then, as he struggled to rise, the shadows around him began to move. He didn't notice, was too busy scraping himself off the ground, but Kate watched, transfixed, as the darkness stretched, and twitched, peeled away from the walls and the street, and pulled itself together, its shape rising up like smoke, face marked only by eerie white eyes that shook the camera's focus, and the glistening of teeth. Its mouth yawned wide and its body wavered, slick and shiny, its limbs ending in talons.

And the man, still on his hands and knees, made the mistake of crawling forward, out of the safety of the streetlight.

The moment he crossed out of the light, it came, a flurry of teeth and claws that sank into the man's flesh and began to shred.

"Violence breeds violence." One of the teachers at St. Agnes had said that, after Nicole Teak tripped Kate, and Kate reciprocated by breaking Nicole's nose. The teacher went on to make a point about how she was only perpetuating the problem, but by then Kate had stopped listening. As far as she was concerned, Nicole had deserved it.

But the teacher had been right about one thing: violence *breeds*.

Someone pulls a trigger, sets off a bomb, drives a bus full of tourists off a bridge, and what's left in the wake isn't just shell casings, wreckage, bodies. There's

something else. Something *bad*. An aftermath. A *recoil*.
A reaction to all that anger and pain and death. That's all
the Phenomenon was really, a tipping point. Verity had
always been violent—the worst in all ten territories—it
was only a matter of time before there was enough mass
and all that *bad* started pulling itself together.

Kate ran her thumb over the medallion pinned to the
front of her uniform, protection from things that went
bump. On her screen, the Corsai continued to feast.
Most of the frenzy was lost in shadow, but here and
there a razor glint of tooth or claw flashed on-screen,
and Kate watched as blood sprayed across the pool of
light. She made a small, disgusted noise, glad the footage had no sound.

Marcus waved from the other side of the partition,
and Kate pulled the earbud from her ear, plunging herself back into a world of black and white, morning light,
and the soft trill of piano keys.

"What is it?" she asked, annoyed.

"Sorry, Miss Harker," said Marcus through the partition. "We're here."

Colton Academy sat at the place where the yellow met
the green and the city streets gave way to suburbs, the
safest zone of the city, where the richest could build their
little shells and pretend that Verity wasn't being eaten

alive. It looked like a photograph, pale stone buildings sitting on a stretch of vivid green grass, all of it showered in crisp morning light. Only a fifteen-minute drive from the dark heart of North City, but you'd never know it by looking at the place. Kate guessed that was the point. She'd rather be at an inner-city institution, in the heart of the red, but most of them had been shut down, and even if it had been an option, her father wouldn't hear of it. If he had to have her in V-City, he was determined to keep her "safe." Which meant out of the way, since there was no such thing as safe in this place, no matter which half you called home.

Marcus held open the door, and she stepped out, shaking off the memory of the Corsai and pulling her features back into alignment. She smoothed the collar of her Colton-issued polo, ran a hand over her pale hair. It was loose, parted to cover the scars where her head had struck the glass. It could have been worse—the hearing loss was partial—but she knew better than to let it show. It was a weakness all the same and weaknesses should never show—that's what Harker told her, back when she was twelve and the scars were all fresh.

"Why?" she'd asked, because she'd been young and stupid.

"Every weakness exposes flesh," he'd said, "and flesh invites a knife."

"What are your weaknesses?" she'd asked him, and Harker's mouth had become something that *almost* looked like a smile, but wasn't one.

To this day, he'd never answered that question. Kate didn't know if it was because her father didn't trust her with his weaknesses, or because he didn't have any. Not anymore. But she wondered if there was another version of Callum Harker in one of those other worlds, and if that one had secrets, and weaknesses, and places where knives could get.

"Miss Harker," said the driver. "Your father wanted me to pass along a message."

She slipped her silver lighter into her shirt pocket. "What's that, Marcus?" she asked blandly.

"If you get yourself expelled, he'll ship you out of Verity. One way. For good."

Kate flashed a cool grin. "Why would I get myself expelled?" she said, looking up at the school. "I'm finally where I want to be."

"*Park Station,*" announced a calm, metallic voice.

August sank back against the train seat and tugged a well-read copy of *The Republic* from his backpack, opening it to the middle. He knew most of the text by heart, so it didn't matter which page he landed on. What mattered was that it gave him a reason to be looking down instead of up. He listened to the stops as they were announced, not willing to risk an upward glance at the grid in case he caught the attention of the cameras above. More little red eyes looking for monsters, even though everyone knew they all came out at night.

Well, thought August. Almost all.

"*Martin Center.*"

Three stops to Colton. The subway car was filling up, and August stood, offering up his seat to an old woman. He kept his head bowed over the book, but his eyes trailed across the passengers, in their nice dresses and slacks, heels and suits, and not a weapon in sight.

A man jostled his shoulder as he squeezed past, and August tensed.

There was nothing unusual about the man himself—suit and tie, a bit slack around the middle—it was his *shadow* that caught August's eye. It didn't behave as a shadow should—in such a well-lit space, he shouldn't even *have* one—but when the man stopped, the shadow kept moving, twitching and shifting around him like a restless passenger. No one else could see it, but to August's eyes, it loomed in the air, a ghostly thing with too many features for a shadow, too few for a man. August knew it for what it was, an echo of violence, a mark of sin. Somewhere in the city, a monster lived and killed because of this man, because of something he'd done.

August's fingers tightened on the pole.

If they were in South City, he would learn the man's name. It would be handed to him—or Leo—on a slip of paper along with an address, and he would find him in the night, silence the echo, and claim his life.

But this was North City.

Where bad people got away with everything, so long as they had the cash.

August tore his eyes away as the old woman sitting on the bench leaned forward.

"I've always wanted to be on stage," she said in a confiding voice. "I don't know why I've never done it. I'm afraid it's too late now. . . ."

August closed his eyes.

"Union Plaza."

Two stops.

"I'm sure it's too late . . . ," the woman rambled on, ". . . but I still dream about it. . . ."

She wasn't even talking to him, not really. Monsters couldn't tell lies, but when humans were around Sunai, they became . . . honest. August didn't have to compel them—if he could compel them *not* to open up, he would—they just started unloading. Most of the time they didn't even realize they were doing it.

Henry called it *influence*, but Leo had a better word: *confession.*

"Lyle Crossing."

One stop.

". . . I still dream . . ."

Confession was without a doubt his least favorite ability. Leo relished it, willing everyone around him to voice their doubts, their fears, their weaknesses, but it just made August uncomfortable.

"Do you dream . . . ?"

"Colton," announced the voice overhead.

The train ground to a halt, and August said a silent

THIS SAVAGE SONG

33

prayer as he fled the subway car, the woman's confession following him out.

If North City was surreal, Colton was something else entirely. August had never been this far from the red. The Academy was fenced in, but unlike the Seam, the walls seemed more aesthetic than functional; beyond the wrought iron gate, Colton Academy sat on a rolling stretch of grass, a line of trees at its back. August had seen trees once before, in a run-down park three blocks south of the compound, but these were different. There were enough of them to make a wall. No, a *forest*. That was the name for so many.

But the trees didn't distract him nearly as much as the *people*.

Everywhere he looked, he saw them, not FTF cadets or North civilians, but teenagers in Colton's trademark blue. Boys and girls walking through the gates, or sitting clustered in the grass. He marveled at the easy way they chatted and hung on one another, elbows bumping, arms thrown around shoulders, head to head and hip to hip. The way their faces broke into broad grins, or pursed in annoyance, or opened with laughter. They made it look so . . . natural.

What was he doing here?

Maybe Leo was right; he should have eaten

something. Too late now. He fought the urge to retreat, tried to remind himself that he'd wanted a way out of the compound, that *Leo* of all people had vouched for him, that he had a *job* to do, one as important as the rest of the FTF. He forced his feet forward, so sure with every step that someone would see through the Colton clothes and the practiced smile, and notice he wasn't human. As if it were written on his face as plainly as the marks down his arm. All of a sudden the hours spent before the mirror seemed ridiculous. How could ever he mimic this? How could he think that he was capable of passing for one of them, just because they were the same age? The thought snagged him. They *weren't* the same age. They only *looked* his age. No, that wasn't right: *he* looked *their* age, because they'd all been born, and he'd woken up in the shape of a twelve-year-old boy because that's how old they'd been, the bodies in the black bags when *it started with a bang*, not the universe only the sharp staccato bursts of gunfire and—

He slammed to a stop, struggling for air.

Someone bumped his shoulder, not a friendly jostle but a hostile jab, and August stumbled forward, regaining his balance in time to see the guy—broad-shouldered and blond—shoot a hard look back.

"What's your problem?" snapped August, the question out before he could think to stop it.

The boy spun on him. "You were in my way," he growled, grabbing August's collar. "You think I'm gonna let some shit newbie mess this up? This is *my* year, asshole, *my* school." And then, to August's horror, the guy *kept talking*. "Think you can scare me with that creepy stare? I'm not afraid of you. I'm not afraid of anyone. I . . ." he shuddered, forcing August closer. "I can't sleep; every time I close my eyes I see them."

"Hey now," said another student over August's shoulder. "There a problem, Jack?"

The blond guy, Jack, blinked a few times, gaze sharpening, and then shoved August backward. The other student caught his shoulder. "Come on, no need for that. My friend here's sorry. He didn't mean to piss you off." His tone was friendly, casual.

"Keep him away from me, Colin," snapped Jack, his voice normal again, "before I break his smug face."

"Will do." Colin shook his head. "Ass," he muttered as Jack stormed away. He turned toward August; a short, slim boy with a widow's peak and warm eyes set in an open face. "Making friends on your first day, huh?"

August straightened, smoothed his jacket. "Who said it was my first day?"

Colin laughed, an easy sound, as natural as breathing. "It's a small school, dude," he said with a grin, "and I've never seen you before. You got a name?"

August swallowed. "Frederick," he said.

"*Frederick?*" echoed Colin, raising a single brow. August wondered if he'd made a mistake, chosen the wrong name.

"Yeah," he said slowly, then added, "but you can call me Freddie."

No one had ever called him Frederick *or* Freddie, but it was the right answer. Colin's face morphed again, from skepticism to cheer in an instant. "Oh, thank God," he said. "Frederick is a really pretentious name. No offense. Not your fault."

They started walking toward the main building together, but a pair of students called Colin's name.

"Hey, I'll see you inside," he said as he jogged over to meet them. Halfway there he twisted around with a grin. "Try not to piss off anyone else before school starts."

August managed a ghost of the boy's smile. "I'll do my best."

"Name?" asked the woman in the registration office.

"Frederick Gallagher," said August, managing what he hoped was a nervous smile as he brushed a strand of hair out of his eyes. "But I go by Freddie."

"Ah," said the woman, pulling out a folder with a yellow band along the top. "You must be one of our new students."

He nodded, tweaked the smile. This time, she smiled back. "Look at you," she said. "Dark hair. Kind eyes. Dimples. They're going to eat you up."

August wasn't sure what she meant. "I hope not," he said.

She only laughed. Everyone laughed so easily here. "You still need to get your identification card," she said. "Go next door, and hand them the top page in your folder. They'll take care of you." She hesitated, looked like she was about to say something more, something personal. He backed away before she could.

Next door, a short line spilled out of a door marked ID REGISTRATION. August watched as a student at the front of the line handed the man behind the counter his paper, then stepped in front of a pale green backdrop. He grinned, and an instant later a flash went off. August cringed. Another student repeated the process. And another. He backed away.

The rest of the students seemed to be heading for a large pair of doors at the other end of the lobby, so he followed them, and found himself at the mouth of an auditorium. There was some unspoken system, a natural order that everyone else seemed to understand. They filed toward their seats, and August hung back, trying not to interrupt the flow of traffic.

"What year?" asked a woman's voice. He turned to

find a teacher in a skirt holding a stack of folders.

"Junior," he said.

She nodded. "You're sitting down front, on the left."

The auditorium was filling with bodies and noise as he found a seat, and the sheer quantity of both left him dizzy, dazed. All around him, hundreds of voices talked over and under and through one another, layering like music, but the cadence was all wrong, less like classical than jazz, and when he tried to pick the threads apart he wasn't left with chords, just syllables and laughter and sounds that made no sense. And then, mercifully, it quieted, and he looked up to see a man in a crisp blue suit striding across the stage.

"Hello," he said, tapping the mic on the podium. "I'm Mr. Dean, and I'm the Head of School here at Colton. I want to welcome our freshmen to a new school, and our returning students to a fresh year. You might not have noticed that we have several new students joining our ranks. And because Colton is a community, I'm going to ask them to stand when I call their names, so that you can make a point of making them feel welcome here."

August's stomach dropped.

"We have two new sophomores. Marjorie Tan . . ." A girl got to her feet a dozen rows behind him, blushing deeply under the collective gaze. She immediately started to sit down again but the headmaster waved his hand. "Please stay standing," he insisted. "Now, Ellis Casterfeld?"

A lanky boy got to his feet, and waved at the room.

"Juniors, we have one student joining your ranks." August's heart pounded. "Mr. Frederick Gallagher." August exhaled, relieved not to hear his name. And then he remembered that Frederick *was* his name. He swallowed, and stood. The juniors to every side shifted in their seats to get a better look at him. His face went hot, and for the first time August wished he could be *less* real. Maybe even disappear.

And then the headmaster said her name, and in a way he did.

"And finally, a new senior, Miss Katherine Harker."

The auditorium went silent, everyone else was forgotten as, near the front, a girl rose to her feet. Every head in the room turned toward her.

Katherine Harker.

The only child of Callum Harker, the "governor" of North City, a man known for collecting monsters like weapons, and the reason August had been sent to Colton.

He thought back to the conversation he'd had with Henry and Leo.

"I don't understand. You want me to . . . go to school? With her?" His nose crinkled at the thought. *Harker was the enemy.*

A murderer. Katherine was a mystery, but if she was anything like her father . . . "And do what exactly?"

"Follow her," said Leo.

"Colton's too small. She'll notice me."

"You won't be you," said Leo. "And we want her to notice. We want you to get close."

"Not too close," cut in Henry. "We just want you to keep an eye on her. In case we need leverage. . . ."

"It's the same reason her people are looking for you," explained Leo. "When this truce breaks—"

"*If* the truce breaks—" said Henry.

"She might come in handy."

"We don't know anything about her," said August.

"She's Harker's daughter. If he cares about anyone, it's her."

August stared at the girl in the front row. Katherine looked like her father: slim and sharp and full of angles. Her hair was different from the photo he'd seen. Still blond, but shoulder length, stock-straight, and parted so it covered half her face. Most of the Colton girls had opted for skirts with their polos, but she was wearing slim-cut slacks, her hands hooked casually in her pockets. All around August, people began to whisper. And then Katherine, who had been looking forward with a cool, empty gaze, turned and looked over her shoulder.

At him.

She didn't know—*couldn't* know—who he was, but her dark eyes tracked over him in a slow, appraising way, the very edge of a smile on her lips, before Headmaster Dean instructed them to take their seats. August sank into his chair, feeling like he'd just escaped a brush with death.

"Now," continued the headmaster, "if you haven't gotten your ID card yet, make sure to retrieve it by the end of the day. Not only can you use the card to pay for lunch and school supplies, but you'll need it to access certain parts of the campus, including the theater, sports facilities, and soundproof music rooms."

August's head shot up. He didn't care about the cafeteria, had little interest in drama or fitness, but a place where he could play in peace? That would be worth an ID.

"An attendant will be in the ID room during lunch and for half an hour after school . . ." The headmaster rambled on for several more minutes, but August had stopped listening.

When the assembly was over, the wave of students carried him out of the auditorium and into the lobby, where it took him roughly thirty seconds to realize he had no idea where he was supposed to go next. The hall was a tangle of uniformed bodies; he tried to get out of the way as he dug his schedule from his bag.

"Hey, *Frederick*."

He looked up and saw Colin jostling through the crowd. He caught August by the sleeve and pulled him out of the current. "I've got you." His gaze flicked down, and he saw August's forearm where the sleeve had pushed up. Those expressive eyes went wide. "Oh, nice tattoos, dude. But don't let Dean see them. He's crazy strict. I wore a temporary one on my face one time—I think it was a bee, I don't remember why—and he made me scrub it off. School policy."

August tugged his sleeve back down, and Colin stole a glance at the sheet in his hand. "Oh, perfect. We have English together. I thought I saw your name on the roster. I check all the rosters ahead of time, just to see who I'm up against, you know?" August did not know, and he couldn't tell if it was his influence making Colin so chatty, or if the boy was just naturally that way, but he suspected the latter. "Anyway, come on," Colin tugged him toward a stairwell door. "I know a shortcut."

"To where?"

"To English, obviously. We could take the hall but there are *too many damned freshmen!*" he bellowed. Several smaller students glanced wide-eyed at him, and the teacher in the skirt shot Colin a dark look. "Get to class, Mr. Stevenson."

Colin only winked at her and stepped into the

stairwell, holding the door for August, who wasn't sure
if he was being helped or abducted. But he didn't want
to be late for the first class of his life, so he followed anyway. Just before the door banged shut, he thought he
saw Katherine Harker walk past, the students around
her parting like a sea.

When people talked about the first day of school, they used terms like "fresh start," and "new beginning," and always made a point of saying it was a chance to define—or redefine—yourself.

In Kate's eyes, the first day was an opportunity, one she'd taken advantage of it at each of her previous institutions, and those first days felt like an education unto themselves, leading up to this. Her first day at Colton was a chance to set the tone. A chance to make an *impression*. She had the added advantage of being on home turf; people here might not know her, but they all knew *of* her, and that was better. It was a foundation, something to be built upon. By the end of the week, Colton would be hers. After all, if she couldn't rule a school, she didn't deserve to run a city.

Kate didn't actually care that much about running a school *or* a city. She just didn't want Harker to look at her and see weak, see helpless, see a girl who shared nothing but a few lines of his face, a shade of blond. She wanted him to look at her and see someone who deserved to be there. Because she'd be damned if she'd let him send her away, not this time.

She'd fought her way here, and she'd fight to stay.

I am my father's daughter, she thought as she walked down the hall, arms at her side and head up, medallion and metallic nails glinting beneath the lights (she thought of the monstrous teeth shining in the footage, and it gave her strength). Eyes followed her through the halls. Lips moved behind cupped fingers. To every side, the students swarmed and parted, rushed forward and drew back like a wave, a flock of starlings. All together. All apart.

"You have to break them early," her father once said. Of course, he'd been talking about monsters, not teenagers, but they had a lot in common. Both had hive minds; they thought—and acted—in groups. Cities and schools were both microcosms of life, and *small* schools came with their own delicate ecosystem.

St. Agnes had been the smallest of the bunch, with only a hundred girls, while Fischer, her first private school, weighed in at a considerable six hundred and fifty. Colton Academy was four hundred strong, which was small enough to feel intimate but large enough to guarantee at least a modicum of resistance.

It was natural—there were always those who wanted to challenge the ruling power, to stake their own claim to authority or popularity or whatever it was they were after, and Kate could usually pick them out within the first few days. They were a disruption to the hive mind, those few, and she knew she'd have to deal with them as soon as possible.

All she needed was an opportunity to establish herself.

And to her surprise, one presented itself almost immediately.

She'd known there would be whispers about her. Rumors. They weren't inherently bad. In fact, some of them were practically propagandistic. As she moved through the halls between classes, she cocked her head, catching the loudest ones.

"I heard she burned her last school down."

"I heard she's been to jail."

"I heard she drinks blood like a Malchai."

"Did you know she axed a student?"

"Psychopath."

"Killer."

And then, as she stepped into her next class, she heard it.

"I heard her mother went crazy."

Kate's steps slowed.

"Yeah," continued the girl, loud enough for her to hear. "She went crazy, tried to drive them off a bridge." Kate set her bag down on a desk, and ruffled through it absently, turning her good ear toward the girl. "I heard Harker sent her away because he couldn't stand to look at her. She reminded him of his dead wife."

"Charlotte," whispered another girl. "Shut up."

Yes, Charlotte, thought Kate. *Shut up*.

But Charlotte didn't. "Maybe he sent her away because she was crazy, too."

Not crazy, Kate wanted to say. No, he thought she was young, thought she was weak like her mother. But he was *wrong*.

She dug her nails savagely into her palms, and took her seat, eyes on the board. She sat like that all through class, head high, but she wasn't listening, wasn't taking notes. She didn't hear a word the teacher said, didn't care. She sat still and waited for the bell to ring, and when it did, she followed Charlotte out, and down the hall. Whatever class she had next wasn't as important as this.

When the girl detoured into the nearest bathroom, Kate followed, throwing the bolt behind her.

Charlotte, pretty in such a boring way, was standing at the sink, retouching her makeup. Kate came up beside her, and began rinsing the crescents of blood from her palms. Then she tucked her hair behind her ear, showing the scar that traced her face from temple to jaw. The other girl looked up, found Kate's gaze in the mirror, and had the audacity to smirk. "Can I help you?"

"What's your name?" asked Kate.

The girl raised a bleached brow, and dried her hands. "Charlotte," she said, already turning to go.

"No," said Kate slowly. "Your full name."

Charlotte stopped, suspicious. "Charlotte Chapel."

Kate gave a small, silent laugh.

"What's so funny?" snapped the girl.

Kate shrugged. "I burned down a chapel once."

Charlotte's face crinkled with disgust. "Freak," she muttered, walking away.

She didn't make it very far.

In an instant, Kate had her up against the wall, five metal-tipped fingers wrapped around her throat. With her free hand, Kate drew the lighter from her pocket. She pressed a notch on the side, and a silver switchblade slid out with a muted *snick*.

Charlotte's eyes went wide. "You're even crazier than I thought," she gasped.

For a moment, Kate thought about hurting her. Seriously hurting her. Not because it would serve some purpose, just because it would feel really, really good.

But getting expelled would negate everything she'd done to get here.

He'll ship you out of Verity. One way. For good.

"When the headmaster hears about this—"

"He won't," said Kate, resting the knife against Charlotte's cheek. "Because you're not going to tell him." She said it in the same way she said everything: with a quiet, even voice.

She'd seen a documentary once, on cult leaders, and the traits that made them so effective. One of the most important features was a commanding presence. Too many people thought that meant being loud, but in truth, it meant someone who didn't *need* to be loud. Someone who could command an audience without ever raising their voice. Kate's father was like that. She'd studied him, in the slivers of time they'd had together, and Callum Harker never shouted.

So neither did Kate.

She loosened her fingers on Charlotte's throat, just a little, and brought the knife to the medallion hanging against the girl's uniform shirt, tapping the engraved *V* casually with her blade. "I want you to remember something, Charlotte Chapel." She leaned in. "That pendant may protect you from the monsters, but it won't protect you from me."

The bell rang, and Kate pulled back, flashing her best

smile. The knife disappeared into the lighter and her hand fell away from the girl's throat. "Run along now," she said icily. "You wouldn't want to be late."

Charlotte clutched her bruised throat and scrambled out of the bathroom.

Kate didn't follow. She went to the sink, washed her hands again, and smoothed her hair. For an instant, she met her reflection's gaze, and saw another version of herself behind the stormy blue, one who belonged to a different life, a softer world. But that Kate had no place here.

She took a long breath, rolled her neck, and went to class, confident she'd made a solid first impression.

August was supposed to be in gym.

Or at least, every other junior was supposed to be in gym, and probably was, but thanks to a health condition—asthma, according to his file—he'd been granted a study hall instead.

August did not have asthma. What he *did* have were four hundred and eighteen uniform lines running the length of one arm and starting to wrap around his back and chest, and Henry was worried that they would draw attention.

So instead, August was in study hall. Or at least, he had been. He imagined a study hall might come in handy, but it being the first day of school, he had nothing to study, so he'd asked the monitor if he could go to the bathroom, and never came back.

Now he was standing outside the ID office.

On the way there, he'd tried to think up an excuse

for not wanting his photo taken—he'd read once about a tribe that believed being photographed would steal their soul—but in the end he didn't need an out.

The office was empty. The lights were on, and when he tried the handle, the door was unlocked. August looked around nervously, then stepped inside, pulling the door shut behind him. The ID form was still up on the computer screen, and he typed in his details: Frederick Gallagher, 16, junior, 5' 10", black hair, gray eyes.

An empty rectangle sat waiting to the right of the information. August knew what it was for. He swallowed and hit the delayed action photo button, then stepped in front of the pale backdrop, just like he'd seen the other students do. He looked straight into the camera lens and the flash went off. August blinked the light from his eyes and held his breath as he rounded the counter, but his heart sank when he saw the photo on the screen. His expression was a little too vacant, but his face had almost all the right components—jawline, mouth, nose, cheekbones, hair. An ordinary boy . . . except his eyes. Where August's eyes should be, there was only a smudge of black. As if someone had drawn his face in charcoal and then smeared it.

Sunai, Sunai, eyes like coal, sang a voice in his head. His stomach twisted.

Retake? prompted the computer.

He clicked *yes.* This time he didn't look straight at the camera, but just above it. No luck. The same dark smudge still obscured his gaze. August tried again and again and again, each time cheating his eyes a fraction to the left or the right, high or low, the smudge of black shifting, sometimes thinning, but always there. His vision filled with dots of light, a dozen flashes every time he blinked. The last take stared back at him from the screen, his eyes obscured by the same black streak, but a small, frustrated crease visible in his brow. He shouldn't have bothered, should have known it wouldn't work, but he'd hoped . . . *for what?*

A chance to play at being human? chided his brother's voice.

Sing you a song and steal your soul.

He shook his head.

Bang.

Too many voices.

Retake? prompted the computer.

August's finger hovered over *no,* but after a moment, he clicked *yes.* One more time. He stepped in front of the screen, took a deep breath, and readied himself for the inevitable flash, the disappointment of a final failed attempt. But the flash never came. He heard the digital click of the camera, but the light must have glitched. He crossed to the screen, heart thumping, and looked.

His breath caught.

The boy on the screen was standing there, hands shoved in his pockets. He wasn't looking at the camera. His eyes were half-lidded, his head turned away, the faintest blur to his edges, a picture snapped midmotion. But it was him. No black streak. No empty gaze.

August exhaled a shuddering breath, and clicked *print*, and a minute later the machine spat out his ID. He stared at the image for several long seconds, transfixed, then pocketed the card, and slipped out of the office just as the bell rang for lunch. He was halfway to his locker when a voice called his name. Well, *Freddie's* name.

He turned to find Colin, flanked by a boy on one side and a girl on the other. "Alex and Sam, this is Freddie," he said by way of introduction. "Freddie, Alex and Sam."

August wasn't sure which one was Alex and which was Sam.

"Hey," said one of them.

"Hey," echoed the other.

"Hello," said August.

Colin swung an arm around his shoulder, which was hard to do considering he was a full six inches shorter. August tensed at the sudden contact, but didn't pull away. "You look lost."

August started to shake his head, when Colin cut him off.

"You hungry?" he asked cheerfully. "I'm starving, let's get some lunch."

". . . gives me the creeps."

". . . party this weekend . . ."

". . . such an asshole."

". . . Jack and Charlotte an item?"

August stared down at his half-eaten food.

The cafeteria was loud—much louder than he'd expected—the constant clatter of trays and laughter and shouts as staccato as gunfire, but he tried not to think about that and instead focused on the green apple he was rolling between his hands. Apples were his favorite food, not because of the way they tasted, but because of how they felt. The cool, smooth skin, the solid weight. But he could feel Sam—that was the girl, it turned out—watching him, so he brought the apple to his mouth and bit down, fighting back a grimace.

August *could* eat, but he didn't enjoy it. The act wasn't repulsive. It was just . . . people talked about the decadence of chocolate cake, the sweetness of peaches, the groan-inducing pleasure of a good steak. To them, every food was an *experience*.

To August, it all tasted the same. And it all tasted like nothing.

"That's because it's *people* food," Leo would say.

"I'm a person," he'd say, tensing.

"No." His brother would shake his head. "You're not."

August knew that he meant, *You're more.* But it didn't make him feel like more. It made him feel like an impostor.

Now, the way other people felt about food, that's how August felt about music. He could savor each note, taste the melody. The thought made his tallies prickle, his fingers ache for the violin. Across the table, Colin was telling a story. August wasn't listening, but he was *watching.* As Colin talked, his face went through an acrobatic procession of expressions, one folding into the next.

August took a second bite, chewed, swallowed, and set the apple down.

Sam leaned forward. "Not hungry?"

Before August could show her the half-eaten contents of his bag, Colin cut in.

"I'm always hungry," he said with his mouth full. "Like, always."

Sam rolled her eyes. "I've noticed."

The boy, Alex, speared a piece of fruit. "So, *Frederick*," he said, emphasizing every syllable in the name. "Colton doesn't get a lot of new blood. You get thrown out of one of the other academies?"

"I heard *she* got kicked out," whispered Colin. He didn't have to say who.

"That's not the only reason people change schools," said Sam, turning to Alex. "Just because *you* got tossed—"

"It was a voluntary transfer!" said Alex, turning his attention back to August. "Well? Expulsion? Transfer? Bang a teacher?"

"No," he answered automatically, and then, slower, "I was homeschooled."

"Ah, no wonder you're so quiet."

"*Alex*," said Sam, angling a kick under the table, "that's rude."

"What? I could have said 'weird.'"

Another kick.

"It's okay," said August, managing a smile. "I'm just not used to so many people."

"Where do you live?" asked Colin around a mouthful of pasta.

August took another bite of apple, using it to force down the words rising in his throat. In those stolen seconds, he sorted through his lines, trying find the right truth. "Near the Seam," he answered.

"Damn," said Alex, whistling. "In the red?"

"Yeah," said August slowly, "but it's North City, so . . ."

"It's only scary if you don't have a medal," added Colin, tapping the embossed pendant around his neck.

Sam was shaking her head. "I don't know. I've heard bad things happen in the red. Even to those with Harker's protection."

Alex shot a look across the cafeteria. "Don't let *her* hear you say that. She'll tell her dad."

Colin shrugged, and started talking about a concert— the boy's mind seemed to jump around even more than his—but August followed Alex's gaze. Katherine was sitting alone at a table, but she didn't look lonely. In fact, there was a small, defiant smile on her lips. As if she *wanted* to be alone. As if the fact people avoided her was a badge. August didn't get it.

"You want to come, Freddie?"

He watched as she picked at her food in a slow disinterested way, as she drew a metallic nail around the edge of her pendant, as she got to her feet.

"Freddie?"

The current of the cafeteria shifted with the movement, eyes drifting her way. But she didn't seem to mind. She kept her head up as she dumped the tray and walked out.

"He's not even listening."

August's attention snapped back. "Sorry, what?"

"Concert, Saturday, you want to come?"

"*None of us* are going," Sam cut in, sparing August from having to answer. "Because there's a *curfew*, Colin. And it's practically in the *Waste!*"

"And we don't want to *die*," added Alex in a gross exaggeration of Sam's tone. He flailed his arms as he said it.

"My mom would skin me," said Sam, ignoring the impersonation.

"Not if a Corsai did it first," teased Alex. Sam gave him a horrified look and punched him in the shoulder.

"Ow!"

"I just think," said Colin, leaning across the table, "that life is short, you know?" His tone was soft, conspiratorial. He had a way of making August feel like he wasn't new, like he'd been there all along. "You can't spend it afraid."

August found himself nodding, even though he spent *most* of his time afraid. Afraid of what he was, afraid of what he wasn't, afraid of unraveling, becoming something else, becoming nothing.

"Yeah," cut in Alex, "life is short, and it will be a hell of a lot shorter if you go wandering at night . . ."

Colin's mouth quirked. "Freddie's not afraid of monsters, are you?"

August didn't know how to answer that. He didn't have to.

"I totally saw one once," added Colin.

"You are so full of it . . ."

"What did you do?"

"I obviously ran like hell."

August laughed. It felt good.

And then, between one bite of apple and the next, the hunger started.

It began as nothing.

Or *almost* nothing, like the moment before a cold starts, that split second of wooziness that warns you a fever is coming. Dwelling on it—Is that a tickle? Is my throat getting scratchy? How long have I been sniffling?—only made it worse faster, and he tried to smother the spike of panic even as it shot through him.

Ignore it, he told himself. *Mind over body*—which would work right up until the hunger spread from body to mind, and then he'd be in trouble. He focused on his breathing, forced air down his throat and through his lungs.

"Hey, Freddie, you okay?" asked Colin, and August realized he was gripping the table. "You look a little sick."

"Yeah," he said, pushing to his feet, nearly tripping as

his legs tangled in the chair. "I just . . . I'm going to grab some fresh air."

August swung his bag onto his shoulder, trashed what was left of his lunch, and pushed through the cafeteria doors, not caring where they led, so long as they led *out*.

He was behind the school, the trees a green line in the distance. The air was cool, and he gulped it in, muttering, *"you're okay, you're okay, you're okay,"* to himself before realizing he wasn't alone.

Someone cleared her throat, and August turned to find Katherine Harker leaning against the building, a cigarette dangling from her fingers.

"Bad day?"

Kate just wanted a moment of peace. A moment to breathe, and think, and not be on display. Charlotte's words were still lodged under her skin.

I heard her mother went crazy. Tried to drive them off a bridge.

The words brought back not one memory but two. Two different worlds. Two different Kates. One lying in a field. The other stretched on the pavement. One surrounded by rustling quiet of the country. The other surrounded by ringing silence.

She brought her fingers absently to the scar beneath her hair, traced a metallic nail around the curve of her ear. Disconcerting, to be able to feel but not hear the drag of nail on flesh.

Just then the doors burst open, and a boy stumbled through. Kate's hand dropped away from her ear. The boy looked a little lost and a little ill, and she couldn't really blame him. He'd come from the cafeteria, and that place was enough to set anyone off balance.

"Bad day?"

He looked up, startled, and she recognized him.

Frederick Gallagher. The new junior. Up close, he looked more like a stray dog than a student. He had wide gray eyes beneath a mop of messy black hair, and a starved look about him, bones pressing against his skin.

She watched him open his mouth, close it, open it again, only to offer a single word. "Yeah."

Kate tapped ash off the cigarette and pushed herself up to her full height. "You're the new kid, right?"

One black brow lifted, just a fraction. "So are you," he shot back.

The answer caught her off guard. She'd expected him to be a mumbler, or maybe a groveler. Instead he looked straight at her when he spoke, and his voice, though soft, was steady. Maybe not a stray dog, then.

"It's Katherine, right?"

"Kate," she said. "Frederick?"

"Freddie," he corrected.

She took a drag on her cigarette. Frowned. "You don't look like a Freddie."

He shrugged, and for a second they stood there, sizing each other up, the moment stretching, the gaze growing uncomfortable until his gray eyes finally broke free, escaping to the ground. Kate smiled, victorious. She gestured to the patch of pavement, the border of grass. "What brings you to my office?"

He looked around, confused, as if he'd actually intruded. Then he looked up and said, "The view."

Kate flashed a crooked grin. "Oh really?"

His face went red. "I didn't mean you," he said quickly. "I was talking about the trees."

"Wow," she said dryly. "Thanks. How am I supposed to compete with pine and oak?"

"I don't know," said Freddie, cocking his head. Stray dog again. "They're pretty great."

She tucked her hair behind her ear and caught Freddie's glance. It didn't linger. There was a flush in his cheeks, but it wasn't all embarrassment. He really did look ill.

"I'd offer you a chair," she said, tapping ash on the pavement.

"It's all right," he said, slumping back against the adjacent wall. "I just needed some air."

She watched his chest empty and fill and empty again, gray eyes leveled on a low bank of clouds. There was something about those eyes, something present and distant at the same time.

Where are you? She wondered, the question on the tip

of her tongue. "Here." She held out the cigarette. "You look like you could use one."

But Freddie waved his hand. "No thanks," he said. "Those things'll kill you."

She laughed, soft, soundless. "So will lots of things around here."

A rueful smile. "True."

The bell rang, and she pushed off the wall. "See you around, Freddie."

"Do I need to schedule an appointment?" he asked.

She waved a hand. "My office is always open."

With that, she stubbed out the cigarette and went inside.

By the end of the day, Kate was untouchable.

Word had obviously spread—at least through the senior class—about her stunt with Charlotte in the girls' bathroom. Most kept their distance, went quiet when she passed, but a few took a different tactic.

"I love your hair."

"You have great skin."

"Your nails are amazing. Is that *iron*?"

Kate had even less patience for the would-be minions than the Charlottes. She had seen people grovel at her father's feet, try to plead and con and worm their way into his graces. He told her once that it was why he preferred monsters to men. Monsters were base, disgusting things, but they had little interest and less talent when it came to gaining favor or telling lies. They were hungry, but that hunger had nothing to do with ambition.

"I never have to wonder what they want," he'd said. *"I already know."*

Kate had always hated monsters, but as half the school steered clear and the other half tried to make advances, she began to see the appeal. It was exhausting, and she was relieved when the last bell finally rang.

"Look," she said to Marcus when she reached the black sedan. "Not expelled."

"It's a miracle," deadpanned the driver, holding open her door.

Shielded by the tinted windows, she finally let the cold smile slide from her face as the car pulled away from Colton and headed home.

Home, that was a word that took some getting used to.

The Harkers lived on the top floor of what was once the Allsway Building and was now known ostenta-tiously as Harker Hall, since her father owned it from sidewalk to spire. Marcus stayed with the car, while two men in dark suits held open the glass doors and ushered Kate inside. Classical music wafted through the air like perfume, fine in small doses, but quickly becoming noxious. The place itself was decadent: the lobby vaulted overhead, the floor a stretch of dark marble, the walls white stone with gold trim, and the ceilings awash with crystal chandeliers.

Kate had read a sci-fi novel once about a shimmering future city where everything was glamorous on the outside but rotten to the core. Like a bad apple. She sometimes wondered if her dad had read it, too (if so, he'd obviously never read to the end).

A dark suit fell in step behind her as she crossed the lobby, which was brimming with men and women in lush attire, many obviously hoping for an audience with Harker. One—a gorgeous woman in a cream-colored coat, tried to slip an envelope of cash into Kate's hand, but she never made it past the suit. (Which was too bad. Kate might have taken the bribe. Not that it would have made it to her father.) Instead she kept her eyes ahead until she reached the golden elevator. Only then did she turn, survey the room, and offer the edge of a smile.

"People are users. It's a universal truth. Use them, or they'll use you."

Another line from Callum Harker's manual for staying on top.

And Callum Harker *had* been on top, or at least on his way up, for a *very* long time. He was a man good at making three things: friends, enemies, and money (most of it illegal). Long before the Phenomenon and the chaos, before the territory wars and the truce, he was already becoming a kind of king. Not on the surface, no, that title belonged to the Flynns, but all cities were icebergs, the real power underneath, and even in those days Harker had half of V-City in his pocket. So when the shadows started growing teeth, when the neighboring territories shut the borders, when panic drove people out of the city and then the people outside the city drove them back, when everyone was terrified, Harker was there.

He had the vision—had *always* had the vision—and then suddenly he had the monsters, too. And it seemed so simple: go with Flynn and live in fear, or go with Harker and pay for safety.

And it turned out, people were willing to pay *a lot*.

The Harker penthouse was minimalist and sleek: more marble and glass, interrupted by dark wood and steel. There were no servants up here. No suits. Everything about the apartment was cold, full of sharp edges, no place for a family. And yet, they had been one here. They'd lived in the penthouse, all three of them, in those short months after the truce and before the accident. But when she dragged through her memories, searching for *home*, the images were all mixed up, open fields and distant trees, broken glass and buckling metal.

It didn't matter.

She was here now. She would make it hers.

"Hello?" Kate called out.

No one answered. She hadn't expected a welcoming party, a how-was-your-day-sweetheart. They'd never been *that* kind of family. Her father's private office was attached to the penthouse, but it might as well be its own apartment, its own world. The massive doors were shut, and when she brought her good ear to the wood, she heard only a low and steady hum. Soundproofing. Kate pushed off the doors and turned back toward the rest of the loft.

Beyond the floor-to-ceiling windows, the sun was just starting to sink behind the taller buildings. She tapped a panel on the wall, and the lights came on, flooding the space with artificial white. Another tap, and the heavy silence was broken by music pouring out of speakers across the apartment. She kept her eyes on her father's office and held her finger down; the volume rose and rose until the sound vibrated in her chest and made the empty space feel full. Her steps were lost under the beat as she made her way to the kitchen, climbed onto a stool at the counter, and unpacked her bag. The Colton workload was daunting, but she'd spent years at boarding schools that seemed to have nothing better to do than assign homework. In among her papers was a handout on university preparations titled, "Life after Colton" filled with options, most inside Verity, but a few beyond. The borders had reopened two years ago on a heavily restricted basis—the territory was still a closed zone, under Quarantine Code 53: Other—but Kate imagined a few of the Colton kids had enough connections to get transport papers to go with a university invite.

After all, the other territories *wanted* Verity's brightest minds.

They just didn't want their monsters.

She tossed the booklet aside.

A stack of fresh medallions sat on the marble counter, heavy iron disks with the ornate *V* branded onto the front. Kate spun a pendant absently between her fingers. Iron. It was true that monsters loathed the stuff, but it wasn't the metal that bought safety. It was Harker. Anyone could hang a piece of metal around their neck and hope for the best, but these were special.

The back of every medallion was engraved with a number, and every number was—or would be—assigned to a person; a ledger in her father's office kept track of every soul who purchased his protection from the things that waited in the dark. Not because the monsters feared the metal. Because the monsters feared *him*.

She snapped her fingers, spinning the medallion again, watching the two sides flash past over and over.

No pendant, no protection. That was Harker's law.

As the disc wobbled, she felt something move behind her. She couldn't hear it, not over the pounding beat of the stereo system, but she knew, instantly, in that hairs-standing-up-on-the-back-of-your-neck way, that she wasn't alone anymore.

Her hand drifted under the lip of the counter, and closed around the handgun strapped against the granite. By the time the medallion fell, she was on her feet, the safety off, and the gun raised. She looked down the sight, and found a pair of bloodred eyes staring back.

Sloan.

Six years ago, she'd come home to V-City, to her father, and found *Sloan* at his side. Dressed in a tailored black suit, her father's favorite Malchai looked almost human. He had Callum Harker's height, if not his build, and Harker's deep-set eyes, though Sloan's burned crimson where Harker's shone blue. But if her father was an ox, Sloan was a wraith, the dark bones of his skeleton just visible through the thin vellum of his skin. With his pallor, Sloan looked sick. *No*, thought Kate. He looked *dead*. Like a corpse on a cold day.

An *H* was branded into the monster's cheek, just below his left eye, the letter the size and shape of a college ring. (Her father wore it on his left hand, above his wedding band.)

Sloan's thin lips drew back to reveal sharp teeth, like a shark's, each filed to a point.

Malchai, Malchai, sharp and sly,
Smile and bite and drink you dry.

Sloan was saying something, but she couldn't hear his words over the blaring music. She didn't want to hear them. Sloan's voice was all wrong, not a rattle or a growl, but something soft and cloying. She had never seen the Malchai feed, but she could imagine him, covered in gore, his voice still sickly sweet.

I can't hear you, she mouthed, hoping he would go away. But Sloan was too patient. He reached out and touched a panel on the wall with a single sharp nail, and the beat collapsed, plunging them back into silence.

Kate didn't lower the gun. She wondered what kind of rounds were loaded. Silver? Iron? Lead? Something that would make a dent.

"Home for less than a week," he said, his voice so low in the wake of the music that she had to strain to hear, "and you've already found the weapons."

Kate smiled grimly. "What can I say?"

"Do you plan to shoot me?" he asked, taking a prowling step closer, red eyes bright with interest, as if it were a game.

"I've considered it," she said, but she didn't fire, and then she felt a weight on the gun, and looked down to see Sloan's hand resting casually on the weapon's barrel. She hadn't even seen him move. That was the way with Malchai, slow until they struck.

Sloan clicked his tongue against his sharp teeth. "My dear Kate," he said. "I'm not your enemy."

His fingers slid forward, brushing hers, cold and slick, almost *reptilian*, and she jerked away, surrendering the gun. He set it on the counter between them. "No problems today, I assume."

Kate gestured to herself. "Home in one piece."

"And the school?" As if he cared.

"Still standing." The temperature in the kitchen was falling, as if Sloan were sucking all the heat out of the room. Kate crossed her arms. "You're up early."

"A vampire joke. How original." He never cracked a smile, but Sloan had her father's dry humor. Only the Corsai were truly nocturnal, allergic to the light of day. The Malchai drank blood and drew their strength from the night, but they weren't vampires, didn't shrink away from crosses, wouldn't catch fire in the sun. A piece of pure metal through the heart, though, that *would* still take them down.

Kate watched Sloan eye the stack of medallions on the counter and recoil ever so slightly before he turned toward the floor-to-ceiling windows and the thinning light.

She had a theory about Sloan, that he wasn't just Harker's servant, but *his* Malchai. The product of some awful crime, an aftermath, just like those Corsai in the clip she'd watched. Something that slithered out of Harker's wake. But who had he killed to gain a creature like Sloan? And how long had the Malchai been there, at her father's side when Kate *wasn't*? The question made her want to put a silver bullet through the monster's eye.

Her gaze flicked to the brand on the Malchai's cheek. "Tell me something, Sloan."

"Hmm?"

"What did you do to become my father's favorite *pet*?" The Malchai's face stiffened, as if freezing into place. "Have you learned any tricks since I left? Can you sit? Lie down? Play fetch?"

"I only have one trick," he said, lifting a bony hand to the air beside her head. "I know how to listen."

He snapped his fingers next to her bad ear. Kate went for the gun, but Sloan got there first. "Uh-uh," he warned, waving it side to side. "Play nice."

Kate held up her hands, and took a step back. "Who knows," said Sloan, twirling the weapon. "If you behave, maybe Harker will finally claim you, too."

August felt like hell.

Every one of his four hundred and eighteen tally marks was humming faintly by the time he slumped into the subway seat and closed his eyes. His pulse pounded in his head along with the steady, distant sound of gunshots. He tried not to think about it, but it was like trying not to scratch an itch.

"How *could* you?" snapped a woman across the aisle. She was standing over a man reading a tablet. When he didn't look up she slammed her hand down on the screen. "*Look at me.*"

"Dammit, Leslie."

"I work with her!"

"Do you really want to do this right now?" he growled. "Fine, let's make a scorecard."

"You are *such* an ass."

"There was Eric, and Harry, and Joe, but are we

counting the ones who didn't want you—"

She slapped him, hard—the sound was a crack in the subway car, a bang in August's skull. Heads turned toward the fight. He swallowed hard. His influence was spreading, radiating off of him like heat. Two seats down, a man began to sob. "It's all my fault, all my fault, I never meant to do it. . . ."

"You really are a *bitch*."

"It wasn't worth it."

"I should have left."

"It's all my fault."

The noise in the subway car grew louder, and August gripped the seat, knuckles white, and counted the stops until the Seam.

"You okay?" asked Paris when he reached her apartment. She had that extra sense, the one that knew when things weren't right.

"I'm alive," he said, swapping the blazer back for his FTF jacket.

She reached out, brought a hand to his cheek. "You're warm."

His bones were heating up, his skin stretched too tight over them. "I know."

The cellar downstairs felt blissfully cool and dark, and part of him just wanted to lie down on the damp floor and close his eyes, but he kept going, through the tunnel and into the building on the other side, up, and out, and four blocks south through the broken streets to home. In the elevator he found his reflection, and did his best to smooth his hair, compose his features. He looked peaked, but otherwise, the sickness wasn't showing yet.

Henry was waiting for him in the Tower. "August?" he chided. "You were supposed to text when you left school."

"Sorry," he mumbled.

"Are you okay?"

God, he hated that question.

"I'll be fine," he managed. It wasn't a lie. He would be fine, eventually.

"You don't look fine," challenged Henry.

"Long day," he muttered through clenched teeth.

Henry sighed. "Well, perk up. Emily's making a nice dinner tonight to celebrate your first day."

"That's ridiculous," he said. "Three of us don't even eat."

"Humor her."

August rubbed his eyes. "I'm going to take a shower."

He left the lights off in the bathroom, peeling the uniform away in the dark. The water came on cold, but he didn't turn it up. He stepped in, and gasped as it hit his bare skin, shivering under the icy stream. He stayed until his bones stopped hurting, until the cold loosened the fire in his chest and he didn't feel like he was swallowing smoke with every breath. He leaned his forehead against the shower wall. *You're okay, you're okay, you're okay.*

By the time he got out of the shower, the sun had gone down.

Everyone was waiting for him in the kitchen.

"There he is," said Emily, wrapping him in a hug. "We were starting to worry." His skin was still cool from the shower, so she didn't notice the fever. Still, he pulled free and made his way to the table.

August cringed; the overhead lights were too bright, the scraping of chairs too sharp. Everything was heightened, like the volume on his life was turned up but not in an exciting way. Noises were too loud and smells too strong and pain—which he *did* feel—too sharp. But worse than the senses were the emotions. Agitation and anger burned under his skin and in his head. Every comment and every thought felt like a spark on dry wood.

The table was set. Two plates had food on them; the other three were garnished only by napkins. This was ridiculous. It was a waste of time. Why were they even *trying* to pretend like—

"Sit by me," said Ilsa, patting the seat to her left.

August sank into the chair, fists clenched. He could feel Leo's gaze on him, heavy as stone, but it was Henry who spoke.

"So, did you see her?"

"Of course I saw her," said August.

"And?" pressed Emily.

"And she looks like a girl. She doesn't exactly exude murderous kingpin." Sure, she tried to, but there was something about the performance that rang false. Like it was a piece of clothing. His own clothing felt too tight. August closed his eyes, a bead of sweat sliding down his back. He felt like he was made of embers, someone blowing faintly on the—

"Anything else?"

They were both looking at him so expectantly. August tried to focus. "Well, I think I might have . . . accidentally . . . made a friend."

Ilsa smiled. Leo raised a brow. Henry and Emily exchanged glances. "August," said Henry slowly. "That's great. Just be careful."

"I *am* being careful," he snapped. He could hear the annoyance in his voice, but he couldn't calm down any more than he could cool off. "You wanted me to blend in. Wouldn't I stand out more for *not* making friends?"

"I'm all for you making *acquaintances*, August," said Henry evenly, "but don't get too close."

"You think I don't know that?" The anger rose in him, too fast. "Do you really think I'm that stupid? Just because you've kept me cooped up in this place for four years, you think I don't have any common sense? What am I going to do, *Dad*? Invite them over for *dinner*?" He shoved up from the table.

"*August,*" pleaded Ilsa.

He heard his parents push up from their chairs as he fled the room, but it was Leo who followed him into the hallway.

"When's the last time you ate?" he demanded.

When August hesitated, Leo came at him. He cringed back, away, but his brother was too large, too fast, and he only made it half a step before Leo pinned him against the wall. He took August's chin in his hand and wrenched his face up, black eyes boring down into his. "*When?*"

Leo's influence bled through his voice and his touch at the same time, and the answer forced its way out. "A few days ago."

"*Dammit, August,*" said Leo, stepping back.

"What?" he challenged, rubbing his jaw. "You go a week, sometimes more. And Ilsa doesn't even seem to need it. Why should I—"

"Because you do. This is a foolish, futile pursuit. You have a fire in you, little brother. You should embrace its heat instead of trying to dampen it."

"I don't want—"

"This isn't about what you *want,*" cut in Leo. "You

cannot build up resistance by starving yourself. You know what will happen if you don't eat. All those precious little tallies will go away and you'll have to start again." But that wasn't what August was afraid of, and Leo knew it. It wasn't about losing the marks. It was about what he'd lose with them. What Leo had already lost. "How many are you up to now, little brother?"

August swallowed. "Four hundred and eighteen."

"Four hundred and eighteen days," echoed Leo. "That's impressive. But you can't have it both ways. You feed or you go dark. How many died last time you fell? Eight?"

The number clawed its way up August's throat. "Nine," he whispered.

"Nine," repeated his brother. "Nine innocent lives. All because you refused to eat." August wrapped his arms around his ribs. "What do you want?" chided Leo. "To be ordinary? To be *human*?" He said the word as if it stained his tongue.

"Better human than a monster," he muttered.

Leo's jaw tightened. "Take heed, little brother," he said. "Do not lump us in with those base creatures. We are not Corsai, swarming like insects. We are not Malchai, feeding like beasts. Sunai are justice. Sunai are balance. Sunai are—"

"Self-righteous and prone to speaking in third

person?" cut in August before he could stop himself.

Leo's black eyes narrowed, but his calm did not waver. It *never* wavered. He pulled out his cell and dialed. Someone answered. "Tell Harris and Phillip to take a walk," he said, then hung up. He drew a folded piece of paper from his pocket and pressed it into August's hand. "Go eat before you lose more than your temper." Leo wrapped his fingers around the base of August's neck and pulled him close. "Pretend it's chicken," he said softly. "Pretend you're normal. Pretend whatever you like, little brother. It does not change what you *are*."

And with that Leo let go and returned to his place at the table.

August didn't follow. He stayed in the hall until his heart settled, and then he went to find his violin.

By the time Harker's office door finally opened, the sun had gone down, the last echoes of light streaked violently across the sky. Kate was still sitting at the kitchen counter, less out of academic diligence—her homework was done—than a stubborn determination to be there when her father emerged. He'd been avoiding her all week, ever since the black transport had deposited her in the hours before dawn.

That first good-bye—when she was five and the city was tearing itself apart, and Harker was bundling them into a car, and she was sobbing because she didn't want to go—he'd taken her chin in his hand and said, "My daughter does not cry."

And she'd stopped, right then and there. But when she came back after the truce, the first words he said to her were, "Make me proud," and somehow, then, she'd let him down. Now Kate was here again, and this time she wouldn't fail.

Charlotte's words rang in her ears.

He can't stand to look at her.

But it wasn't true. He just didn't understand yet—she wasn't the little girl he'd sent away twelve years ago, the one who set bugs free instead of killing them and was afraid of the dark. She wasn't the girl who'd come back six years later, the one who cried when she had bad dreams and got sick at the sight of blood. She wasn't weak like her mother, wouldn't break down and try to vanish in the middle of the night.

She was her father's daughter.

Kate sat very still at the counter, her head turned so she could hear the sound of Harker's heavy steps across the paneled floor. She waited, listened as the steps moved *away* instead of toward her. Listened to the sound of the elevator being called, the scrape of its arrival, the hush of its descent. When it was gone, Kate got to her feet, and turned to follow, only to find Sloan blocking the doorway.

It was dark out now, and Sloan seemed more *real*, solid in a way that put her on edge. His skeleton stood out like a bruise beneath his skin, and his teeth looked longer and sharper and silver as knifepoints. "Hungry?"

Kate shook her head. "Where did he go?"

"Who?" asked the Malchai, narrowing his red eyes. Surely he had better things to do than babysit her. His expression certainly said so.

"Is this how Harker has you spending your time?" she goaded.

"Let's play a game," he said amiably. "You can tell me to get out of your way. You can call me a monster and I can call you a sheltered little brat and we can have a quarrel. It will be entertaining. Maybe when it's over you'll even storm off to your room and slam the door like an ordinary teenager."

Kate gave him a cold smile. "I'm not an ordinary teenager."

Sloan sighed. "Would that you were."

"Tell me where he—"

Sloan shot forward, caging her in against the counter. The sudden force of it was like a blow to the ribs, knocking the air from her lungs.

"Down, dog," she snarled, trying to keep the fear out of her voice.

The Malchai didn't move. His crimson eyes dragged over her. "Can't you see," he whispered. "Harker doesn't want you here."

"You don't know that—"

"Of course I do." A single cold finger came to rest against her cheek. The nail was filed to a point.

She swallowed, held her ground. "I am not a child anymore."

"You will always be our little Katherine," he murmured. "Crying herself to sleep. Begging her mother to take her away."

"Mom wanted to leave, not me."

"You can lie to yourself, but I can't."

A drop of blood welled above Sloan's nail, but she didn't pull away. "I am a Harker," she said slowly. "I belong here. Now tell me where he is."

The Malchai sighed and turned his gaze away, considered the thickening dark beyond the windows. "In the basement." Kate swallowed, and started toward the elevator. "But you really shouldn't go there."

The doors opened. Kate stepped in, and turned back toward the Malchai. "Why not?"

He flashed a savage smile. "Because that," he said, "is where the real monsters are."

Harris and Phillip joined August on the way down.

The elevator paused at the fifteenth floor and the two brawny guys in black fatigues climbed in. Harris was eighteen, dark hair spilling out beneath his cap, and Phillip was twenty, buzz-cut, and like most of the young men in South City, they'd apparently jumped at the chance to join the FTF. They were both cheerful guys, the kind to get a bounce in their step at the first sign of trouble, to run *toward* it instead of away. The kind to high-five after taking out a Corsai with an HUV beam to the head or driving a metal spike through a Malchai's heart.

"So we're on level three, you know that corridor, the one where the cameras don't quite reach, and—oh, hey, August!"

"Saved by the elevator," said Phillip. He flashed August a warm grin. "You holding up?"

August nodded tightly. The anger was bleeding out of him, which wasn't a good sign. What came after was worse.

"You look like you could use a boost," said Harris, pulling off his FTF cap and settling it over August's black curls. Only a few handpicked members of the FTF knew who—and, more important, *what*—August really was. "I was just telling Phil about this prime—"

"She's out of your league, bro."

"Harsh."

"No," said Phillip as they hit the lobby. "I mean she is *literally* out of your league. Second-class team captain, and you're a what—didn't you just get bumped back to mindless drone?"

Harris rolled his eyes. "What about you, August? Good-looking mons—" Phillip shot him a look. "—kid like you. Anyone special?"

"Believe it or not," said August as they stepped out into the night. "My options are limited."

"Nah, you just gotta expand your parameters. Look beyond your—"

Phillip cleared his throat. "Who're we visiting tonight?" he asked, scanning the street. August shifted the strap on his shoulder—he'd moved the violin into a different case, one that looked like it was made for a weapon instead of a musical instrument—and unfolded the paper Leo had given him. It was a profile. A victim. August tried not to use that word—victims were innocent, and this man was not—but the term kept getting stuck in his head.

"Albert Osinger," he read aloud. "259 Ferring Pass, 3B."

"That's not too far," said Phillip. "We can walk."

August considered the paper as he fell into step behind them. A grainy photo was printed below the words, a capture from a video feed.

Sometimes people brought cases to Henry Flynn, looking for justice, but most of the targets came from the footage. South City had its own surveillance, and Ilsa spent most days scanning the feeds, searching for shadows other people couldn't see, ones that shouldn't be there. The mark of someone whose violence had taken shape. A sinner.

Corsai fed on flesh and bone, Malchai on blood, and whose it was meant nothing to them. But the Sunai could feed only on sinners. That's what set them apart. Their best-kept secret. It was the seed of Leo's righteousness, and the reason all FTFs were required to be shadow free. It was also why, in the early days of the Phenomenon and the mounting chaos, Leo had chosen to side with Henry Flynn instead of Callum Harker, a man with too many shadows to count.

"We are the darkest acts made light," Leo liked to say.

August supposed they were a kind of cosmic clean-up crew, created to address the source of the monstrous problem.

And Albert Osinger had officially been labeled a source.

The boots ahead of him came to a stop, and August folded the paper, and looked up. They were on the corner of a gutted street, most of the lights dead or flickering. Phillip and Harris had their HUVs out, beams slicing back and forth on the pavement. They were looking at him expectantly.

"What?"

Phillip cocked his head. Harris jabbed a finger at a building. "I said we're here."

The apartment building looked run-down, five stories of chipping paint and cracked brick. Broken window glass littered the curb where it had been bashed out and boarded over using iron nails. A nest, that's what they called places like this, where people burrowed down as if waiting out a storm.

There was no telling how many people were holed up inside.

"You want us to come in?" asked Harris.

They always offered, but August could tell they'd rather keep their distance. The music couldn't *hurt* them, but it would still take its toll.

August shook his head. "Watch the front." He turned to Phillip. "And the fire escapes."

They nodded, and split up, and August made his way up the front steps. A metal *X* had been fashioned across the door, but it wasn't pure, and even if it had been, it wouldn't have stopped him. He pulled an access card from his coat pocket. An FTF tool, skeleton-coded. He swiped it, and inside the door, a lock shifted, but when he turned the handle, the door barely moved. Stiff or barricaded, he didn't know. He put his shoulder into the metal, and shoved, felt the bottom lip scrape the floor for several grating inches before finally—suddenly—giving way.

Inside, the stairwell itself was a mess of boxes and crates, anything that could be used to help hold back the night if it found a way in. UVR lights glared down from the ceiling, giving the hall an eerie glow, and a single red dot flickered in the corner. The security cameras in South City were all wired into the same closed grid, but August still pulled the FTF hat down over his eyes as he climbed to the third floor, the violin slung over his shoulder.

Sunai, Sunai, eyes like coal,

Sing you a song and steal your soul.

He could hear voices through the walls, some low and others loud, some distorted—television or radio noise—and others simple and real.

When he reached 3B, he pressed his ear to the door. The hungrier he got, the sharper his senses tuned. He could hear the low murmur of the TV, the floor creaking under the weight of steps, the bubble of something cooking on the stove, the inhale-exhale of a single body. Osinger was home, and he was alone. August pulled back; there was no peephole on the door. He took a deep breath, straightened, and knocked.

The sounds in 3B stopped abruptly. The footsteps stilled. The TV went dead. And then, a bolt slid free, the door opened, and a man peered out into the hall, too thin in a half-buttoned shirt. Behind his back, his shadow coiled. Behind his shadow, the room was a maze of towering paper and books, half-collapsed boxes, bags of trash, clothing, food—some of it rotten.

"Mr. Osinger," said August. "May I come in?"

When Albert Osinger met August's eyes, he knew. Somehow, they always knew. The man paled, then slammed the door in August's face. Or tried. August caught the wood with his hand, forcing it inward, and Osinger, in a panic, turned and ran, toppling a stack of books, pulling over a shelf of canned food as he scrambled to get away. As if there were anywhere to run.

August sighed and stepped inside, closing the door behind him.

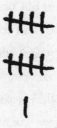

The elevator doors slid open, and the veneer of wealth fell away. Up above, Harker Hall might be all veined marble and gold trim, but down here in the basement there were no polished floors, no glittering chandeliers, no soothing Bach. Those were just layers, the waxy skin of the apple. This was the rotting core.

The basement of the Allsway Building housed an "event space." A decade earlier, a bomb had stripped the paint and taken the lives of seventeen people but left the steel and concrete bones intact, and it was here, the echoes of terror still ghosted on the walls and soaked into the bare floor, that Callum Harker held court. Not with his citizens—his *subjects*—but with his monsters.

Kate hung back, watching from the bank of elevators. The basement lights had all been directed away from the walls and toward the center of the massive room, spotlighting the raised platform in the middle. In the darkened corners, dozens of Corsai gathered. All around the basement's edges the monsters rustled like leaves, or debris, a death rattle in the shadows, a hoarse chorus of whispers, their voices coalescing from many into one.

beat break ruin flesh blood bone beat break

They were nightmare creatures, the stuff of bedtime stories gone wrong, the things that lurked under the mattress and in the closet, given life and teeth and claws. Be careful, parents told their children, be good, or the Corsai will come, but the truth was the Corsai didn't care if you were careful or good. They swam in darkness and fed on fear, their bodies sick, distended shapes that looked human only if you caught them out of the corner of your eye. And by then, it was usually too late to run.

Kate looked straight at the nearest one, focusing until her eyes adjusted and she could make out its milky pupils, its shadowed edges and sharpened teeth. Almost impossible to kill. A blast of sunlight to the head—anything less just dispelled them—but you had to *find* the head for that to work, which was harder than it seemed when their edges ran together, blurring in the dark.

The Corsai had a hive-mind—you ruled them all, or none—and somehow, Harker had bent them to his will. Apparently he'd lured them down into the underground, and cut the lights, but what happened next was story made legend. Some said it was his fearlessness that had cowed them. Some said he'd rigged the sprinklers with liquid metal, and when the Corsai had finally recovered days—weeks—later, they bowed to him.

Harker's Malchai stood closer to the action, skeletal arms crossed over their dark clothes and eyes burning like embers in their gaunt faces. Most looked male, a few vaguely female, but none of them remotely human. They seemed to radiate cold, leeching all the heat from the air (Kate shivered, remembering Sloan's icy grip), and each and every one of them bore the same brand— an *H* on their left cheekbone. Nearby, a Corsai got too close to one and it hissed, flashing row after row of jagged teeth. Men and women dotted the crowd, thugs with hardened bodies and scarred cheeks, their very presence a show of strength—but next to them, the Malchai looked far more monster than human.

The only things missing from Harker's collection were Sunai. Those rare creatures—the darkest things to crawl out of the Phenomenon—had aligned themselves with Flynn down in South City. Some said the Sunai refused to be controlled; while others said they refused only to be controlled by *Harker*. Either way, Harker's were many and Flynn's were few, and their absence didn't make a dent. Everywhere Kate looked, the basement was brimming with monsters, every set of eyes—white, red, or ordinary—focused on the platform, and the pool of light, and the man standing at its center.

Callum Harker had the kind of face that cast shadows.

His eyes were deep-set and blue—not light blue or sky blue or gray blue, but dark, cobalt blue, the kind that looked black at night—paired with an aquiline nose and a severe jaw. Tattoos—bold tribal patterns—snaked out from under his collar and cuffs, black ink trailing onto the backs of his hands and tracing up his neck, the sweep and curl ending just below his hairline. Harker's hair was the only part of him that didn't fit. It was fair, a warm, sun-kissed blond, like Kate's, that swept across his forehead and trailed along his cheeks. That one feature made him look like a "Cal." But only Kate's mother, Alice, had called him that. To everyone else, he was Sir. Governor. Boss. Even Kate thought of him as Harker, though she made an effort to call him Dad. The way his face twisted—discomfort? disdain? dismay?—was its own kind of victory.

Harker wasn't alone up on the platform; a man was on his hands and knees before him, begging for his life.

"Please, please," he said in a shuddering voice. "I'll find the money. I swear."

Two Malchai hovered at the man's back, and when Harker motioned, they wrenched the man to his feet.

Their nails sunk into his skin and he let out a stifled cry as Harker reached forward, and took hold of the metal pendant that hung from the man's neck.

"You can't," he pleaded. "I'll find the money."

"Too late." Harker tore the pendant free.

"No!" cried the man as one of the Malchai holding him yawned wide, revealing rows of jagged teeth. He was about to sink those teeth into the man's throat when Harker shook his head.

"Wait."

The man let out a sob of relief, but Kate held her breath. She knew her father, watched as he considered the medal and then the man.

"Give him a head start," he said, tossing the medal aside. "Five minutes."

The monsters let go, and the man crumpled to the floor, clutched at Harker's legs. "Please," he cried. "Please. *You can't do this!*"

Harker looked down coldly. "You'd better start running, Peter."

The man paled. And then he scrambled to his feet, and stumbled down off the platform, and *ran*. The crowd of men and monsters, held quiet by Harker's command, now burst into noise, laughing and hissing and jeering as they parted to let the dead man through. A few peeled away from the group and followed him toward the concrete steps that led up to the street, into the dark.

Back onstage—that's what it really was: a stage, a performance—Harker held up an iron walking stick, its grip shaped into a gargoyle like the one on the front of their car (cult leaders, Kate had read in that same book, had a flare for the dramatic, the pomp and show). Now rather than raise his voice to quiet the crowd, Harker drove the pointed end of the walking stick down against the concrete platform. The sound reverberated through the basement, and the crowd fell to whispers, the murmurs sinking from a wave into an undercurrent.

"Next," he said.

Kate's eyes widened as a Malchai was dragged up onto the platform. The monster twisted and writhed, strength dampened by the iron chains circling his wrists and throat. Where his brand should have been, there was a patch of ruined skin, as if he'd clawed the mark away.

"Olivier," said Harker, his voice carrying across the event space, "you've disappointed me."

"Have I?" snarled the monster, his voice a rasp. "It is *we* who are disappointed." A ripple went through the basement hall. *We*. The Corsai rattled and the Malchai began to whisper. "Why should *we* starve because of deals *you* make, human? We did not make such deals ourselves. The Corsai may speak as one, but the Malchai are not yours."

"You're wrong," said Harker, bringing the iron gargoyle up beneath the Malchai's chin, smiling as the monster recoiled at the metal's kiss. "I give each and every one of you a choice. Stay in North City, under my command, or go south, and be slaughtered by Flynn's. You chose to stay in *my* city, you chose to take my mark, and then you chose to bleed a family dry. A family under my protection." The Malchai's eyes burned angrily, but Harker's calm smile never faltered. He looked up, and addressed the cavernous space. "I have a system. You all know what happens to those who disrupt it. Those who follow me reap the rewards. And those who defy me"—Harker looked down at the Malchai—"die."

The crowd began to rile again, nervous energy and violent excitement, while the Malchai strained against his bonds. Even monsters feared death. At least the Malchai didn't beg. Didn't plead. He only looked up at Harker, flashed his sharp teeth, and said, "Come near me, and I will rip your throat out."

Harker took a casual step back, and turned away. A table stood near the edge of the platform, littered with a variety of weapons, and Harker ran his fingers over them, considering his choices.

"Hear me!" growled the Malchai behind him, his voice echoing through the hall even as his throat burned beneath the iron. "We are not servants. We are not slaves. We are wolves among sheep. Monsters among men. And we will rise. Your time is ending, Harker!" roared the Malchai. "Our time is coming."

"Well," said Harker, selecting a blade. "*Yours* is already here."

He drew the knife from its sheath, and Kate saw her chance.

"I'll do it," she called out, loud enough for her father to hear. The crowd stilled, searching for the source of the words. An elevated strip ran like a catwalk between the elevators at the back of the hall and the platform in the center, and Kate stepped out of the shelter and into the light.

She kept her head up, focused on her father instead of the crowd, and caught the vanishing shadow of his surprise as it crossed his face—she'd been hoping for pride, but she'd settle for that.

He considered her for a moment, clearly dissecting her move—ostentatious, public, brash to the point of brazen—and they both knew he'd either have to welcome her involvement or punish her insolence. A dangerous play, and one she might pay for later, but to her immediate relief, he smiled and gestured to the table of tools as if it were a banquet.

"Be my guest."

Kate strode forward slowly, confidently, every inch

aware of how important it was to keep her emotions in check, her nerves in control. She mimicked her father's cool smile as she made her way toward him, careful not to look down at her audience. When she reached the platform, Harker brought a hand to rest on her shoulder, and squeezed, a small, unspoken gesture, not of warmth, but of warning. And then he stepped aside to watch.

"What is this?" hissed the Malchai in chains. "You send a *child* to dispatch me?"

"I send my daughter," replied Harker coolly. "And if you think that's a mercy, you don't know her."

Kate smiled at the praise, even if it was an act. She'd show him. She could be strong. She could be cunning. She could be cold.

"Send me a girl," said the Malchai, "and I will return a corpse."

Kate kept her good ear toward the monster, but pretended not to hear. She considered the table, her back to the crowd. Her fingers danced across the objects as she pictured the smooth bone plate that ran down a Malchai's chest in place of a sternum and ribs. She'd done her homework. Those who didn't know better tried to drive a weapon *through* the bone shield, pierce it with bullet or blade.

"Anytime now, little Katherine," said the Malchai,

and Sloan's words shuddered through her.

You will always be our little Katherine.

Kate's hand closed around a crowbar. It took more force than a blade, but the length would act in her favor. She took it up by one end and dragged it casually off the table, letting it scrape, metal on metal, drawing out the moment the way Harker would.

She took up a knife as well, then approached the monster.

Her fourth school, Pennington, had a zero tolerance policy when it came to fighting, but the others had paid off. Back at Fischer, she'd taken karate, then kendo at Leighton, fencing at Dalloway, kickboxing at Wild Prior. St. Agnes didn't have anything like that, but they were big on quieting the mind, allowing room for God. Or in Kate's case, for focus.

Kate twirled the crowbar. The basement went quiet.

"Lean in, pretty," said the Malchai, "show me your throa—"

Kate thrust the hilt of the knife between the monster's teeth and drove the crowbar up and under his ribs. There was a wet sound, and the grind of metal on bone, and then the Malchai shuddered horribly, wretched a mouthful of black blood onto her shirt, and slumped. Kate lowered him onto his back, and his red eyes gazed up at her, dull and dead. She drew the crowbar free with a slick scrape, then strode back to the table, and returned the weapons carefully to their places, leaving a trail of gore in her wake.

And then she met her father's gaze. And smiled.

"Thank you," she said. "I needed that."

Her father raised a brow, and she thought she saw the barest flicker of respect before he gestured to the basement. "Want me to find you another one?"

Kate considered the hall, still crowded with silent, shocked faces, burning eyes, coiling shadows. "Thanks," she said, wiping her hands. "But I have homework." And with that she turned and strode out of the basement.

When the steel elevator doors closed, she caught sight of her reflection. She was still in her school uniform. Her face was dotted with blackish blood, her shirtfront and hands slick with it. She met her own cold, blue gaze and held it as the elevator rose up through Harker Hall, floor after floor until it reached the top.

Sloan was nowhere to be seen, and Kate wove silently through the empty loft to her bedroom and closed the door behind her. Her hands were shaking as she tapped the radio on, and turned the volume *up up up* until the sound vibrated off the walls of the room, drowning everything.

And then, only then, safe beneath the sound, did Kate sink to the floor, gasping for air.

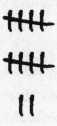

The first time August killed a man, it was entirely by accident.

He'd come to—been born, manifested—at the school, with the black body bags and the worried woman who tried to shield his eyes as she pulled her coat around his narrow shoulders and loaded him into a car. The car took him to a building where other children were being collected by their families. But he didn't have a family, and he knew with a strange, bone-deep certainty that he shouldn't be there, so he slipped out through a back door, and onto a side street.

And that's when he heard the music—the first beautiful thing in an ugly world, as Ilsa would say. The song was thin, unsteady, but loud enough to follow, and soon August found its source: a weary-looking man on a packing crate, wrapped in a ratty blanket. He was tinkering with the instrument, and August made his way toward him, wondering at the man's shadow, which stretched behind him on the wall, moving even when he didn't.

It had too many hands, too many teeth.

And then the man beneath the shadow held the instrument up to the light.

"Who throws out a violin?" he murmured, shaking his head.

Back at the building, they'd given August a pack of cookies and a carton of juice. The food tasted like white noise on his tongue, so he'd shoved the rest in the pockets of the woman's coat. Now he dug them out and offered them to the stranger. It must have tasted better to the man, because he devoured both, and then looked up at the sky. August looked, too. It was getting dark.

"You should go home," said the man. "South City's not safe at night."

"I can't go home," he answered.

"Neither can I," said the man, dropping the violin. It made a horrible sound when it landed, but didn't break. "I did a bad thing," he whispered as his shadow writhed against the wall. "I did such a bad thing."

August knelt to retrieve the instrument. "It'll be all right," he said, fingers curling around the wooden neck.

He didn't remember what happened next. Or rather, he did, but it was a set of photos, not a film, stills without the space between. He was holding the violin, running a thumb over the strings. There was light. There was darkness. There was music. There was peace. And then, there was a body. And sometime later, there was Leo, who found him sitting cross-legged on the packing crate, fiddling with the strings, while the corpse lay at his feet, mouth hanging open and eyes burned black. It took August a long time to understand the vital thing that had happened in the gaps.

"Mr. Osinger?" he called now, stepping into the cluttered apartment. His violin case caught on a teetering stack of papers, and sent them sprawling in his wake. Across the room, Albert Osinger was fighting his way up a narrow set of stairs so crammed with junk he almost couldn't pass. August didn't bother trying to follow. Instead he shrugged the case from his shoulder, and clicked it open. He withdrew the violin with practiced ease, and nestled it under his chin, his fingers finding their positions.

He exhaled, brought the bow to the strings, and drew the first note.

The moment August began to play, everything eased. The headache loosened and the fever calmed, the tension went out of his limbs and the sound of gun-shots in his head—which had become a constant static— finally ceased as the melody slid out and twined through the room. The music wasn't loud, but August knew it would reach its target. Beyond the chords he could hear Osinger's footsteps overhead drag to a stop, and then reverse, no longer frantic but slow and even. August played on as Osinger descended the stairs in measured steps, the music reeling him in.

The song dipped and rose and spiraled away, and he could picture the people scattered through the building, their bodies dragging to a halt as they heard, their souls rising to the surface, most of them bright but untouchable. August's eyes were still closed, but he could feel Osinger in the room with him now; he didn't want to stop playing just yet, wanted to finish the song—he never got a chance to finish—but the sickness was still rolling through him, so he let the melody trail off, the sound dying on the bow as he raised his head. Albert Osinger stood in front of him. His shadow had gone still, and his soul shone like a light beneath his skin.

It was stained red.

August lowered the violin. He set it on a chair as Osinger looked at him, eyes wide and empty. And then the man spoke.

"The first time it happened, I was broke," he confessed quietly. "I was high. I'd never held a gun before." The words spilled out, unhindered, and August let them. "I just wanted the cash. I don't even remember shooting them. Now the second time . . . ," the man smiled grimly. "Well, I knew what I was doing, down to the number of bullets. I kept my eyes open when I pulled the trigger, but I still shook like a baby after." The smile spread, sickening in the red light. "The third time—that was the charm. You know what they say: It gets easier. Living doesn't, but killing does. I'd do it again. Maybe I will."

When he was done, he fell silent. Waiting.

Leo probably made some speech, but August never said anything. He simply closed the gap between them, stepping over and around the clutter, and pressed his hand to Osinger's collar, where his half-buttoned shirt split open, giving way to weathered flesh. The instant August's fingers met the man's bright skin, the red light flooded forward. Osinger's mouth opened and August gasped, catching the man's breath as the energy surged into him, cooling his body and feeding his starved veins. It was blood and air, water and life. August drank it in, and for a moment, all he felt was relief.

Peace.

A glorious, enveloping sense of calm. Of balance.

And then the light was gone.

August's arm fell back to his side, and Albert Osinger's body crumpled, lifeless, to the floor. A shell. A husk with no light, no shadow, its eyes burned to black.

August stood very still as the man's energy rolled

through him. It didn't feel electric, didn't leave him high with power. If anything, it simply made him feel . . . *real*. The anger and the sickness and the strain were gone, washed away, and August simply felt *whole*.

Is this what it was like to be human?

And then he looked down at the man's corpse, and a quiet sadness crept through him like a chill. Suddenly normal felt so far away. It was a cruel trick of the universe, thought August, that he felt human only after doing something monstrous. Which made him wonder if that brief glimpse of humanity was really just an illusion, an echo of the life he'd taken. An impostor sensation.

Leo's voice came to him, simple and steady.

This is what you do. What you are.

Ilsa's rose to meet it.

Find the good in it.

August took a deep breath, and returned the violin to its case. He might not be human, but he was alive. The hunger was gone. The fever had broken, his skin was cool, and his head was clear again. He'd bought himself a few more days. A few more tallies. And he'd delivered justice. He'd made the world a little better, or at least, prevented it from getting worse. That was his purpose. That was his point.

Someone would come for the body.

He was about to leave when he heard a quiet shuffle from the corner of the room. A box toppled sideways, a can rolled across the floor, and August glanced back but saw nothing. And then, from the shadow beneath an old chair, a pair of glowing eyes.

August tensed, but realized, as the thing crept forward, that it wasn't a monster.

It was a *cat*. All black, except for a tuft of white above a pair of bright green eyes. It navigated the cluttered room with feline grace, then came to a stop several feet away. August stared at the creature. The creature stared back. He glanced at the remains of the cat's owner on the floor. The cat did the same.

"I'm sorry," he said aloud.

He'd seen animals go primal against monsters (it usually didn't end well for the animal) but the cat didn't hiss or attack. It padded around the body and then brushed up against August's leg. He shifted the violin case onto his shoulder and cautiously knelt to pet it, and to his surprise, the cat purred against his hand. He didn't know what to do. He got to his feet and opened the far window onto the fire escape.

"Go on," he said, but the cat only looked at him. It wasn't a fool. There weren't many animals running loose in the city. The Corsai made sure of that.

Reluctantly, August made his way to the front

door. This time, the cat followed.

"Stay," he whispered.

He squeezed out into the hall, shutting the door before the cat could follow. He started to walk away, but heard the cat crying on the other side, scratching to get free. August paused, hoping the sound would stop, but the plaintive meow continued, and after a long moment, he sighed and turned back.

Harris was standing on the curb, leaning against one of the half-working streetlights and humming faintly to himself.

Monsters, monsters, big and small.

He trailed off when he saw August coming. "Hey."

"Hey," echoed August.

"What's with the cat?" asked Harris.

August had stashed the creature inside his FTF jacket; its head was sticking out the top. "I couldn't just leave it," he said. "Not after . . ." His gaze went back to the building.

Harris shrugged. "Suit yourself. But just so you know, that's not what I meant when I said you should expand your parameters."

August let out a tired laugh.

"Home?"

August nodded. "Home." He looked up, wishing they

could see stars, then heard the sound of Phillip's boots jogging over.

"We good?"

"All done," said Harris.

"Then we need to go," said Phillip. "Just caught word on the comm of a flare-up near the Seam."

"Should we go help?" asked August, straightening.

"No," said Phillip, eyes flicking to the cat in August's coat. He didn't even ask. "We need to get you back."

August started to protest, but it was no use. Phillip and Harris had their orders—they'd drag him back to the compound if they had to—so August zipped the jacket up over the cat and fell into step between them.

Henry was in the kitchen when August got home, a blueprint rolled out across the counter, a comm device buzzing in his hand. Leo's voice crackled on the other end.

"Under control . . ."

Henry lifted the comm to his mouth. "Casualties?"

"Two . . . can't ignore . . . signs . . ."

"Return home."

"Henry—"

"Not now." Henry flipped the switch and tossed the comm aside. He ran a hand through his hair, which was graying at the temples.

August scuffed his shoe, and Henry's head snapped

up. For an instant, his face was a tangle of surprise and anger, frustration and fear. But then his features went smooth, the shadows pushed back under the surface.

"Hey," he said. "Feeling better?"

"Much," said August, heading toward his room.

"Then why is your stomach moving?"

August dragged to a stop and looked down at his FTF jacket, which was indeed beginning to shift and twist. "Oh," he said. "That."

August unzipped the coat a little, and a small, furry face poked out the top.

Henry's eyes widened. "What is that?"

"It's a cat," said August.

"Yes," said Henry, rubbing his neck. "I've seen them before. But what is it doing in your jacket?"

"He belonged to Osinger," explained August, freeing the cat from his coat. "I felt responsible—I *was* responsible—and I couldn't . . . I tried to leave but . . ."

"*August.*"

He switched tactics. "You've taken in your share of strays," he said. "Let me have this one."

That earned him a relenting smile. "Who will take care of it?" asked Henry.

Just then someone made a sound—something between a gasp and a delighted squeak—and Ilsa was there between them, lifting the small creature into her arms. August nodded at Henry as if to say, *I can think of someone who would love to.* Henry just sighed, shook his head, and left the room.

Ilsa brought the cat an inch from her face and looked it in the eyes. It responded by reaching out a single black paw and bringing it to rest on the bridge of her nose. The cat seemed mesmerized by her. Most things were. "What's its name?" she whispered.

"I don't know," said August.

"Everybody needs a name," she cooed, sinking cross-legged to the kitchen floor. "Everybody deserves one."

"Then name it," said August.

Ilsa considered the small black cat. Held him to her ear. "Allegro," she announced.

August smiled. "I like that," he said, sitting down across from her. He reached out, and scratched the cat's ears. Its purr thrummed under his fingers.

"He likes you," she said. "They can tell the difference, you know, between good and bad. Just like we can." Allegro tried to climb into her hair, and she dragged him gently back into her lap.

"Will you look after him, while I'm at school?"

Ilsa folded herself around the cat. "Of course," she whispered. "We will look after each other."

They were still sitting on the floor with Allegro when Leo returned, a steel guitar strapped to his back, and a streak of blood—not his—across his cheek. He took one look at Allegro and frowned. Allegro took one look at him and put its ears back. Ilsa broke into a laugh, as sweet as chimes, and right then August knew, for sure, that he was keeping the cat.

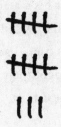

Kate sat on her bedroom floor until the music stopped.

Her hands were shaking a little as she lit a cigarette; she took a long drag, leaned her head back against the door, and looked around. Her room, like the rest of the penthouse, was sleek and sparse, made of sharp edges and hard lines. There were no traces of her childhood, no height measurements or nicks, no stuffed animals or old clothes, no fashion ads or posters. No field beyond the window.

When she was twelve, it had felt sterile, cold, but now she tried to embrace the room's austerity. To *embody* it. The blank walls, the unshakable calm.

One of the few pieces of decoration was a folding frame with a pair of photographs inside. She plucked it from the table. In the first photo, a five-year-old Kate stood with one arm thrown around her father, the other wrapped around her mom. Above her head, Callum kissed his wife's temple. Alice Harker was beautiful—not just in the way that all children think their parents are—but concretely, undeniably *gorgeous*, with sun-kissed hair and large hazel eyes that lit up whenever she smiled. The picture had been taken two months before the Phenomenon.

The second photo was a reenactment, taken the day they returned to V-City after the truce. Together again. A family reunited, made whole. She ran her thumb over the faces. An eleven-year-old Kate with her arms around her parents, reunited after six years apart. Six years of chaos and fighting. Six years of quiet and peace.

The changes showed on all of them. Kate was no longer a round-faced child, but a freckled youth. Her mother had tiny wrinkles, the kind you got from laughing. And her father still looked at Alice, his gaze intense, as if afraid that if he looked away, she would vanish again.

And she had.

"Get up, Kate. We have to go."

Sloan was wrong. Kate had wanted to come back to V-City, had wanted to stay.

"I want to go home," she'd whispered.

"I want to go home," she'd begged.

It was her *mother* who couldn't adjust. Her mother who dragged her from bed in the middle of the night, eyes red and lipstick smeared across her cheek.

"Hush, hush, we have to be quiet."

Her mother who bundled her into the car.

"Where are we going?"

Her mother who drove into oncoming traffic.

Her mother who slammed the car into the concrete rail.

Her mother who died with her head against the wheel.

And after the accident, it was her *father* who wouldn't look at her. She would float in and out of sleep, would wake to see him standing in the doorway, only to realize it wasn't him at all, just a monster with dark bones and red eyes and a too-sharp smile.

And when she was finally better, it was her father who sent her away. Who buried her mother, and then buried her. Not in the ground, but in Fischer. In Dalloway. In Leighton and Pennington and Wild Prior and St. Agnes.

At first, she'd pleaded and begged to come home, to stay home, but over time, she stopped. Not because she stopped wanting it, but because she learned that pleading didn't work on Callum Harker. Pleading was a sign of weakness. So she learned to bury the things that made her weak. The things that made her like her mother.

Kate returned the picture frame to the bedside table

and looked down at her hands. Her lungs hurt from the smoke but her hands had stopped shaking, and she considered the black blood staining her fingers, not with horror but with grim determination.

She was her father's daughter. A Harker.

And she would do whatever she had to do to prove it.

VERSE 2

MONSTER SEE, MONSTER DO

1

"Valor, Prosperity, Fortitude, Verity," recited the teacher, a middle-aged man named Mr. Brody, as he tapped the four central territories on the map. Combined, they took up more than half the space, the six remaining territories filling in the land on either side. "These are, of course, the four largest of the Ten Territories, with populations ranging from twenty-three to twenty-six million. Can anyone tell me the smallest?"

Grace, thought August as he scribbled a rough map in his notebook and carved it into ten, mirroring the divisions on the board.

"Fortune?" asked a girl, pointing to the northwest corner.

"I'm talking about population, not landmass, so no. Fortune has almost seventeen million."

It also had *mountains*. August looked out the window,

tried to imagine the blue haze of peaks in the distance. He couldn't.

"Charity?" guessed a boy in the back, pointing to the southeast corner, where oceans bordered two sides of the territory. Mountains. Oceans. All Verity had were plains, interrupted here and there by hills, which were little more than undulations according to the topographic map.

"Nine point three million. Getting closer."

"Grace?" ventured a girl at the front, pointing to a mass on the northeast coast.

"*That* is correct. Can anyone tell me how many—"

"Six million three-hundred and fifteen thousand, at last count," said Kate without raising her hand. She was sitting one desk over.

Of all the classes they could have shared, they'd ended up with History. The irony wasn't lost on him.

"Very good, Miss Harker," said Mr. Brody with a shit-eating grin (a term August had learned from Harris). "Luckily for the rest of you, this course will focus primarily on our own illustrious territory . . ."

August might have found his current situation flat-out *funny*—being in a room with his enemy's daughter, learning about the balance of power and politics in Verity—if he didn't have to focus every ounce of energy on keeping his mouth shut as the teacher went on about their *esteemed* capital, skipping over any mention of the monsters that ran it in the light of day or the ones that roamed its streets at night. It wasn't as if he expected the class to be objective, but it was still hard to listen to the skewed narrative. Every time the teacher referred to the city as V-City instead of North City, as if the southern half wasn't worth mentioning, as if it didn't exist beyond the Seam, August felt his chest tighten. People weren't really this deluded, were they?

The class wasn't the only thing making him tense; he'd overheard a conversation that morning between Henry and Leo. They were talking—heatedly—about the latest incident at the Seam. A handful of Corsai had found a crack and come through, and no one knew if Harker had sent them or if the monsters on his side were getting restless. August had hovered outside the office to listen.

"*It doesn't matter why they came,*" Leo was saying. "*It doesn't matter who sent them. Either Harker did, in which case he is actively breaking the truce, or they rebelled, in which case Harker is failing to control them and the truce is forfeit.*"

"*We've come so far,*" said Henry. "*I will not put this city through another war.*"

"*We made a promise,*" said Leo.

"*A threat.*"

"*—that if Harker broke his covenant, we would see his empire razed.*"

"*Those were your words, Leo. Not mine.*"

"*We must remind him of the weapons at our disposal.*"

"*People will die,*" challenged Henry.

"*People are always dying.*"

August had shivered at the cold detachment in his brother's voice.

At the front of the room, Mr. Brody was droning on. ". . . marked forty years since the dissolution of the federal government—you should all know this—in the wake of the war in . . ." he trailed off, waiting for an answer.

"Vietnam," announced a boy.

"Indeed," said the teacher. "National unrest, a strained economy, and depleted morale resulted in the federal collapse and subsequent reconstruction of the once-United States." He tapped the center of the map. "Now, can anyone tell me how many of the antiquated states now make up Verity? Anyone?"

August continued to shade in his own map, the names drifting through his head. *Kentucky. Missouri. Illinois. Iowa.* They sounded like nonsense words.

"And in the aftermath of these tumultuous events?"

August was halfway through labeling the map when he felt a pair of eyes, and glanced over to find Kate staring at his paper. He hadn't defaced the territories, but he'd started a running list in the corner of the page with other, more fitting, names for each.

Greed, Malice, Gluttony, Violence.

Kate frowned slightly. August held his breath. All around them, the class rambled on, but for him, the room was receding, leaving only the two of them in focus.

". . . states combined to form fewer, independent territories," said a girl near the front.

"Good." Mr. Brody turned to write the answer on the board, and Kate reached across the aisle. He tensed, wondering what she was about to do, when she brought her pen to his paper and drew a second *V* beside the one at the beginning of *Verity*. He frowned, confused.

By the time the teacher looked back, her hands were folded on her desk.

"What else?"

"States became self-governing," added a boy.

"And then condensed into the Ten Territories."

"Power concentrated in the capitals."

"And so did the people."

Every time someone called out an answer, the teacher returned to the board, and every time he did, Kate leaned over and added another mark—a jagged line, a swoop, a pair of dots. It took him half the class to figure out what she was doing, and then, between one scribble and the next, it came together.

The body. The mouth. The claws.

Kate had turned *Verity* into a monster.

He stared at her, and then, he couldn't help it.

He smiled.

11

Kate enjoyed the sliver of time between classes, the five minutes Colton afforded its students to get from *A* to *B*. Being in class was exhausting: half the teachers treated her like she had a loaded gun, the other half like she had a crown. The walk was the only time she could really breathe, so she was more than a little annoyed when one of the girls from History looped an arm through hers on the way to Gym.

"Hi," chirped the girl in a voice that was way too bright for ten A.M. "I'm Rachel."

Kate's stride didn't falter, but she said nothing.

"I heard what you did to Charlotte Chapel."

"I didn't do anything to Charlotte." *Yet*.

"Hey, I think it's great," she said cheerfully. "That bitch totally deserved a check."

Kate sighed. "What do you want?"

The girl's smile went full wattage. "I just want to

help," she said. "I know you're new here, and I thought you could use a friend."

Kate raised a single pale brow. Being liked was a perk, not a necessity. She supposed she could take a different tactic, try to conform, go out for homecoming queen, establish a more traditional form of popularity, but it all seemed so . . . juvenile. She could still feel the blood beneath her nails. How could anyone care so much about which table they sat at when Malchai were ripping out throats in the red? Then again, that's why they lived in North City. That's what their parents were paying for. Ignorance. "You don't want to be my friend, Rachel."

The girl's cheer settled into something colder, more calculating. "Look, Katie."

"*Kate.*"

"Everyone needs an ally. You can go around acting invincible, but I'm willing to bet you'd rather be liked."

"Is that so?" asked Kate dryly.

Rachel nodded solemnly. "We all know who your father is, but you don't have to be like him." She took Kate by the shoulders and looked her straight in the eyes, as if she was about to say something vitally important. "You're *not* your father."

Kate tensed imperceptibly at that, then managed to draw her mouth into a small, cruel smile. "Can I tell you a secret?"

"Of course," said Rachel.

Kate leaned in and brought her lips to the girl's ear. "I'm much worse."

She pulled back, taking a moment to savor Rachel's expression before walking away.

The first week of Gym was supposed to be a segment on self-defense—Kate had several issues with Colton's interpretation. The first—and biggest—of which was that there were no weapons. Kate couldn't imagine someone stupid enough to wander the streets of V-City without at least a knife on them, but Colton insisted on a "safe" environment (she was starting to hate that word).

She could have skipped, but watching students try to defend themselves (poorly) against imaginary attackers was more interesting, so she sat on the stands with the rest of the class and pretended to pay attention.

"Who can tell me what S-I-N-G stands for?" asked one of the instructors.

"Sing?" offered a girl, chewing gum. A few people snickered. Kate hoped she was joking but feared she wasn't.

"Um, yes," drawled the teacher, "but I meant, what do the letters *stand* for?"

Stomach. Instep. Nose. Groin.

A brawny boy raised his hand. "Stomach, instep, nose, groin?"

"Very good!"

Kate wanted to point out that Corsai didn't have stomachs, insteps, noses, *or* groins, and if you got close enough to hit a Malchai, it would probably rip your throat out. But she kept the observations to herself, and focused on the *second* most frustrating thing about this alleged self-defense course, which was the fact that the teachers were doing it *wrong*.

The moves they demonstrated likely wouldn't stop a human, let alone a monster. Their form was off, as if they didn't really want to teach the Colton students how to fight. It was just a performance, all for show, something to make the children—or probably the parents—feel safer.

Five of Kate's six schools—St. Agnes excluded—had taught self-defense courses, since many of the students who boarded there were sons and daughters of influential people—territory ambassadors, big-business owners, some old money and others new—the kind of people whose kids make good targets. No one had ever had the guts to try and kidnap Kate, but over time she'd amassed an arsenal of defensive techniques—as well as a few offensive ones—which just made the current display of ineptitude even more annoying.

When one teacher demonstrated how to disarm an attacker, it was so slow and clumsy that Kate actually laughed. Not loudly, but the gym was basically an echo chamber, and the sound carried far enough for an instructor to hear.

"Is something funny?" he asked, scanning the students. He wouldn't have known she was responsible if everyone near her hadn't leaned away.

Kate sighed. "No," she said, speaking up. "But your form's all wrong."

"Well, then, missy," he said, pointing at her. "Why don't you come down and give us a proper demonstration?"

A murmur ran through the class. The instructor clearly didn't know who she was. One of the other teachers shot him a look, but Kate only smiled and got to her feet.

Ten minutes later, Kate was sitting in the counselor's office. Not for laughing at the instructor, but for breaking his collarbone. She hadn't *tried* to hurt him. Not badly. It wasn't her fault he had poor stance and an inflated sense of ability.

"Miss Harker," said the counselor, a round man named Dr. Landry, with glasses and a spreading bald spot. "Here at Colton we try to provide a *safe* learning environment." There was that word again. "We have a zero tolerance policy when it comes to violence."

Kate choked back another laugh. Landry pursed his lips. She coughed, swallowed.

"It was a self-defense segment," she said. "And he asked me to participate."

"You were asked to demonstrate a defensive maneuver, and in so doing you *accidentally* fractured the instructor's collarbone?"

"That's correct."

Landry sighed. "I've read your file, Miss Harker. This isn't an isolated incident." Kate sat back, half expecting him to read the list of her offenses, the way they did in movies, but he didn't. Instead he took off his glasses and began to polish them. "Where do you think this aggression is coming from?" he asked.

Kate met his gaze. "Is that a joke?" But Landry didn't seem to be the joking type. If anything he seemed painfully sincere. He opened his drawer and slid a vial of small, white pills across the table. She didn't reach for them.

"What are those for?"

"Anxiety."

Kate sat up straighter, making sure her shoulders were level, her face even. "I don't have anxiety," she said stiffly.

Landry gave her a strangely weighted look. "Miss Harker, you've been rapping your fingers on your knees since the moment you sat down." Kate pressed her hands flat on her thighs. "You're tense. Irritable. Defensive. Intentionally distancing."

Kate offered a very cold smile. "I live in a world where shadows have teeth. It's not a particularly relaxing environment."

"I know who your father is—"

"So does everyone."

"—and I've read about your mother. About the accident."

Her mother's face flashed in her mind, lit by the oncoming car, those wide hazel eyes, the screeching tires, the crunching metal—Kate dug her nails into her slacks, and resisted the urge to let him talk into her bad ear. "So?"

"So I know it must be hard. Suffering that kind of loss. The subsequent alienation. And now this: a new school, a fresh start, but also what I have to imagine is a great deal of stress." He nodded to the pills. "You don't have to use them. But take them with you. They're less harmful than cigarettes, and you never know, they might actually help."

Kate considered the vial. How many of the students were on these pills? How many of the citizens in North

City? Did the medicated calm keep them from fanning the flames of violence? Did it help them pretend the world was *safe*? Did it hold them together? Did it help them sleep?

Kate frowned but reached for the pills. She doubted anything would help, but if the gesture got the good Dr. Landry off her back and kept the incident off the school record (and her father's radar), it was worth it.

"Am I free to go?" she asked. Landry nodded, and she escaped out from under his gaze and into the empty hall.

Kate shook a white tablet into her palm. She looked down at the pill, hesitated.

Where are you? she asked herself.

Away. Whole. Sane. Happy. A dozen different selves with a dozen different lives, but she wasn't living any of those. She had to be *here*. Had to be strong. And if Dr. Landry saw the fraying edges, then so would her father.

Kate swallowed the tablet dry.

She looked around the empty hall. Too late to go back to class. Too early to go anywhere else. Through the nearest set of doors, the bleachers stood, soaked invitingly in sun. She pocketed the pills and went to get some air.

III

August heard her coming.

People were made of pieces—looks and smells, sure, but also sounds. Everything about Emily Flynn was staccato. Everything about Henry was smooth. Leo's steps were as steady as a pulse. Ilsa's hair made the constant hush-hush of blankets.

And Kate? She sounded like painted nails tapping out a steady beat.

August was leaning back against the warm metal bleachers, chin tipped toward the sun, when she sat down in the row behind him. The steel bench thrummed from the sudden weight, and August decided that even if she hadn't made a sound, he'd still have guessed it was her. She had a way of taking up space. He could feel the soft pressure of her gaze, but he kept his eyes closed. A gentle breeze ran fingers through his hair, and he let himself smile, a small almost-natural thing. A shadow slid across the red-white glow of sun, and his eyes drifted open and there she was, looking down at him. There was a softness to her features from this angle, a distant quality to her eyes, like clouds muddling a crisp blue sky.

"Hello," he said.

"Hello," she said. And then, absently, "Where were you?"

He squinted. "What?"

But Kate was already shaking her head, edges sharpening. "Nothing."

August sat up, twisting slowly around to look at her. "Tell me," he said, regretting the words the moment they were out. He could see her gaze flatten, the answer rising to her lips. "Or don't," he added quickly. "You don't have to tell me if you don't want to."

Kate blinked, her gaze focusing again. But then she said, "It's just a game I sometimes play. When I want to be somewhere else."

"Like where?"

A small crease appeared between her brows. "I don't know. But you're telling that if you could be anywhere right now, you'd be here on the Colton bleachers?"

August smiled. "It's pretty nice." He gestured to the field, the distant line of trees. "And of course, there's the view."

She rolled her eyes. Up close, they were blue. Not

sky-bright, but dark, the same shade as her navy Colton polo. She had her hair twisted over one shoulder, and again he saw the teardrop scar in the corner of her eye, the silvery line that traced her face from scalp to jaw. He wondered how many people got close enough to notice. And then, before he could ask, she was leaning back, stretching her legs out on the bleachers.

"Shouldn't you be in class?" she asked.

"I have study hall," he said, even though he obviously wasn't there, either. "What about you?"

"Gym," she said. "But I got kicked out for *misconduct*." August raised both brows, the way he'd seen Colin do when feigning surprise. "Did you know they teach self-defense here?" she went on. "It's a joke. I mean, S-I-N-G tactics, really? As far as I know, a kick to the groin isn't going to stop a Corsai from tearing you apart."

"True," he said, resting his elbows against the bench behind him. "But there are plenty of bad humans in the world, too." *Like your father.* "So, did you get kicked out for lecturing the teacher?"

"Even better," she said, running a hand through her sandy hair. "I got kicked out for breaking his collarbone."

Something escaped August's throat, a soft, breathless laugh. The sound took him by surprise.

"According to the counselor," continued Kate, "I have a violence problem."

"Doesn't everyone?"

Neither one of them mentioned his map sketch or the monster she'd drawn across Verity, and soon an easy quiet settled over the bleachers, interrupted only by Kate's nails, which she rapped in a soft, constant way against the metal bench, and the distant sounds of students running on the track. It wasn't supposed to feel like this, thought August. He was sitting inches away from the daughter of a bloodthirsty tyrant, the heir to North City. He should feel disgusted, repulsed. At the very least, unnerved. But he didn't.

He wasn't sure *what* he felt. Frequency. Consonance. Two chords that went together.

Don't push her away, said one voice, while another warned, *Don't get too close*. How was he supposed to do both?

"So, Freddie," she said, dragging herself upright, "what brings you to Colton?"

"I was homeschooled," he said, and then, struggling to find words that weren't a lie, "I guess my family thought . . . it was time for me to socialize."

"Huh, and yet every time I've seen you, you've been alone."

August shrugged. "I guess I'm not really a people person. What about you?"

Her eyes went wide in mock surprise. "Didn't you

hear? I burned down a school. Or did drugs. Or slept with a teacher. Or killed a kid. It really depends on who you ask."

"Is any of it true?"

"I did burn down a school," she said. "Well, part of a school. A chapel. But it was nothing personal. I just wanted to come home."

August frowned. "You got out of V-City." It was no small feat, with the border cities capped and the Waste in the way. "Why would you want to come back?"

Kate didn't answer right away. Which was strange— most of the time he couldn't *stop* people from talking— but she tipped her head back and looked up at the sky. It was a cloudless day, and for a second she seemed lost, as if she expected to see something up there, and didn't. "It's all I have left." The words came out soft, like a confession, but she didn't seem to notice. Her gaze drifted back to earth. "Are those real?"

August looked down and realized that his sleeves had ridden up enough to reveal the lowest line of tallies. Four hundred and nineteen.

"Yes," he said, the truth across his lips before he even thought to stop it.

"What do they stand for?"

This time August bit back the answer, and ran a thumb over the oldest marks around his wrist. "One . . ."

he said slowly, "for every day without a slip."

Kate's dark eyes widened in genuine surprise. "You don't strike me as an addict."

"Well," he said thoughtfully, "I didn't strike you as a Freddie, either."

She cracked a smile. "So what's your poison?"

He sighed dramatically, and let the truth tumble off his tongue. "Life."

"Ah," she said ruefully. "That'll kill you."

"Not as fast as cigarettes."

"Touché," she said, "but—"

She was cut off by a scream. August tensed, and Kate's hand went straight for her backpack, but it was just some student on the field faux-tackling his girl-friend. She squealed again, beaming even as she fled.

August let out a low breath. He would never under-stand why people screamed for fun.

"You okay there?" asked Kate, and he realized he was gripping the bleachers, knuckles white. Gunfire crackled like static in the back of his head. He pried his fingers free.

"Yeah. Not a fan of loud noises."

She pursed her lips, gave him a look that said *how cute*, then gestured to the case at his feet. "Violin?"

August looked down, nodded. He'd smuggled the instrument out of the compound this morning, slipping out before Leo could stop him. His fingers were itching to play again. He'd gone to the music room only to discover that an ID card wasn't all you needed to use the practice space. He was halfway through the door when a girl cleared her throat behind him.

"Excuse me," she said, "but the room's mine."

August hadn't understood. "Yours?"

She pointed out a clipboard on the wall. It was a sign-up sheet. "My time," she explained. August's heart sank. He held the door open and let her pass, then examined the list of times and names on the sheet. It was Wednesday, and the space was booked solid until Friday afternoon. August wasn't supposed to stay after school—Henry had been insistent, wanting him back across the Seam before the gates closed at dusk, even though he didn't *use* them to get home—but in a rare moment of defiance, August had signed himself up.

"I've always liked music," said Kate, picking at the metal polish on her nails. August waited for her to go on, but the bell rang and she shook her head, settling her hair back over one eye. "Are you any good?"

"Yes," he said without hesitation.

"Will you play for me?"

August shook his head, and the look she gave him made it clear—she wasn't used to being told no.

"Performance anxiety?" she said blandly. "Come on."

She was looking at him through the sweep of blond, waiting, and he couldn't exactly say that he played only for sinners. He swallowed, struggled to find a lie that skirted truth.

"Go on," she insisted. "I promise not to—"

"Freddie!" shouted a voice, and August turned to see Colin waving him toward the cafeteria. He rose gratefully to his feet.

"I better go," he said, taking up the case as casually as possible.

"I'll get you to play for me," she called as he descended the metal steps. "One way or another."

He didn't say anything, didn't dare look back as he jogged over to Colin, who was staring baldly. When August reached the sidewalk, the boy patted him down. "He lives!" he announced with feigned shock.

August waved him off, and Colin fell into step beside him. "But seriously, Freddie," he said, shooting a glance back at the bleachers. At Kate. "Do you have a death wish? Because I'm pretty sure there are faster, less painful ways to go. . . ."

||||

Kate got through the rest of the day without hurting anyone, so that was something. She didn't know if it was luck, odds, or Freddie. Even though she'd teased him, there had been a moment on the bleachers where the answer to *Where are you?* had really been *Here*. She wasn't sure why, only that for the first time in ages, sitting in that strange but comfortable silence, she felt like herself. Not the Kate who grinned at the rumors, or the one who held a knife to a girl's throat, or drove a crowbar through a monster's heart.

The Kate she'd been *before*. The version of her that made jokes instead of threats. The one that smiled when she actually meant it.

But this wasn't the right world for that Kate.

She tossed her bag onto the bed, and the vial from Dr. Landry tumbled out.

Maybe it was the pills, smoothing her edges.

Maybe . . . but there was still something about Freddie. Something . . . disarming, infectious, familiar. In an auditorium full of stares, his was the gaze she felt. In a classroom full of students learning lies, he scribbled the truth in the margins. In a school that clung to the illusion of safety, he didn't shy from talk of violence. He didn't belong there, the way *she* didn't belong there, and that shared strangeness made her feel like she knew him.

But she *didn't*.

Not yet.

She sat at her desk, tapped her computer awake, and logged into the Colton Academy website.

"Who are you, Mr. Gallagher?" she wondered aloud, pulling up the student directory and scrolling through profiles until she found the one she was looking for. She clicked on Frederick Gallagher's page. His information was listed on the left-hand side—height, age, address, etc.—but the photo on the right was odd. She'd had half a dozen pictures taken, one for every school, and they always insisted on front and center, eyes forward, big smile. But the boy on-screen wasn't even looking at her.

His face was in profile, eyes cast down, edges blurred, and lips parted as if he'd been caught midbreath as well as midmotion. If it wasn't for the barest edge of a black tally mark where his cuff was riding up, she wouldn't have been sure it was him.

Why hadn't the office retaken the photo?

There was something teasing about the blurred shot, and Kate found herself craving a better picture, wanting the luxury of being able to stare at someone without being stared at. She booted a new browser on the city's updrive, went onto a social networking site the students all seemed to use, and typed in his name.

Two matches came up in the V-City area, but neither one was the Freddie she'd met. Which was odd, but Freddie said he was homeschooled. Maybe he'd never joined the site. She opened a third browser and typed his name into the search engine. It landed half a dozen hits—a mechanic, a banker, a suicide victim, a pharmacist, but no match for *her* Freddie.

Kate sat back in her chair, and tapped a metal nail against her teeth.

These days, *everyone* left a digital mark. All day, every day at Colton, people were snapping photos, recording every mundane moment as if it deserved to be preserved, remembered. So where was he?

Something twinged in her mind. Maybe she was being paranoid, searching for a complicated answer when the simple one—that he was that rare teen who preferred staying off-grid—was probably true.

Probably. But it was like an itch, and now she'd started scratching . . .

The drive wasn't the only place that information was logged, not in North City. She logged into her father's private uplink, clicked on the archive labeled *human*. The screen filled with thousands of thumbnails, each with a name and date. Freddie wasn't like the other kids at Colton, and maybe she wasn't the only one who'd noticed. She typed his name into the search bar, half hoping his face would show up with a tag for some disturbance, even just an anomaly, but—nothing.

Exasperated, she clicked back to the school directory and reconsidered the picture, staring at it for several long minutes as if it might come to life, complete the arc of motion, meet her eyes. When it didn't, Kate scrolled through his profile, scribbled down his address, and got to her feet.

There was still one place she hadn't looked.

"Hello?" she called out as she crossed the penthouse. No answer. She did a quick lap through the open layout. No sign of Sloan or Harker. The door to her father's office was locked, but when she pressed her good ear to the wood, she didn't hear the hum of the soundproofing system that Harker activated when he was inside. She keyed in the code—she'd set up a camera on her second day, caught the motion and order of his fingers—and a second later the door opened under her touch.

The lights came up automatically.

Callum Harker's office was massive, and strangely classic, with a broad, dark desk, a wall of bookshelves, and a bank of windows overlooking the city. She crossed to the shelves and ran her hand over the large black books that ran the wall. Ledgers.

Harker was a careful man; he kept both physical and digital copies of the information on all his citizens. The computer was locked—Kate hadn't been able to crack the access code—but the beautiful thing about books was that anyone could open them. The ledgers were alphabetical, and retranscribed every year. When people lost Harker's protection in the course of that year, their names were blacked out. If they *gained* protection, their names were written in at the back of the book.

Kate pulled the G ledger from the wall and opened it on the desk, paging through until she found the name: *Gallagher.*

Eleven Gallaghers were listed under Harker's protection in North City, and there was even a Paris Gallagher whose address matched the one on Freddie's profile, but there was no mention of Freddie himself. But she'd *seen* the pendant around his neck. She turned to the back of the ledger, hoping to find his name in the additions.

It wasn't there.

"Where are you?" she whispered, right before someone cleared his throat.

Her head snapped up. Her father was standing in the doorway, wiping his hands on a black square of silk. "What are you doing, Katherine?"

The air stuck in Kate's lungs. She forced it out, hoping the exhale might pass for an exasperated sigh. "Looking for a name," she said, leaning against the desk, as if she had every right to be there. "There's a girl at my school who's driving me crazy. She had a medal, and I was hoping it was stolen or expired, but alas," she said, letting the ledger fall shut, "she's still under your protection."

Harker's dark eyes hung on her. She tried to ignore the dried blood on his cuffs. "Sorry," she added. "I should have waited for you to get home, but I didn't know when that would be."

"I didn't think I'd left the room unlocked."

"You didn't," said Kate coolly, pushing off the desk and walking out. She was relieved when he didn't follow.

Back in her room, she sank into her chair, Freddie's student profile still up on her screen. It made even less sense now, a blurred photo beside a name that, according to her father's records, didn't exist. Could he be using an alias? But *why*?

The only people who hid were the ones with something to hide.

So what was Frederick Gallagher hiding?

August hated blood—hated the sight, hated the smell, hated the slimy, too-thick feel—which was unfortunate, since he was currently *covered* in it.

It wasn't his, of course.

It was Phillip's. The FTF with the warm smile and the buzz cut, the one who treated August like a friend, and glared at Harris whenever he used the word *monster*.

"Hold him still," ordered Henry. "I need to tourniquet the wound."

Phillip's shoulder had been torn from the socket. Visibly. His FTF gear had been shredded, and August could have reached out and traced his fingers over the Corsai's claw marks—teeth marks? It was always hard to tell—if Phillip hadn't been writhing around so much on the steel medical table.

August had been sitting at the counter doing homework, Allegro playing with his laces, when they got the call. Another attack. But this one wasn't at the Seam. And it wasn't random. It was an ambush. Harker's monsters knew exactly where the FTF would be patrolling, and when. Someone had *told* them. And now four FTFs were dead and Phillip seemed hell-bent on going down in a blaze of obscenities and blood.

"For God's sake, hold him *still*."

Leo and August pinned Phillip down while Henry moved with careful, decisive motions over the vicious wound. His partner, Harris, stood to the side, blood streaked across his face, looking numb from shock while Emily stitched up a gash on his bicep. She didn't have Henry's surgical grace, but her hands were just as steady.

Henry drew a syringe full of morphine and sank the needle into Phillip's functioning arm. His cursing trailed off and his head lolled to the side, the pain and tension finally going out of him.

"This cannot stand, Henry," said Leo, a smudge of Phillip's blood along his jaw. "We have suffered enough insult. It is time to—"

"*Not now*," snapped Henry as he pulled on a pair of surgical gloves and set to work. August looked down at the wreckage of Phillip's shoulder, the slick red pool spreading across the metal table, and felt ill. Under the glare of the lights, Phillip looked suddenly young, delicate. Humans were too fragile for this fight, but the Sunai were too few to do it alone, and even if three *could* wage a war on thousands, the Malchai and Corsai weren't foolish enough to get close, opting instead for prey they could catch, and kill. And so the Sunai focused on hunting sinners in order to stem the flow of violence, and the slaying of the monsters fell to the humans, and the humans, invariably, fell to them. It was a cycle of whimpers and bangs, gruesome beginnings and bloody ends.

August's gaze traced the claw marks. Messy. Brutal. This was a *monster's* work. The lingering scent of the Corsai—fetid air, stale smoke, and death, always death— still clung to the torn flesh and turned his stomach. Leo was right. August was *nothing* like the thing that did this. He couldn't be.

"August," said Henry a minute later. "You can let go now."

He looked down and realized he was still pinning Phillip's limp body to the table. His hands slid off, and he went to wash them in a nearby sink while Henry worked.

Blood ran into the sink, and August looked away, trying to find something—anything—else to focus on, but it was everywhere, on the wall, and the counter, and the floor, a trail leading back through the doors to the steel elevators marked with a *19.*

The nineteenth floor of the Flynn compound had been nicknamed the Morgue by some of the more morbid members of the FTF. Even though it was the second highest floor in the building, directly below the Flynns' own apartment, there was no view. The windows had all been bricked up, the furniture removed in favor of sterile space. The nineteenth floor housed two essential things: a private interrogation chamber (the rest being on the sublevels with the cells) and an emergency medical suite.

"Where is he?" asked Henry, looking up from the wreckage of Phillip's shoulder. He was referring to the traitor. The man who'd sold the information to Harker. He was a cousin of someone in the FTF, and after he'd sold them out, he'd tried to escape across the Seam and claim some kind of sanctuary in North City. But Harker didn't keep rats, so he'd thrown him back. A squad had hunted him down and hauled him in, but not before he put two bullets in their captain. Two minutes with Leo, and he'd confessed to everything.

Leo stood before a mirror, wiping the bloodstains from his face. His black eyes went to the scar through his brow and glanced off, the way August's had around the blood, as if disgusted by the sight.

"Cell A," answered Harris dully, all trace of his boyish humor gone. Taken.

"He's guilty," added Leo evenly, and they all knew what he meant. A red soul. A reaping.

"All right." Henry nodded to his wife. "Go get Ilsa."

The man in Cell A looked rough.

His nose was broken, his hands were bound behind his back, and he was lying on his side, chest hitching in a wounded way. August stood, staring, trying to understand what made men break like this. Not in a physical way—human bodies were brittle—but heart and soul, what made them jump, fall, even when they knew there was no ground beneath.

He felt a gust of air, and then the soft warmth of Ilsa's hand in his as she looked through the Plexiglas insert in the cell door.

"Can you feel it?" she asked, sadly. "His soul is so heavy. Who knows how long the floor will hold. . . ."

Her hand slipped away, and she made her way barefoot into the cell. August shut the door behind her but did not leave. It was a rare thing to see another Sunai reap a life. And Ilsa had a way of making everything beautiful. Even death.

Steps sounded behind him, heavy and even. Leo. "Henry is a fool not to let her out."

August frowned. "Who? Ilsa?"

Leo lifted his hand, brought it to rest against the door. "Our sister, the angel of death. Do you know what she is? What she can *do*?"

"I have an idea," said August dryly.

"No, you don't, little brother." Within the cell, Ilsa sank to her knees beside the traitor. "Henry would keep you in the dark, but I think you deserve to know what she is, what you could be, perhaps, if you let yourself."

"What are you talking about, Leo?"

"Our sister has two sides," he said. "They do not meet."

It sounded like a riddle, but Leo wasn't usually one for talking in circles. "What—"

"Do you know how many stars she has?"

August shook his head.

Leo's fingers splayed. "Two thousand one hundred and sixty-two."

August started to do the math, then stopped. Six years. Six years since Ilsa had last gone dark. Six years since *something* ended the territory war.

Leo must have seen the understanding register. He traced a circle with his index finger. "Who do you think made the Barren, little brother?"

Beyond the door, the traitor was confessing in a broken whisper. Ilsa took his face in her hands and guided him down to the concrete floor. She lay on her side, stroking his hair.

Somewhere in the city was a place where nothing grew.

"That's not possible," whispered August. The last time he'd gone dark, he'd taken out a room of people. The idea that Ilsa could level a city block? Leave a scar on the surface of the world? If that was true, no wonder Henry didn't want the truce to break. The FTF thought Flynn had a bomb.

And they were right.

Behind his eyes, August saw the stretch of scorched earth at the center of the city. Did she . . . did she mean to do it? Of course not—he hadn't meant to hurt anyone, either—but things got lost in the darkness. When Sunai went dark, lives ended. There were no rules, no boundaries: the guilty and the innocent, the monstrous and the human—they all perished.

A *culling*, that's what Leo called it.

How many had died that day in the square? How many innocent lives lost among the guilty? It wouldn't come to that again. It couldn't. There had to be another answer.

"Her confinement was part of the truce," continued Leo. "But memories are short, and it seems our Northern half needs to be reminded."

The way he spoke of her made August's skin crawl. "She isn't a *tool*, Leo."

His brother looked at him with those terrifying

black eyes, their surfaces too flat, too smooth. "We are all tools, August."

Inside the cell, Ilsa began to hum. The sound barely reached him, a muffled song that still sent a tremor through his bones. Unlike August, who relied on his violin, or Leo, who could make his music with almost anything, Ilsa's only instrument was her voice.

August watched, a dull hunger rolling through him as the red light rose to the surface of the man's skin and spread through hers like a flush. He'd just fed, and still it ached, his constant need, a hollowness he feared would cease to exist only when *he* did.

Twin tendrils of smoke rose from the man's hollowed eyes as the last of his life escaped. The corpse went dark.

"One day you'll see," said Leo calmly. "Our sister's true voice is a beautiful, terrible thing."

Beyond the Plexi and steel, Ilsa ran her hand along the man's hair like a mother putting a child to sleep.

August felt ill. He backed away, turned, and retraced his steps to the medical wing, where Harris hadn't moved, and Henry was still working on Phillip's shoulder, and Phillip looked halfway to dead. Suddenly, August was unbearably *tired*.

He almost asked if it was true about Ilsa, but he already knew.

Instead he said, "We have to do something."

Henry looked up from the table, exhausted. "Not you, too."

"Something to *stop* the truce from breaking," said August. "Something to stop another war."

Henry rubbed the back of his arm against his eyes, but said nothing. Harris said nothing. Leo, now standing in the doorway, said nothing.

"Dad—"

"August." Emily brought a hand to his shoulder, and he realized he was shaking. When she spoke, her voice was low and steady. "It's late," she said, wiping a smudge of blood from his cheek. "You better go upstairs. After all," she added, "it's a school night."

A strangled sound clawed up his throat.

He wanted to laugh at the absurdity of this life, with all its farces. He wanted to take up his violin and play and play and play until all the hunger was gone, until he stopped feeling like a monster. He wanted to scream, but then he thought of his sister's voice turning the city to ash, and bit his tongue until pain filled his mouth in lieu of blood.

"Go on," urged Emily, nudging him toward the elevator.

And he went, following the trail of blood, like bread crumbs, through the door.

"Rough night?" asked Kate, climbing the bleachers.

Freddie's head was bowed over a book, but she could see the shadows under his eyes, the tension in his jaw.

He didn't look up. "That obvious?"

She dropped her bag. "You look like hell."

"Why, thank you," he said dryly, raking a hand through still-damp hair.

He kept his eyes on the book, but never turned the page.

Questions swam through her mind, each one trying to surface, but she held them under. She started rapping her fingers, then remembered Dr. Landry's observations and forced herself to stop. She was going to bring up the violin, but he didn't have it with him today. She tried to see what he was reading, or pretending to read, but the words were too small, so she sat there, trying to re-create the feeling she'd had the day before, the comfortable quiet they'd shared. But she couldn't sit still. Exasperated, she dug her earbuds out and had them halfway to her head when Freddie spoke.

"What did you do?" he asked, turning the page.

Kate tensed a fraction, glad he couldn't see. "What do you mean?"

Finally, he put the book aside. Plato. What kind of junior read philosophy for fun? "To get kicked out of another gym class."

"Oh," she said, touching her abdomen. "I have a terrible stomachache."

Amusement flickered in his pale gray eyes. "Is that so?"

"Yeah, I hope I'm not coming down with something," she said, slumping back against the bleachers with a smirk. "But you know what they say."

"What do they say?"

"Fresh air is the best medicine."

It would be too generous to call his expression a smile, but it was warm enough. She tucked her hair behind her ear and felt his gaze go straight to the scar. It wasn't the first time he'd noticed, but it was the first time he asked. "What happened?"

Weakness invites a knife. But the words rose up before she could stop them. "Car accident."

Freddie didn't automatically say *sorry*, as if it were his fault. (She hated when people did that). He only nodded and ran a thumb over the black lines on his wrist. "I guess we all have our marks."

She reached out and brushed her fingers over the nearest tally, feeling him tense under the touch. "How many days sober?"

He pulled gently free. "Enough," he said, tugging the cuff down to cover the skin.

The questions rattled in her head.

Who are you?

What are you hiding?

Why are you hiding it?

They were trying to get out, and she was about to let them, when Freddie spoke.

"Can I tell you a secret?"

Kate sat forward. "Yes." The word had come out faster than she'd planned, but he didn't seem to notice. His eyes found hers, and there was something heavy about his gaze. Like she could feel it weighing on her. "What is it?" she pressed.

He leaned in. "I've never seen a forest up close." And then, before she could say anything, he was pulling her down the bleacher steps and toward the trees.

"They smell like candles," said Freddie, kicking up leaves.

"I'm pretty sure candles smell like *them*," said Kate. "What kind of guy hasn't seen *trees*?"

He lifted a crimson leaf, twirled it between his fingers. "The kind who lives in the red," he said, letting it fall, "and has very protective parents."

Kate's pulse ticked up at the mention of family, but she kept her voice even. "Tell me about them."

Freddie only shrugged. "They're good people. They mean well."

What are their names? she wanted to ask.

"What do they do?"

"My dad's a surgeon," he said, stepping over a fallen log. "Mom grew up in Fortune. She was just on the wrong side of the border when it closed."

"That's awful," said Kate, and she meant it. It was bad enough that the Verity citizens were trapped inside; she often forgot about the foreigners. Wrong place, wrong time, a life erased because of bad luck.

"She doesn't let on," he said absently. "But I know it weighs on her."

The mention of weight pulled Kate's thoughts back to the iron pendant and the black ledgers.

Where did you get your medallion?

She swallowed. "So, only child?"

"Inquisitor?" he shot back, and then, to her relief, he said, "Youngest. You?"

She liked that he asked, even though he had to know.

"Only," she answered.

In the distance the lunch bell rang, and Kate hesitated, but Freddie showed no signs of turning back. Instead he slumped down against a tree, his back against the trunk. Kate sank against its neighbor and mirrored the pose. Freddie dug a crisp, green apple from his bag and held it out.

Who are you?

She reached for the fruit, fingers purposefully brushing his, and again she relished the small shiver that went through him, as if the contact were something foreign, something new.

She took a bite and handed the apple back. He rolled it between his palms.

What are you hiding?

"I wish the rest of the city were like this," he said softly.

"Empty? Green?"

"Peaceful," he said, passing her the apple. He never took a bite.

She traced her thumb along her own teeth marks. "Have you ever seen a monster up close?"

Freddie chewed his lip. "Yes. You?"

Kate raised a brow. "My father keeps a Malchai as a pet."

His eyes narrowed, but all he said was, "I prefer cats."

Kate snorted and tossed the apple back. "So do I."

Their voices trailed off, and for a second it was there, that glimpse of easy silence. A gust of wind rustled the branches overhead, sending down a shower of dying leaves, and between the fruit in his hand and his colorless eyes and the golden leaf stuck in his black curls, Freddie Gallagher looked more like a painting than a boy.

Who are you? she wanted to ask.

Instead she reached for the apple, and took another bite.

All afternoon, the questions ate at her. The longer they'd stayed in the forest, the louder the doubt. About him. About her. Maybe there was a simple answer for the alias. Maybe he didn't have a choice. Maybe sometimes people had good reasons to hide. To lie.

But Kate wanted to know the truth.

She was halfway down the hall when she heard the violin.

She'd gotten out of her last class a few minutes early from a test and was killing time until the final bell. Her steps slowed as she listened, assuming—hoping—it was Freddie. A glimpse of truth among the mysteries. The music was coming from a classroom down the hall; as she reached the door, it stopped, followed by the screeching of chairs and equipment. She peered in through the glass insert and saw the orchestra students packing up.

The bell rang, and as they poured out, she scanned the class for Freddie, but she didn't see him.

"Hey," she said to a guy hauling what looked like a cello. He blanched a little when he realized she was talking to him. "Is there a Gallagher in your class?"

"Who?"

"Freddie Gallagher," she said. "Tall, thin, black hair, plays the violin?"

The guy shrugged. "Sorry, never seen him."

Kate swore under her breath, and the cellist took the opportunity to escape.

The halls were thinning, and she backtracked to the lockers, reaching them in time to see Freddie packing up his bag. She shot a look at the student one locker down and the girl fled. Kate leaned her shoulder against the metal.

"Hey."

"Hey," he said, shuffling his books. "I keep finding pieces of forest stuck to my clothes."

"I brushed myself off," she said. "Wouldn't want to give anyone the wrong idea."

He stared at her blankly. "What do you mean?"

She stared at him. He stared back. And then a streak of color shot across his cheeks. "Oh."

She rolled her eyes, then remembered her purpose and nodded at the locker. "No violin?"

"It's at home."

"I figured you were in orchestra."

Freddie cocked his head. "I never said I was."

"Then why bring it?"

"What?"

She shrugged. "Why bring the violin to school, if you're not in orchestra?"

Freddie closed the locker, not with a crash like everyone else, but with a soft, decisive click. "If you really want to know, I can't play at home because the walls are too thin. Colton has music rooms, the soundproof kind. So, that's why I brought it."

Kate felt her conviction slipping. "Okay," she said, trying to keep her voice light, teasing. "But if you're not in orchestra, when am I supposed to hear you play?"

A wall went up behind Freddie's eyes. "You're not."

The words landed like a blow. "Why not?" she asked, temper rising.

He slung his bag onto his shoulder. "I told you, Kate. I don't play for *anyone*."

"I'm not *anyone*," she snapped, flushing, suddenly hurt. "I'm a Harker."

Freddie gave her a disparaging look. "So what?"

"So you don't say no to me, not like that."

He actually laughed—a single, icy bark—and shook his head. "You really believe that, don't you? That this whole city revolves around what you want, because you have money and power and everyone's too afraid to tell you no." He leaned in. "I know it's hard to believe, Kate, but not everything in this world is about *you*." He pulled back. "Honestly, I thought you were better than this. I guess I was wrong."

Kate recoiled, stunned. Her face burned, and anger flared through her, hot as coals. Freddie turned to go, but her hand hit the locker beside his head, barring his path. "Who are you?"

Confusion spread across his face. "What?"

"Who. Are. You?" He tried to knock her hand away, but she caught his wrist and pushed him back against the locker. She'd had enough. Enough games. Enough dancing around the point. "You know what I mean, Freddie." She brought her metal-glossed nails to the pendant on his shirt. "You *really* don't look like a Freddie. Or a Frederick. Or a Gallagher."

His eyes narrowed. "Let go of me, Kate."

She leaned in. "Whoever you really are," she whispered, "I'm going to figure it out."

Just then another body came crashing, an arm thrown around Freddie's shoulders.

"There you are!" said the boy loudly. "Been looking for you everywhere!" The kid flashed Kate an apologetic smile while pulling Freddie free of her grip. She let her hand fall away. "We're going to be late. For that thing. You know. The party thing." He tugged Freddie down the hall. "You didn't forget, did you? Come on . . ."

The other boy waved good-bye without a backward glance, but Freddie cast a last, unreadable look her way before the two disappeared around the corner.

Anger rolled through her as Kate stormed out of the school.

She tapped another pill out of the vial Dr. Landry had given her and tossed it back, berating herself for letting Freddie of all people crack her calm. Stupid, stupid, stupid—but she thought he liked her, thought he *got* her, let him get under her skin. Idiot. If she'd learned *anything* from her father, it was that composure was control. Even if it was just an illusion.

I know it's hard to believe, but not everything in this world is about you.

The rage flared fresh.

I thought you were better than this.

Who did he think he was?

I guess I was wrong.

Who *was* he?

Kate reached the lot, but the black sedan wasn't there yet. She paced and tried to take a few steadying breaths, but it didn't help. She could feel her nerves rattling like loose change inside her chest. She perched on a bench and dug a cigarette out of the box in her bag, shoving the filter between her lips as she watched the students pour out of the school like ants.

"Miss Harker!" called an administrator as she reached for her lighter. "We have a strict no-smoking policy on campus."

Kate considered the man. She was in the mood for a fight, but the more logical part of her recognized this wasn't the right one. "Let me guess," she said, returning the cigarette to its box. "It's a health . . ."

She was going to say *risk*, but something caught her eye.

They were striding across the lawn, Freddie and the short boy and a girl she didn't know. The boy and the girl were smiling, and Freddie was doing that the thing people do—the flickering grin and the nod—when they want you to think they're paying attention but they're not.

And then Kate watched as the girl skip-stepped a few paces ahead and turned back, lifting her phone to snap a picture of the boys. At the last minute, Freddie held up his hand in front of his face. He did it with a smile, but there was something to the gesture, and when the girl teasingly tried again, Freddie closed his eyes and looked away. Just like in his school photo.

It was such a small thing, really.

But as she watched him deflect, a ghost of panic

crossing his face, a single word hissed through her head.

Monster.

It was ridiculous—absurd, paranoid—but it was there, and suddenly her thoughts were spiraling past the blurred picture on the Colton Academy page to the lack of photos anywhere on the updrive and the false name and the words scribbled in the margins and his protective parents and the stolen medal and his refusal to play for her and his rebuke and the way he looked at her, as if they shared a secret. Or as if he was keeping one.

Sunai, Sunai, eyes like coal.

Sing a song and steal your soul.

Kate reached for her phone. The girl gave up trying to snap photos, and Freddie disentangled himself from the other boy, waved good-bye, and began to walk away. Kate didn't hesitate. She pulled up the camera on her cell and held the button down, snapping a sequence of shots before he could turn away.

A car honked behind her. It was the black sedan.

Kate climbed in, heart racing, fingers clenched around the cell's screen. She didn't look, not right away. She waited until the car pulled away from Colton, waited until the world began to blur beyond the windows.

And then, slowly, she looked at the phone.

It was a crazy theory, she knew, and she scrolled through the photos, half-expecting to see nothing but

Freddie's face staring back at her. In the first few shots, he was already looking away, and she swiped back through the rapid-fire sequence with nervous fingers, rewinding until the moment when his head was turned enough to show his face.

Her eyes tracked over the image, sliding over his uniform slacks and his crisp Colton polo to the bag on his shoulder and the dark hair falling across his cheeks and into his eyes . . . but there the illusion ended. Because his eyes weren't their usual gray.

They were nothing but a smudge of black, a streak of darkness the camera couldn't catch.

Have you ever seen a monster up close?

Kate slumped back against the seat.

Freddie Gallagher wasn't an ordinary student.

He wasn't even human.

Who are you?

Kate's voice followed him onto the subway.

You don't look like a Freddie.

It trailed him through the city.

I'm going to figure it out.

It tailed him on the street.

August was relieved when he made it to the top floor of the Flynn compound and found the place empty. He dropped his bag onto the bed next to Allegro, and sank into his chair, his thoughts spiraling.

I know it's hard to believe, but not everything in this world is about you.

Why had he said that?

I thought you were better than this.

What had he *done*?

Not with a bang but a whimper.

A question.

Who are you?

Whoever you are . . .

I'm going to figure it out.

He tore off the iron pendant and lobbed it at the wall. It hit hard enough to dent the plaster before rolling across the floor. August put his head in his hands.

Who are you?

Who are you?

Who are you?

There was a knock on his door, and his head snapped up. Leo was standing there, filling the frame. "Get your coat," he said. "We're going out."

August glanced at the window and was shocked to see the sun had gone down.

"Where?" he asked.

Leo held up a piece of paper. "Where do you think?"

August scrubbed his eyes. "I'm not hungry."

"I don't care. Phillip's in critical and Harris is out of commission, so tonight you're with me."

He didn't know what he'd done to deserve his brother's attention, but he didn't want it, not now, not like this. Leo had a reputation when it came to hunting.

"Everyone knows your face," said August, scrambling. "If I go with you—"

"They'll assume you're a subordinate. Now *get up.*"

August swallowed and got to his feet. He reached for his violin case, but Leo stopped him. "Leave it."

August blinked. "I don't under—"

"You won't need it tonight."

He hesitated. His brother didn't have any of his instruments, either. "Leo . . ."

"Come," ordered his brother.

August's hand slid from the violin case. As he trailed Leo through the apartment, he cast around, hoping to catch sight of Henry or Emily, a lifeline, someone to stop them. But his parents were nowhere to be found and Ilsa's door was shut.

He didn't ask where they were going. Away from the Seam and the city center, that much was obvious, into the grid, a tangle of darkened streets, broken buildings never salvaged. A place for addicts and ex-criminals looking to hide from FTF and Sunai alike.

"You're quiet," said his brother as they moved down the street. "What are you thinking about?"

August hated when Leo phrased questions that way, leaving little room for evasion. His head was a mess, and the last person he wanted near it was his older brother, but the answer still drifted to his lips. "Kate Harker."

"What about her?"

A harder question to answer, because he wasn't sure. Everything had been going fine. And then something had tipped, the balance had faltered, fallen. Why did everyone have to ruin the quiet by asking questions? The truth was a disastrous thing.

"August," pressed Leo.

"She knows I'm keeping a secret."

Leo glanced back. "But she doesn't know what it is?"

August fidgeted. "Not yet."

"Good," he said, his voice infuriatingly calm.

"How is that good?"

"Everyone has secrets. It's normal."

"*None* of my secrets are normal, Leo." He shoved his hands in his coat. "I think I should pull out of Colton."

"No."

"But—"

Leo stopped. "If you suddenly pull out of school, they'll figure out why. Your identity will be forfeit. I'm not willing to trade the possibility of trouble for the certainty of it."

"She's not going to stop digging," said August.

Leo started walking again. "If she learns the truth, you'll know. She'll tell you herself. Until then, you stay in school."

"And if she figures it out? Then what?"

"Then we deal with it."

The way he said it made August nervous. "She's an innocent."

Leo shot him a black-eyed look. "No," he said, "she's a *Harker.*"

Kate didn't turn the music on when she got home.

For once she didn't want to drown out her thoughts. She needed them all, loud and clear. She went straight to her room and locked the door. Set the phone facedown, pulled the tablet from her bag, and booted the updrive.

Sunai, Sunai, eyes like coal.

The whole ride home her mind had spun over what little she knew about the third breed of monster.

What little *anyone* knew.

Sunai—the word alone seemed to rile the other creatures and annoy her father. But there was more to it than that. The Sunai were *rare*—much rarer than the Corsai or Malchai—but they still made Harker nervous. It had to be because of the catalysts. The Corsai seemed to come from violent, but nonlethal acts, and the Malchai stemmed from murders, but the Sunai, it was believed, came from the darkest crimes of all: bombings, shootings, massacres, events that claimed not only one life, but *many.* All that pain and death coalescing into something truly terrible; if a monster's catalyst informed its nature, then the Sunai were the worst things to go bump in the night.

It didn't help that South City probably fed the rumor

mill itself. Some said Flynn kept the Sunai like rabid dogs. Others said he treated them as family. Others still claimed the monsters were buried in the ranks of the FTF. Another, more frustrating, theory held that they could change their faces. Control minds. Make people forget they'd met them . . . if those people ever lived to tell.

Sunai were sadistic. Sunai were evil. Sunai were invincible.

And on top of it all, Sunai *looked human*.

What little Harker and his men actually knew about the Sunai came from one monster. The only one they'd ever managed to catch on camera.

Kate logged into her father's private uplink, and typed the name into the footage search.

LEO

He'd been part of the initial fight, Flynn's right hand when Harker tried to take the city twelve years back. And he wasn't shy. Kate scrolled through more than a dozen video thumbnails that tracked across the screen, all dating from before the truce. They fell into two categories.

Leo_Music

Leo_Torture

She chewed her lip, hesitating a moment before clicking on one of the videos labeled *Music*. The footage was more than a decade old, and it was shot from a security camera at an odd angle, but there he was in the frame, not stalking through shadows or down a back alley, but perched on a stool beneath a spotlight. Leo was sitting on stage in what looked like a bar, one foot up and a steel guitar balanced on his knee. Even at this angle, she could tell he was tall and blond and handsome, and aside from his eyes, which raked black lines across the camera every time his gaze drifted up, he didn't look like a monster at all.

Kate supposed that was what made him so dangerous.

There was no sound in the feed, but when he began to play, she still found herself turning her head, good ear toward the screen, *wanting* to hear the song. And even with the grainy footage and the darkened room, she could see the crowd sit forward.

Only the room wasn't so dark anymore. At first she thought the overheads must be switching on, but as she watched, she realized the audience itself was beginning to glow. The people didn't seem to notice the light, didn't seem to notice anything. They sat so still Kate thought the footage must be frozen. But it couldn't be, because Leo's fingers were still plucking at the guitar strings.

Movement caught her eye as two people rose from their chairs, not fast, but slowly, as if drifting up through water. The light coming from their skin was different, sickly, and they both moved toward the stage with the simple, steady steps of those in a trance, their lips moving but their expressions empty.

When they were nearly to the stage, Leo stopped playing.

He rose from the stool, set aside the guitar, and stepped down off the platform to greet the two glowing forms as if they were fans.

And then he closed his hands around their throats.

They didn't fight back, didn't thrash, even when he dragged them up so that only their shoes skimmed the floor. She watched as the light beneath their skin flickered, and then began to drift, out of their bodies and into Leo's, infusing him with that strange glow. She watched as the last of their light guttered and died, watched as their eyes shriveled black in their sockets, and even then Leo didn't let go. He stood there, eyes closed and head back, looking almost peaceful as the men went limp, turned from living, breathing people into empty shells. At last he let the bodies fall and returned to the stage, where he took up his guitar and walked out.

The glow from the audience faded, and one by one they began to move again, as if shaking off sleep, slowly at first, and then frantically as they saw the corpses on the floor.

Kate sat there, chilled. It wasn't the act of killing that

bothered her—monsters and men both did that—and it wasn't even the chilling serenity on the Sunai's face. It was the fact that he killed them with a *sound*. Those men were dead the minute he started playing. Pulled like puppets on strings.

She thought of Freddie's violin, suddenly grateful he'd refused to play, even if she wasn't sure why. Was he trying to spare her? Or just waiting for Flynn's signal?

Her attention flicked back to the screen. She wasn't like the people in that crowd, walking straight into the hands of death. No, Kate had an advantage, knew her monster's face, his weapon. Now all she had to do was find his weakness.

She closed out of the video and was about to exit the page when she remembered the second tab.

Torture.

If a Sunai used *music* to lure its prey, then what was this?

She pulled her hair back, lit a cigarette, and clicked on the next video.

"Who are we hunting?" asked August.

They were standing on the front porch of a row house, its windows boarded, its siding warped. The door had been tagged with red paint that read *STAY AWAY*.

As if words had that much power here.

"Two men," said Leo, rolling up his sleeves, revealing the short bands of black crosses that ran like cuffs around both forearms. The marks were too few in number, washed away every time he went dark. Leo didn't turn because he lacked control—that he had in spades—but simply because he *liked* the way it felt. *Like shedding a coat on a hot day.* The thought made August shudder.

"Brothers," continued Leo. "Responsible for the deaths of six. Gang politics. Drugs. I expect they'll be armed."

"And you had me leave my violin at home?"

Leo reached into his jacket. August assumed he was

fetching one of his own instruments. Instead, he withdrew a long, thin knife, and passed it to August.

"What is this for?" he asked.

Leo didn't answer. He was staring down at his hand, now empty, and August watched as darkness began to roll up his fingers and across his palm. August recoiled instinctively, but only Leo's hand blackened to shadow. The way he did that, slid between the two forms, that worked only because he'd torn away the walls between. August tried to imagine what Leo must have been like, back before he burned through his humanity, but he couldn't. He watched as Leo reached out his shadowed hand and gripped the rusted doorknob. The metal crunched like paper under his touch and fell away. The door swung open.

"Do what I say, little brother," he said, his voice lower, stranger, more resonant.

"How do you know they're here?" whispered August.

"I can smell the blood on their hands," said Leo, the darkness receding from his skin, his voice returning to its usual pitch. He strode inside, and August followed, nudging the door shut behind him.

The house was dark and smelled of stale smoke and liquor, and when they moved, the boards creaked under their feet. August cringed. Leo didn't. They reached the center of the room and stopped. Leo cocked his head,

listening. And then August heard it, too. The floorboards groaned again. They were both standing still.

The first guy came out of nowhere. He lunged at Leo,
but his brother was too fast; he plucked the man out
of the air and slammed him down against the rotting
boards so hard they split. The man squirmed and spat
obscenities, but Leo crouched calmly over him like a cat
pinning a mouse, but without the playful glee.

"What is your name?" he asked, and the air vibrated
with his will.

"Foster," spat the thug. His shadow writhed beneath
him, clawing at the broken floor.

"Foster," repeated Leo. "Are you here alone?"

The man thrashed, coughed, answered, "No."

August's grip tightened reflexively on the knife, but
his brother looked unconcerned as he hauled Foster to
his feet and spun him around so his back was pressed to
Leo's chest. "Pay attention, August," he said. "There is
more than one way to bring a soul to surface."

With that, Leo wrenched Foster's arm up behind his
back, and the man cried out. August cringed, but Leo
remained calm, unmoved. He kept twisting until August
heard the tearing ligaments, and the man let out a scream.

"Why are you doing this?" asked August.

"To educate you," said Leo simply. He twisted harder,
and Foster keened. Bones broke audibly and August

watched, horrified, first as sweat broke out across the man's face, and then as his skin began to glow red. The light rose like blood to the surface, and as it did, it began to pass from Foster's body into Leo's.

"I'm sorry," gasped the man, his confession spilling out through ragged breaths. "I'm sorry. I did what I had to do. If I didn't kill them, they'd have killed *me*." Leo twisted further, and the man sobbed between the crack and splinter of bone. The sound turned August's stomach.

"Stop this, Leo," he said. "Why make him suffer?"

Tears streamed down Foster's face as the life seeped out of him. "I'm sorry," he cried. "Please, I'm sorry. . . ."

Leo was unmoved. "Why *shouldn't* he suffer?" he challenged, meeting August's eyes as the man wailed. "These are bad people, little brother. They do bad things. They hurt and they murder and they taint this world with blood and darkness and evil." He had to raise his voice over Foster's screams. "Why *should* they go gently? Why shouldn't they suffer for their sins?"

"I'm sorry . . ." Foster's voice faded, along with the light beneath his skin. His eyes burned, collapsing inward.

"Our purpose is *not* to bring peace," said Leo, letting the broken body fall to the floor. "It is to bestow penance." August opened his mouth to protest, when Leo said, "Watch out."

It happened too fast. A second man lunged at August from behind. He didn't have a chance to think, to stop, to let go of the weapon and step out of the way. He turned just in time for his knife to bury itself in the attacker's stomach. August looked down at the blade disappearing between the man's ribs with a mixture of shock and horror as the man let out a strangled sound of pain. His life surged to the surface, and August gasped as the energy hit him like a bucket of ice water, sudden and bright and achingly cold. His fingers tightened on the knife, and the man went for his throat, but his hands faltered, landed on August's collar, nails digging uselessly into his skin.

"They deserved it," coughed the man, blood already staining his lips. His legs started to buckle but August held him up, his life coursing between them, sharp and electric. "They all deserved it. This messed up . . . world . . . we're all . . . gonna . . ."

The man's words fell apart as he slumped into death, and August stood there in the dark, shaking from the force of it, feeling as if he'd taken on the man's evils as well as his life. This was the opposite of peace. He felt alive—so alive—but tarnished, his senses screaming and his head a tangle of dark thoughts and feelings and power, and he was drowning and shivering and burning alive. He had to close his eyes and force air into his lungs until the sensations dulled and his mind stopped spiraling, and he could drag it back into his head, back into his skin. When the room took shape around him again, the first thing he saw was the blood-covered knife. He felt a hand on his shoulder and saw Leo there beside him, looking proud.

Which only made August feel worse.

"It'll get easier," promised Leo, taking the blade.

But August looked down at the corpses, their shadows still, their bodies broken.

"Should it?"

Kate stared at the screen, where a man's body lay twisted on the floor, a bloody, contorted corpse. It had taken him a long time to die. Or rather, Leo had taken a long time to kill him. He'd used only his hands, which meant they didn't need music to steal a soul. What was the saying? More than one way to skin a cat.

She'd never really understood the phrase.

Now she did.

The only thing she didn't get were the marks. Leo had them, too, short bands of crosses circling his wrists.

One for every day without a slip, that's what Freddie had said. Which obviously wasn't the whole truth, but it couldn't be a lie, either. Monsters didn't lie.

"Our Kate, always a dreamer."

She jumped, and saw Sloan standing in the doorway, a

wicked smile smeared across his sickly face. She didn't know how long he'd been standing there—or how long she'd been sitting, for that matter, staring at the frozen image of Leo amid the wreckage and thinking about Freddie. She tapped out of the updrive, and set the tablet aside.

"What is it?" she asked.

He drew a pointed nail absently down the wooden door frame, eliciting a screech. Kate resisted the urge to touch the nick he'd made on her cheek. "Your father won't be home tonight."

Her grip tightened on the chair. "Oh?" The thought of being left alone with the Malchai gave her chills, but she knew better than to let it show. If Sloan knew how uncomfortable he made her, he would only torment her more. "Nothing too serious, I assume?"

"Nothing he can't handle," said Sloan.

She watched him go, hesitated, then grabbed her phone and surged after him.

"Hey," she called, following the Malchai out into the penthouse. But he wasn't there. "Sloan?" Nothing. Then a cold breath against her neck.

"Yes, Kate?" said a voice near her bad ear. She didn't jump, but turned, stepping carefully back out of his reach. She focused on the branded *H* instead of his red eyes, reminding herself that he belonged to her father. To *her*.

"I want to ask you something."

Sloan's dead lips pursed in distaste. "I would rather you didn't," he said evenly.

"What do you know about Sunai?"

The Malchai stilled. A shadow flickered across the planes of his face before they went smooth again. He tilted his head, considering her. But he couldn't lie. "They are as different from *us*," he said, "as we are from the Corsai." His nose crinkled when he spoke of the shadow beasts. "They can appear human, but it is not their true form."

Kate frowned. There had been no files, no footage of the monsters in another shape. What did a Sunai look like, behind its skin?

"Is it true they feed on souls?"

"They feed on *life force*."

"How do you kill one?"

"You don't," said Sloan simply. "The Sunai appear to be indestructible."

"There's no such thing as indestructible," said Kate. "Everything has a weakness."

"I suppose," he acquiesced, "but if they have a weakness, it does not show."

"Is that why the other monsters fear them?"

"It is not a matter of *fear*," snarled Sloan. "We avoid them because we cannot feed on them. Just as they cannot feed on us."

"But *you* can be killed." His red eyes narrowed, but he said nothing, so she went on. "How many are there?"

The Malchai sighed, clearly tiring of the interrogation. "As far as we know, there are three."

Only child?

Youngest.

"The first, Leo, is known to all," said Sloan. "He fancies himself judge, jury, and executioner."

"Have you met him?" asked Kate.

Sloan's expression darkened. "Our paths have crossed." He unbuttoned his collar, pulled the shirt aside to reveal sickly blue-white skin raked with scars, as if someone had try to claw their way through the bone shield of his chest.

"Looks like he won," said Kate.

"Perhaps." A rictus grin spread across Sloan's face as he touched a single, sharp nail to the place above his eye. "But I left my mark."

She had seen a recent photo of Leo, seen the narrow scar that cut through his left brow like a piece chipped from a statue, the only blemish on a flawless face.

"And the other two?"

"The second Sunai made the Barren." Kate's eyes widened. She'd seen the dead space at the center of the city, heard about the catastrophe, the hundreds of lives lost, but she'd assumed it was the result of a force, a massive weapon, not of a single monster. "She is bound to her tower by the truce.

"The third," continued Sloan, "is a mystery."

Not to me, thought Kate, clutching the phone.

She could see the truce was failing, knew it was only a matter of time before it broke. The monsters were restless, and her father's attention was drifting again to the Seam. The Sunai had always been Flynn's best weapon. If they could be hunted down, if they could be *killed*, even captured, South City wouldn't stand a chance.

Sloan was still watching her. "You are very curious tonight, little Katherine."

She met his gaze. "The more you know," she said casually, grabbing a drink before retreating to her room. Once inside, she locked the door, and considered the phone.

She could give her father this, the identity of the third Sunai . . . or she could give him something better. She could give him Freddie Gallagher.

Show him that she was a Harker to the core.

Sloan's words sang through her mind.

You will always be our little Katherine.

Kate held down the *delete* key and watched the photos vanish, one by one by one.

Not anymore.

August wanted to crawl out of his skin.

They walked back to the compound in silence . . . well, *he* walked back to the compound in silence. Leo was preaching. That's how August thought of it, when his brother gave one of his sermons about the natural order of the world. As if there was anything natural about them. About what they'd just done. He could feel the man's blood drying on his fingers. Could feel the man's soul swimming in his head.

"Your problem, August, is that you resist the current. You fight against the tide instead of letting it carry you. . . ." Leo's black eyes were rimmed with light and bright with zeal. But at least when he got like this, he wasn't forcing August to answer questions about his hunger, his thoughts, his need to feel human. "Just as you fight against your inner fire. You could burn so brightly, little brother."

August shivered, cold to his bones. "I don't . . . want to . . . ," he said, teeth chattering. This was the opposite of hunger. This was worse.

"Stop being selfish," said Leo. "We were not made for *want*. It has no place in us."

It has no place in you, August wanted to say, *because you burned it out*.

They reached the compound, passed the guards, and stepped into the elevator. He clenched his teeth as it rose, afraid that if he opened his mouth, something would escape. Maybe a sob, or a scream. The man's life was buzzing inside of him like bees.

What have you done to me?

What have you made me do?

The moment the elevator doors opened, he stormed out, carving a line toward his room.

"Where have you two been?" asked Henry.

"Is that blood?" added Emily.

August didn't stop.

"Leo?"

"I was giving him a lesson."

"What—"

"Don't worry, Henry. He'll be fine. . . ."

August closed the door, and slumped back against the wood. There was no lock, so he stayed there until he was sure no one would follow, then let out a shuddering breath and tore off the FTF jacket. He left the lights off and collapsed onto the bed. His fingers dug into his ribs, trying to stop the buzzing, but it didn't work, and as soon as he closed his eyes, the buzzing rose to screams. He fumbled in the crumpled sheets until he found the music player and shoved the buds into his ears.

Something landed on the bed, and he rolled over to see Allegro padding toward him, but the cat paused just out of reach, bright eyes narrowing with suspicion, and when he went to pet him, the cat recoiled and darted away.

They can tell the difference, you know, between good and bad.

"I'm sorry," he whispered into the dark. "I had no choice."

The words left a sick taste in his mouth. How many times had someone said those things to him? It never made a difference. A confession didn't undo the crime, nothing could, so August folded in on himself and turned the music up until it drowned out everything.

It was the middle of the night, but he couldn't sleep.

The buzzing had finally stopped, but his nerves were frayed, and he padded out into the kitchen, and poured himself a glass of water. He wasn't thirsty, but something about the gesture calmed him, made him feel normal.

His attention wandered over a stack of folders on the

counter, and he was about to reach for them when he heard something scratching in the dark. August set the glass aside untouched, and found Allegro pacing back and forth in front of Ilsa's door.

He knocked, but the door wasn't pulled all the way shut, and it fell open under his touch. Inside, the lights were off, and the first thing he saw were the stars. Every surface of Ilsa's room was covered in them, tiny dots of fiber-optic light splashed across the ceiling and walls and floors. His sister stood in front of the window, her strawberry hair loose but strangely weightless, twining through the air around her face. Her fingers were splayed across the window glass, and in her sleeveless shirt, her own tiny black stars trailed across her shoulders and down her arms.

Two thousand one hundred and sixty-three.

August couldn't reconcile the Ilsa in front of him, gentle and kind, with the monster whose true voice somehow leveled a piece of the world and everyone in it.

Our sister, the Angel of Death.

He wanted to ask her about that day. Wanted to know what happened, what it felt like, to live with so much death. He wanted to, but he wouldn't.

Allegro padded toward the bed, and August was about to retreat when his sister spoke, so softly he almost didn't hear.

"It's falling apart," she whispered. Her fingers twitched on the glass. August padded forward carefully, quietly. "Crumbling," continued Ilsa. "Not ashes to ashes and dust to dust, like things should go, but wrong, like when a crack starts deep inside a stone and then spreads and spreads and spreads, and you don't know until the day it . . ." She pressed against the window, and hairline fractures began to web out across the glass.

August brought his hand to rest over his sister's.

"I can feel the cracks. But I can't tell . . ." She squeezed her eyes shut, and then opened them wide. "I can't tell if the cracks are out there or inside of me or both. Is it selfish, to hope they're out there, August?"

"No," he said gently.

They stood for a while in silence. When she spoke again, her voice was steadier. "Thirteen. Twenty-six. Two hundred and seventeen."

August frowned. "What's that?"

"Thirteen Malchai. Twenty-six Corsai. Two hundred and seventeen humans. That's how many died in Lyle Square." He stiffened, didn't realize he was still holding her hand until she let it fall from the glass. "That was its name, before *the Barren*. They were holding a rally; that's why there were so many people there. I didn't mean to do it, August. But I had to do something. Leo wasn't there, and the rally was turning, and . . . I just wanted to help. I'd never gone dark before. I didn't know what would happen. Leo makes it look so simple, I thought we all burned the same way, but our brother burns like a torch, and . . ."

And Ilsa burned like a wildfire.

And August?

You could burn so brightly, that's what Leo told him. *If you let yourself.*

"It was night," whispered Ilsa, "but they all left shadows." When she met his gaze, her eyes were haunted, dark. "I don't want to burn again, August, but if the truce breaks, I'll have to, and more people will die." She shuddered. "I don't want them to die because of me."

"I know," he whispered, drawing her away from the splintered window. "We'll find another way."

If it came to war, thought August, how many would he kill to spare her the task? How brightly *could* he burn? He thought of the knife, of the life lurching through him, the sickness, and Leo's promise it would get better. Get easier.

Ilsa sank onto the bed. Allegro hopped up, and nestled against her. She didn't notice. "I'll stay with you," said August. "Until you fall asleep."

She curled up on her side, and he sat down on the floor, his head back against her bed. Her fingers wove absently through his hair.

"I can feel the cracks," she whispered.

"It's okay," he whispered back. Allegro bounded down, considered him with his green eyes, then curled up in his lap. His chest loosened with relief.

"Everything breaks. . . ," murmured his sister.

"Hush, Ilsa," he said, looking up at the stars across her ceiling.

". . . breaks apart . . ."

"Hush . . ."

He fell asleep like that, surrounded by Ilsa's voice and Allegro's purr and hundreds of stars.

Kate spread her tools on the bed.

Duct tape (the utility of which really couldn't be over-estimated), half a dozen copper-threaded zip ties, and a set of iron spikes the length of her forearm (at the very least, they might slow him down). She considered the meager selection, feeling like she was going into battle with a toothpick, then packed the tools into her backpack and headed out.

She was halfway through the kitchen, shrugging on her Colton jacket, when she noticed Callum Harker sitting on the couch.

She'd barely seen her father since the trials in the basement, but there he was, arms stretched along the back of the sleek leather sofa. A step toward the couch, and she realized he wasn't alone—Sloan was kneeling at his side, head bowed and stiff as a statue, or a corpse. Harker was speaking softly to the Malchai—Kate couldn't hear the words—and she hesitated, feeling like an intruder. But this was *her* house, too. She fetched a mug and poured herself a cup of coffee, making no effort to be quiet. Harker clearly heard. He made a short motion with his hand, and Sloan withdrew and went to stand by the window. Morning light streamed in against his blue-white skin, and seemed to go straight through it.

"Good morning, Katherine," said her father, lifting his voice.

Kate took a long sip of coffee, ignoring the way it burned her throat. "Morning."

She imagined him asking her how she was settling in, imagined telling him that she didn't need Sloan keeping tabs. Maybe he would ask her about school, and she could tell him that she'd met a boy and planned to bring him home. But of course, he didn't ask her any of those things, so she couldn't answer. Instead she said, "You're up early."

"Actually," he said, "I've been up all night." His arms slid from the couch as he stood. "I figured I would stay up a little longer to see you off."

Hope flickered through her, followed almost immediately by distrust. "What for?" she challenged, blowing on the coffee.

Harker crossed the room, moving with the sure steps of someone who expected the world to get out of his way.

"I'm your father," he said, as if that were an explanation. "Besides, I wanted to give you something." He held out his hand. "Something more fitting for a Harker."

Kate looked down and saw a new pendant glittering in his palm. It looked like a large coin on the end of a thin chain, the V embossed and filled with nine garnets, each shining like a drop of blood. "The metal is silver," he said. "More delicate than iron, but still pure."

Kate tried to find the meaning in the gesture. The trap. "Was it my mother's?"

"No," said her father sternly. "It was mine. And now it's yours." He crossed behind her and swept her hair aside to unfasten her standard medal. "And one day . . . ," he said, sliding the silver chain around her throat. "Perhaps you'll have more than my pendant." She turned to face him, this man who'd given her his eyes, his hair, and little more, this father who'd always been a shadow at the edges of her life, more legend than real. The knight in a story, strong and stoic and always somewhere else. He was all that she had now. Was she all that he had, too?

Behind her father, Kate met Sloan's red eyes.

"I know," she said, holding the Malchai's gaze, "that you don't want me here."

She waited, half-expecting Harker to deny it, but he didn't. "No father wants his daughter in harm's way," he said. "I already lost your mother, Katherine.

I don't want to lose you, too."

You lost my mother to fear, she wanted to say. *To her own monsters, not the ones that follow you.*

"But," continued Harker, "you deserve a chance. That's what you want, isn't it? To prove you belong here, with me?"

The Malchai's red eyes narrowed.

"I want a chance to show you," she said, finding her father's gaze, "that I'm *your* daughter."

Harker smiled. No teeth, just a quiet curl of his lips. "You better go," he said. "Or you'll be late for school."

The elevator was waiting. When the doors closed, Kate considered her reflection and brought her fingers to the silver pendant.

I have something for you, too, she thought, clutching the medallion.

She couldn't wait to see the look on her father's face when she laid a Sunai at his feet. Then he would know—without a doubt—that she was a Harker.

"Hey, want a lift?"

The morning air was heavy and stale, and August was standing on Paris's front steps, trying to shove the Colton jacket into his bag when he looked up and saw the black sedan idling on the curb, Kate Harker leaning against it. His fingers tightened on his violin case.

"Um." He glanced back at Paris's building. "How do you know where I live?"

She gave him a look that said *I'm a Harker* before opening the door. "Come on. Get in."

In response, August actually took a step *back*. Not a large one—it could have been mistaken for a shuffle, a shift of weight—but he still cursed himself.

"Oh," he shrugged, "that's okay. I don't need—"

"Don't be ridiculous," she cut in. "We're going to the same place. Why suffer the subway when there's a perfectly good car?"

Because the perfectly good car comes with a perfectly dangerous girl, he thought, but he managed not to say it out loud. He hesitated, unsure what to do. There could be cameras in the car. It could be a trap. It could be—

"For God's sake, Freddie. It's just a ride to school."

She turned and climbed in without closing the door, an obvious invitation—or maybe a command—to follow.

Bad idea bad idea bad idea thudded his heart as he approached the sedan. He hovered in the open door, then took a breath, ducked his head, and climbed in, closing the door behind him with a click that made fresh panic flutter in his chest.

You're the monster, he thought, followed rapidly, reflexively, by *you're not a monster*, and then, in desperation, *be calm be calm be calm,* because his thoughts were threatening to spiral out.

The car had two bench seats, one facing forward and the other back, and Kate had already claimed the rear bench, so he took the other one. Putting his back to the driver made him *almost* as nervous as putting his front to Kate, but before he could say anything, do anything, the car pulled into traffic, and moments later Paris's building vanished from sight. He could feel Kate watching him, but when he went to meet her eyes, they were leveled on his shirt.

"You're not wearing your medal," she said.

August's pulse stuttered. He knew even before he looked down that she was right. There was no prickle of iron, no weight, because the medallion was still on his bedroom floor where he'd thrown it the night before.

He groaned, and leaned his head back on the seat. "My dad's going to kill me," he muttered.

Kate shrugged. "It's okay," she said, flashing the ghost of a smile. "But make sure you're home before dark." He couldn't tell if she was joking.

The car cut through the streets, a blur of speed, the city tunneling behind Kate's head. Her nails, usually tapping their short, metallic beat, were curled into her palms.

If she learns the truth, you'll know.

He watched her chest rise, her lips part.

She'll tell you herself.

August braced himself, but when she spoke, all she said was, "I want to apologize."

"For what?" asked August, and Kate gave him one of those looks that wasn't really surprise. "Oh," he said, "you mean, for assaulting me in the hall."

Kate nodded, opened her mouth, then closed it again. He tensed. She seemed to be struggling to find the right words. Was she trying to hold back? Could she? He watched as she fiddled with the medallion around her own throat. It was new, polished silver and bloody red stones. "Look," she said at last, "growing up the way I have, I guess it makes a person . . ."

"Paranoid?"

Her dark eyes narrowed. "I was going to say guarded. And yes, okay, a little paranoid." Her hand slipped from the coin. "There's not a whole lot of trust in my family. I don't expect you to understand."

August wanted to say that he did, but he couldn't, because it wasn't true. For all their differences, Ilsa and Leo were like family, and so were the Flynns. He trusted them.

"The moment I met you," she said. "I knew you were different."

August dug his fingers into his knees, silently

begging her not to say more, not to confess to this.

"So am I," she added.

He held his tongue, focused on his breathing.

"We don't fit in," she went on. "Not just because we're new. We see the world for what it is. No one else does."

"Or maybe they do," he cut in, "but they're too afraid of you to say it."

Kate gave him a withering smile, and shook her head. "I make them uncomfortable, because I'm a reminder that it's not real. That it's just this . . ." she waved her metal-tipped fingers. "*Veneer.* They'd rather close their eyes and pretend. But our eyes . . ." she trailed off, her dark blue gaze weighing him down. "Our eyes are open."

And then she flashed a strange, private smile, and he was back in the hall again.

Whoever you are . . . I'm going to figure it out.

August felt dizzy. The things Kate was saying, they were the truth, they had to be, and yet it all felt like a line to reel him in. It was too clean and too messy at the same time. Was she flirting with him? Or trying to tell him she *knew*? Did she mean what she was saying, or was she saying something else? August felt himself scrambling for purchase as the car filled up again with silence.

"You're right," he said at last, throat dry. "About us

being different . . . But I'd rather be able to see the truth than live a lie."

"Which makes you the only bearable person at that school." Her smile widened when she said it, shifting into that genuine, contagious grin. Watching her, it was like watching a flickering image, two versions that shifted back and forth depending on how you turned your head. He waited for her confession to spill out, but it didn't.

"I was wondering," she said, tapping a metal nail against the pendant, "about your marks."

August swallowed, rubbed his wrist. "What about them?"

"You said they were for sobriety, but they're permanent."

"Yeah. So?"

She cocked her head, revealing the silvery edge of her scar. "So what if you relapse?"

He looked at her, unblinking. "Well, that would suck."

She laughed, but her attention was still fixed on him—she wasn't going to settle for a brush-off—so he swallowed, trying to find a way to tell the truth. "If I could just wipe them off at the end of the day," he said, "they wouldn't mean anything. They wouldn't matter. And they do. I was in a dark place, once, and I don't ever want to go back. I'd rather die than start over." She stared at him, a slight furrow between her brows, and he could imagine her thinking, *So this is what it looks like when he tells the truth*, and he thought, *So this is what it looks like when she believes you.*

Which was almost funny, seeing as he'd never lied, but it also scared him, because it was the first time he'd seen her make that face, and the others now looked empty by comparison.

Do you know? Do you know? Do you know?

He could ask her. Force her to answer. But the question was damning, and the car was too small, and he didn't know what he was supposed to do if she said yes.

The violin case sat on the floor between his feet, and Leo was right—if he tried, he could smell the blood on the driver's hands, but not on Kate, and she didn't have a restless shadow, and—

"Freddie?"

He blinked. She was looking at him expectantly. The car was idling in front of Colton.

"Sorry," he said. He climbed out first, and held the door open for Kate. At the last moment he offered his hand to help her from the car, and to his surprise, she actually took it. He fought back a shiver when her nails brushed his skin.

"Hey, Marcus." She leaned her head back into the

sedan. "I have a counseling session, so I might be a little late."

The man in the driver's seat only nodded, and drove away.

Kate set off toward the front gate, glancing back when he didn't follow. "You coming?"

"I'll catch you around," he said, nodding at a random cluster of juniors as if they were his friends.

Again, the edge of a smirk, the raise of a brow, the careful composure that he now realized went with disbelief. "I'm glad we talked, Freddie," she said, her voice sliding smoothly over the name.

"Me, too," he said, pulling his cell from his pocket the moment she turned away.

He dialed Henry, but it was Leo who answered.

"Where's Dad?" he asked.

"Flynn is stitching someone up. What is it?"

"She knows."

"Knows what?" pressed Leo.

"Something. Everything. I don't know. But she *knows*, Leo."

His brother's voice was stiff, impatient. "What changed?"

"I don't know, but yesterday she threw me against a locker, and today she wants to be my friend. It's off, something's off, and the way she said my name—not my name, I mean, Freddie's name, it's wrong, and I look at her and I see two people and I can't tell which is real and—"

"Stay put, August."

"But—"

"Stay. Put."

August dug his nails into his palms. "I forgot my medal."

A sigh. "Well," he said slowly, "try to stay away from monsters. In the meantime—"

"Leo—"

"You're letting your head get away from you. If Kate Harker knew what you were, she would have felt compelled to tell you."

"I know, but . . ." August closed his eyes. But she *did* tell him. Didn't she? What was she trying to say? "I have a bad feeling. Could you just have Henry call me when he's done? I need to talk to him."

"Fine," said Leo. "But in the meantime, little brother, take a deep breath, and try not to lose your head."

"Okay, I'll—" he started, but Leo had already hung up.

Kate slammed her hand into the bathroom counter.

She glared at her reflection. "What the *hell* is your problem?"

A girl behind her jumped. "Um, nothing!" she whimpered before scurrying off.

Kate exhaled as the bathroom door swung shut, and slumped into a crouch, resting her forehead against the cold counter. "Dammit, dammit, dammit. . . ."

She hadn't done it.

He'd been right there in front of her, but every time she thought of crossing to his seat, of reaching for the copper ties in her pocket, she couldn't do it. She tried to picture black-eyed Leo torturing that man until his life welled up like blood, but all she saw was Freddie sitting there folded in on himself like *she* was the monster.

The images didn't line up.

But she'd *seen* the photo on her phone, she *knew* what he was; knew the thing sitting across from her was just a trick of the light, a façade.

Freddie might look innocent, but he wasn't.

He was a Sunai.

But he didn't know that she knew. She still had the upper hand, the element of surprise. But for how long?

It was okay. She'd prepared for this, given herself another chance. Kate would just offer him a ride home. She didn't really have a meeting after school, but she'd seen his name on the practice room sheet, in smooth cursive. *Frederick Gallagher. 4 p.m.*

"What are you *doing*?" came a voice, the words like a whine. *Rachel*. The girl who'd cornered her on the way to the gym.

Kate forced her grip to loosen on the counter. "Praying," she said, straightening slowly, composing her features.

Rachel arched a brow. "For what?"

"Forgiveness," said Kate. "For the things I'm about to do if you don't *get out of my way*." Rachel had the good sense to back up and let her pass without another word.

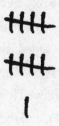

By the end of the day, August was beginning to think he'd overreacted about Kate. She'd sat beside him in History, doodling monsters in the margins of her own work instead of his. They'd passed in the hall, exchanged a nod and an awkward smile, a murmured *hey there*, and that was it. He'd waited on the bleachers during study hall—found himself *wanting* her to show—but she didn't come. At lunch, August sent Leo a text that simply said, *Feeling better*, and got back a single word: *good*.

By the last class, he was glad he hadn't left—it was finally his turn in the practice studio. As soon as the bell rang, he grabbed his violin from the locker and headed straight for the room. He was breathless by the time he reached it, heart tight with the panic that it would be locked, or taken, but it wasn't; the only name left at the bottom of the page was his own.

He knew he should go home, talk to Henry, and he

would, but Leo was probably right, he was overreacting, and the chance to play—*really* play—was too tempting. Besides, the longer he stayed, the less likely he was to run into Kate on the way out. A win-win, that's what he told himself. And he believed it.

August swiped his ID, and the door gave a small beep of approval before letting him in. The studio itself was a cube so white it swallowed the corners and made him feel like he was standing in a void, the emptiness interrupted only by a black stool, a music stand, a bench. When the door closed behind him, it sealed, and he felt as much as heard the soundproofing kick in—a subtle vibration followed by sudden, absolute quiet.

Of course, it was never quiet in his head. Within a heartbeat or two, the gunshots started up, distant but relentless, and August couldn't wait to drown them out. He laid the case on the piano bench and took out his phone, setting the timer for forty-five minutes—he'd still have plenty of time to get home before dark. The violin case clicked open at his touch, the sounds short, staccato in the silence. He drew the instrument and bow free, then lowered himself onto the stool.

With a deep breath, August brought the violin beneath his chin, the bow to the strings and . . . hesitated. He'd never done this before. There were so many days when he ached to pick up the violin and just *play*.

But he never could. Music wasn't idle in the hands of a Sunai. It was a weapon, paralyzing everyone it touched.

He would have loved a place like this at the compound, but resources were always stretched, every inch of space was given over to the FTF—housing, training, supplies— and Leo said he didn't *need* practice; if he wanted more chances to play, all he had to do was hunt more often. Once or twice, August had fantasized about stealing a car, driving past the red and the yellow and the green, out into the Waste, with its empty stretches of field, its open space. He'd park on the side of the road and start walking out, go until he was sure no one could hear his song.

But that fantasy came with its own dangers. No people meant no souls, and he'd calculated how long it would take to get that far out, and back, and knew it was too risky.

"Pack a meal," Leo had said dismissively.

August had wanted to say several things back, none of them kind.

But now . . .

Now it was just him and the white walls and the violin, and August closed his eyes and began to play.

Kate lingered after school, watching the campus empty. The students left in a wave, heading for the subway or peeling out of the lot as if they were racing against the darkness, which she supposed they were. Curfew was technically sundown—7:23 today, according to a helpful chart outside the main office—but nobody ever cut it that close, not even the teachers. As long as they had a medallion, they would be safe—that was the idea—but no one seemed eager to test the theory, and twenty minutes after the 4 p.m. bell, the only people still on campus were a handful of sophomores retaking a quiz, a pair of seniors loitering in the parking lot, and the monster in the music room.

Kate perched on a bench inside the gate, waiting for the black sedan to show. The copper-lined zip ties jabbed at her through her back pocket, a nagging reminder of what she needed to do. She glanced back at the school— the car needed to get here before Freddie.

Thirty minutes after the bell, there was still no sign of either.

Kate rapped her nails on the bench. She'd told Marcus she'd be late, and she tried to still the nervous prickle in her chest, but fifteen minutes later, with Colton going quiet around her and no sedan in sight, she broke down and phoned the driver.

He didn't answer.

Fear flashed through her, sudden and sharp.

It was almost five.

The light was already starting to weaken. Kate got

to her feet, began to pace. She thought of calling her father, but couldn't bring herself to do it. She wasn't a child. But Freddie was still inside, and without the car she had no way of getting him to go with her anyway. Abandoning the mission, she shifted the backpack on her shoulder and headed for the subway entrance across from campus.

But when she got there, it was locked.

Kate's pulse quickened as she wrapped her fingers around the metal bars.

This wasn't right. The subway lines were supposed to run until sundown, but the gate had already been pulled across the entrance and padlocked shut. Her bad ear started ringing, the way it did when her heart was going too fast. She closed her eyes for a moment, tried to slow it down, but it was telling her, over and over, to *run*.

No. Kate closed her eyes, took a breath. Think, *think*. She let go of the bars and turned back toward the school, dragging her phone from her pocket and phoning a cab.

The guy didn't want to dispatch, and she didn't blame him, but it was after five and the sun was getting lower, and she had no intention of being trapped alone on campus with a monster after dark.

"My name is Kate *Harker*," she snapped. "Name your price. Just get here fast." She hung up, and dug the iron spikes out of her backpack, the sound of metal on metal a reminder of how quiet Colton had become. She shoved one spike into her sock and gripped the other near the blunted top, knifelike point away.

She headed for the front doors, but they were locked; tried to swipe in, but nothing happened. She rattled the handles, just to make sure, and then, through the glass, she saw the body.

He was lying twisted on the floor, his head craned back so she could see his face.

It was Mr. Brody, the history teacher, his neck broken and his eyes burned black.

For the first time in ages, August finished his song.

And then he played it again.

And again.

The melody—this strange, incredible thing that had come to him that first day in the alley and never left, never let go, sang in his head beneath the gunfire, always waiting to be set free—poured from him now through skin and bow and string. It thrummed through muscle and bone, wove through heart and vein, and made him feel human, and whole, and *filled* with life.

Maybe it wasn't the soul he fed on.

Maybe it was this.

Each chord hung in the air, shimmering like dust caught in beams of sun, and as the song ended a third time and the melody trailed off, he stood there savoring the perfect moment.

The timer chirped, a shrill sound that shattered the last lingering notes and dragged August back to the world and all the troubles waiting in it. He sighed and took up the phone, silencing the alarm, then frowned. He'd sent Henry a text to say he'd be home a little late, but there was no reply. Not even from Leo.

That's when he noticed there was no signal, either. Damn. He reluctantly returned the violin to its case, slung his bag onto his shoulder, and went for the door.

It didn't open.

August tried to put his weight behind it, but the door wasn't just stiff, or stuck.

It was *locked*.

He looked around, wondering if there was some kind of card swipe in the studio, but there was nothing. The access pad was on the other side. Panic chewed through him, but he swallowed and pressed his face to the glass insert, straining to see something—anything—and what he saw was the access pad busted open, spilling cut wires like innards down the wall.

He was trapped.

Kate staggered back from the main doors, the corpse's black eyes staring blankly out at her. She fought back a shudder, tried to think. Three Sunai. Logic said it was Freddie. But if it *was* Freddie, how had he gotten out and locked the subway gate without her seeing him? And if it *wasn't* Freddie, and the second Sunai never left the compound, then that meant . . . Leo.

Multiple Sunai on the grounds, circling like sharks. Her chest tightened, but she couldn't panic. Panic served no purpose. It clouded your head, led to fatal mistakes. She was a Harker, she thought, clutching the iron spike. She would find another way out. She set off, fighting the urge to run as she rounded the corner of the school, heading for the back gate, digging out her cell with her free hand and—

Something hit her, *hard*.

The phone went skittering away as she stumbled, a steel grip vising around her shoulders from behind. She didn't hesitate, but drove the iron spike back and down into the creature's thigh. It let out a wet hiss, its arms loosening enough for her to drop to one knee and fling it over her shoulder. The body hit the ground, rolled up, and spun with a strange grace, the spike still buried in its leg.

Kate froze.

It wasn't a Sunai.

It was a Malchai.

A skeletal shape, red eyes swiveling in a skull that

looked black beneath his slick dead skin. Half the Malchai's face was a mass of angry lines—the *H* on his sunken cheek had been clawed off, just like the one on the monster she'd killed in the basement. His lips dragged into a crooked grin, his voice a wet rattle.

"Hello, little Harker."

She opened her mouth to say that her father would have his head but never got the chance. A second shape hurtled forward, too fast to dodge, a blur that caught her in the chest and slammed her back into the brick side of the school. Something inside her cracked, and a scream tore free before the second Malchai's grip tightened around her throat, cutting off the air.

The monster's mouth split into a smile full of sharp teeth.

"This is going to be fun."

No service.

Of course there was no service. August shoved the cell back in his pocket, took a deep breath, and then threw his shoulder against the door. He was rewarded with nothing but an echo of pain. Just because he didn't bleed and break like a human didn't mean he could out-muscle reinforced steel. He wasn't a battering ram.

He looked down at his hands and thought of Leo the night before, the way the darkness had licked up his fingers, the doorknob crumbling in his grip, but August didn't have that kind of control. It was all or nothing.

He rubbed his hand over the tallies on his wrist.

Four hundred and twenty-one days.

But it wasn't the marks he was afraid of losing.

There had to be another way. He retreated into the center of the room, scanned the walls, the floor, the ceiling. Smooth. Smooth. *Tiled.* Standing on the stool, he was just tall enough to reach the insulated squares overhead; they were heavy, but when he pressed against one hard enough, it lifted, and he was able to slide it up, and over.

August sniffed, recoiling faintly at the stale air, then retrieved his violin and hoisted himself up into the grimy dark.

The fingers were icy steel around Kate's throat, and before she could twist free, she was being thrown down against the sidewalk. She hit hard, the wind knocked out of her lungs and her palms burning where they scraped against concrete. She scrambled to her hands and knees, but the Malchai were too fast, and one of them was on her, forcing her down onto her back.

Her shoulder flared with white-hot pain as the monster pinned her to the sidewalk.

"Feisty thing," he murmured as the other Malchai

freed the spike from his leg with a wet sound and tossed it aside. The monster on top of her had those same deep scratches running down his cheek, ruining the *H* and cutting all the way to bone. The marks looked fresh.

"She killed Olivier," said the other, shaking the burn of iron from his bony fingers.

"Indeed she did," whispered the first, bringing his lips to her cheek. She wrenched her head away and felt cold breath on her face as he whispered something in her bad ear, too low for her to hear. She drove her knee into his groin, but the monster only chuckled. So much for SING.

They were strong, but it was still light out, and if she could just get to her feet, put her back to the wall—

"I can hear your blood pulsing," said the Malchai on top of her as her fingers scrambled for the second spike shoved in her sock. "I bet you taste sweet." The monster's mouth yawned wide, flashing jagged, silvery fangs.

"No teeth," warned the second, and the Malchai pinning her frowned but closed his mouth with a click. The other one produced a small, handheld torch, snapped it to life. The flame hissed, and Kate thrashed beneath the monster's grip, until his nails dug into her skin, drawing blood.

"I'm going . . . to kill you," she snarled.

"Humans, humans, full of lies," sang the one on top of

her, red eyes dancing with delight. "Should we kill her first, like the others?"

The Malchai with the torch seemed to consider. "No. There's no one to hear. We should take our time, like he would."

This was wrong.

This was wrong, wrong, wrong.

Her hand clawed at the grass, trying to reach the second spike. The monster on top of her smiled, and the one with the torch turned the dial, focusing the heat into a white-hot knife.

"She has her father's eyes," he said, and Kate shuddered, remembering the teacher on the ground, his sockets scorched black. "Hold her still."

August dropped out of a ventilation duct and into the hallway, his uniform smudged with dust and cobwebs. His shoes hit the polished Colton floor, and as he straightened, his relief at being free quickly reverted to fear. This hadn't been some random prank. Someone had wanted to keep him in that room. But who? And *why*?

Right now, that didn't matter as much as getting out. He headed for the nearest exit, pulling the phone from his pocket, but staggered to a stop when he saw the girl's body. She was young, a freshman, her head twisted at an awkward angle, but it was her face that made him gasp.

She had no eyes. They'd been burned out.

He dialed Henry as he hit the emergency door override and burst out of the building.

"Come on," he muttered as the phone began to ring. He let it ring three times, four, then hung up, and was about to dial Leo when he heard the strangled scream.

It wasn't a high-pitched cry, more a muffled shout. August rounded the corner and slammed to a stop. Two creatures huddled over a girl, their lines too long and lean, their skin too pale and bones too dark. He'd never seen a Malchai before. Not face-to-face. They cast no shadows, but the air around their bodies shivered in his vision, their teeth jagged silver points.

They looked . . . monstrous.

And the girl beneath them—the one who'd cried out—was Kate.

For an instant, the world went still, and time slowed, the way it did between chords, the moment drawn out like a note.

He had to help her.

He shouldn't help her.

If he did, she would know what he was.

If he didn't, she would die.

They were killing her.

They were framing him.

She was an innocent.

She was a Harker.

And then, too fast, the moment collapsed, and he dropped to his knees and opened the violin case.

The torch burned the air above Kate's face.

The Malchai's nails were digging into her jaw, and a sound like a whimper escaped her throat. The noise, so foreign, so pitiful, was enough to shock her back to her senses.

Her fingers brushed the edge of the spike. And then she heard it.

Music.

A single note that rang out across the grounds and filled the air, a note that seemed to take up more space than it should. And then another, and another, weaving together into a song. The music was strange and haunting and beautiful, and it took all of Kate's focus to cover her good ear, but somehow, she could still hear it, crystal clear. The Malchai dropped the torch and staggered as if hit, and the one on top of her froze, and clutched his skull in pain as something began to blossom like a bruise across his skin.

Her fingers finally found the spike in her boot, and she drove the iron up into the Malchai's chest, past the blackish substance breaking out on his skin like sweat, and under the bone plate, and into his heart. The monster screamed, clawing at himself, but it was too late. The spike was buried all the way to the blunted grip, her fingers slick as black blood spilled from his lips and he slumped onto her. Kate shoved him off and staggered to her feet, swaying from pain, her thoughts clouded by the threads of music.

And then, abruptly, it faltered, and she heard Freddie scream, "Watch out!"

She turned too slowly, and found herself face-to-face with the second Malchai. The monster caught her wrist despite the oily darkness oozing from its skin, and before she could tear free, his knife-like fangs sank into her shoulder.

Pain shot through her. And then, an instant later, the monster's fangs were gone, and he was being hauled backward. Freddie's arms were wrapped around the Malchai's shoulders, one of his hands pressed flat against the pale skin at the monster's throat; and Kate stood there, dazed, thinking about how young he looked—how small—before she remembered that he was a monster, too. Freddie's eyes were shut, his teeth clenched as he pinned the Malchai back against him, the darkness soaking from the monster's skin into his own like a stain.

Kate's senses finally snapped back, and she broke into motion, taking up the discarded spike and driving it up into the Malchai's heart. He didn't fight. He was already slumping against Freddie's chest, the red light flickering out of his eyes by the time the iron struck home.

Freddie let go, and the monster collapsed between them, little more than teeth and bones, and for a second they just stared at each other, covered in blood and gore and gasping for air.

Neither moved.

Freddie's gaze rolled unsteadily over her, and the corpses, before drifting to his violin, discarded in the grass. Kate's fingers tightened on the spike in her hand.

Run, said a voice in Kate's head.

She didn't.

Freddie's eyes found hers, and he swayed a little on his feet.

"What the—" Kate started, but then he doubled over and began to retch.

What came up was black, glistening like oil. He tried to straighten, but stumbled forward, collapsing to his hands and knees and heaving inky liquid onto the pale concrete of the Colton sidewalk.

Get back, said the voice, but she was already sinking to her knees in front of him. "What's wrong?"

He opened his mouth, as if trying to speak, but choked as more darkness heaved out onto the concrete. When he looked up, his eyes were no longer gray, but black. Black, and full of pain. Veins stood out on his hands and wound like black cords over his skin, climbing his throat.

What had Sloan said?

We cannot feed on them. They cannot feed on us.

Then why? Why had he done that? She wanted to ask him, but Freddie's eyes were sliding out of focus, his body shaking. He reached weakly for his violin, but it was too far away, and moments later he crumpled to the pavement. He wasn't moving. Was he dead? Did she want him to be dead? A small part of her thought, so *that's* how to kill a Sunai, but no, his chest was still lurching up and down with shallow, staccato breaths.

Her cell phone rang. It was still sitting on the sidewalk where it had been knocked from her hands, and she rushed forward and answered.

"Hello?" she asked, breathlessly. But it wasn't her father. Or Marcus. It was the cab company. The car was waiting in front of the school. The meter was running.

Kate looked around at the wreckage of the fight: the two Malchai corpses, the torch scorching a black line into the sidewalk, the unconscious Sunai at her feet. She was covered in drying blood and streaks of blackish gore. She swallowed.

"Stay there," she told the cab. "I'm on my way."

RUN, MONSTER, RUN

1

When August woke up, everything hurt. Pain had always been a fleeting thing, something that skimmed along the surface of his senses, but this was deep, knotting around every muscle and bone. The last time he'd gone dark, it had hurt to the core, burned through him like a fever, but even that was different. Now he felt hollowed out. It hurt to breathe. It hurt to *be*. And for the first time in his life he wanted to crawl back into the darkness of his dreams.

Instead, August dragged his mind to the surface where his body waited and opened his eyes.

He was sitting on a concrete floor, propped up against an unfinished wall, a tangle of metal girding and wooden beams against his back. His vision swam, then focused, then swam again; he tried to move, but his wrists were bound to the metal framework on either side with zip ties.

Kate Harker was sitting in the middle of the concrete floor, arms around her knees, watching him. She was wearing his Colton blazer over her blood-streaked polo. A bruise was coming out along her jaw, and she held one arm in front of her at a protective angle, her polo torn where the Malchai's teeth had sunk in. She looked shaken, but when she saw him staring, she stiffened, her face unreadable.

"Welcome to my new office," she said. Her voice was cold, distant. Maybe it was shock. He'd seen FTFs go through that, after a brush with death. "I was starting to wonder if you'd ever wake up."

August tore his eyes away and looked around the room. They weren't alone. A man was slumped in the corner, unconscious, hands bound, and mouth covered in duct tape. A label on his shirt read "V-City Cab."

She followed his gaze. "You're heavier than you look," she explained. "I needed his help getting you up here. And then . . . well . . . I didn't think I should let him go. But I paid him pretty well before . . . well."

August tried to swallow. His throat felt like it was coated in sand. "My violin."

Kate rapped her nails on the case beside her. He sagged with relief, and she gave him a look he couldn't parse. Her attention drifted to the windows, empty frames covered in plastic sheeting. Even through the plastic, he could tell it was getting dark. He should have been home by now. Where was his phone? He couldn't feel it in his pocket. Had he dropped it?

"Where are we?" he asked.

"My father has safe houses set up around the city."

A wave of panic hit him like nausea. "And you *took* us to one? After his Malc—"

Kate shot him a withering look. "They weren't my father's anymore," she said icily. "But I'm not stupid. We're in a renovation project around the corner from the safe house. I have a lot of questions, Freddie."

He swallowed again. "August," he said tiredly. "My name's August."

"August," she said, as if testing it out. "That does suit you better. August Flynn."

So she did know.

"How long?" he asked, and she must have understood the question because she said, "Yesterday." August nodded. He'd been right. He'd probably feel vindicated, if he weren't in so much pain.

"I thought your kind were supposed to be invincible." She said *kind* like it was a dirty word.

He cringed. "Nothing is invincible."

A dry smile flickered across her face. "That's what I thought."

"Kate—"

"No," she cut in, "you don't get to talk yet."

He fell silent. The blood pounded in his head.

Kate scraped black gore from her metallic nails. "Why did you help me?" The question came out fast and sharp, like this was the one she'd been waiting to ask.

He closed his eyes. "It was a trap. Those Malchai weren't just trying to kill you. They were trying to make it look like a Sunai execution. They would have pinned the death on me—on my family—and used it to break the truce." He dragged his eyes open again. The illness was finally, mercifully, receding. "I meant what I said in the woods. About wanting peace."

"I'm supposed to believe the monster's a pacifist?"

"I never lied to you."

"But you didn't tell the *truth*."

"How could I?" he asked. "Would you?"

Kate didn't answer. She was staring at the floor, her face taut with pain.

"Are you all right?" he asked softly.

Her head snapped up. "Are you fucking with me?"

August shrank back, confused. "I was just ask—"

"Stop talking." She got to her feet, revealing the iron spike she'd tucked beneath her knee. "I know what your kind can do. I've seen the footage, seen the way you toy with your victims, playing some sick game of cat and mouse. . . ." *Footage?* thought August. "I am not a mouse, August Flynn, do you understand? I know what you are."

She was coming toward him. The metal girding she'd bound him to ran vertically up the wall, and he dragged himself to his feet, wrists sliding up the bars until he was at full height.

"I saved your life," he said.

In response, Kate brought the tip of the iron spike to his throat. It was still stained with Malchai blood, and the scent turned August's stomach. Kate's eyes were feverish, but her hand was steady.

"A thank-you would suffice," he said.

"Why were you at Colton?" she demanded.

"My father sent me."

"You mean *Flynn*."

"Yes."

"Did he want you to kill me?"

"No. He wanted me close to you in case the truce broke. There aren't many things in this world Callum Harker cares about, and Leo thought you might prove valuable as leverage in the fight." August leaned forward against the metal tip. "And for the record, it's going to take more than this to hurt me." As if rising to the challenge, Kate pressed down, but the point didn't break the skin.

Just then, a cell phone buzzed on the concrete floor

beside the violin case. Kate turned toward it, and horror washed over August. "You left it *on*?"

"I took out the GPS," she said, crouching to retrieve the cell. She frowned at the screen.

"Kate," he said, tugging against the zip ties. He swore. They were threaded with metal. "Who is it?"

She straightened. "Home."

"Don't answer," he said, wishing for the first time he could change a person's mind instead of just loosening their thoughts. Her thumb hovered over the screen. "Kate, *someone* sent those Malchai to kill you."

Kate stared down at the cell. It stopped buzzing. And then started again. "They broke their oaths," she said. "Just like Olivier."

"Who's Olivier?"

"They're hungry and restless," she went on, voice half lost beneath the phone's ringing. "And sick of following orders."

August twisted against the ties. "That wasn't some random attack back there. It was calculated. Someone went to a lot of trouble to make sure you died and I was there to take the fall."

Kate hissed a single word under her breath. The phone was still going but instead of answering, she turned it over, and slid the battery out. The buzzing died. She said the word again, and August realized it was a name.

"Sloan."

He'd heard that name before. Leo spoke of him the way he spoke of most monsters, only worse.

My father keeps a Malchai as a pet.

"Would this *Sloan* start a war?"

Kate shot him a look. "Death and violence, isn't that what all monsters want?" August didn't rise to the bait. "Look, I don't know," she said, pacing, "but I'm pretty sure he wants me gone, and if he could frame Flynn in the process—I don't know anyone else who'd think that many steps ahead. Most of the Malchai are single-minded killers. Sloan's . . . different."

"Do they listen to him, the other Malchai?"

"I've been home for nine days, August. I haven't really noticed. So far his favorite hobby seems to be torment-ing *me*."

"If he's involved, then you can't go home. You . . ."

He trailed off as he heard the sound of cars coming to a stop, an engine cutting off. The sounds were low, muted, and Kate hadn't heard them yet. She was still pacing.

"Kate."

Car doors opened and closed.

"Kate."

Footsteps.

"*Kate*."

She turned toward him. *"What?"*

"You have to untie me," he said, trying to get his hands free. The zip ties were too tight, and even though the metal didn't *hurt*, it made the bonds hard to break.

"Why would I do that?"

"Because someone's coming."

A door slid open somewhere below, the sound loud enough, finally, for her to hear.

"They must have tracked you here."

"No," she said, shaking her head. "I took the GPS out of the phone."

In the corner, the cab driver stirred. A cell jutted out of his pocket.

"Shit."

Footsteps echoed on stairs. Kate hurried to the window, shouldering her backpack. She drew a lighter from her pocket, a small silver knife snicking open from one end, and sliced through the plastic sheeting with the small but vicious blade, revealing a bruised sky beyond. For a second he thought she was going to leave him there, pinned to the wall for Harker's men to find, but then she came back.

"I was going to turn you in to my father," she said. "When you got in the car this morning." She slid the knife between the zip tie and his skin. "It would have been so easy."

"So why didn't you?"

She looked up. Swallowed. "You didn't look like a monster."

August held her gaze. He wanted to say *I'm not*, but the words got stuck. "And now?"

Kate only shook her head and gave the knife a swift pull.

But the zip tie didn't break.

She frowned and tried again. Nothing.

August paled. "Please tell me you have a way of getting these off."

"I didn't plan on getting them off," she snapped. August began to fidget with panic, but Kate simply raised her shoe and slammed it into one of the metal bars. The noise was loud—too loud—but the bar buckled and gave, and August managed to weave his zip-tied wrists free. Kate kicked the second bar, but it was stronger, or the angle was wrong. It bent but didn't break. The footsteps were getting louder. August wrapped his hands around the bar and so did Kate, and together they pulled with all their weight until it finally came free, and the two went crashing to the concrete floor.

Kate landed on her injured side and gasped in pain, but when August went to help her up, she pulled back as if his touch were poison, and managed on her own. August caught up the violin case as she was reaching the torn plastic on the window, and he climbed through after her, expecting a fire escape of some sort and finding only a six-inch lip before a three-story fall.

The air caught in his throat.

"Don't tell me you're afraid of heights," she said, shimmying along the edge.

"Not heights," he murmured. "Just falling."

He looked around, trying to figure out how they were supposed to get down, when Kate took a breath and *jumped*.

11

Kate launched herself forward, off the wall and across a six-foot gap between the construction project and the roof of a low building. She landed, stumbled a few steps, and took off, not even looking back. The message was clear: keep up or get lost. August took a breath, gripped the violin case, and leaped. He cleared the roof's edge and slid, scrambling upright as Kate disappeared behind a rooftop structure. August followed, and when he rounded the corner, she caught his shoulder, pressing him back against the wall beside her, out of the line of sight.

"You do this often?" he whispered. "Jumping between buildings, running over rooftops?"

Kate raised a blond brow. "You don't?" She almost smiled, though it could have been a grimace; when she leaned forward, he could see the jagged line the Malchai's teeth had cut into her shoulder.

August scanned the buildings. "Where are we?"

"Outer edge of the red."

"I have an access point near the Seam. If we can get to South City—"

"*We?*" She pushed open the rooftop door and started down the stairs. "You saved me. I saved you. The way I see it, we're even."

August frowned. "I'm not leaving you."

"And I'm not going to Flynn."

"We could protect you."

She let out a sound like a laugh but colder. "Oh, I'm sure."

He followed her down the stairs. "Fine, don't believe me, but it isn't safe *here*."

"It isn't safe *anywhere*," she snapped, the truth welling up. "I can't go home. Harker Hall is in the center of the red, and whether or not my father's there, Sloan will be, and—"

August caught the scent of blood and pressed his hand over her mouth, tilting his head toward the street. Kate started to protest, but must have seen the answer in his eyes, because she went silent. He strained, trying to make out the voices.

"*. . . not in the building. . .*"

"*. . . call it in . . .*"

"*. . . check the cameras . . .*"

"...*signal*..."

August and Kate stood in the stairwell, perfectly still, until the voices trailed away, blending with the hum of engines and the other city sounds. When he lowered his hand, Kate wiped her face with the back of her sleeve. "What did they say?" she asked.

"Give me your phone."

She dragged the cell from her pocket and handed it over. August set it on the stairs and crushed it underfoot. Kate scowled. "Necessary?" she whispered.

"Couldn't hurt," he whispered back. "Is all of North City wired?"

Kate nodded. "Cameras on almost every block."

"Almost?"

Kate considered him. "There are some exceptions."

"I don't suppose you've memorized them all?"

Kate raised a brow. "I've only had a week."

August's spirits sank. And then her lips twitched, the barest edge of a smile, tired but knife-sharp. "I got through the ones in the red."

August straightened. "If you want to run, I won't stop you, but first, help me find another phone."

The sun had dipped below the skyline, and the city was beginning to fold in on itself. Not like in South City, where everything was boarded up and everyone shrank inside their armored shells, but even here the streets were emptying, as anyone without Harker's protection headed home and even those with medallions went inside. The restaurants and bars were filled with people brave enough to venture out but not linger on the sidewalks, which meant that, even avoiding cameras, every moment they were in the street, they were standing out.

August followed Kate through a network of streets and into a nearby café.

She beelined for the bathroom, and came out a few minutes later wearing someone else's clothes and holding someone else's cell phone. She handed him back the Colton jacket. "Hope you don't mind, I got a little blood on it."

August wrinkled his nose. "Thanks," he said, shrugging it on over his polo. She passed him the cell, and they hovered in the dark hall between the kitchen and the tables and out of the line of the restaurant's camera as he dialed.

After two rings, someone answered. "FTF."

It caught him off guard. He was so used to calling from his own cell, which went directly to the family line. But they'd gone over this, along with every other fallback and safety net, before he started at Colton.

"Flynn," said August.

"Code?"

"Seven eighteen three."

"Status."

"Red."

"Hold."

The line went silent, and August was starting to worry they'd dropped the call when he heard a click and then Henry's voice, sharp with worry.

"August? August, is that you?"

His chest tightened. "It's me, Dad."

Something crossed Kate's face at the use of the word.

"Where are you? What's going on? Are you all right?"

"I'm okay, but something's happened and I need to—"

"August," cut in another voice. Leo.

"Leo, I need to talk to Henry right now. Put him back on."

"Are you alone?" His brother's voice was low and steady, his will as solid as a wall.

The answer tumbled out before August could stop it. "No."

"Who is with you?"

"Kate," he answered, trying to focus. "Leo, listen, someone tried to kill her at Colton today. They killed others, too. It was two Malchai, but they tried to make it look like us. We both managed to get away, but they're still looking for her and I think—"

"Leave her."

The rest of August's words snagged in his throat. *"What?"*

"Leave her and come home."

"No. I'm not doing that."

He could hear Henry say something in the background, and he desperately wanted Leo to put his father back on the line, but the other Sunai kept talking. "You've acted beyond your orders and compromised your position. Your identity is now clearly forfeit, so our priority has to be protecting *you*."

"And what about *her*?" he snapped. He could feel Kate's attention trained on him.

"You are more important," said Leo smoothly. "Now, where are you?"

The question hit August like a punch. He had to hold the phone away from his face to keep from answering. He forced air into his lungs. He didn't want to tell him that, and he wasn't entirely sure why.

"Where. Are. You?" repeated his brother, the patience evaporating from his voice.

August bowed his head, and clenched his teeth, but he could feel the answer clawing its way up his throat, so he hung up.

"What the hell was that about?" asked Kate as he stared down at the phone. "August?"

He shook his head. There had been something in

Leo's voice, something he didn't like. He thought of the way his brother spoke of Kate, as if she deserved to suffer for Harker's crimes just because she was his daughter. As if crimes were something that could be passed on like a genetic trait.

"I can't take you South," he said grimly.

"Great," said Kate, plucking the phone out of his hand. "Well, that's settled."

But it wasn't. Nothing was settled. Everything was falling out of order, out of balance.

August closed his eyes to clear his mind and heard Kate typing something rapidly into the phone.

"What are you doing?"

"I have to get a message to my father, let him know it was a setup."

"What if Sloan sees it?"

Kate showed him the screen. It was a jumble of letters with dashes scattered between. "When we first came back to the city, after the truce, he taught me a cipher."

"That's . . . sweet?"

"Hey, kids," said a waitress, "you're going to have to order something or go."

"Sure thing," said Kate. "We're just waiting on a friend."

The woman didn't look like she believed it, but she let them be.

"What does it say?" asked August. "Your message."

"Kidnapped by vicious Sunai. Please start a war in my name." August frowned. The bells over the front door chimed. "Relax, it's just my name and this cell number."

The smell and the sound hit him at the same time. He caught his breath. "Kitchen."

"What?" asked Kate, disabling the phone's GPS. "Are you hungry?"

August shook his head. "Go toward the kitchen," he whispered.

Gasps were moving through the restaurant. Kate twisted toward the noise, but August pulled her back into the corridor.

"Everyone," said a voice like wet marbles in the main room. A Malchai. "Please stay in your seats."

"You aren't supposed to come in here," said the manager. "We have a deal, and—"

The clean snap of a breaking neck.

Chairs scraping and stifled cries as people began to rise.

"*Stop*," ordered the Malchai. "Sit. Down."

August cheated another step toward the kitchen. His violin case knocked into a folding tray, nearly toppling it, but Kate lunged and caught the edge before it fell. The moment they were through the kitchen doors, August turned and shoved some kind of cooking tool through the handles.

"Hey!" shouted one of the chefs with a booming voice. "You can't be back here."

The sound echoed against the stainless steel, and August grabbed Kate's hand and ran. They reached the back door just as the first Malchai slammed into the one on the restaurant side. The barricade held long enough for them to burst out into the alley.

"We can't stay here," said Kate, scanning for cameras.

"Is there anywhere we *can* stay?" asked August, pushing a Dumpster in front of the doors.

Kate shook her head, but she was already pulling him out of the alley and around the corner, putting as much space between them and the restaurant as possible. As they reached the street, she looped her good arm through his, and pulled him close, nestling into his side. August startled but didn't pull away. He didn't understand at first, and then he did. The only people on the street were walking in pairs or groups, and suddenly the two of them looked less like frantic, fleeing teens and more like a young couple. Eyes that might have snagged slid off.

August bent his head casually, as if sheltering her from a breeze.

"We have to get out of the red until I hear from my father," she said.

We, he noticed. "And how are we supposed to do that?"

"I don't know," said Kate, leaning against him. "Every building in North City has cameras, and soon the streets are going to be swarming with Malchai, and God only knows how many are now working for Sloan."

And then, all of a sudden, she stopped.

"What is it?"

She spun on him, eyes wide. "The Malchai are working for Sloan."

"I thought we already knew that."

"Right, but that means we just have to go somewhere the Malchai *won't*." August opened his mouth to ask where in North City the Malchai could possibly refuse to go, but then he followed her gaze down, down to the ground beneath their feet, to the curl of steam rising from a grate in the pavement.

"Oh hell."

III

"Just for the record," said August as they climbed down the pipes and bars into the bowels of the subway tunnel, "I think this is a *terrible* idea."

"The Malchai hate the Corsai," said Kate, dropping the last few feet to the tunnel floor, "and from what I've seen, the feeling is mutual."

"Yes, well," August hit the ground beside her, "the Sunai aren't fond of either of them."

"You wanted to come along," said Kate, secretly relieved he had—the thought of doing this alone made her ill. Her shoulder ached with every breath, and August might be a monster, but at least he didn't want her dead. The tunnel was dangerously dark; thin street-light streamed in through the metal grates overhead, and box lights hung at intervals down the tunnel walls. They weren't UVRs, weren't even fluorescents, just rect-angles emanating a dull red glow.

Beneath their feet, the floor wasn't solid; gaps ran down the center and along the walls, the ground plunging away into darkness. August kicked a pebble over the side and it fell, fell, fell for three solid seconds before landing with a splash.

"What's down there?"

Kate dug an HUV from her backpack, and switched it on, angling the beam into the gap. Far below, a broad stretch of water slid past. "Looks like a river." She tapped her foot on the concrete. "I think this used to be a bridge."

August started to say something, but Kate swung around, the beam tearing a single solitary line of compressed light through the tunnel. Her right ear registered nothing but white noise, but with her left she could make out the distant murmur of shadows, the scratch of claws on concrete, and the constant whisper. Judging by August's face, he heard it, too.

beat break ruin flesh blood bone beat break

There were rumors that the Corsai told secrets, that their nonsensical murmurings took shape right before they killed you. Others claimed they merely parroted the sins that made them, whispering atrocities, mimicking the gruesome sounds of metal against skin, breaking bones, muffled screams.

Now wasn't the time to lose her nerve. Kate focused

on her breathing, reminding herself that Corsai fed on fear. She faced the tunnel, flashlight burrowing away into black, and tried to focus her eyes on the center, the darkest point, as it began to *move*.

"I am the daughter of Callum Harker," she called into the dark.

Harker, Harker, Harker, it echoed.

And then the word was taken up and carried, and when it came back, it was different. *Not our Harker, Harker, Harker.*

Kate shivered, fought the urge to take a step back, her eyes still trained on the place where her light ended, and the shadows took hold.

Beside her, August was kneeling, clicking open his case.

"Do you have another flashlight in there?" she asked softly.

"No," he said, "but I have something better." He held up the violin. "Besides, you said you wanted to hear me play."

She remembered the eerie chords, the way the Malchai had screeched and recoiled and covered their ears, the strange calm that settled over her like snow.

Beyond them, the tunnel's red glow caught on teeth and claws, and the darkness began to churn. "Remember when I said this was a bad idea?" he muttered, fixing a strap to the case and swinging it over his shoulder.

"The good news," she said, gripping the light, "is that I don't think they're going to tell Sloan we're here."

"And the bad news?" asked August, tucking the violin under his chin.

Kate swung the flashlight in an arc, and there was a flutter, like wings, as the Corsai parted and reformed. "The bad news," she said, "is I don't think they're very happy to see us."

She slashed again, and the beam must have finally connected with a creature's head, because a single shadow screamed and toppled forward from the mass, white eyes winking out, teeth raining down on the damp floor like loose stones.

"Any time now," snapped Kate as the Corsai rattled and hissed.

"Can't rush art," said August as he rested the bow on the strings. The darkness barreled toward them like a train, edges raking the air, but just as Kate faltered and took a step back, he finally began to play.

A single, resonant note swept through the tunnel, and everything *stopped*.

Sound vibrated through the air as he drew a second sound, and then a third, the chords fusing together as they formed. The music was like a blade, knifing through the dark. The melody sang through her head, and the Corsai arced back as one, as if repelled by a single, massive beam. They hissed like steam, and broke apart, and fell away beneath the music, and Kate could feel her thoughts begin to fall, too, her head swimming with the notes the way it had at Colton.

Now, in the darkness, she could *see* the music, too. It threaded through the air like wisps of sunlight, ribbons of color that twisted and swirled and held the shadows at bay. She reeled, suddenly dizzy, and her feet dragged to a stop. She couldn't move, couldn't look away. Her senses tangled in the chords as the song filled her head, swallowed her sight.

And then she looked down and saw that *she* was glowing, too, a strange pale light rising to the surface of her skin. She marveled at it, at the way it moved when she did, danced like steam, even though it was beneath the surface. It was like silver and smoke, pulsing faintly in time with her heart.

Was this her life?

Was this her soul?

In the distance, August's voice reached her, soft and fluid and woven through the music. "Come on, Kate."

The music faltered, fell away, leaving only the echoes as he reached for her arm, and in that moment she found enough sense to be afraid.

"Don't," she said, trying to pull away before he could

steal her soul. She was too slow, but when his fingers closed around her wrist, nothing happened.

"It's okay," he said, his voice careful, taut. "I can't hurt you. . . ." She looked down at the place where his skin met hers, the way the silver light seemed to bend around his fingers like a stream around a stone.

"But you need to stay close." He drew her hand to the edge of his coat and picked up the song before the last tendrils of music could fade from the air. "Follow me."

And the truth was, Kate probably would have followed him right over a cliff, as long as he kept playing. The words left his mouth and tangled with the music and became real, became truth. The two of them moved through the tunnel, the shifting center in a sphere of melody and light. Kate's mind sank. She tried to swim to the surface but it kept stretching out of reach. It was like the cusp between waking and sleep, where you couldn't hold on to your thoughts. Couldn't hold on to anything.

But she held on to him.

The darkness thinned as they reached a station, the tunnel unfolding into an arched ceiling, a set of platforms. Tiles glittered like teeth as the light from August's song reflected off them.

CASTER WAY, the sign flickered in the ghostly glow. They were heading northeast.

The subway tunnels thinned and opened and thinned

again as tracks merged and diverged and merged again. They passed a depot of darkened cars disabled until the morning shift.

Kate wasn't sure how long the song lasted. She couldn't hold on to the minutes, felt herself say something, felt her mouth forming words, felt them spill out over her lips, but she couldn't hear her own voice, only the music, and if August heard her, he didn't respond, didn't turn. He kept his head forward, violin up, and hands moving.

This wasn't the boy from the bleachers or the one folded in on himself in her car. This wasn't the one coughing black blood onto the pavement or tied to the half-constructed wall.

This was a different August Flynn.

Confident.

Mesmerizing.

And Kate felt her lips forming those words, too, but she was cut off by a sharp *twang* as one of the violin strings broke. August faltered, his face flashing with panic. He started up again, and the melody returned, still entrancing, but there was something . . . thinner about it. Fewer threads of light wove around them, and as the glow caught August's face she saw a line of worry.

And then, too soon, a second string broke. August caught his breath. Now the sound was *noticeably* weaker.

She felt its presence retreating from her mind and had a feeling that was a bad sign.

"August," she said, an edge of warning in her voice.

"I never play this long," he explained, eyes narrowed in focus. "My song needs all four strings."

She could see the strain on the final two, the place where the bow met the string pricking with light, like heat. The threads in the air were starting to dim, and the darkness—and the things that writhed inside—began to press forward.

Up ahead, the tunnel opened onto another cavernous space. A shape glinted in the middle. Not eyes, or teeth, but the metal corners of a train car.

Something scratched the walls of the tunnel at Kate's back, the *skritch skritch* cutting through August's faltering song. She didn't turn. She wouldn't turn. Seeing wouldn't help. It would only make it real.

"Kate," said August, right before the third string broke.

"Yeah?"

"*Run.*"

IIII

They ran.

As fast as they could, the last tendrils of music and light trailing behind them like streamers, dissolving too quickly into the dark. The music had kept the Corsai at bay, but they were patient, they were waiting, and as soon as the song gave way, they were on them, surging forward in a mass of claws and teeth.

August kept his eyes ahead, and Kate slashed with the flashlight, trying to keep them back as they raced for the subway car. They reached the door hand in hand moments before the first monsters reached them.

August leaped up the steps, but Kate stumbled beside him, letting out a cry before he could haul her up. He threw his arms around her, shielding her body with his own as the Corsai hit the train car in a wave of *breakruinbone*. They hissed and tore at the air, claws raking the steel, but they wouldn't touch August, so they couldn't reach Kate.

"The door!" he shouted as a creature tried to tear the violin from his hands. "Hurry!"

Kate was shaking and pale, but she twisted in his arms, curled her fingers around the door, and pulled.

The metal slid sideways with a resistant groan. They tumbled in and tried to force it closed. A Corsai's clawed arm stretched through, but when August pressed his hand against the shadowed flesh the thing recoiled as if burned, and the door ground shut.

Kate and August stood in the darkened car, gasping for breath as the shadows swarmed outside, gnashing and throwing themselves against the Plexiglas, but the walls were striped with iron, and soon the monsters shrank back into the tunneled dark. Their scent lingered, a mix of ash and damp decay.

Kate collapsed onto a bench seat. "You were right," she said. "Worst plan ever."

"Told you," said August, sinking onto his knees. He examined the violin, wincing at the sight of the large scratch running down the wood. He dug around in the case until he found the pouch of new strings,and set to work by the light of Kate's HUV beam.

"Why the violin?" she asked, her voice shaking.

August didn't look up. "Sunai use music to bring a soul to surface," he said, freeing the broken strings.

"I get that," she said. "But why a violin? Can you use

anything?" She drummed fingers on the subway seat. "If you made a beat, would that count as music?"

August shook his head. "Hold the light a little higher." He hooked the first string and threaded it through the peg.

"We each have a song," he explained. "A piece of music that belongs only to us, something we're born with, like a fingerprint." He tightened the string. "Leo can use almost anything to play his song—guitar, piano, flute—but Ilsa's doesn't work with anything except her voice. And my song only comes out right when I use this." He plucked at the one taut string. "My sister thinks it's about beauty. That our music correlates to the first beautiful sound we heard. I heard a violin. She heard someone singing."

"And Leo?"

August hesitated. By Ilsa's logic, Leo must have found beauty in everything. But he couldn't imagine his brother seeing the world as anything but broken. Something to be fixed.

"Who knows . . ."

He worked in silence for a few moments, replacing the second and third strings.

"There's a big difference, you know," said Kate, "between can't and won't."

"What?" He glanced over. Even in the near-black car, she looked pale.

"When you took my hand, you told me not to worry. You didn't say you *wouldn't* hurt me. You said you *couldn't*." August turned his attention back to the violin. This wasn't the time.

"I've seen footage," she continued, a strange tremor in her voice, "of Leo reaping. He touches people and takes their souls. But when you touched me, nothing happened. Why?"

August hesitated, tightening the final string. "We can only take the souls of those who've harmed others."

"I've harmed people," said Kate defensively, as if it were some kind of badge.

"Not like that."

"How do you know?"

"Because your shadow doesn't have a life of its own, and your soul doesn't glow red."

Kate went quiet for a few moments, then said, "What do your tallies really stand for?"

August plucked each string, tuning it by ear. "Days."

He returned the violin to its case, and Kate turned the flashlight off, plunging them both into the pale red glow of the box lights on the tunnel walls. "Wouldn't want it to burn out," she whispered.

August didn't argue. He sat on the floor across from her, his back against the seat, and rubbed the tallies on his wrist. Even lost inside the song earlier, he'd felt the latest mark, a new day, a line of heat against his skin.

"How many?" she asked.

"Four hundred and twenty-two."

"Since what?"

He swallowed. "Since I last fell."

"What do you mean, *fell*?"

"It's what happens if Sunai stop feeding. They . . . go dark. They lose the ability to tell the difference between good and bad, monster and human. They just kill. They kill everyone. It's not even about feeding, when that happens. It's just . . ." he trailed off with a shudder. He didn't say that every time Sunai went dark, they lost a piece of their souls—if they *had* souls—a part of what made them feel human. That every single time they fell, something didn't get back up.

"What does it look like," pressed Kate, "when you go dark?"

"I don't know," he said shortly, "I can't exactly see myself."

"But you said, before, that you'd rather die than let it happen again."

No hesitation. "Yes."

Kate's eyes danced in the low light. "How many times has it happened, August?"

Her questions were easier to bear when he couldn't

really see her. "Twice," he said. "Once, when I was much younger, and then . . ."

"Four hundred and twenty-two days ago," she finished for him. "So what happened?"

August hesitated. He didn't talk about it. He never talked about it. There was no one to talk *to*. Henry and Emily didn't understand—couldn't understand—and Leo thought the soul was a distraction, had burned it away on purpose, and Ilsa, well, the last time she went dark, she apparently took a chunk of V-City with her.

"I stopped eating," he said at last. "I didn't want to do it anymore. Didn't want to feel like a monster. Henry and I got into a fight, and I stormed out. Spent most of the day wandering the city in a daze, stuck in my own head." His eyes drifted shut as he remembered. "I was finally heading back when a fight broke out and I— you know when you're hungry, and the smell of food is intoxicating? When you're famished, and it's all you can think of? I could smell the blood on their hands, and then . . ." His voice wavered. "I remember feeling so empty. Like there was a black hole inside, something I had to fill and couldn't. No matter how many people I killed." The words left his throat raw and his fingers shaking. "So yes, I'd rather die than face that again."

Kate had gone quiet.

August dragged his eyes open. "What, no quip?"

She was slumped on the bench, her eyes closed, and he thought for a second she'd just nodded off, but her arm, which had been crossed over her stomach, had fallen into her lap, and it was slick with something blackish and wet.

Even in the dim car, he knew it was blood.

####### ||||

"*Kate.*"

August scrambled over, knelt in front of her, and took her face in his hands. "Kate, wake up."

"Where are you?" she murmured.

"I'm right here."

"No . . . ," she mumbled, "not how it works . . ." but she was already sliding back into unconsciousness.

"I'm sorry," he said, right before he squeezed her wounded shoulder. Her eyes flashed open as she let out a cry and kicked him in the chest. He stumbled backward, rubbing his ribs as she muttered, "I'm *okay.*"

"Why didn't you say anything?" he asked, squinting to see the damage in the low light.

Kate shook her head, and he couldn't tell if that was an answer or if she was trying to shake off the haze.

He grabbed the flashlight. "Let me see," he said,

snapping it on, and then wishing he hadn't. Her stomach was slick with blood.

"I'll be okay . . . ," she said, but the words were dulled, and she didn't fight him as he guided her onto her back along the bench, only swore when he peeled the shirt up from her hip. He told himself the cussing was a good sign; it meant she was conscious, but when he saw the wound, he still cringed. Two razor-sharp gashes—claw marks—ran from the curve of her ribs to her navel. They hadn't torn anything vital, but the cuts were deep, and she'd lost a lot of blood.

"Listen to me," he said, pulling off his coat. "You need to stay awake."

She almost laughed, a shallow chuckle cut short by pain.

He tore the lining from the Colton jacket. "What's so funny?"

"You're a really shitty monster, August Flynn."

He pressed the lining against Kate's stomach, eliciting another string of curses. Then he got up and scoured the car for an emergency kit.

"Talk to me, Kate," he said, searching. "Where are you?"

She swallowed, then said, "On a lake."

"I've never been to a lake." He found a first-aid box mounted behind a set of benches on the back wall and, returning with some disinfectant spray and some gauze, knelt beside her. "Tell me what it's like."

"Sunny," she said sleepily. "The boat is rocking and the water's warm and blue and full of"—she hissed at the disinfectant— "fish."

"You need stitches," he said, cinching the gauze around the wound.

"No problem," she said, a fresh edge in her voice. "We can just pop up to street level and over to the nearest hospital. I'm sure no one will notice that Kate Harker and a Sunai—*owwww*," she cut off as August put pressure on her stomach.

"We don't need a hospital," he said calmly. "But we do need a suture kit."

"If you think I'm letting you near me with a needle and thread—"

"My father is a surgeon."

"Stop calling him that," she snapped, leveraging herself up to a sitting position with a hiss. "He's not your father. He's a human, and you're a monster working for him."

August went still.

"What? Nothing to say now? Oh that's right, you can't tell lies."

"Henry Flynn is my family," he snarled. "And I'm willing to bet he's been a better father than yours."

"Fuck off." Kate slumped back, breathing through gritted teeth. "Why would you even *want* to be human? We're fragile. We die."

"You also *live*. You don't spend every day wondering why you exist, but don't feel real, why you look human, but can't be. You don't do everything you can to be a good person only to have it constantly thrown in your face that you're not a person at all."

He stopped, breathless.

Kate looked at him hard. He waited, gave her a chance to speak, but she didn't. He shook his head, turned away.

"August," she started.

And then a loud hum filled the air.

Electricity crackled through the tunnels and Kate and August both looked up sharply as the power was reconnected, and the lights in the subway car flickered and came on.

"Oh no," said August at the same time Kate said, "Finally."

She looked paler in the full light of the car, the blood a violent red where it dotted the metal floor and streaked the bench.

"We have to go," said August, getting to his feet. "Now." He pointed up when he said it, and Kate looked at the ceiling and noticed the series of small red dots. Surveillance cameras.

"Shit," she muttered, hauling herself to her feet with the help of a pole. She let out a hiss of pain, and August started back toward her but she cut him off. "Just get the door."

He slung the violin onto his shoulder, and pried the train door open. The tunnel beyond wasn't fully lit, but bands of UVR light now ran like tracery down the length of the walls, and the Corsai were gone.

August offered Kate a hand down from the train car but she didn't take it, and he had to catch her arm when she landed and nearly fell. She shook him off and started down the tunnel toward the nearest station, careful to keep her feet on the wood between the rails. August picked his way behind her, ears tuned for the sound of moving trains, but the service clearly hadn't started yet, or if it had, it hadn't reached them. Where were they? How far had they made it in the night? Not to the end of the line, that much was clear, but he could hear the pulse of the city fading with every step.

They reached the nearest station and climbed off the tracks and onto the platform—Kate finally let him help—as the grates across the subway doors above began to grind open, and people spilled in.

They were the only ones moving up the stairs instead of down, and August looped his arm gingerly around her, remembering the way they'd knitted together the night before, turning themselves from two people into a couple. But it felt different now, with Kate leaning into him a little too hard, his jacket pulled tight around her, and his bloodstained hand shoved in the pocket, and he felt the eyes lingering instead of sliding off.

People shook rain from their coats and folded their umbrellas as they descended from the street, and August nicked one from a newsstand near the base of the steps, opening it over them as they climbed the stairs toward the promise of morning light.

As soon as they reached the surface, August stopped.

Buildings rose around them, but they weren't the massive skyscrapers that filled the red. These were shorter, shoulder to shoulder, but squat enough that they could see the sky over the rooftops. There were even trees here and there. Not massive stretches, like at Colton, but a row along the street, each with its own little fence. The city center carved its outline in the distance, and from here, North and South didn't look so different; he couldn't see the Seam.

Kate shivered against him, and August dragged his attention back, eyes lighting on a pharmacy across the street.

"Stay here," he said, passing her the umbrella. She offered a weak nod, but said nothing.

He held his hands out in the rain, rinsing off as much

of the blood as he could before he went inside. He dug a handful of folded bills from his pocket—he didn't carry much, only what Henry made him keep on hand in case of emergency—and made his way up and down the aisles, avoiding the gaze of the security cameras as he grabbed a suture kit, antiseptic, painkillers, adhesive strips.

His fingers itched to call his father, to let Henry know he was all right, that he was trying to *help*. But what if Leo answered? Or worse, what if his brother was on his way? What would he do if he found Kate?

"There's a clinic down the road," said the woman behind the counter.

August looked up. "What?"

She nodded at the supplies, and he realized how obvious they were. He should have added other things, to make it all look less suspicious, but he didn't have much cash. He fumbled for a version of the truth. "Friend took a fall," he said. "Doesn't want her family to find out."

The woman nodded absently and bagged the supplies. "Overprotective?"

"Something like that." August paid, and pulled up his collar as he headed back out into the rain. He looked up, expecting to see Kate waiting beside the subway entrance where he'd left her.

But she wasn't there.

"No, no, no," murmured August as he jogged across the street, holding his breath until he reached the exact place she'd been, as if that would somehow make her reappear. The puddle at his feet was stained red. Rain soaked into his hair and dripped from his case as he spun in a circle, resisting the urge to call out her name. Umbrellas swirled around him as people came and went.

And then, at last, he saw her, standing beneath an awning down the block. Relief washed over him. The force of it caught him off guard.

"I thought you'd left," he said, jogging over.

Kate gave him a long look and said, "I thought about it," before her eyes went to the bag of supplies in his hand. "But this sounds like *so* much fun."

They walked three blocks to a motel—the kind you paid for by the hour—and used the majority of Kate's cash to pay for a room. The place claimed it wasn't linked to Harker's feeds—only a closed loop, for security purposes—and the man at the front desk gave her a seedy smile as he handed her two keys.

"This place is dirtier than the subway," said Kate, lowering herself onto the edge of the bed while August laid out the medical supplies. She thought of yesterday morning before school, the way she'd laid out the zip ties and duct tape and iron spikes. How had it only been a day? "Do you really know what you're doing?" she asked when he tore open the suture kit. And then when he started to answer, she held up her hand. "Flynn. Surgeon. Got it."

He tossed her a bottle of painkillers and she swallowed three dry, then peeled off the jacket and shirt.

August didn't even try to sneak a glance as he pulled on a pair of plastic gloves. She should have known he wasn't human.

The tooth marks on her shoulder weren't deep, but the gashes across her stomach were angry and red. Kate lay back, wincing as August cleaned the cuts and sprayed the area with a numbing agent. She drew a steadying breath as he took up the needle.

"I'm sorry," he said softly. "I'll try to be quick."

"Wait." She dug the pack of cigarettes out of her bag. The package was a little soggy, but they still lit.

August shook his head. "Of all the ways to die—"

"I'll be lucky if I live long enough for these to be a problem." She put the cigarette between her lips and took a drag. "Okay. Let's do this."

The whole thing hurt like hell, but Kate had to hand it to August: He was careful. Gentle. As gentle as someone could be when they were stabbing you with a needle and thread. But he obviously wasn't trying to hurt her—if anything, he seemed put off by the whole thing. Great. A squeamish monster. Go figure.

But halfway through, Kate felt her resolve failing. The room was too quiet and the pain too sharp, and before she knew it, she was talking. She didn't know why, but the words just started coming, and she didn't stop them.

"I grew up with stories of my father," she said, trying

to keep still. "That's all he was really, for years, a good story. But I wanted him to be real. Mom made him sound so strong, invincible, and I could barely remember him myself—I was so young when we left the city—so over time, all I wanted was to see him again. To be a family again." She winced, continued. "And then we finally came back to V-City, and it was all wrong. None of it was like the stories. Dad was never around, and when he was, it was like he was a stranger. Like we were strangers in his house. Mom couldn't take it."

"The night she died," continued Kate, "she dragged me out of bed. Her mouth was too red, and she'd been crying."

Get up, Kate. We have to go.

Where are we going?

Home.

"She kept looking back. But no one stopped us. Not when we snuck through the penthouse. Not when she took the car. Not when the city blurred past."

He's going to be mad, Mom.

Don't worry, Kate. It's going to be okay. Sit back. Close your eyes. Tell me where you are.

It was her favorite game, a way to turn where you were into where you wanted to be.

Go on, Kate. Close your eyes.

She squeezed her eyes shut, but before she could come

up with a place, she heard the *skritch* of claws on metal, saw the sudden flash of headlights. The horrible shift of gravity before the crash. The deafening screech of metal and tires and breaking glass and then . . . silence. Her mother's face, cheek against the wheel, and in the glass behind her mother's head, the fractured light of two red eyes.

Kate gasped, and tried to sit up.

"I'm sorry," said August, a hand against her good shoulder. "It's over. I'm done."

No, no, what had . . . Kate scrambled for the memory, but it was already falling apart. It was like waking up too fast, the dream crumbling before you could grab the threads. She'd seen something, something . . . but she couldn't catch it. The pieces were broken again. Her bad ear was ringing.

"What was I saying?" she asked, trying to shake off the strange panic.

August looked down, embarrassed. "I'm sorry."

Her head spun. "For what?"

"I can't control it," he said. "Trust me, if I could . . ."

"What are you *talking* about?"

August ran a hand through his black hair. "It's just something that happens around me. Around *us*. People open up. They tell the truth. Whether they realize it's happening or not."

Kate blanched. "What did I *say*?"

He hesitated. "I tried to tune most of it out."

"How considerate," she growled. "You really should have told me about this up front."

One dark brow twitched up. "Well, it's only fair. *I* can't lie to *anyone*."

He turned his attention back to her stomach. "You're going to have scars," he said, pressing an adhesive over the stitches.

"Not my first," said Kate. She looked down at the lines of white tape tracing lines across her stomach. "Your father would be proud."

August winced a little.

"How does a surgeon end up running South City?"

"His whole family dies."

An uncomfortable silence, and then August said, "What about *your* father? Any word?"

Kate looked at the cell. There were a handful of messages, all for someone named Tess, who was probably the girl she'd stolen the phone from back in the restaurant bathroom. She hadn't stopped to get her name.

"Not yet," said Kate, deleting the texts.

They both knew that was a bad sign. Harker should have seen the message. Should have known it was her. Should have called by now. She'd tried a second time while August was in the pharmacy. Now she tried a third.

She tried to draw a deep breath, and winced; she was still waiting for the pain to blur into a blanket, something she could ignore, or for the comforting numbness of adrenaline and shock. So far, no luck.

Her stomach began to ache in a different, hollow way. "You didn't pick up any food in that pharmacy, did you?"

August frowned. It obviously hadn't occurred to him. Of course. He didn't eat food. Only souls. And maybe it was the pain, or the blood loss, or the exhaustion, but Kate started to laugh. It hurt, God it hurt, but she couldn't help it.

"What's so funny?" asked August, pushing to his feet.

"What's a Sunai's favorite food?"

"What?"

"Soul food."

August just stared at her.

"Get it? Because—"

"I get it," he said flatly.

"Oh come on, it's funny." He just shook his head, but she saw the edge of his mouth twitch as he turned to go.

"How often do you . . . you know . . . eat?" she asked, and just like that, the smile was gone.

"When I need to," he said in a way that made it very clear he didn't want to talk about it. He rattled the change in his pocket. "I'll go see if there's a vending machine."

The moment he was gone, the cell phone rang.

August stood in the alcove, staring at the vending machine.

His vision unfocused, and refocused, and this time instead of the shelves of packaged processed foods, he saw his reflection in the glass.

You are not a monster.

He ran a hand through his hair, trying to push the damp curls out of his face.

He's not your father, August. He's a human.

His rain-slicked shirt clung to his narrow frame, the sleeves pushed up to the elbows, black tallies spilling down his left forearm.

Four hundred and twenty-two.

He leaned his forehead against the glass and closed his eyes, fatigue washing over him. He wanted to go home. Wanted to take Allegro into his arms and sit on Ilsa's floor and look at stars. What were they doing? What was *he* doing? Maybe they should have gone south. Maybe they still could.

"Did it eat your money?" asked an old man.

August straightened. "No," he said wearily. "Just trying to decide."

He fed coins into the groove, punching numbers at random, and collected the contents from the bottom drawer. And then, just as he was turning back toward the room, he saw it.

A pay phone.

It was mounted to the wall, one of those old-fashion machines that took coins.

He looked down, considering the last of the loose change in his palm.

He didn't even know if it would be enough.

August picked up the receiver, listened to the empty tone, like white noise in his ears.

He wanted to call Henry. Wanted to know that he was doing the right thing. But what if Leo answered? Or worse, what if Henry told him to abandon Kate, to let Harker's monsters have her? No. He couldn't do that. She was an innocent. He was a Sunai. He was supposed to make the world better, not worse, and wasn't letting someone die just as bad as killing them? Henry would understand, and Leo . . .

August put the receiver back.

"Katherine? Is that you?" She was caught off guard by the urgency in Harker's voice. His usual calm had splintered, and he sounded worried.

"Dad." It was the only word that came out.

"Thank God." An audible exhale, like a wave breaking. "Are you all right?"

Her voice wavered and she clutched the silver pendant around her neck. "Yeah."

"What happened? Where are you?" He was actually raising his voice. Her father never raised his voice.

"There was an attack yesterday," she said, trying to stay calm, focused. "At Colton."

"I know. I've been trying to reach you ever since I heard. Four students and a teacher dead, along with two of my Malchai. It looks like one of Flynn's—"

"No," Kate cut in. "They weren't your Malchai. They'd clawed off their brands. And it wasn't a Sunai. It was a setup."

Silence. Then, "You're certain?"

"They were after me," she said. "Dad, they brought a blowtorch, for my *eyes*."

"But you got away," he said, and there was something in his voice, surprise, or grudging respect. "Are you alone?"

Kate hesitated, eyes flicking to August's violin case against the chair. "Yes."

"Where are you? I'm sending a car."

Kate rolled her head on her shoulders. "No."

"Katherine, wherever you are, it isn't safe."

"It isn't safe there, either."

An exhale. A beat of silence. She could hear the words he wasn't saying. *I should never have brought you back. I should have kept you away.*

She swallowed. "Where is Sloan?"

"He's out. *Why?*" challenged Harker.

"*Someone* tried to have me killed, Dad. *Someone* tried to break the truce, and that *someone* had enough power to bend other Malchai to his will. And logically—"

"Sloan has always been loyal."

"Confront him, if you're so sure," she said icily.

Silence again. When Harker spoke, his tone was careful. "You're right, it isn't safe here. You need to get out of the city until the problem is solved. . . . Do you remember the coordinates?"

She stiffened. "Yes."

"I'll call when I know more."

Her fingers tightened on the cell. "Okay."

"I promise, Katherine, the problem *will* be solved—"

"I killed them," she said, before he could hang up. "The Malchai at Colton. I drove my spikes into their hearts, and when you find the monster behind this, I want to be the one to kill him, too." *Even if it's Sloan. Especially if it's Sloan.*

A single word in answer. "Done."

And then he was gone. It was the most she'd spoken to her father in five years.

Kate stayed on the line and listened to the silence until August came back.

August stood at the hotel window, watching the sun arc over the city skyline. The rain had stopped, the clouds broken from a solid pane of gray into a hundred slivers, blue shining through. Kate had burned through the last of her cigarettes, and when he refused to buy her more, she'd stretched out on the bed, and stared up at nothing, turning her silver pendant over in her fingers.

She said she had to get out of the city. She didn't say where she was going, only pushed herself up from the bed and nearly tore her stitches when she fell. Between the blood loss and the painkillers and the lack of sleep, she wasn't fit to go anywhere right now.

One night, he told her. They'd paid for the room. She could leave in the morning.

She. As if August was just supposed to walk away. That's what Leo wanted him to do. That's what Henry would probably tell him to do, if he actually phoned home.

"You should get going," said Kate, as if she could read his mind. With his luck, it was probably the only thing written on his face.

"Yeah," said August, sinking into a chair. "I probably should."

"I'm serious," she said, the faintest tremor in her voice. "Go while it's still light out."

"I'm not leaving you," he said.

"What if I don't want you to stay?" she asked, which wasn't the same thing as asking him to go.

"Too bad," said August. "I'm not staying just for you. Whoever's behind this, they tried to frame my family. Do you have any idea what will happen if this truce breaks? If the city's plunged back into territory war?"

"People will die," she said hollowly.

"People will *die*," he echoed, thinking of Ilsa. Ilsa in her room, surrounded by stars. Ilsa in the Barren, surrounded by ghosts.

"People are already dying," muttered Kate. But she didn't talk any more about him leaving, only sank back against the cushions and returned her attention to the silver pendant.

August shivered, his clothes still damp with rain. He turned away, and felt Kate's eyes on his back as he stripped the shirt over his head, revealing the black tallies that had circled his forearm and were making their way like roots across his chest and back.

He drew the curtains against the sunlight, dizzy with fatigue. There was only one bed, so he sank to the floor beneath the window, his back against the hotel's faded wallpaper. Kate said nothing but dropped a pillow over the side of the bed. August stretched out on the dingy carpet, tucking the pillow behind his head.

It was so quiet.

The motel was a nest of muffled noises: dripping water and far-off voices and the electric hum of appliances, and beyond, the growl of engines and tap of shoes on concrete. He missed his music player, missed the hundreds of more familiar sounds that came with living in the compound, every one of them helping to drown the gunshots that now rose to fill the silence in his head.

And then, mercifully, music.

He looked up to see Kate fiddling with the radio beside the bed.

". . . hate quiet," she mumbled, turning past a classical station to something with a low, heavy beat. She found his eyes in the curtained dark, and flashed him a tired almost-smile back before sinking gingerly back to the bed. Within minutes, her breathing had evened, and he knew she was asleep.

August let himself sink into the songs, drift past the words and into the instruments, picking apart the threads of sound as he tried to sleep. He couldn't remember ever being so tired. The ceiling swam in his vision, and a shiver passed through him, like the cusp of a cold.

And then, just as he was drifting off, the hunger started.

August woke from fever dreams to cool air and the smell of mint.

His skin ached and his bones were humming, and a shape hovered over him, a nest of hair blocking out the last light beyond the window. His dreams had been a tangled mess of teeth and shadows, and for a second, he thought he was still asleep, still dreaming, but then he felt the cheap motel carpet beneath his back, and the shape leaned closer, revealing blue eyes and strawberry curls and skin covered in stars.

"Ilsa?" he asked, throat dry. But Ilsa couldn't be here. His sister didn't leave the compound. He tried to blink away the phantom, but she only grew more solid.

"Shh, little brother." She pressed her fingers against his mouth and turned his face toward the bed. "Someone is sleeping."

Kate was curled up on her side with her back to

them, a blanket slipping to reveal the bandages wrapped around her waist, and it hit him in a wave, where he was, what had happened. Colton. The Malchai. The tunnels. The hunger. August sat up, and the room tipped. "You can't be here."

"Can't, shouldn't, wouldn't, won't," she whispered. "No one saw me go. No one thinks to look for someone who's always there. They are all looking for *you*."

"How did you find us?"

"You tick, I tock," she said, her voice so soft that only his ears could pick it up. "I would hear you anywhere." A breeze blew through the window. It was open, twilight streaming in. He'd slept all afternoon, and he winced as his pulse thudded in his skull, and Ilsa pressed her cool palm to his cheek. "You're warm."

He brushed her hand away. "I'm all right," he mouthed, because it was still true. "Is anyone with you?"

She shook her head. Her eyes were wide, the skin tight over her bones, her edges haloed by the thin light from the window. She looked wrong outside the compound, as if she'd left some part of herself behind.

Our sister has two sides. They do not meet.

"Ilsa," he whispered. "You can't be here."

"Henry is worried. Leo is angry. Emily wanted me to come. She didn't say the words, but I heard them anyway."

"You need to go back home. If Harker's men see you, if they *catch* you—"

"I told you everything was breaking." Ilsa sank down next to him, curled up right there on the floor with her cheek to the carpet, picking at the fibers. "I could feel it," she murmured. "And I'm glad it's not inside me, but that means it's out here. I'm sorry. I'm sorry I let the cracks into the world."

He rolled toward her. "Hush, Ilsa. It wasn't you."

"I told Leo about the cracks, and he told me everything breaks. But I wish it didn't have to. I wish we could go back instead of forward."

"I wish we could stay the same," whispered August.

She gave him a rueful smile. "Nobody gets to stay the same, little brother." She nodded at Kate. "Not even them." She took his hand and folded it in hers, the way she had with the traitor's back at the compound, just before she took his soul. "Please come home."

"I can't, Ilsa. Not yet." His eyes went to the bed.

"Do you care about her?" The question was simple, curious.

"I care about *us*. About our city. Someone tried to kill her. To frame us. To break the truce." A shadow swept across Ilsa's face.

I don't want to burn again.

"She's an innocent," he added. "I'm just trying to keep her safe."

Ilsa's features smoothed. "All right," she said. "Then I'll help."

August shook his head. "No. Please go home, Ilsa."

I need you safe, he thought. *There is too much to lose. I can't risk you.*

A small crease formed between her eyes. "But someone has to keep the shadows back."

August tensed. "What shadows?"

"The ones with teeth."

He sat up. "Malchai?"

Ilsa nodded. "They are coming. They are on their way."

"How do you know?"

"I can feel the cracks they make and—"

He took her by the shoulders. "But how do you *know?*"

"—the man downstairs, he told me," she went on, as if she hadn't heard him. "It spilled right out of his mouth, little brother. He couldn't keep it in. He went back and forth, back and forth, but then he broke, like all things do. . . ."

August let go, pushed his hands through his hair. "Kate," he said. "Kate, wake up."

She made a muffled sound but didn't stir.

Ilsa slid to her feet, and crossed to the bed. "No, Ilsa, *wait*." But it was too late, she was already reaching out, wrapping her fingers around Kate's shoulder. She must have squeezed it, because Kate gasped and jerked forward, the lighter in her hand transforming into the small, sharp knife, the silver edge pressed to Ilsa's throat. His sister looked down at the girl, but didn't move.

"You're hurt," said Ilsa simply.

"Who are you?" demanded Kate.

"We have to go," said August, pulling on his shirt. But Kate was still staring at Ilsa as if entranced. Which made sense; Ilsa was entrancing. "This is my sister, Ilsa. Ilsa, Kate."

Kate's eyes went to the stars pouring down Ilsa's bare arms. "You're the third one."

Ilsa cocked her head. "No," she said sweetly, "I'm the first."

Kate lowered the knife, her free hand against her injured stomach. August could see the pain etched into her features. "What's going on?"

"Malchai. Coming. Now."

Kate pitched to her feet, swaying before Ilsa caught her. Kate stared down at the place where the Sunai's fingers met her skin.

"Listen for me, Ilsa," August pulled on his shoes,

slung the violin over his shoulder. His sister pressed her ear to the wall. "Tell me if they—"

"They're here."

August paled, caught the distant sound of steps, the wet rattle of voices, the scent of rot. She was right. Kate swore, maneuvering her shirt back on. She headed for the door, and August took a step, but turned back when his sister didn't follow. "Come on."

"Go, little brother," she said, her ear still to the wall. "I will stay here until you are gone."

"It isn't safe," he said, holding out his hand.

But Ilsa reached up, and touched his cheek instead. "Safe," she said with a hollow smile. "That is a pretty word."

"Come *on*," snapped Kate beside the door.

"But—"

"Don't worry, August. I'm not afraid of the dark."

Our sister has two sides.

He took his Ilsa's face in his hands. "Please be careful."

They do not meet.

"Go," she said. "Before the cracks catch up."

Kate had an iron spike out by the time they reached the hall.

The lighter's hidden knife was well and good for threatening schoolgirls, but it wasn't long enough to bypass the ribs of a Malchai and hit the heart. She hadn't had a chance to clean the spike since the attack at Colton, and the edge was still crusted with blackish blood.

August was there at her side, one hand up as if he thought she would fall. As if he planned to catch her. There was an elevator and two stairwells, one on either end of the hall. A one-in-three chance of choosing wrong, but she wasn't about to get caught in a box. Pain burned across her stomach as she raced for the nearest set of stairs.

August kept looking back toward the room and the other Sunai, with her sad eyes and her skin covered in stars.

"She'll be fine," said Kate as they plunged into the stairwell, and it came out sounding hollow even though the girl wasn't just a girl of course, she was a monster. She'd made the Barren, torn a hole in the world. Surely she could face a few Malchai, if it came to it.

They hit the second floor landing right as a door slammed open below, and the air went cold.

August must have felt the difference, too, because he grabbed her hand, and they burst out onto the second floor, sprinting for the other set of stairs.

Down, down, steps echoing through the concrete chamber as they passed the first floor and kept going. A door thrown open overhead. They hit the basement level just as a shape dropped like a stone over the stairs and landed before them in an elegant crouch.

The fall should have shattered the creature's body, but the Malchai rose fluidly, red eyes little more than violent cuts in her skull. A gash ran down her cheek, obscuring the *H* once branded into her skin.

"Foolish little Harker," she said, her mouth twisting into a rictus grin, "doesn't know when to die." The Malchai's red eyes cut to August, and she let out a wet hiss. "Sunai."

August started to put himself in front of Kate, but someone was stomping down the stairs. He appeared, a human rippling with muscles, a metal baton clutched in one meaty hand. Just like the Malchai, the man's face bore her father's brand, and just like the Malchai, it had been *clawed off.* Angry red welts ran down his cheek.

The sight of him made Kate's head spin. A human? The dissenters were gathering steam. And *men.* But that made no sense; Olivier's whole point had been—

The man's baton slashed toward her, and August pulled her out of the way and got his arm up in time to block the blow. When the metal cracked against his forearm, electricity arced and crackled over his skin. August gasped but didn't buckle.

Kate felt a shudder of movement at her back and spun, slashing at the Malchai with the iron spike, but the creature ducked and dodged, her motions terrifyingly fast and impossibly fluid. Beside Kate, August's fist connected with the man's face, and his head cracked sideways, but he didn't fall. He struck again with the baton, and this time August caught it in one hand, the energy arcing over him and filling the stairwell with static. For an instant, his gray eyes burned blue with the power, and then he tore the weapon from the man's grip.

Kate stepped too close to the Malchai, trying to get under her guard, but the monster's skeletal fingers caught her by the jaw and shoved her back into the wall. Light burst across her vision from the force of the blow, and the Malchai's mouth yawned into a smile.

Kate smiled, too, then drove the metal spike down into the Malchai's sinewy forearm. The monster hissed and slammed Kate back again, but this time Kate hit the door instead of the wall and went stumbling backward into the basement garage, landing hard on the concrete. Pain seared through her injured shoulder and across her stomach, and she could feel fresh blood welling against the bandages as the Malchai appeared, pulling the spike free and casting it aside.

Another crash, and August and the man came tumbling into the garage, a tangle of limbs. The baton went skidding away, and Kate was halfway to her feet when the Malchai sent her sprawling backward to the concrete with a vicious kick. She felt stitches tear, and stifled a cry, eyes blurring. Before she could force herself up, the monster was on her, slight but dense, unyielding.

Kate strained to reach her back.

"Oh dear," said the Malchai, pinning her to the cold ground, her razor teeth shining in the artificial light. "It seems you've lost your toy."

Kate's fingers closed over the metal against her spine. "That's why I keep two," she said, driving the second spike up into the Malchai's chest.

The monster gasped as Kate forced the spike home, greasy black blood spilling over her fingers as the Malchai collapsed onto her, more bones than body. She freed herself from the dead weight, recovered the two spikes, and staggered to her feet in time to see August force the baton up below the human's chin. There was an electric crackle, a spasm of blue, and the man went down with all the grace of a cinder block.

August looked shaken, eyes wide and strangely bright, but he was already moving again. He plunged back into the stairwell and reemerged a moment later clutching his violin case. Kate didn't waste time. She turned and started moving briskly, deliberately, between the rows of vehicles.

"What are you looking for?" he asked. A car alarm was going off in the distance, and he cringed as if the sound were deafening.

"A ride," she answered. Some of the cars were too new, others too old. She finally stopped in front of a black sedan, nice enough, but not one of the models with fancy security and keyless entry.

"Break that for me," she said, nodding at the driver's side door.

"The window?" asked August, and she gave him a look that said *yes, obviously the window*, and he gave her a look that said *I don't commit petty crimes very often* before he slammed his elbow into the glass to shatter it. The sound wasn't loud, but it echoed through the garage as Kate reached in and unlocked the doors. She brushed the pebbles of broken glass from the seat and slid in as gingerly as possible, using the lighter's hidden knife to pry open the panel beside the steering wheel. August rounded the car and sank into the passenger seat, the violin case between his knees as she sliced wires and began stripping them.

"Is this something they teach at boarding school?" he asked, craning to watch the garage behind them.

"Oh yeah," she said, crossing two wires together. Nothing. "This, breaking and entering, monster killing. It's all standard." She stripped another pair and tried again. There was a spark, and the car's engine thrummed to life.

"Impressive," said August dryly.

She lifted both hands to the wheel, then winced as the pain caught up. "I don't suppose you know how to drive?"

August shook his head. "No. I can probably figure it out—"

"That's okay," she said, shifting into drive. "We already have plenty of ways to die."

She put her foot on the gas, and the car shot forward with surprising power, letting out a squeal that made August groan. *It wasn't* that *loud*, she thought. Maybe Sunai had sensitive hearing. She gripped the wheel— growing up, she'd always liked cars, the fresh air racing past, the feeling of freedom, of motion. She wasn't that fond of them since the accident, but driving was a handy skill, like physics and combat. She rounded the corner of the parking structure, and hit the brakes. There was a gate over the exit, a man in the booth.

She reached for the seat belt, then remembered the stitches and decided to leave it.

"Hold on," she said, gunning the gas.

The car surged forward. August gripped the door. "Kate, I don't think this is a—"

But the rest of his words were cut off by the satisfying crack of the front bumper connecting with the garage gate, the former denting and the latter snapping off as they burst through and onto the darkened street.

The car swerved for an instant before righting itself, and Kate smiled as she revved the engine, drowning the attendant's shouts in their wake.

August twisted in his seat and looked back at the wreckage and the motel, and she wondered if he was thinking about Ilsa. She shifted lanes, following the traffic lights as they changed from red to green so that no matter what, they were always moving. "Is anyone coming?"

August slumped back against the seat with a ragged sigh. "Not yet." His eyes were closed, his muscles tense, fingers white on the handle of the door as if he might be sick.

"You okay?"

"I'm *fine*." She didn't believe him, but his tone was clipped in that way that said to let it go. She had more important things to worry about right now than his mood, so she headed east and watched V-City shrink in her rearview mirror until it was a steel hill, a speck, and then, nothing.

"Tell me something," said Kate.

The pain in her body had finally settled into something low and pervasive, but that was proving to be worse, because it made her want to fold in on herself, on the world, and that didn't work behind the wheel of the car. August sat silently beside her, looking out into the darkness as they passed from the yellow into the green, and finally from the green into the Waste. If he noticed the shift, he didn't say anything.

There wasn't a strict boundary, some bright billboard to announce that you were now leaving V-City. There didn't need to be. It was the transition from manicured lawns to wild grass, the change from streetlights and nice houses to *nothing*.

UVR lines carved out the road—not from overhead but set into the pavement below—and made the night beyond look solid. They were on the Eastern Transit, one of four supply roads that led from the capital all the way to the Verity border. Kate tried to imagine what they looked like from the sky, ribbons of light running like compass spokes away from V-City. From that angle, the Waste would register as a massive black ring, a two-hundred mile buffer between the capital and the subcities that hugged the periphery, each little more than a speck of light compared to V-City's beacon.

Apparently the transit roads used to be packed, back in the days before the Phenomenon, when travel in and out of the territory wasn't restricted, and then after, when people tried to evacuate the city, only to be pushed back by those who already lived outside it. These days the Waste roads were largely bare, save for the semis carrying shipments between subcities and the capital.

It was a dangerous job. The Waste *looked* empty, but it wasn't. Not many Malchai came this way, but the Corsai loved to hunt in the dark and pick off anything they could, from a cow to a family of five. The monsters that ventured this far out served no master, and the people who braved the Waste were just as lethal. Survivalists, mostly, scavengers who raided homes and stole from semis. These were the people who didn't have the money to buy Harker's protection, the ones who didn't want to fight for Flynn and his task force, or die on his moral high ground. They didn't want anything to do with V-City. They just wanted to stay alive.

But the dead zone didn't go on forever. She'd spent most her life on the other side of the Waste, and she knew that out ahead there was a place where razor wire gave way to open fields, and the high beams trailed into starry nights, and a girl could grow up in a house with her mother afraid of nothing, not even the dark.

"Tell me something," she said again.

August had been sitting there, his eyes fixed on the night, his fingers tapping out some kind of short, staccato rhythm against his leg. Now he glanced toward her. His face looked strangely hollow, his eyes feverish. "Like what?"

"I don't know," she said. "A story?"

August frowned. "I don't like stories."

Kate frowned, too. "That's weird."

"Is it?" asked August.

Kate drummed her nails on the wheel. The paint was chipping. "Yeah. I mean, most people want to escape. Get out of their heads. Out of their lives. Stories are the easiest way to do that."

August's gaze escaped to the window. "I suppose," he said. It was maddening how little he talked, how much she wanted to. She switched on the radio, but the signal was already full of static, so she snapped it back off. The quiet gnawed at her already fraying edges.

"Say something," she whispered. "Please."

August's jaw clenched. His fingers tightened on his pants. But he cleared his throat and said, "I don't get why people are always trying to escape."

"Really?" said Kate. "Take a look around."

In the distance beyond August's window, the nothing gave way to something—a town, if it could be called a town. It was more like a huddle of ramshackle structures, buildings gathered like fighters with their backs together, looking out on the night. The whole thing had a starved dog look about it. Fluorescent lights cut glaring beams through the darkness.

"I guess it's different for me," he said, his voice taut. "One moment I didn't exist and the next I did, and I spend every day scared I'll just stop *being* again, and every time I slip, every time I go dark, it's harder to come back. It's all I can do to stay where I am. Who I am."

"Wow, August," she said softly. "Way to kill the mood."

That won her a small exhausted laugh. But by the time it left his lips, it was already fading. He turned his face away, and Kate flexed her fingers on the wheel and kept her eyes ahead. Pain sparked across her stomach every time she breathed. Beside her, August was quiet, coiled, eyes on the night.

"What happened to her?" she asked, trying to distract them both.

"Who?"

"Ilsa," she said. "She doesn't seem . . . all there."

August rubbed his fingertips over the tallies above his wrist. "She's never been *all there*," he said. "For the longest time I thought . . . I thought that was just her way. Scattered. I didn't get it until recently."

"Get what?"

"It's who she is," he said. "It's *what* she is. Cause and effect."

"You mean it has to do with the catalyst?"

August nodded. "Sunai are the result of tragedies," he said, "acts of horror so dark they upset the cosmic balance. Leo came from some kind of cult slaughter in the first weeks of the catalyst. This whole group thought the world was ending, so they threw themselves off a roof. Only they didn't go alone; they dragged their families with them. Parents. Children."

Kate let out a shallow breath. *"Christ."*

"No wonder my brother is so righteous," he said softly.

"Ilsa was different," he continued. "Emily—Henry's wife—she told me the story. Ilsa came from a bombing in the basement of a big hotel in North City."

The Allsway Building, thought Kate. *Harker Hall.* You could still see the scorch marks on the walls.

"It was right after the chaos started," he said. "Not

even weeks, *days*. Days of confusion and terror. They didn't even know yet what was going on, but something got inside that place, and the people who managed to get away all went to the basement. They huddled down, just trying to stay alive. Barricaded the doors. But someone decided that if they were going out, it wasn't going to be at a monster's hand. That someone brought a homemade bomb into that basement with them and lit the fuse." August shook his head. "No wonder my sister broke apart."

"And you?" asked Kate. "Your brother is righteous, your sister is scattered. What does that make you?"

When August answered, the word was small, almost too quiet to hear. "Lost." He exhaled, and it seemed to take more than air out of him. "I'm what happens when a kid is so afraid of the world he lives in that he escapes the only way he knows how. Violently."

Silence, so heavy it hurt.

August leaned his head against the window, and the glass began to fog with steam. A bead of sweat ran down his cheek, and Kate reached to turn on the air, when the car made a sound.

It wasn't the kind of sound a car should make.

August straightened.

The engine stuttered.

"What was that?" he asked.

The car began to rapidly lose speed.

"Oh no," she said.

And then it died.

A light on the dash was blinking. The high beams were still on.

The rest of the car was dead.

"Shit," muttered Kate.

"Kate," ground August through his teeth. "What's wrong with the car?"

"It's out of gas," she said, already swinging open the door. She was digging in the trunk by the time he got out and joined her.

The night was cool but it wasn't enough to dampen the fever. "You couldn't have picked one with a full tank?"

"I'm sorry, I was a little busy trying not to die." Something like a groan escaped his throat. "It's fine," she said, producing an HUV flashlight.

"How is this fine?" he growled, anger burning through his chest, flaring with every breath.

"We'll find a ride," said Kate, keeping her voice even, as if the calm would help.

August wheeled on her. "Do you *see* a ride?"

"What the hell's gotten into you?" she shot back.

August opened his mouth to say *"nothing"* but he couldn't, and the urge to shout was fighting with the urge to hit something, so he turned and walked away, trying with every step to steady his breathing, calm his heart, knowing that panic would only spread the sickness faster.

His feet carried him down the line of light at the edge of the road. He wasn't going anywhere really, just moving.

Mind over body.

He knotted his fingers in his hair and stared out into the dark. They were in the middle of nowhere. The light from V-City was nothing but a ghost against the distant clouds, and the night around them black as pitch. They'd passed some kind of fortress a few miles back. It hadn't looked welcoming. In the distance somewhere, gunfire echoed like far-off thunder, and he didn't know if it was real or just the phantoms in his head.

Hunger plucked at his muscles and sang through his bones, and it felt like something was trying to claw its way out.

He should have eaten the man back in the garage— *would* have, if he'd had the chance—but to his dismay, the human hadn't been a killer. Of all Harker's men, what were the odds of Sloan sending an innocent? Did the Malchai *know* Sunai could only feed on sinners? Or was it just bad luck?

After several deep breaths, August had the anger under control. He turned back to the car and saw Kate leaning against the driver's side door, arms crossed carefully over her ribs, clearly fighting back the cold. August couldn't feel it, not through the fever.

"Here," said August, setting the violin case on the ground and shrugging off his jacket.

"Keep it," she said, but he was already settling it around her shoulders. He could see her relax beneath the added warmth.

His hand lingered a moment on her good shoulder. Something about the contact—simple, solid—made him feel steadier. He started to pull away, but Kate caught his fingers. Her eyes were dark, and the way her lips were parted, he could tell she wanted to say something, but when she spoke, all she said was, "Your hand is hot."

August swallowed, and pulled free as gently as possible as something flickered across the sky above Kate's head. He looked up, and the air caught in his throat. It was a clear night, and the sky was *filled* with dots of light.

Kate followed his gaze. "What?" she drawled. "You've never seen stars before?"

"No," he said softly. "Not like this." The sky was on fire. He wondered if Ilsa had ever seen stars—not the black icons across her skin, but the real things, which were so strange and perfect. One streaked across the sky, trailing light.

"I read somewhere," said Kate, "that people are made of stardust."

He dragged his eyes from the sky. "Really?"

"Maybe that's what you're made of. Just like us."

And despite everything, August smiled.

It was such a hard-won smile, but it was worth it.

And then, all of a sudden, it was gone, and August shuddered, bracing himself against the car. Something like a chill went through him, a tremor that seemed to run from his limbs to his core.

Her hands hovered in the air around him, helpless. "What's wrong?"

"I'll . . . I'll be okay," he said.

"Bullshit."

In response, he tugged aside his collar and she saw the edge of light, not bright but burning against his chest like the lit end of a cigarette. It drew a single line, the ember red darkening to black. A new tally. A new day.

"How many is that?"

He was still shaking, but when he looked up, there

was something in his eyes, a kind of grim triumph. "Four hundred and twenty-three."

Just then, truck lights cut through the darkness, coming from the direction of V-City.

Kate waved the HUV, and to her relief, the truck slowed and hauled itself onto the shoulder. It was a semi, obviously reinforced for the trek through the Waste, its grill and flanks framed by grates with iron striping, its windows coated to make them bulletproof. There were several scores along its sides, and they probably weren't from Corsai. The monsters targeted humans. The humans targeted supplies.

Kate tucked the ornate silver pendant under her shirt and stepped up onto the truck's footboard as the passenger window inched down.

"What the hell are you kids doing out here?" asked the driver. He was middle-aged and had the cropped, weathered look of someone who'd spent too much of his life on edge.

"Car trouble," she said, flashing her best smile. "Can you give us a lift?"

He looked past her to August, and Kate tried to see him as the driver would, just a lanky teen boy with an instrument case slung over his shoulder. "Where you going?"

Kate nodded at the road heading *away* from V-City.

She dug up the name of the easternmost subcity. "Louisville."

He shook his head. "That's on the other side of the Waste," he said. "You're better off trying to catch a lift back toward the capital."

"We saw a town or something a little ways back," she said, filling her voice with naiveté. "You think we should head there?"

The man grimaced. "You try to get inside a fort at night, the only thing you're gonna get is shot." He ran a hand through his short hair. "Dammit." He wasn't wearing a medallion. Kate swallowed, then tugged her pendant over her head.

The weight of the silver was solid, reassuring. She didn't want to get rid of it, but she couldn't stay here on the side of the road, either. She held it up for the driver to see. "Look, we don't want to cause trouble. We haven't got much cash, but if you can at least give us a lift in the right direction, I'll give you this."

The driver's eyes went wide, and Kate knew she had him. After all, a Harker medallion was safety, and safety was a luxury, a commodity more valuable—and more expensive—than a truck, a house, a life.

The man's fingers closed around the silver. "Get in."

Kate climbed into the front seat, and August slid onto a bench that looked like it also functioned as a cot. He knitted his fingers and bowed his head. Kate wasn't an idiot. Something was obviously wrong. But every time she asked he just got mad, as if she was making it worse. He looked ill. Did monsters get ill? Or did they only get hungry? How long had it been since he'd eaten?

"Look," said the driver. "I'm not in the smuggling business, okay? I'm a trucker. I only go as far as the sub-cities, so if you're looking for a way through the border, I can't help you."

"It's fine," said Kate. "We're not trying to cross."

"Then what the hell *are* you doing out here in the dark?"

And it was weird, but Kate almost told him the truth. It seemed to bubble up, out of her mind and out her mouth, the words rising so fast she had to bite her tongue to stop them. What had August said, about Sunai and truth? She shot him a look, but he was sitting hunched forward, elbows on knees, staring at the ground.

"It was a dare," she said. "We were with some friends."

"There was a concert tonight," added August from the back seat. "At the edge of the green."

"Yeah," chimed in Kate. "Our friends bet us twenty bucks we wouldn't drive into the Waste when it was over. Forty if we brought something back from the subcity on the other side. Stupid me," she added. "I didn't check the tank."

The driver shook his head. "Kids these days," he said, guiding the semi back onto the road. "You got too much time and too little sense." His sleeves were rolled up, and his right forearm bore several nasty scars. Corsai marks. "I'll take you as far as the next truck stop. It's about as safe as it gets out here. After that, you find your own way back into the green."

Kate nodded. "Works for us," she said, casting a glance at August. But she couldn't see his face. It was lost in shadow.

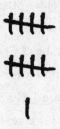

August felt the semi slow, and dragged his head up off the backseat.

The truck was pulling off the UVR strip and onto a second, smaller road. For an instant the road light faded, then it redoubled as a building came into sight.

It was more a fortress than a truck stop. High metal fences topped with razor wire circled the structure, and massive UVRs cut a swathe through the darkness, a moat of light that stretched across the tarmac, erasing every shadow. A sign over the building—which really looked like several buildings stacked together—announced that this place was the Horizon.

The driver stopped in front of the fence and honked once, then waited. Two men stood on either side, weapons in hand. One held an HUV and some kind of machete, the other a machine gun. One weapon for the monsters, August realized, and one for the raiders.

The gates hissed open and the semi rumbled forward into the lot. August heard the metallic grind of gates closing again, and his chest tightened at the thought of being penned in.

"This is as far as we go," said the driver as he parked. "Plenty of guys here'll give you a ride back. You got any cash?"

"A little," said Kate, even though August was pretty sure they were down to spare change. The man chewed his lip, then held out the medallion she'd given him. "Give 'em this, then."

Kate hesitated. "We had a deal."

"I was going this way," said the driver. "Go on. Take it."

Kate took the pendant and tucked it into her pocket with a quiet thanks. Outside, the night had gotten crisper, the cool air washing over August like a salve. Around them, a dozen trucks were parked in even rows, like black tallies, shadowless against the pavement. His eyes floated closed, his mind sliding into four hundred and twenty-three lines, into echoes ghosted on barren ground, into gunshots and screams and blazing hunger.

And then he was being pulled, and he opened his eyes to see Kate dragging him toward the fluorescent haze of the rest stop.

"Come on," she said, "I'm starving," and he tried to laugh but the sound stuck in his throat like glass.

The Horizon was apparently the place to be at 4 A.M. It was like its own small, self-contained city, with a cafeteria and bathrooms with showers and supply stores, the whole space so well lit that it hurt Kate's eyes.

August had gone to the bathroom, mumbling something about freshening up, and Kate wandered the aisles, trying to pretend she had more than five dollars in her wallet as she perused the shelves. Credit cards she had in abundance, but cards were traceable, and she'd used most of her cash to pay for the motel.

She was thinking about palming a granola bar when she saw the watch. It was hanging on a low display with a few maps and other travel supplies, an ordinary digital watch except for the fact it showed not only time and temperature but coordinates. She didn't have an address for where she was going. But she had the numbers, latitude and longitude.

38° 29.45

−86° 32.56

Kate pulled the watch from the display as casually as possible, examining it for several long moments before slipping it into the pocket of her coat. Only it wasn't her coat, but August's. And when she shoved the watch into the pocket, her fingers came up against something metal and smooth: the stolen cell phone. Her eyes flicked up, but there was no sign of August, and the rest of the patrons were busy pouring too much sugar in their coffee or looking glassy-eyed at the row of television screens mounted along the wall.

Kate drew the cell phone from her pocket. It was off, to save power, and she held the button down until it booted, hoping for a message. Nothing.

She looked around. Maybe they didn't need to keep going. Maybe they could stay here, in the Horizon. It was warded six ways against monsters. No Malchai would ever get in, and the place was big enough to keep them from looking too conspicuous. Maybe—

And then she heard her name, not coming from August or anyone in the store, but from the television on the wall.

She looked up and saw a picture filling the screen.

A picture of *her*.

August clutched the sink, his vision sliding in and out of focus.

It was getting worse.

He stared at the mirror, and his reflection stared back, eyes wide and cheeks hollow. His bones were on fire; when he looked down at his hands, he thought he could see them through the skin, not dark like a Malchai's but glowing white, alive with heat. The fever was burning out the anger, leaving something else in its wake.

He fumbled with the tap and ran his hands under the cold water. Tendrils of steam rose from where the moisture met his skin.

They were so far from the city, and the absence— of people, of monsters, of energy—was making him woozy.

Pack a snack, Leo had said.

August groaned inwardly.

Mind over body.

Mind over body.

Mind over body over bodies on the floor over tallies seared day by day by day into skin until it cracked and broke and bled into the beat of gunfire and the melody of pain and the world was made of savage music, made and was made of, and that was the cycle, the big bang into the whimper and on and on and none of it was real except for August or all of it was real except for him. . . .

He surfaced with a gasp—it was getting harder and harder to stay afloat—and clenched his hands into fists on the rim of the sink. He could feel his nails denting his palms, threatening to break the skin.

August had done this before, had starved himself, determined to believe that he was stronger than this, disgusted by the fact he wasn't, by the way the hunger ravaged him when it barely seemed to touch his siblings, desperate to find something on the other side, something besides darkness. August had gone to the edge of his senses, and over, had memorized the steps, the stages, as if knowing them was half the battle to overcoming, to outwitting—out*willing*—the need. First came anger, then madness, then joy, then sorrow. They should make a nursery rhyme about *that*, anger, madness, joy, sorrow, anger, madness, joy, sorrow, ang—

He was sliding again.

You're okay, you're okay, you're okay.

"You okay, kid?"

He looked up and saw a man standing there, the left half of his face creased with scars.

August swallowed, found his voice. "Tired of fighting," he said.

The man shook his head, the gesture sympathetic as he washed his hands.

"Aren't we all?"

The headline on the screen read:

KATHERINE HARKER ABDUCTED, FLYNN FAMILY SUSPECTED

"Henry Flynn is denying any responsibility in the abduction," the news anchor was saying, "but sources close to the case confirm that a member of the Flynn family was attending school with Katherine Harker and was seen with her immediately preceding her disappearance. "What's more"— the news anchor's eyes went bright with morbid glee—"evidence suggests that a *Sunai* was responsible for the attack at the esteemed school, which left three students and a teacher dead, and Harker's only child missing."

Kate's stomach lurched. Several men were standing around, looking up at the screens. One muttered something vile underneath his breath; another said there better be a reward. "Turn this trash off," grumbled the third.

"Can't," said the old woman working the till. "It's on every channel."

The screen then cut to footage of her father, who was standing before a podium in a crisp black suit, as if he didn't know what was happening, as if his own rogue monsters weren't to blame. "I will have my daughter back," he said, "and I will see the perpetrators—*whoever they are*—punished for their crimes against my family and against this capital. We in North City see this for what it is: an act of war."

The news anchor was back. "If you have any information about Katherine Harker, contact the number below . . ."

Kate was already coding a message into the stolen cell.

Call. Urgent.

She backed away from the line of televisions, ducking behind a display of some nondescript, nonperishable food. One minute passed. Two. And then it rang.

"Katherine," came her father's voice, only a ghost of his former panic in his voice. He'd regained his usual composure. "Are you all right?"

"Why would you say that on TV?" she snapped. "I told you it wasn't them!"

A measured exhale. "I don't know that. Not for sure."

"*I* do," she whispered angrily.

"So he *is* with you."

The question threw her. "What?"

"Frederick Gallagher. Also known as August Flynn. Henry's third Sunai." Her chest tightened. She would have told him, was planning to tell him. Hell, she was planning to deliver the monster to her father's feet. Now she couldn't bring herself to say his name. "Has he been with you the entire time?" pressed Harker.

But Kate didn't give. This wasn't *August's* fault. *August* hadn't tried to kill her. *August* had saved her life.

"Katherine—"

"Where is Sloan?"

"Hunting down those who moved against me."

"*He's* the one moving against you!" she snarled.

"No," he said evenly. "He's not. I questioned him myself. Sloan says he had no hand in the attack."

"That's a lie!"

"We both know he *cannot* lie."

Her thoughts spun. It had to be Sloan. Who else would have done this?

"Dad—"

"Stay out of the city until you hear from me."

"So you can let people think I've been abducted?"

"So I can keep you *safe*." His tone was hardening. "And you need not code the messages, Katherine. This is *my* phone, after all. Who else would see it?"

Your shadow, she wanted to say.

Instead, she hung up.

"You're letting out the cold," snapped a rasping voice. August drew his head out of the beverage case to see a wiry old woman in a Horizon uniform.

"Sorry," he said, shutting the fridge doors. "I meant to let it in." The words sounded wrong on his tongue, but they were already out.

Nearby, a woman's voice started rising as she talked into a cell.

A man dropped his cup of coffee, spilling it on another trucker. The second swore, and shoved the first back, a little too hard. Tension rose like pressure in the store around him.

The woman hurried away, and then, between one burning heartbeat and the next, August caught the scent of crime—old blood, a chill in the air that rustled against his fevered skin. August swayed, his fingers tightening on the strap of the violin case as his gaze slid across the store, over shelves and faces until . . . *there*. The whole world came into focus around the man. He was stocky, with a mud-splattered coat, a short, uneven beard, and a head too small for his shoulders.

But August didn't care about any of that. All he cared about was the shadow coiling like a cape behind the man, restless and wrong, and the fact he was already out the front door, taking the promise of cold bones and clear thoughts with him.

August moved to follow but someone gripped his arm. Kate. "We have to go," she snapped. *"Now."*

"Kate, I . . ." He couldn't drag his eyes from the man's shrinking form. "I need to . . ." But before he could finish, she took his jaw in her hand—he was amazed it didn't burn her fingers—and turned it toward a bank of televisions mounted on the wall. Her face was plastered on the screens—*all* the screens—above the headline:

KATHERINE HARKER ABDUCTED, FLYNN FAMILY SUSPECTED

He felt himself surface, a painfully sharp moment of clarity as he took in the headline. *"No,"* he said, the word knocked out of him like a breath. "I didn't—"

Just then the front doors chimed open, and the driver, the one who'd given them a lift, came in and saw the screens and stopped. "What's this?"

"Shit." Kate pulled August down below the rim of the shelves. "Go. Now." She shoved him in the direction of a hall. He cast a last, desperate glance toward the front doors, but the man with the sin-made shadow was already gone.

"Come *on*," said Kate, pushing him past the bathrooms and through the back exit, out onto the other side of the truck stop's tarmac. The UVRs rained down on them, and August winced, head pounding.

"I didn't *abduct* you," he said. "I saved your life. You're the one who decided to run."

"And you're the one who decided to come with me." Kate was already walking away. Away from the truck stop. Away from him. She disappeared around the nearest corner, and he forced himself to follow.

"We have to tell someone," he said, jogging to catch up. "We have to let them know you're okay."

"In case you forgot," she called back, "someone is still trying to *kill me*."

"They don't even have to!" August knew he had a

point. He was fighting to hold on to it. "This is exactly what they wanted, Kate. To blame my family for breaking the truce. And it's going to work if we don't—"

Kate spun on him. "What do you want me to do, August? I can't just go back—"

A set of doors burst open behind them.

"Hey, you," called a voice.

August and Kate both turned. It was one of the truckers from inside the store, a hard-looking man with a pistol hanging loosely from his fingers, a second, unarmed man trailing in his wake. August started to shift in front of Kate when another pair of doors flew open behind her, and two more figures spilled out into the pool of light. The man had a bat, the woman a knife, edge glinting in the glaring light. Beneath the UVRs, they cast no shadows—four more people, and none of them were sinners.

The ground tipped dangerously beneath August's feet.

He started to slide the violin case from his shoulders, hoping he could at least disarm them, when the first man moved, swinging up his gun and firing. The bullet ricocheted off the tarmac inches from August's feet. The sound was deafening, and for a moment he was back in a school cafeteria staring down at the small black tallies on the floor before Kate's voice brought him back.

"What the fuck is wrong with you?" she snapped at the man.

"Is it true?" said the trucker, his gun leveled on August's chest, but his gaze on Kate. "You're Harker's kid?"

"Does that make *you* the monster?" cut in the man behind him.

Before August could answer, the man with the bat caught Kate's wrist and dragged her toward him. She kneed him, and he went gasping backward, but the woman with the knife grabbed Kate and forced her back, shoving the blade beneath her chin.

August started forward, and the gun went off again, this time nearly grazing his cheek.

The woman with the knife smiled, her teeth half metal. "Finders keepers, boys. Reward's mine."

"Only reward you're gonna get is a bullet." August almost wished the man would follow through. He was having trouble staying on his feet, his focus swinging from the bat to the knife to the gun while the tension rose around them all like heat.

"Tell you what," said the man with the bat. "We'll take the girl, you can take the boy."

"I think we'll take 'em both," said the one with the gun.

Kate hissed as the knife pressed against her throat.

"How do you plan to do that?" asked the woman.

The air was humming now, the woman with the knife and the man with the gun locked in a kind of standoff; the man with the bat and the one with nothing but fists inching closer.

Their eyes were shining strangely, the way people's did when they spoke to August, greed and violence all starting to surface . . . as if they were feeding on his hunger. August's head spun; he knew he couldn't quiet the chaos as long as it was rising in him . . . but maybe he didn't have to. Leo knew how to twist these feelings in people, how to sharpen and focus them.

Mind over body.

Instead of fighting the influence, trying to rein it in, he turned the volume up, let it roll across the tarmac and over the men.

Kate must have also felt the shift in the air, in the attackers, in herself, because her eyes met his. Her fingers twitched, and an instant later he caught sight of metal in her palm.

"I'll take the bitch with the knife," said Kate, driving the switchblade into the woman's thigh. She shrieked, and Kate got her hands up and shoved the woman's arm, ducking out from under the blade. At the same moment, August lunged, knocking the man with the gun back as hard as he could into the one behind him. The gun went off, then clattered to the tarmac as the two went down, a foot away from where the others grappled and swore, knife and bat forgotten. August heard the rumble of an approaching truck, the short, sharp burst of its horn, and grabbed Kate's hand and ran. Shouts rang out after them, along with the sound of a body hitting pavement and muffled curses, but August didn't look back as he and Kate sprinted around the corner of the truck stop and across the glaring tarmac toward the open gate.

The truck pulled through, and the barricade began to close. The guards were turned away, eyes fixed on the darkness beyond the semi, and by the time they saw August and Kate coming, it was too late. They were out, and through, moments before the gate slid home and locked.

They veered off the light-lined road and into the fields, August straining to hear the sound of tires over his pounding heart, but the trucks didn't follow, the guards didn't fire, and the gate didn't open.

Still, they didn't stop. Didn't look back.

August lost track of the seconds, lost track of the fact that Kate's hand was still tangled in his, lost track of the fever and the pain. Was he crazy, or was it actually starting to fade?

They ran, cutting a jagged path through wild grass, past bunkers and lines of trees, and by the time they finally slowed to a walk and then at last a stop, they were alone, surrounded by nothing but darkness and the distant glow of the road.

Kate gasped for breath, pressing a hand to her wounded stomach, and August sank to his knees, fingers splaying in the cool, damp dirt.

He wanted to lie down. To press his cheek to the ground, the way Ilsa did, and just listen. Kate dropped to her knees beside him, her shoulder against his, and for several long moments they sat there, swallowed up by the wild grass. The night was so quiet, the world so calm; it was hard to believe there was any danger in it.

August caught the distant grumble of trucks and tensed, but the semis held to the road, none of them bold enough to venture beyond the safety of the light.

When they finally got to their feet, the first light of dawn was beginning to break across the horizon, turning the world a bruised purple instead of black. His vision swam, and Kate reached out a hand to steady him. "You okay?"

The question echoed in his head, rippling his thoughts like a stone in a pond, becoming an answer as it spread. *Okay. Okay. Okay.*

And it was crazy, it was impossible, but he *was*. The pain was thinning, his muscles and bones finally starting to loosen. He drew in a shuddering breath, shock mixing with joy. Leo was wrong. He'd done it. He'd come through.

"August?" pressed Kate. "Are you *okay*?"

"Yes," he said, the word filling his body and mind. It was the truth.

"Good." She had something cupped in her hand. She turned it toward the thin dawn light, and then started walking.

"Where are we going?" he asked, falling in step behind her.

Kate didn't look back, but the answer reached him, catching on the air and carrying like music.

"Home."

VERSE 4

FACE YOUR MONSTERS

1

For six years, home had been a house at the eastern edge of the Waste, far enough from the darkness that no one came, far enough from the nearest town that the lights didn't reach.

V-City was a place from the past, a place for the future, but Kate and her mother lived in the present. She wanted to remember it as boring, dull, restless, but the truth was, it was perfect. And she was *happy*. The kind of happy that smoothed time into still frames.

Arms wrapped around her shoulders while she read.

A warm voice humming while fingers braided her hair.

Wildflowers in vases and cups and bowls, wherever they would fit.

Color everywhere, and sunsets turning the fields to fire.

Somewhere else, the world was really burning.

Somewhere else, shadows had claws and teeth, and nightmares came to life.

But there, in the house at the edge of the Waste, it hadn't reached them. There it was easy to forget that the world was broken.

The only thing missing was her father, and even he was there, in the photographs, in the shipments of supplies, in the promises that soon they could come home.

After, she told herself a lot of things. That she'd always wanted to leave. That she was sick of the little house. That when she spoke of home, she meant the capital.

The sun rose against Kate's back, showering the fields ahead of her with light. Dew glittered on the tips of the grass, and dampened her pants from shoe to knee, and the world smelled fresh and clean in a way the city never did. August walked a few steps behind, and Kate watched the coordinates on the watch shift up and down, inching closer.

He was quiet, but so was she.

They skirted factories and storage facilities, each guarded as heavily as the Horizon, and caught the wary gaze of a haggard-looking woman standing outside a squat compound, checking to make sure she hadn't lost anything in the night. Midmorning Kate saw a skeletal town in the distance, light glinting off the metal roofs and outer walls. They steered clear, kept to the tree lines when there were trees and the tall grass when there were none. And the whole time, Kate kept her eyes on the watch, the numbers edging closer, closer, closer.

Up ahead, the woods came into sight. Memory flickered behind her eyes. The barricade of trees that looked dense but gave way to a smaller field, half a mile in.

And a house.

They crossed the tree line before Kate realized that she couldn't hear August's steps behind her anymore. She turned and found him a little ways back, running his fingertips thoughtfully over a chestnut tree.

"Come on," she called. "We're almost there." He didn't move. "August?"

"Shhh," he said, closing his eyes. "It finally stopped."

She walked back toward him. "What stopped?"

"The gunfire," he whispered.

Kate frowned, looked around. "What are you talking about?"

August's eyes drifted open again, his gaze fixed on the rough bark. "Leo was wrong," he said softly, his voice strangely musical. "He told me it was who I was, what I was, and I believed him, but he was wrong, because I'm still here." He broke into a boyish grin. She had never seen him smile, not like that. "I'm still here, Kate."

"Okay, August," she said, confused, "you're still here."

"The hunger hurt so much at first, but now—"

Kate froze. "How long have you been hungry?"

He just laughed. A simple, delighted noise that sounded so wrong coming from his lips. And then his gaze met hers and Kate caught her breath. His eyes were *burning*. Not just fever-bright, but *on fire*, the centers icy blue, the edges licked with gold.

It was like staring into the sun. She had to look away. *"August—"*

"It's okay," he said cheerfully, "I'm better now, don't you see, I'm—"

"About to set the woods on fire," she said, coming toward him with her hands up. "Why didn't you tell me?" She looked around, as if there might be a sinner conveniently waiting, but of course, there were no sinners nearby, because there were no *people* nearby. They were in the middle of a *fucking forest* in the middle of the *fucking countryside*. Kate closed her eyes, trying to think, and then felt a flash of heat and opened them to find August's fingers grazing her cheek.

"It's okay," he said gently.

She pulled back. "Your hand."

"My hand," he echoed, considering it. "It looks like yours but it's not because I'm not, I'm not like you, you look like me . . . but that's wrong isn't it—"

"August."

"—I look like *you*, but you were born and grew and I wasn't and then was, not like this, not exactly, smaller, younger . . . ," he rambled, a kind of manic energy rising in his voice, ". . . but I start from nothing and then all of a sudden I'm something, all at once, like the opposite of death, I've never thought of it that way. . . ."

She touched his forehead, jerked away. "You're really burning up."

He smiled, that dazzling, delighted smile. "Just like a star. Did you know that all the stars are burning? It's just a whimper and a bang, or a bang and a whimper, I can't remember, but I know that they're burning. . . ." She turned, and started pulling him through the trees. Heat wicked off him now, and flowed over her skin where it met his sleeve. "So many tiny fires in the sky, and so much dark between them. So much darkness. So much madn—" He cut off. "No."

"What is it?"

He jerked free, brought his hands to his head. "No, no, no . . . ," he pleaded, folding to his knees. "Anger, madness, joy, I don't want to keep going."

"Come on," whispered Kate, crouching beside him. "We're almost there."

But he'd started shaking his head, and couldn't seem to stop. She could feel the anxiety rippling off him like heat, seeping into her skin. His lips were moving, and she could just make out the words. *"I'm okay, I'm okay, I'm okay."*

She wrapped her arm around his waist to help him up. His shirt was slick and she thought it must be sweat, but the rest of him looked dry and when she pulled back, her fingers came away black.

"August," she said slowly. "I think you're bleeding."

He looked down at his body as if he didn't recognize it, and when he didn't move, Kate reached out and guided up his shirt. She could see the place where a bullet had graze his ribs. He touched his side and stared at the streak of blackish blood on his hand as if it was a foreign thing. The manic smile was gone, and suddenly he looked young and sad and terrified.

"No," he whispered. "This is wrong."

He was right.

Sunai were supposed to be invincible.

Nothing is invincible.

It had to be the hunger, somehow wearing away at his strength.

"Let's go," she said, trying to help him up, but he pulled her down instead. Her knees sank into the mossy earth, and his fingers dug into her arms. He was shaking now, the short-lived euphoria plunging into something else. Tears streamed down his face, evaporating before they reached his jaw.

"Kate," he said with a sob. "I can't keep going toward the edge—don't let me fall." His breath hitched. "I can't I can't do it again I can't go dark again I'm holding on to every little piece and if I let go I can't get them back I don't want to disappear—"

"Okay, August," she said, trying to keep her voice calm and even. "I won't let you fall."

He buried his burning forehead on her shoulder. "Please," he whispered. "Promise me."

She reached up, and stroked his hair. "I promise," she said.

They'd made it this far. They would get to the house. Cool him down. Get the money from the safe. Get the car from the garage. And they would drive until they found something—*someone*—for him to eat.

"Stay with me," she said, taking his hand and rising to her feet. "Stay with me."

Heat prickled through her fingers, at first pleasant, and then painful, but she didn't let go.

II

They made it to the house.

Gravel crunched beneath her feet as Kate half led, half dragged August across the field and past the over-grown drive and up the front steps. The blue paint on the front door had faded, the garden plants had all gone wild, and a spiderweb of a crack ran across a pane of glass, but otherwise, the house looked exactly as it had.

Like a photograph, thought Kate, edges frayed, color fading, but the picture itself unchanged.

August slumped against the steps as Kate scavenged under weedy grass for the drainpipe and the small magnetic box with the key hidden inside. She'd knock the door in if she had to, but it had lasted this long, and she didn't like the thought of being the one to break it now.

"Tell me something," murmured August, echoing her words from the car. His breathing was ragged.

"Like what?" she asked parroting his answer.

"I don't know," he whispered, the words trailing off into a sob of grief or pain. He curled in on himself, the violin case slipping from his shoulder and hitting the steps with a thud. "I just wanted . . . to be strong enough."

She found the box and fumbled to get it open. She didn't realize her hands were shaking until the sliver of metal went tumbling into the weeds and she had to dig it out. "This isn't about strength, August. It's about need. About what you *are.*"

"I don't . . . want . . . to be this."

She let out an exasperated sound. Why couldn't he have eaten? Why couldn't he have *told* her? Her fingers found the key and she straightened, shoved it into the lock, and turned. It was such a small gesture, but the muscle memory was overpowering. The door swung open. She knew the place would look abandoned, but the sight still caught her off guard. The stale air, the surfaces covered in dust, the tendrils of weed creeping up through the wooden floorboards. She almost called out for her mom—the urge was sudden and painful—but caught herself, and helped August inside.

Her feet carried her through the front room. She found the generator box in the kitchen, flipped the switches the way she had a hundred times, the gestures simple, automatic. She didn't wait for the lights to hum on but went straight for the bathroom with its warm blue-and-white tiles, its porcelain tub.

She snapped the shower on, praying the rain tanks still worked. There was a groaning sound in the pipes, and moments later, water began to rain down, rust red at first, but then cold and crystal clear.

August was there behind her, swaying on his feet. He set the violin case down, managed to get off his jacket and shoes before stumbling forward, catching himself on the lip of the tub. Kate went to steady him, but he threw out a hand in warning. The tallies were burning up his arm and back, singeing through his shirt. He dragged it off, and she saw four hundred and twenty-three white-hot lines blazing across his skin.

She didn't know what to do.

"Go." The word was a whisper, a plea.

"I'm not leav—"

"Please." His voice was shaking, heat rippling his hair like a breeze, and when he looked over his shoulder at her, the bones of his face were glowing white hot, while his eyes were turning darker, black pressing in on the flames. She took a step back, and August climbed into the shower half dressed, gasping as the cold water struck his skin and turned to steam.

She turned toward the bathroom door and heard a voice through the hiss and crackle of the shower, little more than a breath, but still somehow audible. "Thank you."

Kate's hand was throbbing as she ran it under the kitchen tap. It looked like she'd put it on a stove. It felt that way, too. All she'd done was take August's hand and not let go.

Anger, madness, joy . . . I don't want to keep going.

That's what he'd said in the woods.

Whatever he was going through now wasn't joy. How long had he been suffering? She'd noticed the temper, when the car broke down, but he'd managed to keep most of the madness to himself. The joy he couldn't. And now . . . the sound of his pained voice clawed inside her head.

I don't want to disappear.

She set the bloodstained spikes in the sink, cut the tap, and wove back through the house. The bathroom was clouded with steam, but August was no longer standing in the shower, and she panicked until she noticed his mop of dark hair cresting the wall of the tub.

I can't keep going toward the edge.

His eyes were closed, his head tipped back, his body dangerously still beneath the shower's stream as the water rose over his hips.

Don't let me fall.

"August?" she said quietly.

He didn't answer. Didn't move. Kate forced herself forward, holding her breath until August gave a small shudder. She exhaled, relieved by the subtle motion. His teeth were clenched, his eyes squeezed shut against the fire.

She watched as he took a breath, and went under.

He didn't come back up.

His bones had stopped glowing, easing the skeletal effect that made her think of Malchai, of monsters. Beneath the water, August looked so . . . human. A teenage boy, his long limbs folded up and his black curls floating around his face. She counted the seconds, watching the last of the breath leave his lips, wondering if she'd need to pull him out.

And then, at last, he surfaced.

He gripped the rim of the tub and dragged himself up, water streaming into his eyes. They were no longer on fire, but they hadn't returned to pale gray, either. They were darker, the color of charcoal, set too deep in his hollowing face.

Kate knelt and curled her fingers over his. His hand tensed beneath hers, but his skin had cooled enough to touch, and he didn't pull away. "Kate," he murmured, his vision sliding in and out of focus.

"I'm here," she said. "Where are you?"

August closed his eyes, took a long breath. "Lying on

my bed," he whispered. "Listening to music while my cat chews on the corner of a book."

Kate almost laughed. It was such an ordinary answer. His hand was getting hot again, so she let her fingers slide from his and sank back against the tub wall. Behind her, the shower almost sounded like rain, and she dug the silver medallion from beneath her collar, rubbing a thumb absently over the surface.

"Your house," said August tiredly, and she couldn't tell if it was a question.

"It was," said Kate, turning the pendant between her fingers.

A small, shuddering sigh from the tub. "Why are there so many shadows in the world, Kate? Shouldn't there be just as much light?"

"I don't know, August."

"I don't want to be a monster."

"You're not," she said, the words automatic, but as she said it, Kate realized that she believed it, too. He was a Sunai—nothing was going to change that—but he wasn't evil, wasn't cruel, wasn't monstrous. He was just someone who wanted to be something else, something he wasn't.

Kate understood the feeling.

"It hurts," he whispered.

"What does?" asked Kate.

"Being. Not being. Giving in. Holding out. No matter what I do, it hurts."

Kate tipped her head back against the tub. "That's life, August," she said. "You wanted to feel alive, right? It doesn't matter if you're monster or human. Living hurts."

She waited for him to say more, wondering why *she* no longer felt the urge to talk. Maybe she was finally out of secrets, or maybe she was just getting used to him. When she couldn't take the silence anymore, she got to her feet, stiff from the tile floor, and made her way down the hall to the first door on the left.

Beneath the film of dust, her bedroom walls were yellow—not sunflower yellow, but pale, almost white, the color of the sun, the real sun, not the one kids drew. The bed was narrow but soft, and there were drawings tacked up on one wall.

She rifled through the drawers and found an old journal and a few discarded pieces of clothing, things she hadn't bothered to take with her back to V-City. They were all too small, of course, but Kate had to get out of her ruined clothes, so she continued to her mother's room at the end of the hall.

The door wasn't shut all the way, and it swung open under her touch.

The room beyond was simple and dark, the curtains

drawn, but the sight of the bed, with its nest of pillows, sent an ache through her. If Kate closed her eyes, she could see herself sprawled on that bed, reading, while her mother playfully covered her with those pillows one by one.

She stepped slowly across the floor, over a weed growing up between the floorboards, and sank on the edge of the bed, ignoring the plume of dust. Beneath the dust, it still smelled like her mother, and before she knew what she was doing, Kate had curled up in the sea of pillows, burying her face in the nearest one.

Home, she thought, as the memory reached up and dragged her under.

They'd been back in V-City for four months, and Kate still couldn't sleep. Every night she dreamed of monsters—teeth and claws and crimson eyes—and every night she woke up screaming.

"I want to go home," she told her mother.

"We *are* home, Kate."

But it didn't feel right. It wasn't like the stories her mother had told her when she was growing up. There was no happy family, no loving father—only a shadow she hardly saw, and the monster in his wake.

"I want to go home," she pleaded every time she woke.

"I want to go home," she begged every time her mother put her back to bed.

"I want to go home."

Her mother was getting thinner, her eyes rimmed with red. The city was eating her, piece by piece. And then one night, she said, "Okay."

"I'll talk to your father," she promised. "We'll work it out."

The night of the accident, Kate was still dreaming, still trapped in a room of violent shadows, when her mother shook her awake.

"Get up, Kate. We have to go."

An angry red mark flared on her mother's cheek, a welt with an *H* in the middle, the echo of Callum Harker's ring where it had struck her face. Weaving through the darkened penthouse. A shattered glass. A toppled chair. The office doors sealed shut and sleep still clinging to Kate, tripping up her feet.

"Where are we going?" she asked in the elevator.

"Where are we going?" she asked in the garage.

"Where are we going?" she asked as the car's engine came to life, and her mother finally answered.

"We're going home."

They never made it.

Kate sat up. Tears were streaming down her face, making tracks in the dust. She scrubbed her cheeks with the back of her hand.

I want to go home.

The words had been hers. Always hers. She'd said them a hundred times. When had they gotten twisted, tangled, confused?

That plea, that night, her father's *H* bruised into her mother's skin . . . what else had she forgotten?

The accident spiraled through her mind, pieces fitting into the gaps. The sudden headlights, as if they'd veered into oncoming traffic—but they *hadn't*. It was the other car that swerved. And then her mother's gasp, her sudden jerk on the wheel as she tried to get out of the way. Too late. The horrible momentum of the crash, the sound of crushed metal and broken glass, and the blinding force of her skull meeting the window. Her mother, slumped against the wheel, broken lungs fighting for air once, twice. The world suddenly so still, white noise in her ears and blood in her eyes and, beyond the broken glass, her father's pet just standing there, his crimson gaze sharp and his mouth curled into a rictus grin.

Kate surged up off the bed, and retched on the old wood floor. She crouched there, forcing air into her lungs. How could she forget so much?

But she remembered now.

She remembered everything. And those memories didn't belong to a different Kate. They were hers. Her life. Her loss. And one way or another, she would have Sloan's heart.

Shaking, she got to her feet, steadied herself, and rounded the bed. She rolled the rug up with her shoe, fingers skimming the wooden floor until she found the lip of the loose board and shifted it aside. Nestled in the darkness beneath she found the metal case and lifted it free. She spun the lock, lining up the numbers until the case clicked open. Inside she found a clip of cash, a set of border papers, and a handgun. Her mother hadn't wanted to take it, but Harker insisted, so she had put it here, with the other things she didn't need. Kate pocketed the cash, checked the gun's magazine— it was full of silver-tips—and slid it into her waistband, tucked against her spine, before turning to the papers. She thumbed through the stack, hesitating when she saw Alice Harker's face staring up at her. She put her mother's papers back in the box, folded her own, and got up.

In her mother's chest of drawers, Kate found a dark sweater and when she held it up, she was surprised to see how close they were in size. Another reminder of how much time had passed. She set the sweater on the chest of drawers and stripped off August's jacket and the shirt beneath, cringing at the way her stitches tugged as she pulled on the clean clothes, the silver medallion warm against her bare skin. She closed her eyes and brought the sweater cuffs to her nose, inhaling the fading scent of lavender. Her mother had tucked it into all the drawers to keep the clothes fresh.

She found a T-shirt for August and slung it over her shoulder.

The bathroom was still quiet in that heavy way, so she hung the shirt on the door and went outside, padding across the tangled grass and ruined garden toward the small garage. The sun was already starting to sink, but the light caught on something in the distance, beyond the line of trees and back in the direction of the Waste.

Kate squinted.

It looked like some kind of warehouse, or an industrial barn. It was new—at least, it hadn't been there six years ago—but the whole thing was still, no smoke rising from the chimneys, no trucks coming and going, no perimeter. Either it had been abandoned or raided.

Inside the garage, she found the car. It had gone unused, even when they lived here, but her mom had insisted on having one, in case of emergencies. The day they returned to V-City, Harker had sent a small entourage to pick them up, so there'd been no reason to take it. She disconnected the battery from the generator and closed the hood. She tipped a gallon of gas into the tank and tried the door. It creaked, but came open, and Kate lowered herself into the driver's seat, and found the key tucked against the visor. She slid it into the ignition, held her breath, and turned. On the first try the motor shuddered. On the second, it started.

A victorious sound escaped her throat.

And then, as she turned the car off, she heard the rumble of a second engine. A distant truck. She held her breath and reminded herself that the main road lay on the other side of an incline and beyond the line of trees. She reminded herself that no one could see the house from there, but she still stayed in the car, gripping the wheel, until all she could hear was her heart.

III

August knew he was losing his mind.

The worst part was he could *feel* it happening.

The sickness had taken over his body, infecting his thoughts, and now he was trapped inside himself, caught in the haze like a dreamer trapped at the edge of sleep. He could feel the corner of the dream but he couldn't reach it, couldn't pull himself out.

He couldn't hold on to his words, either. They slid through his thoughts and out of his mouth and then they were gone before he could grasp their meaning.

The pain had faded for a while, smothered by madness and joy, but now the tallies seared across his skin again, pulsing hotly, and the gunshots rang through his head in a barrage of white noise. He pressed his burning forehead against the cold tiles, his skin hissing like doused fire as the cold fought against the fever.

His body finally cooled and he slumped back against the wall of the tub, letting the cold water rise over his shins, up his spine, closing over his ribs.

Kate came and went, her dark eyes floating in the steam, here and gone and here again.

She was here now.

"Listen to me," he said, trying to hold on to the words before they got away. "You need . . . to go."

"No."

"You can't . . . be here . . . when I fall."

Her hand on his again, one of them cold and the other hot and he didn't know which was which. Lines were blurring. "I'm not going to let you fall, August."

Again, the fear, the wrenching sadness. "I . . . can't . . ."

"You can't hurt me," she cut in. "Not as long as you're you, right? So I'm going to stay."

He clenched his teeth, closed his eyes, and tried to focus on his heart, his bones, his muscles, his nerves. Picked himself apart piece by piece, cell by cell, tried to feel every little atom that added up to him.

Every one of those atoms begged him to let go, to give in, to let the darkness wash over him. He felt himself sliding toward unconsciousness and forced himself awake, scared that if he went under now, something else would surface.

◈

Kate perched on the edge of the couch, a cigarette between her teeth.

She'd scavenged and come up with half a pack, her mother's old stash.

Those things can kill you, he'd said that first day.

Kate's lips quirked around the cigarette. She clicked the silver lighter, watched the flame dance in front of the tip, then put the fire out, and tossed the cigarette aside, unlit.

Plenty of other ways to die.

She clicked the television on, cringing at the sight of her face on the screen.

". . . the hours since Harker's press conference," the news anchor was saying, "there has been a rise in unrest along the Seam, and FTF and Harker forces have reportedly come to blows. We go now to Henry Flynn . . ."

The screen cut to a press conference. A slim man stood behind a podium, back straight.

A dark-skinned woman stood at his left, her hand on his shoulder—his wife, Emily. On his other side, an FTF with his arm in a sling. Thousands of task force members, and Flynn had picked a wounded one. Clever, thought Kate grudgingly, casting himself as the victim. Then again, he was: His son was missing, framed for a crime he didn't commit. Because of her father. Because of her.

"My family had *nothing* to do with the attack on Katherine Harker."

"Is it true you planted a spy at her school?"

"Is it true one of your Sunai is missing?"

"Is it true—"

Kate clicked the television back off, dug the cell from her pocket, and was halfway through a message to her father when a sound cut through her thoughts.

Tires. On gravel.

Her head snapped up. The sound had been muffled by the TV and the hiss of the shower, and by the time she got off the couch and looked out the window, the car was pulling to a stop out front. A man climbed out of the driver's side, young and lean in a black FTF cap. Kate tensed. A member of Flynn's task force? She tugged the gun from her back, and switched off the safety as the man climbed the steps, and knocked.

Her stomach dropped as she saw the handle. She hadn't locked the door.

"August Flynn?" called the man, and then, "Are you in there?"

Kate held her breath.

What was he doing here?

She hesitated. Maybe it was safe. Maybe he didn't mean them any harm. Maybe she could go with August to South City. . . .

The man started knocking again, and she began to creep across the living room, unsure of whether she was going toward the door or the hall. Maybe . . . but how had he found them?

The knocking stopped.

"Katherine Harker?" called the voice.

Her chest tightened.

"I know you're in there."

Her eyes were trained on the front door, so she didn't see the side table, the one she *always* used to catch her knee on. Her shin caught the wooden leg, and the framed photo on top fell facedown with a hard snap.

The handle began to turn, and Kate took off toward the hall.

She was halfway there when the door burst open.

August heard a sound beyond the shower.

A heavy beat. He thought it could be one of Kate's songs but there were no words, only the repetitive *Thud. Thud. Thud.*

August dragged himself into a sitting position. It hurt to breathe, hurt to move, but he was still here, still him.

He got to his feet, pants plastered to his skin with water, and swayed, then steadied himself against the tile wall as he turned the shower off, straining to hear over the pulse of the gunfire in his head. But beyond the harsh staccato, he heard his name, and then the sound again, and he realized it had the steady cadence of a fist against wood.

Thud. Thud. Thud.

He stepped out of the tub, feeling like his body was made of glass—one wrong move and it would simply shatter. He braced himself a moment on the edge.

"Kate?" he called.

And then he heard the crash.

The door burst open as Kate crossed the entryway. The man caught her around the waist, and the two went down struggling. He landed on top of her hard, wrenching her wrists over her head, but she got her knee up into his stomach, and then her foot, sending him back into the wall as she rolled over and up, and leveled the gun.

"Don't move," she growled, heart racing, but hands steady. His hat had fallen off, and his hair fell into his eyes, but not before she saw the ruined *H* on his cheek. Not FTF, then. One of Sloan's. "Put your hands up."

"Miss Harker," he said smoothly, half raising one hand, the other still behind his back. "I'm not here to kill you."

She cocked the gun. "Hands. Up."

"There's no need for this," said the man, but his eyes were hard, calculating. "Your father sent me."

Her eyes flicked from the hat on the floor to the scar on his forehead. "Bullshit."

"It was just a disguise," he said evenly. "In case the monster came to the door." An almost arrogant smile. "How else would I know your location, Miss Harker?"

"Why would he send you?"

"He was worried."

"And the scar?"

He tilted his head, hair falling aside to reveal the mark. "Quick, aren't you? Now put that down and—"

"Show me your other hand."

Slowly, smoothly, his hand emerged, holding a cell phone. "See?" he said smoothly.

"Put it on the—"

More tires on gravel. Kate glanced away for an instant, but that was all it took. The man lunged for her weapon, and she swung back toward him as his fingers brushed the barrel, and she fired.

The blast recoiled up her arms, and the sound tore through the room, turning the sound in her good ear to static. It wasn't a clean shot—the bullet took the man in the neck, burrowed a hole straight through into the wall behind him. The cell phone tumbled from his fingers, skidding across the floor as he clutched his throat, but blood was already spilling between his fingers and down his front, dripping to the wood.

Red.

Not the black blood of monsters, but the vivid red of human life.

His lips moved, but Kate couldn't hear, and by the time she could, it was too late. He took a single, staggering step back into the wall, and then the life went out of his eyes and he fell, a body before he hit the floor.

Kate couldn't tear her eyes from the spreading pool of blood.

It should have been like killing a monster.

It wasn't.

A shiver went through her, and then she heard a ragged breath, and looked up to see August standing at the mouth of the hall, soaking wet and doubled over in pain.

No, not pain.

Hunger.

"Kate," he gasped. When he dragged his head up, the light was gone. His eyes were wide and black. "What have you done?"

IIII

August's vision tunneled.

The shadows in the room were bending, peeling away from the walls and the floor and tangling together around Kate. Her own shadow writhed around her as she moved toward him.

"I didn't—he came at me—I thought—"

She reached for his arm, soul pulsing like red light beneath her skin, and he staggered back. Away, away, away.

He tried to make the words but they were stuck in his throat.

It felt like the gravity in the room was tipping, like any second the wall behind Kate would become the ground and he'd fall forward into her. But she just stood there, waiting, and all he had to do was reach out and grab her, dig his nails into her wounded shoulder and drag her soul to the surface and the pain would stop everything would stop and—

"Run," he pleaded as his flesh burned and his bones sang.

"August, I—"

"*Run.*"

This time she listened. She staggered backward into the door and sprinted out into the dusk just as a second car pulled up.

Kate skidded to a stop on the gravel drive as a black sedan blocked her way.

A Malchai she didn't know climbed out of one side.

And Sloan stepped out of the other.

His gaze tracked over her, his mouth drawing into a smile. "Hello, Kate."

The crashing car. That rictus grin. Those bloodred eyes.

She raised the gun. "What are you doing here?"

He spread his arms, as thin as wire. "I've come to take you home."

"My father didn't send you."

"But he *did*, Kate. Despite all the bad things you've been whispering in his ear."

Her fingers tightened on the gun. "I'm not going anywhere with *you*. You sent those monsters to kill me, didn't you?"

Sloan considered her. "And?"

"You said you didn't do it—"

His smile was vicious. "*I never said that.*"

Her father's words. *I questioned him myself. We both know he cannot lie.*

It hit her like a blow. Sloan couldn't lie, but Harker could.

"Oslo," said Sloan, addressing the other monster. "Go get the Sunai. I'll handle this."

The Malchai started toward the house, and Kate swung the gun and fired. The silver-tipped bullet buried itself in the monster's shoulder, and he snarled as black blood stained his shirt. Kate turned the gun back on Sloan, but he was already there, cold fingers vising around her wrist and wrenching the barrel up. "This game again?" he said dryly. "Did you really think you could turn my master against me?" An edge of disdain on the word *master.* He pulled her toward him, and her free hand went for the lighter in her pocket just before his fingers closed around her throat.

The moment they did, she drove the switchblade up into his wrist. Sloan recoiled at the silver, and she drew the knife free and tried to slash at his throat, but he was too fast, and before she could get in another shot, his fist connected with her jaw, and she went down hard, spitting blood into the gravel.

The lighter skidded out of reach, and cold fingers curled around her wounded shoulder as he forced her onto her back and wrapped both hands around her throat.

"Our little Katherine, all grown up."

She clawed at his wrist, but it was like fighting stone.

"You think you deserve a chance to rule the city? It doesn't belong to you, or Callum Harker—not anymore. Soon the monsters will rise, and when they do . . ." he leaned close, "the city will be *mine*."

He knelt on her wounded ribs and she tried to cry out, but there was no air. Her lungs screamed.

"You've made a mess of things," he went on. "Can't even die when you're supposed to. Even *your mother* could do that much."

She kicked and squirmed, trying to gain purchase, to get a leg up as her vision swam, tunneled. "I should kill you now," he said wistfully. "It would be a kindness. But—"

He slammed her head back into the ground, and everything went dark.

August stumbled into the bathroom. He fell to his knees on the tile, and pulled the violin case onto the floor in front of him, fumbling with the clasps as a shadow appeared in the doorway, its red eyes reflected in the mirror.

August wasn't fast enough—his fingers barely brushed the strings of the violin before a boot connected with his ribs and sent him hard into the base of the sink.

Porcelain cracked against his spine, knocked the air from his lungs.

"Well, well," came the Malchai's wet rasp, "not so scary now, are you?"

August struggled up onto his hands and knees, and crawled back toward the case, but the creature's boot came down on his wrist, grinding it into the tile floor. Pain flared through him, too bright, too human. Sharp nails hauled him up, and then he was flying backward into the wall so hard the tiles cracked, and rained down around him when he fell.

August tasted blood, staggering upright as the Malchai's hand closed around the neck of his violin.

No.

"Sunai, Sunai, eyes like coal," sang the monster, running a nail along the string. *"Sing you a song and steal your soul."*

August lunged forward, but at the same moment the Malchai wound up and swung the violin at August's head.

He tried to get his hand up to stop the blow, or at least save the instrument, but he was too late, and the violin shattered against his skull, turning the world to splintered wood and broken strings and silence.

||||

The world came back in pieces.

Concrete beneath his knees.

Iron around his wrists.

A shifting pool of light.

A metallic *tap tap tap*.

The echo of large, empty spaces.

The world came back in pieces, and so did August. For a moment he was terrified that he'd lost himself, but the pain in his head, the ache in his wrists, and the searing heat across his skin told him that he hadn't gone dark. Not yet.

He was kneeling on the floor of a warehouse, surrounded by glass and dust and a single harsh light, the edges so sharp that the space beyond registered as a wall of black. His arms had been wrenched up over his head. Pain flared around his wrists, and August could feel the metal chains cutting into the base of his hands, rubbing the flesh raw in a way they shouldn't be able to.

Where was he?

Where was Kate?

The tapping continued from somewhere beyond the pool of light, and when August squinted, the first thing he saw wasn't the glint of metal or the smudge of skin but the blazing red of the Malchai's eyes.

August fought to get his feet under him as the creature in the black suit stepped forward, a long metal bar dangling from one hand, its edge sharp, jagged, as if broken off from some large machine. The torn end dragged along the concrete with a screech, and August winced as the sound knifed through his head.

There was something strange about the monster. He was all bone, of course, but the lines of his face, the width of his shoulders, the way he carried himself, was almost human.

Almost.

August got one foot beneath himself before an electric droning started up and the chains overhead drew taut, dragging him the rest of the way to his feet and then onto his toes. He fought for purchase, his shoulders straining in their sockets. Since when did he feel the subtle tests of muscle and bone? His whole body felt fragile, breakable, and some distant part of his mind wondered if *this* was what it truly felt like to be human.

"August Flynn," said the Malchai, rolling the name off his tongue. "My name is Sloan."

Of course. Harker's pet.

"You know," continued Sloan, examining his fingers, which tapered into pointed nails, "you don't look very well." He leaned forward. "How long has it been since you fed?"

August tried to say something and realized that he couldn't. His teeth were jammed together, his mouth sealed shut with tape.

"Oh, yes, that," said the Malchai. "I know the power of a Sunai's voice. Especially if they turn. Leo and I have a bit of a history." A thoughtful pause. "You know, between your brother and your sister, I'm learning *so* much about your kind. But I'm getting ahead of myself."

A second pair of red eyes floated in the darkness behind him, but Sloan's attention was on the metal pole in his hands. He brought the bar to rest against August's ribs, where the bullet wound from the truck stop was leaking a single line of black.

"You're bleeding," he said, tone twisted into a sick pantomime of worry. "Isn't that strange?" The bar fell away. "You know, they say that Sunai are invincible, but we both know that isn't true."

Sloan wound up and swung the bar into August's ribs. The pain was shattering, and he could feel the bones threaten to crack, his consciousness fracturing around the blow. A groan escaped the gag. It felt like the tape was melting, fusing to his skin, the fumes choking his senses as he fought for air. His head swam.

"No, the hungrier you get, the closer you are to human. But close is not enough." The jagged edge of the bar came up beneath his chin, forcing his head up. "You can hurt, you can even bleed, but you just won't *die*."

The bar connected with August's collarbone, and pain exploded through his chest. He choked back a sob.

"You may be wondering," continued Sloan, taking the bar between both hands, "what I want from you right now, August."

He glared, trying to steady his breathing.

"It's really very simple." His red eyes danced like flames in his skull. "I want you to go dark."

The other Malchai, who'd edged forward to the rim of the light, shot Sloan a nervous look, but August felt ill.

Sloan's smile sharpened. "I think you know why."

August started to shake his head, and the bar connected with his ribs. An explosion of pain, and August bowed his head, trying to ground himself in it instead of being swept away. Nails dug into his jaw as Sloan dragged his head up.

"*Think*." He tapped August's forehead with a pointed nail, then drew it down through his left eyebrow.

The line of Leo's scar. It had never made sense, because Sunai didn't *get* scars. Not when they were flesh and blood. Which meant that when Leo got it, he hadn't been.

"*I* think," said Sloan in his slick wet voice, "that a Sunai's most powerful form is also its most vulnerable. I think that if you go dark, I'll be able to drive this bar right into your heart." And then Sloan leaned in, close enough that August could feel the cold rot of the monster's soul against his fevered skin. "In fact," he whispered, "I *know*, because I put my theory to the test last night. With Ilsa."

August's heart stuttered.

Bile rose in his throat.

No.

The darkness welled up, threatening to surface, and the Malchai hummed with pleasure.

"So many stars," said the monster.

Don't worry, little brother.

"I watched them all go out."

I'm not afraid of the dark.

"Right before I cut her throat."

When Kate opened her eyes, the world was still dark.

No, not just dark.

Black.

The heavy black of interior spaces without external light.

Her head was pounding and her throat felt raw from where Sloan's fingers had clamped around it. She drew a ragged breath and tasted the damp of abandoned places exposed to elements, the tang of metal and earth and stone.

A shiver went through her, and she realized she was sitting on a floor, slumped against a wall, both surfaces concrete, and cold was soaking into her back and legs. Metal pressed against her wrists, and when she tried to pull away, she heard the clink of steel on steel. Her hands were cuffed to something to her right. She turned until she was facing it and raised her hands, questing with her fingers, until she found a flat metal bar, like a piece of scaffolding. Kate pulled as hard as she could, but it didn't give.

She curled her fingers around the metal and hoisted herself to her feet, slowly, in case the ceiling was low. Three feet up, her cuffs caught on a crossbar, forcing her to stop, so she sank back to her knees, and followed the vertical line of the pole to the concrete floor, where it was screwed down with some kind of metal plate. She wasn't going anywhere with that. She twisted her head, straining to hear something—anything—over the sound of her pulse in her good ear. At first, there was nothing, but then, muffled by concrete and metal and whatever else stood between her and the outside world, she heard a voice.

Sweet, and smooth, and on the verge of laughter.

Sloan.

Kate gritted her teeth, torn between shouting his name until he showed up and staying silent until she had a way to *kill* him. As she listened, more sounds reached her, muffled by the walls between—a scrape of metal, a stifled groan of pain—and her stomach turned.

August.

August trembling in the hall, his black eyes wide with fear and hunger.

Get the Sunai.

Kate dragged in air, forced herself to focus. She had to get out of here. Her lighter was gone, lost during the fight, which meant no weapon, and no way to see what she doing. She didn't have anything to pick the handcuff locks, and—

Another muffled scream beyond the walls.

She cringed, fought back the shudder of fear. Somewhere a different Kate could be terrified, but *she* didn't have time, so she forced it down and felt her way back to the place where the pole was screwed into the floor. She felt four screws, all half rusted into place. The frame was solid enough, but if she could get the base free she might be able to torque it and slide the cuffs beneath the frame. She'd worry about getting them off later. Being handcuffed wasn't as bad as being handcuffed *to* something. Kate took a deep breath, and exhaled, her breath catching as another sob carried on the air.

She tried to turn a screw free, but it didn't budge. She pried until her fingers ached, twisted until her nails cracked.

Nothing.

She closed her eyes, and tried to think, her fingers drifting to the pendant against her sternum. Her eyes flashed open. She pressed herself against the bar until she could reach the medal's chain and dig it out from under the sweater's collar. It wasn't a very elegant gesture, but soon she got the pendant up over her head and wedged the medal's edge into the screw's groove, praying it was the right size. It fit. She twisted, as hard as she could. Twice her fingers slipped, skinning her knuckles raw.

But then, at last, the first screw began to turn.

And several curse-filled moments later, it came free.

One down, she thought. *Three to go.*

Sloan's voice rose and fell beyond the door.

She jammed the silver disc in the next screw.

A horrible thud, like metal against flesh, bar against *bone.*

She twisted, slipped, twisted again.

A stifled sob.

"Hold on, August," she pleaded as the second screw began to turn. "Hold on."

A drop of blood hit the concrete, viscous and black.

"There's only one way this ends," said Sloan, running a nail along the bar's jagged edge.

August tried to drag in air. The Malchai had struck him across the face, and blood was running from his nose and over the tape across his mouth. He was choking—on blood, on terror—and every time his vision slipped, he thought of Ilsa.

Ilsa standing in front of the window, fingers cracking the glass.

"So many stars."

Ilsa's reflection in the mirror, chin resting on his shoulder.

"I watched them all go out."

Ilsa lying on the floor of the traitor's cell, singing him to sleep.

"Right before I cut her throat."

His lungs ached. His vision swam.

Hold on, he begged his body.

And then an electric buzz filled the air, and whatever was holding August up disappeared. The chains went slack, and he crumpled, hitting the ground hard, his wrists still raw and wrapped in chains.

"Sloan," warned the other Malchai.

August tried to get to his feet, and failed. The warehouse twisted and blurred until it was a bedroom, an alley, a school. Someone was calling a name, his name, and then he was standing in the forest brushing his fingers against the trees and he could hear music, humming, and Kate looked back with a frown and then—

Pain exploded against his side, and he crumpled. He tried to roll onto his back, but the concrete was cold and rising over him like water and he was in the bath his fingers curled around the edge and Kate's over his while the water fell like rain and he was burning burning burning from the inside and the darkness was waiting waiting waiting just beyond the light.

Sloan was towering over him, all shadow save for those vivid red eyes. He raised the bar to strike, but as he brought it down, August's hands flew up and caught the metal.

Darkness curled up around his fingers like steam.

"Let go, August," said Sloan, putting his weight

behind the bar. Cold wicked along the metal, meeting the heat of August's touch. His grip tightened, his vision fixed on his fingers, wishing he had the control to slide between the forms like his brother.

Leo could turn a part of himself without losing the whole.

Because there was no whole left.

Nothing human.

Nothing real.

Somewhere beyond the pool of light, metal scraped across the concrete. August squinted and saw that the darkness wasn't solid after all. Massive objects loomed in the shadows, and a corridor branched off toward the noise, a pair of doors at the very end giving way to the paler dark of night.

"Oslo," said Sloan, still leaning on the bar above him. "Go see to Kate."

August's pulse pounded in his broken chest. *Run*, he willed her, even now.

The other Malchai turned to go.

"And *don't* kill her," added Sloan.

"Don't worry," smirked the monster, "I'll leave you some of—"

"You'll leave me *all* of her," warned Sloan. His tone was icy and slick, his dead lips tight over his teeth. Heat flared through August's skin.

"You can end this," said the monster, his attention back on the bar. And August knew he could, but he also knew that the moment he did, the Malchai would drive the metal down into his chest, and it would tear past what had been flesh, and what would be smoke and shadow, and into his burning heart.

And he would be gone.

Whatever he was made of—stardust or ash or life or death—would be gone.

Not with a bang, but with a whimper.

In with gunfire and out with smoke.

And August wasn't ready to die.

Even if surviving wasn't simple, or easy, or fair.

Even if he could never be human.

He wanted the chance to matter.

He wanted to *live*.

By the time Kate got the last screw free, her hands were shaking, and sweat was running down her face.

She yanked the screw out, grabbed the metal frame, and *pulled*.

It didn't move. She swore and wrenched, putting all her weight behind it, but the bar was still stuck. Exhausted, Kate leaned her head against the metal, and felt it slip forward off the base. Her breath caught in surprise, then relief, as she gripped the metal and *shoved*.

The bar ground forward, scraping over the concrete with a screech, and Kate cringed—so much for stealth. She managed to torque the bar enough to get the cuffs beneath, and scrambled to her feet.

Footsteps echoed in the hall beyond, and she held her breath, back pressed into the wall beside the door, wishing she had a weapon. Something. *Anything.* But she wasn't going down again, not without a fight.

The metal door slid open, casting a skeletal shadow into the room.

Thin light fell on the warped bar, the cast-off screws, the place where Kate *should* be.

The monster hissed and started forward, but something wrenched him back into the hall.

There was a choking sound, and the wet slick of a wound, and then nothing. Kate held her breath as a second shadow passed before the door, then disappeared.

In the distance, Sloan's voice echoed, sickly sweet.

Kate counted to ten, then peeled herself away from the wall and went to find him.

August was slipping, edges blurring into shadow. He lay onto his side, his face against the floor, and listened for the heartbeat of the world.

He didn't hear it.

But he heard footsteps. Soft, steady.

And then a shadow moved beyond the ring of light. He squinted.

It wasn't the Malchai.

It wasn't Kate.

It moved too slowly, its stride was too even.

The shadow drew itself together out of the darkness and became a man, tall and handsome with blond hair and eyes as flat and black as night.

Leo.

His eyes found August's, and black blood dripped from his fingers as he brought them to his lips in a command for silence. His expression was even, assessing, as he drifted silently forward to the edge of the light.

August coughed, tried to push himself onto his hands and knees as Sloan loomed over him, red eyes fixed and waiting.

Look at me, thought August tiredly. *Look at me.*

Leo stepped noiselessly into the light as darkness pooled beneath August like smoke.

A smile crept across Sloan's face. "It's over, little monster," he said, lifting the metal bar.

August braced himself, but before Sloan could strike, the pole was gone. One moment it was in his hand, and the next it was in Leo's, and then, in a single, fluid motion, his brother drove the metal up through the Malchai's back. Sloan let out a strangled scream and staggered forward, nails clawing at the jagged metal edge protruding from his collar as black gore dripped down his shirt. He spun toward Leo, but lost his balance, staggered, and fell to one knee.

"My brother's death," said Leo as Sloan doubled over, retching blood, "wasn't part of the deal."

Sloan's lips curled back, teeth bared as he tried—and failed—to form words. And then his body shuddered, bones twitching before he finally collapsed to the concrete.

August rested his forehead on the ground. Leo's shadow fell over him, and he rolled onto his back, and looked up, meeting his brother's gaze. For a moment, all he felt was relief. And then, for some reason, a prickle of fear. The look in Leo's black eyes wasn't shock, or vindication. It was disappointment.

"Hello, little brother."

Leo knelt, and tore the duct tape from August's mouth, and August gasped, choking on the cold night air. He coughed, spit black blood onto the floor. He tried to speak, but the words had no sound.

Leo tilted his head. "What was that?"

August tried again. "I said . . . ," he managed between ragged breaths, "what deal?"

Leo gave August a pitying look. As if it should have been obvious.

A deal with Sloan. A deal between two monsters who wanted to start a war.

"What have you done?"

Leo took hold of the chain around August's wrists and hauled him to his feet. "What needed to be done."

August swayed. "You . . . you told them about me . . . you sent me to that school and then you told Sloan I was there." He didn't deny it. "Does Henry know?"

"Henry Flynn has grown tired and weak," said Leo. "He is no longer fit to lead us."

"But Ilsa—"

"Our *sister* should have stayed out of the way." He shook his head. "Her loss hurts our mission, but I have hope for *you*."

August started shaking his head and couldn't stop. "You betrayed our family."

"They lost sight of our cause," he said, grip tightening on the chains. "The city needs us, August. Not just South or North. The *whole* city. Poison spreads. Violence spreads. *Everything spreads*. We cannot hide behind these truces and Seams, and wait. We are Sunai. We were made to cleanse this world, not hide and let it rot. We have a purpose, August. It is time you rose to it."

"Henry will never forgive you."

"I do not need his forgiveness. He is a *human*." Leo

sounded disgusted. "He cannot see beyond his own fear. His own desire to survive."

"You're just another monster."

August tried to pull free, pull *away*, but Leo didn't let go. "I am Sunai," he said. "I am holy fire. And if I have to burn the world to cleanse it, so help me, I will." He took August's face in his hand, a gesture that could have been gentle, but wasn't. A thumb beneath his jaw forced August's gaze up to meet his own, the black of his eyes at once flat and endless. "Where is she, little brother?"

Kate.

August saw the truth in his brother's eyes. Leo was going to finish what he started. He was going to kill her. But August couldn't answer what he didn't know. He shook his head.

Leo hissed. "You protect a *sinner*."

"To protect our family. Our city. Killing her will start a war."

A small, grim smile. "The war is already starting. And I'm not going to kill her, little brother. You are."

The first thing Kate saw was the body.

The second Malchai was slumped across from the open door, black gore dripping down its front where its chest had been torn open, the shield of its ribs shattered. Kate crouched and picked up a shard of bone, slick but sharp in her fingers. It wasn't a knife, but it would have to do.

She straightened, looked around: In one direction, beyond the warehouse's open doors, the night waited, an empty dirt lot giving way to fields. In the other direction, slumped in a pool of light, knelt August. August, bruised and bleeding, smoke trailing from him like a dying fire. Someone was standing over him, and at first she thought it must be Sloan, but as she drew closer, she saw the Malchai's body crumpled on the ground. And then she registered the new figure's height, the breadth of his shoulders, the glint of light on fair hair, and realized it was *Leo*.

Relief flooded through her at the sight of August alive, and Sloan dead, but then Leo hauled his brother to his feet, and she saw the pain written on August's bloody face, heard it threading through his broken voice as he pleaded with his brother, and tried to pull away.

Kate took a step back, and it must have been the blood-shined surface of the bone in her hand, or her movement against a still backdrop, but August's eyes found hers in the dark, and even from the distance she could see them widen, not with relief, but *fear*.

An instant later, Leo's head swiveled, too, his black eyes narrowing.

There was no kindness in that look. No mercy.

Kate stumbled backward and nearly fell over the body of the other Malchai as Leo let go of August and drew something from his coat. At first she thought it was a gun, the metal glinting in the pool of light, but then she saw.

It was an instrument. A flute, no bigger than his hands.

He raised it to his lips, and Kate drew in a breath, waiting for the music before she realized it was meant for her.

"Run!" shouted August, throwing himself at his brother.

The two went down on the concrete as Kate turned and sprinted out toward the night.

August was no match for Leo. He was too young, too hungry, handcuffed and broken, and the older Sunai threw him off and stormed out of the circle of light into the corridor. August struggled to his feet and surged after his brother with the last of his strength.

"Stop!" he called as Leo stepped out into the night. August stumbled after him, one knee buckling as he reached the doors. He dragged himself back up, but fell again as Leo lifted the flute to his lips, and played the first note.

A soft, sweet sound that whistled through the air like wind.

"No!" screamed August, trying to break the melody, but it was no use.

Kate was running, her hands up against her ears, but as soon as the music started, her steps faltered, slowed, stopped. Her hands slipped from her head, drifting calmly back to her sides.

"No." August tried to stand again, but couldn't. He knelt there, watching the red light drift to the surface of Kate's skin as she turned back toward them, Leo's music unmooring her soul and August's mind at the same time. When Ilsa had hummed, he felt peace. But when

Leo played, he felt like he was breaking apart, dissolving into darkness.

Which he was.

Somewhere beneath the heat and pain, he felt the scratch of a new mark, another day, four hundred and twenty-four, and none of it mattered because he was burning. Falling.

Kate's lips moved, and as she drifted closer, he could hear the words. Her confession.

". . . thought he was going to hurt me. I didn't have to shoot him, but it seemed like the easiest thing to do . . . He could have been lying. I've forgotten what the truth looks like. I don't know who to trust anymore. . . ."

"Let her go, Leo," begged August. "Please."

The Sunai stopped playing, and Kate stood there, a few paces away, her features lost beneath the blaze of light.

"Take her."

"No."

"Her soul is red."

"*No.*"

"You, too, have sinned, little brother," said Leo. "Sinned against your nature and against our cause." His words forced their way into August's fracturing mind. "You have such potential. Together, we will do great things. But first, you must atone. Now stand up."

August rose, shaking, to his feet. Darkness curled around his body and drifted like steam from his limbs. The tally marks across his skin were fading one by one.

I am not a monster.

"Enough, little brother."

I am not . . . his heart lurched in his chest.

"Give in to it."

I am . . . he could feel himself crumbling.

"Embrace your true form," ordered Leo, and his words rolled through August, sweeping away the last of his strength.

August knew that he was right, knew what he had to do.

He stopped fighting.

And as soon as he did, the pain dissolved, and the fire went out, and he fell down, down, down, into darkness.

Kate stood alone in the night, and felt . . . nothing.

No panic. No fear. Even when the music stopped, it kept playing in her head, twining with the light . . . the red light. . . . Did everyone have the same amount, like blood? There was so much of it. . . .

She heard herself speaking, but couldn't focus on the words, couldn't focus on anything but the man in front of her, and the boy behind him.

The boy knelt there on the ground, wrists bound, looking so hurt, so scared, and she wished she could give him her calm. The boy . . . who was he . . . not a boy, but a monster . . . not a monster, but a boy . . . and then the music finally began to fade, withdrawing from her head, and Kate's thoughts seeped together into a name.

August.

Why was August on the ground? And who was the man? Kate fought against the haze. Everything was far away, but her mind was shifting and sorting, finding order. It was Leo, standing before her, and August behind him. Only he wasn't on his knees anymore. He was getting to his feet, darkness wicking off his shoulders like steam.

And then, between one moment and the next, he *changed*.

His face went smooth, and all the tension vanished from his mouth and eyes, the weight falling from his shoulders. His head tipped forward, the black curls swallowing his face as shadows rolled across his skin. They spread out from his chest, spilled down his limbs, blanketed flesh and bone, and for a moment, he was nothing but a plume of smoke. And then the smoke drew in like a breath, began to shift and tighten, carving out the lines of a body, its edges traced with firelight.

Where there had been a boy, now there was a monster.

Tall, and graceful, and terrifying. The chains crumbled from its wrists, blew away like ash, and when it lifted its head, its black eyes gazed wide and empty, lightless, shineless, matte as the sky on a moonless night. Smoke trailed up over the creature's head into horns and billowed behind its back into wings that shed curls of fire like burning paper. And there, in the center of its body, cracking through the darkness like a smoldering coal, its heart pulsed with fiery, inconstant light.

Kate's eyes watered as she stared at the creature. She couldn't look away. The fire crackled and burned in the cavity of its chest, and its edges—limbs, wings, horns—wavered against the dark, and it was mesmerizing, the way the blaze had been in the chapel that night. A thing made, and then set free. That fire had started with the flick of a match, and this, this had started with a boy.

Leo stepped out of the way, and the creature craned its head toward Kate.

"August," she said.

But it wasn't him.

There was no August in its face, only shadow.

No August in its eyes, only ember and ash.

Kate tried to retreat, but under the monster's gaze, she couldn't. She was frozen, not from fear, but from something else, something deeper. Her body was no longer listening, not to her. The red light still danced across her skin, and she marveled at the way a whole life could be distilled into something so simple. The way a death could be folded into a touch.

The Sunai took a step toward her. It didn't move like other monsters, didn't twitch and shudder like the Corsai, or slither and strike like the Malchai. No, it moved like smoke, dancing forward on a breeze she couldn't feel. A song she couldn't hear.

Its hand floated up, fingertips burning. The heat

brushed the air before her, and the fear finally caught up. She tried so hard to pull away, to fight the hold of the red light wrapped around her skin. Tears streamed down her cheeks, but she didn't close her eyes.

"I'm not afraid of death," she whispered, meeting the creature's gaze as it reached for her. She didn't know if August was still inside, if he could hear her, if he would care. "I'm not afraid," she said, bracing herself for the Sunai's touch.

But it never came.

The Sunai took another step, but its hand swept toward Leo, its shadow fingers closing around his throat. Leo gasped in surprise, but couldn't pull away. He fought, clawing at the monster's grip, but its hold was unbreakable, its strength absolute.

"*What are you d—?*" demanded Leo, but then the creature's grip tightened, cutting him off. It leaned in, and whispered something in Leo's ear, and Leo's face went from shocked and angry to blank. Not still, or calm, just . . . empty.

Something began to rise to the surface of Leo's skin, not black like the Malchai's life or red, like a sinner's. What came to the surface of the Sunai's skin, Kate couldn't process. It was light and darkness, glow and shadow, starlight and midnight, and something else entirely. It was an explosion in slow motion, tragedy and monstrosity and resolve, and it swept over Leo's skin, and wove through the monster's smoke, tracing the outlines of a boy-like shape inside the shadow like lightning in a storm.

And then, like lightning, it was gone.

Leo's legs folded, and the Sunai sank with him, its hand still wrapped around its brother's throat. The Sunai knelt over the body as it turned to stone, and then ash, and then nothing. Kate stood, the red glow of her soul still hovering above her bruised and bloody skin, but its light was fading as it began to retreat back into the safety of her self.

The Sunai straightened, the last of Leo's body crumbling away in its hands. A single beat of burning wings, and the ash was gone, and the Sunai lifted its horned head and turned its gaze again on Kate.

It came toward her, crossing the space in two elegant strides. It raised its hand, and Kate closed her eyes at last, and felt the heat of the creature's fingers, not on her skin, but on the cuffs around her wrists. She blinked and saw the metal blacken and crumble under the creature's touch.

The Sunai looked down at her, its hand hovering in the air between them, edges wavering like smoke. And then, it shuddered. A single, animalistic shiver that rolled from horns to wing and down, through its body and into its feet, the darkness retreating like a tide, revealing black hair, and smooth skin, and gray eyes.

August stood there, barefoot and shirtless, chest rising and falling. His wounds and bruises were gone. So were the black tallies that had counted out days, months, years across his skin. And for a long second, his face remained empty, his features too smooth, his expression as blank as his brother's. He looked at her as if they'd never met. As if they hadn't fled together, hadn't fought together, hadn't nearly *died* together.

Then a small crease appeared between his eyes. The faintest edge of a frown.

"Are you all right?" he asked.

His voice was still distant, but there was something in it. A sliver of concern. Kate let out a ragged breath. She looked down at herself, her torn sweater and bloodied hands. "I'm alive."

A tired smile flickered across his face. "Well," he said, "that's a start."

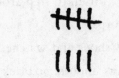

Nothing was different.

Everything was different.

They crossed the field in silence as the first signs of day seeped into the edges of the sky, Kate's eyes on the distant house, and August's on Kate. Her shadow danced behind her, restless, reaching for the world and pulling at his senses, a gentle, persistent tug.

He wanted to comfort her. And couldn't. There was this gap, where something had been, some part of him he couldn't reach. He wanted to believe it was fatigue, loss, confusion. Wanted to believe it would pass.

The house was as they'd left it. The cars on the gravel drive. The front door hanging open. The body in the hall. Kate fetched her lighter from the grass and stepped around the corpse, went into the kitchen. August padded toward the bathroom, where his violin lay splintered on the tiled floor, its neck broken, strings snapped. He forced himself to step around it, the way Kate had with the corpse.

He recovered his shoes and watched his fingers tie the laces. His skin was smooth, no black marks running up his arm. He ran a finger thoughtfully over his wrist.

Four hundred and twenty-four tallies gone.

Erased.

He straightened, his eyes drifting up the mirror. He searched his face, tried to remember the version of himself from hours before, the boy clutching the sink, desperate not to lose control, eyes wild and feverish, face contorted with terror and pain, every feeling sharp and terrible and *real*. He tried, but the memory was more like a dream, the details already fading.

"August?"

He turned to see Kate standing in the doorway, staring down at the wreckage of the violin.

"It's all right," he said quietly. "It's only wood and string." He'd meant the words to sound comforting, but his voice sounded wrong in his ears. Too steady. Like Leo's.

Something rose in him—a ghost of panic, an echo of fear—but then it settled.

Kate was holding out a black T-shirt. When he reached to take it, their fingers brushed, and he drew back sharply, afraid of hurting her. But of course nothing happened. His violin was strewn across the tile floor, and her soul was safe beneath the surface.

The shirt smelled of lavender, he noticed as he slid it on, the fabric soft against his cool skin.

"August," said Kate, her voice brittle. "Are you . . . okay?"

"I'm alive," he said, echoing her answer.

She wrapped her arms around herself, but her gaze was level. "But are you still . . . *you*?"

August looked at her. "I've been tortured, turned, and I just killed my brother. I don't know what I am right now."

Kate chewed her lip, but nodded. "Fair enough." She looked lost.

August ran a hand through his hair. "I have to go back to V-City, Kate. I have to see Henry. I have to help my family—what's left of it. Leo said the fighting has already broken out and—"

"I understand."

"There are two cars. I'll—"

"I'm going back, too."

August frowned. "Is that a good idea?"

"Probably not," she said, fingers closing around the silver pendant at her neck. "But I need to see my father," she said. "Will you come with me?"

August tensed. They'd come this far together, and he

trusted her, but the thought of facing Harker ... "Why?"

Her knuckles went white against the metal. "I need to ask him something," she said. "And I need to know he's telling the truth."

Kate Harker sat on the edge of her father's desk, watching clouds drift past beyond the window, low white streaks over the city. Her heart was pounding, and her whole body ached, but she was here. Where she belonged.

Harker Hall was a fortress; there was no getting in or out without being seen by *someone*.

Which was fine with Kate. She wanted them to know she was here.

Wanted *him* to know.

She'd done her best to keep August a secret, though. Told him exactly where to stand to keep him off the cameras.

And here they were.

It had taken four hours to drive back to the capital, and now the sun was at its peak, the city's monsters at their weakest. Music played from the penthouse's dozen speakers, the volume low but the beat steady. August had wanted something classical, but Kate had chosen rock.

She hadn't bothered to clean off the blood. Hadn't bothered to change clothes. In one hand, she held the gun Harker kept inside his desk. In the other, the silver pendant he'd given her the morning of the attack.

Kate had never been able to figure out how they found her that afternoon, in the bones of a building two blocks from the nearest safe house. Or at the restaurant. Or the house. It wasn't until she was prying the last screw from the metal plate that she understood. The pendant had cracked, the silver case splitting to reveal the chip inside.

Sloan had never lied.

But her father had.

The whole drive back, Kate had tried to figure out what to say. What to do. She knew she should have just run, but she couldn't, not without knowing the truth. Not without *hearing* it.

August was tucked back against the wall beside the door, arms crossed, his fingers dancing absently against his sleeve. His gray eyes were miles away when she heard the penthouse doors open, and a set of strong steps cross the wooden floor. A single set.

Even after everything, he was *still* underestimating her.

"Katherine?" called her father, voice breathless,

tinged with urgency, as if he'd just heard she was here, just heard she was safe.

"I'm in here," she called back, and a moment later he appeared in the doorway. His dark blue eyes raked over the scene, taking in everything except August, and relief swept across his face. It was almost believable. "What are you doing here?" he asked. "You should be at the house."

"I was," she said. "But Sloan came to get me. He said you told him to."

Harker's eyes went to the weapon resting barrel-down on the desk. "Where is he now?"

"Dead." Harker winced. She'd seen her father satisfied, and her father furious, seen him cold and calculating and in control. She'd never seen him caught off guard. "I told you I would do it," she said. "When I found the monster responsible."

"Sloan wasn't—"

"Enough," she said, lifting the broken pendant from the table. "I just want to know, was it his idea, or yours?"

Harker considered her. And then his lips quirked. It was a grim smile, humorless and cold, almost apologetic. And in that gesture, she knew.

"Why?" she asked. "Why break the truce?"

"The truce was failing. Without a war, the Malchai were going to rebel."

"What about the ruined brands? The monsters who clawed off their marks?"

Harker shrugged. "That was Sloan's idea, to shift the blame away from me."

Kate started. It was the truth, it had to be—but it was wrong.

Soon the monsters will rise, and when they do, the city will be mine.

She let out a bitter laugh. "You're a fool," she told her father. "Sloan wasn't *helping* you. He started the rebellion, and you played right into his hands."

The smile slid from his face. "Well then," he said dryly, "thank God you disposed of him." He took a step toward her. "You've proven useful, Katherine. You might be a Harker after all."

Kate shook her head in disbelief. "Blood means nothing to you, does it?"

Harker's face hardened. "I never wanted a daughter, but Alice did, and I loved her, and she said I'd love you. And then you came into this world, and she was right. I did." Kate's chest tightened. "In my own way. They say fatherhood changes a man. It didn't change me. But *Alice* . . . it *ruined* her. Suddenly you were all that mattered. All she could see. And in the end, it killed her."

"No," snarled Kate, gripping the gun. "*Sloan* killed her. I remember."

She'd meant to knock him off balance again, to watch the shock of the betrayal register. But it didn't. He *knew*. "She wasn't really mine anymore," he said coldly. "*My* wife wouldn't have tried to flee in the night. *My* wife was stronger than that."

She raised the gun and leveled it on her father. "Your daughter is."

His eyes narrowed. "You're not going to shoot me."

"You really *don't* know me, Dad," she said, pulling the trigger.

The sound was deafening, but this time, when the gun fired, it didn't take her by surprise.

Harker's body jerked backward, blood blossoming out from his shoulder.

And then, he grinned. It was a terrible, feral thing. "Not a true Harker after all," he chided. "My daughter would have shot to kill."

She squeezed the trigger again, aiming low; the bullet tore through Harker's left knee, forcing his leg to buckle beneath him. He gritted his teeth in pain, but kept talking.

"I thought it might work, you know. If you survived, if you never found out about Colton. It could have been the best of all worlds. Maybe we could have even been a family."

There had been a time when that was all Kate wanted. Now the thought made her sick.

"You're not a father. You're not even a man. You're a monster."

"It's a monster's world," said Harker. "And you don't have what it takes."

She trained the gun on her father's heart. "You're wrong," she said. Her voice was shaking but her hands were steady. But before she could pull the trigger, a shadow stepped in front of her, blocking her shot. "Kate. Stop."

Harker's eyes narrowed. "August Flynn."

"Get out of the way," warned Kate, but he stepped forward until the barrel of the gun came to rest against his ribs.

"No."

"*I have to do this.*" The words came out strangled, and Kate realized she was crying. She hated herself for crying. Crying was weak. She wasn't weak. And she was going to prove it. "He *deserves this.*"

"But you don't." August reached out and rested his hand over hers on the gun.

"It doesn't matter," she said. "My soul is already red."

"That was an accident. You were scared. You made a mistake. But this . . . there's no coming back from something like this. You don't want—"

"I want justice," she snapped. "I want judgment."

August brought his other hand to rest on her shoulder. "Then let me give it."

She met his eyes. They were pale and wide, and in their surface she saw herself, the self she'd tried to be. Her father's daughter. The tremor finally reached Kate's fingers, and she uncurled them from the gun, letting August take the weight, and then—

Movement over his shoulder, a flash of metal as Harker got to his feet and lunged.

He never made it. August turned and caught her father's wrist, wrenching the knife free and slamming him back against the wooden floor. August dug his fingers into Harker's wounded shoulder, and the man hissed in pain. August didn't seem to take any pleasure in the task, but he didn't release him, either.

"You should go, Kate."

"No," she said, but the truth was, watching Harker writhe beneath August turned her stomach. Her father had always looked like such a large man, but lying there, pinned beneath August's knee, pain making the red light surface on his skin like sweat, he looked weak.

"Please," said August. "Make sure no one interrupts us."

Kate took a step back, and then another. She met her father's eyes—dark eyes, her eyes—one last time, and said, "Good-bye, Harker."

And then she turned and left, shutting the sound-proof doors behind her.

◈

It took a long time for him to die.

August didn't draw it out, not on purpose, but the last of the man's life resisted, and by the time it was over, Callum Harker lay in the middle of the floor, his body twisted and his eyes burned black. Beyond the windows, the sun had started its descent.

Blood dripped from August's fingers as he straightened. He still hated the sight of it, and he did his best to wipe it off before stepping out into the penthouse.

Kate was sitting on the black leather couch, an unlit cigarette between her fingers.

"Those things will kill you," he said gently, not wanting to startle her.

She looked up. Her eyes were red, as if she'd been crying, but they were dry now. "That's why I'm not smoking it," she said. "Plenty of other ways to die." Her gaze flicked past him to the office doors. "Especially now."

She'd showered and changed and packed a bag, the handgun resting on top. Her blond hair was free of blood and grime, scraped back into a ponytail, revealing the silver scar that traced from temple to jaw. She was wearing all black, her nails freshly painted.

"You could come with me," he said. "To South City. We can protect you—"

But she was already shaking her head. "No one can protect me, August. Not in this city. Not anymore.

Harker didn't have friends. He had slaves and enemies. And now he's dead, you think they're going to let me go free?"

No, he didn't. Even with Sloan gone, the Malchai were rising up, Harker's system breaking down. It wasn't safe here. It wasn't safe anywhere.

They took the private elevator to the garage where she'd left Sloan's car. The sun was going down, and it wouldn't be long before someone went looking for Harker and found his body. She set the gun on the passenger seat, on top of the border papers and the cash she'd taken from the house.

"Where will you go?" asked August.

"I don't know," she said. It must have been the truth.

She hesitated in the open door, one foot in the car, one still on the ground. August produced a slip of paper he'd taken from Harker's desk, the corner tinged with blood. On it, he'd written the number for the FTF. The codes to access Henry's private line, since he didn't have his own. "If you ever need help," he said. She said nothing, but took the paper and tucked it in her pocket.

"Be careful, Kate. Stay"—he was going to say safe, but he changed his mind—"alive."

She raised an eyebrow. "Any advice on how to do that?"

August tried to smile. "The same way I stay human. One day at a time."

"You're not human," she said. But the words had no venom. She started to climb in, but he reached out and folded his fingers over hers on the car door. She didn't pull away. Neither did he. It was only a moment, but it mattered. He could tell, even through the haze.

August's hand fell away, and Kate pulled the door shut, rapping her nails on the open window. He took a step back, put his hands in his pockets. "Good luck, Kate Harker."

"Good-bye, August Flynn."

He watched the car pull away. And then he walked out of the garage and onto the street, toward the Seam, and South City, and home.

They saw him coming.

Word must have gone up from the moment he stepped into the compound, or maybe Paris had even called when he came through, because Henry and Emily Flynn were waiting when the elevator doors opened. Before he could say anything, they were there, pulling him into something more desperate than a hug. August sank against their grip and told them everything.

About Kate.

About Sloan.

About Leo.

He told them about Colton.

About running.

About leaving Ilsa.

About the Malchai.

And his brother's treason.

And his death.

He *confessed*, and when he was done, he sank to his knees, and Henry sank with him, and the two sat there on the hall floor, foreheads pressed together.

There'd been a fight, Henry told him, after August's call, and Leo had left, abandoned the Flynns and their mission for his own. They couldn't stop him.

August had.

"I thought I'd lost you," said his father.

You did, he wanted to say, but there was more of him left than there was lost, so he said, "I'm here. And I'm so sorry about Leo. About Ilsa."

"She'll be all right," said Emily, touching August's shoulder.

His head snapped up. "What?"

August felt himself choking on the hope of the words, and then the fear that he'd misheard. "But Sloan—"

Henry nodded. "It was a close thing, August. She got away, but . . . well, she got away. That's what matters."

"Where?" But he was already on his feet and heading past them, toward her bedroom.

He pushed the door open, and there she was, standing at the window with her strawberry curls, watching the sun sink over the city, Allegro watching from the bed. She was wearing a thin-strapped shirt, and even from the doorway, he could see her skin was bare, the thousands of stars that had once turned her back into a sky now gone.

"Ilsa," he said, breathless with relief.

And then she turned toward him, and August tensed—a vicious red line sliced across her throat. Sloan had told the truth, if not the whole truth.

He didn't know how the Malchai had gotten away with his life, but he was glad Leo had put a pole through the monster's back.

Despite the injury, Ilsa's face lit up when she saw him. She didn't speak, only held out a hand and he crossed the room and pulled her into a hug. She still smelled like mint.

"I thought you were gone," he whispered. Still nothing. He pulled away to look her in the eyes. He didn't know how to tell her about Leo. Ilsa had been the first Sunai and Leo the second, and Leo might not have loved her—or anyone—but she loved him.

"Our brother—" he started, but she brought her fingers to his lips.

Somehow, she already knew.

"I'm scared," he whispered against her hand. "I lost myself." And it was more than that, of course. He'd taken in the soul of another Sunai. Even now, it burned through him like a star. "I don't think it all came back."

She shook her head sadly, as if to say *it never does*.

Her lips parted, as if she wanted to speak. Nothing came out, but her eyes, those bright blue eyes, were full of words, and he knew what she would say.

Nobody gets to stay the same.

She turned back to the window, and looked out toward the city, and the Seam. Her fingers drifted to the still-cracked glass, and against the dark she drew a star, and then another, and another. August wrapped his arms around his sister's shoulders and watched her fill the sky.

ELEGY

Kate drove west.

Through the red, and yellow, and green of the city, through the Waste and the towns beyond. The car reached the border before the sun, and she handed the man the papers, and waited while he looked from page to her and back again—she'd pried off the photo of a smiling child from the upper corner, glued one of her school pictures from Wild Prior or St. Agnes, she couldn't remember which. Most of the details lined up, but according to the papers, she was Katherine *Torrell*. It was her mother's maiden name.

She kept her hands on the wheel, fighting the urge to rap her nails while the guard read through her details.

There were three more men at the border control station, one on the ground and two on elevated posts, each decked out in gear and artillery. Her father's gun was strapped beneath the driver's seat. She hoped she wouldn't need it.

"Purpose?" asked the checkpoint guard.

"School," she said, trying to remember which of the boarding schools was out this way, but he didn't ask.

"You know these papers don't grant you come-and-go privileges, right?"

She nodded. "I know," she said. "I'm not coming back."

The man went inside, and Kate tipped her head back and waited, hoping they would hold. Her eyes ached from tears, but they'd stopped falling hours ago, and her shades were down against the glare of the setting sun. The radio was set to a news station, a man and a woman talking about the mounting tension between Harker and Flynn. A riot at the Seam. The fact that Callum couldn't be reached for comment. She shut the radio off.

"Miss Torrell," said the man, handing back the papers. "Drive safe," he added, and she almost smiled.

"I will."

The gates went up, and Kate pulled forward, out of Verity, and into the world beyond. It was ten miles of buffer zone to the nearest crossroads. Ten miles for Kate to decide where she was going.

She switched the radio back on. The Verity news feed was already losing its signal, and a few moments later it crackled out entirely, surging up with a different voice in a different city in a different territory. Gone were the reports of North City, of the Harkers and the Flynns, and she drove on, half listening, until a line caught her ear. *". . . violent murders have people shaken and police stumped. . . ."*

Kate reached forward, and turned the volume up.

"Yes, that's right, James, disturbing reports out of Prosperity, where enforcement is still investigating a string of grisly murders in the capital, originally thought to be gang-related."

She reached the crossroads, and stopped.

Temperance to the left, Fortune to the right, Prosperity straight ahead.

"While the police refuse to release any details, a witness called the murders ritualistic, almost occult. The killings come in the wake of another attack last week that left three dead. Crime in the territory has been on the rise for several years, but this marks a frightening new chapter for Prosperity."

"Scary times, Beth."

"Indeed."

"Indeed," echoed Kate, hitting the gas.

August ran a finger over the single black tally at his wrist.

It was a new day.

A fresh start.

He rose, and dressed, but not for Colton.

He checked himself in the mirror, the dark fatigues hugging the slim lines of his body, the blocky white FTF stitched over his heart. His hair still fell into his eyes, but they were darker now, the color of pewter, and he found himself avoiding their gaze.

August sank on the edge of the bed, Allegro toying absently with his laces as he cinched his boots. When he was done, he lifted the cat onto his knees and looked him squarely in the face.

"Am I all right?" he asked, and Allegro looked at him with his massive green eyes, and cocked his head the way Ilsa did sometimes when she was thinking. And then the cat reached out, and rested a small black paw on the bridge of his nose.

August felt himself smiling. "Thank you."

He got to his feet. A case sat waiting on the stack of books. A gift from Henry and Emily. The violin inside was new, not polished wood, but metal, stainless steel, the strings heavy. A steel bow sat beside it.

It was a new instrument, for a new age.

A new August.

He took up the violin, nestled the cool metal beneath his chin, and drew the bow across the first string.

The note that came out was more than sound. It was high and low, soft and sharp. It filled the room with a steady pitch that vibrated like a bass through August's bones. It was unlike anything he'd ever heard, and his fingers itched to play, but he resisted, lowering the instrument, letting the bow slip back to his side.

There would be time to call the music.

Time to summon the souls.

With Harker gone, North City was already sliding. Malchai with the *H*s torn from their skin were attacking the Seam. Corsai were feeding on anything they could catch, even if it wore a Harker medal. The citizens were panicking. They didn't know how to find safety when they couldn't buy it. It was only a matter of time before the FTF would have to cross the Seam and step in.

And when they did, August would be with them.

He wasn't Leo, but without his brother's strength, his sister's voice, he was South City's last Sunai. And he would do what was needed to save the city.

He could be the monster, if that kept others human.

August had killed Harker so that Kate wouldn't have to. He hadn't relished the murder, but it wouldn't stain his soul, not the way it would have hers. It hadn't been just about the sinner in the end, it was about the sin itself, the shadow that ate away a human's light.

And August wasn't human.

He wasn't made of flesh and bone, or starlight.

He was made of darkness.

Leo had been right about one thing—it was time for August to accept what he was.

And embrace it.

❖

The house beyond the Waste lay empty, except for the corpse.

In the bathroom down the hall, the faucet still dripped into the half-filled tub.

The blue front door hung open on its hinges, and loose leaves blew in across the threshold.

The sun was going down, stretching shadows across the wooden floor.

Most of the shadows stood still, but one began to crawl, spreading like the pool of blood, now stiff, away from the body and up the wall. It stretched, and twisted, and drew itself upright, off the blood-flecked wall and into the room.

She was tall and thin, with pointed nails that shone like metal, and eyes that glowed like cigarettes.

The monster stepped over the corpse and wandered down the hall, into the bathroom where the pieces of a violin lay strewn across the floor. She toed the shards of wood, the broken wire, saw her reflection in the mirror, and flashed a smile full of silver teeth. In the bedroom at the end of the hall, she found a photograph of a man and a woman, with a girl between them. The man and the woman meant nothing to the Malchai, but the girl she recognized.

She took the photo and left, humming as she stepped

out into the dark, crossed the gravel path and the field beyond. The monster ran her hands over the wild grass as she made her way to the glint of the distant warehouse, following the scent of blood and death.

She found the first Malchai in the passageway with his heart ripped out. She stepped over him, and made her way toward the second one. He was lying in a pool of light, a metal bar speared through him, suit and skin and bone.

Suit and skin and bone . . . but not heart.

She cocked her head, considering, then took hold of the blood-slicked pole and drew it free with a wet scrape.

The Malchai didn't move.

Nothing, nothing, and then a sudden rattling sound escaped the monster's chest, and his red eyes flicked open. He sat up and spit a mouthful of black blood onto the concrete before tipping back his head and looking up at her.

"What is your name, little Malchai?"

She thought about it for a long second, waiting for a name to surface. And then it did, welling up like blood, and she answered, "Alice."

The Malchai's lips curled into a wicked smile, and he began to laugh, the sound ringing through the warehouse like a song.

ACKNOWLEDGMENTS

Every time I sit down to write acknowledgments, I freeze. Not because there are so few to thank, but because there are so many, and I know with increasing dread that the harder I try to remember them all, the more of them I will forget. With that in mind, I have taken to using broad strokes, but know that every single reader, supporter, friend, fan, has a hand in this book, and in every book.

To my mother and father. Ten books later, and you still haven't given up on me, or told me to get a real job. I promise never to put you in a book.

To my agent, Holly Root, for your steadfast support and serious hustle. You are the best champion, and I'm so glad that you're mine.

To my editor, Martha Mihalick, for being both a sharp editor and a lovely person, and for demanding the best I can give. It's an honor to work with you.

To my entire team at Greenwillow, from the designers to the marketing and publicity stars. To my UK team at Titan, from Miranda Jewess to Lydia Gittins and so many more.

To the six C's who keep me afloat, three on each side of the ocean. You are my buoys, my bests.

To my housemate Jenna, for somehow turning random ingredients into delicious meals, and for reminding me to leave the house.

To the incredible network of writers and readers in the Nashville area, for making this community a true joy to be a part of.

And most of all, to my readers. Through thick and thin, high and low, you're with me.

SUNAI, SUNAI,

EYES LIKE COAL,

SING YOU A SONG

AND STEAL YOUR SOUL.

READ ON FOR THE FIRST NOTES IN

OUR DARK DUET,

THE NEXT—AND FINAL—VERSE

IN VICTORIA SCHWAB'S

MONSTERS OF VERITY DUOLOGY.

IF YOU DARE.

Out in the Waste stood a home, abandoned.

A place where a girl had grown up, and a boy had burned alive,
where a violin had been shattered, and a stranger had
been shot—

And a new monster had been born.

She stood in the house, the dead man at her feet, stepped over
his body, wandered out into the yard, drew in fresh air as the
sun went down.

And started walking.

◆

Out in the Waste stood a warehouse, forgotten.

A place where the air was still full of blood and hunger and heat,
where the girl had escaped and the boy had fallen,
and the monsters were defeated—

All except for one.

He lay on the warehouse floor, a steel bar driven through his
back. It scraped his heart with every beat, and black blood
spread like a shadow beneath his dark suit.

The monster was dying.

Dying, but not dead.

◆

She found him lying there, and pulled the weapon from his
back, watching as he spit black blood onto the warehouse
floor, and rose to meet her.

He knew that his maker was dead.

And she knew that hers was not.

Not yet.

1

Kate Harker hit the ground running.

Blood dripped from a shallow cut on her calf and her lungs were sore from the blow she'd taken to the chest. Thank god for armor, even if it was makeshift.

"Turn right."

Her boots slid on the slick pavement as she rounded the corner, peeling onto a side street. She swore when she saw it was full of people, restaurant canopies up and tables out despite the brewing storm.

Teo's voice rose in her ear. "It's catching up."

Kate backtracked and took off down the road. "If you don't want a mass casualty event, find me somewhere else."

"Half a block, then cut right," cut in Bea, and Kate felt like the avatar in some MMRPG of a girl being chased by monsters through a massive city. Only this massive city was real—the capital at the heart of Prosperity—

435

and so were the monsters. Well, *monster*. She'd taken out one, but the second was heading her way.

The shadows wicked around her as she ran, a bitter chill twisting through the March night. It started to rain again, fat drops that dripped under her collar and ran down her back.

"Left up ahead," instructed Bea, and Kate bolted past a row of shops and down an alley, leaving a trail of fear and blood like breadcrumbs in her wake. She reached a narrow lot and a wall, only it wasn't a wall, it was a warehouse, and for a splintering second she was somewhere else, cuffed to a bar in a blacked-out room while somewhere beyond the door metal struck bone and someone—

"Left."

Kate blinked the memory away as Bea's instruction came again. But the warehouse's door was ajar, so instead she went straight, out of the cold rain and into the vacant space, her breath pluming.

There were no windows in the warehouse, no light at all save that of the street behind her, which only reached a few feet ahead—the rest of the interior was plunged into solid black. Kate's pulse pounded in her head as she cracked a glorified glowstick and tossed the bar into the shadows, flooding the warehouse with a high-density UV light.

The HUV stick had been Liam's idea. Just a kid with a high-wattage smile and thick glasses, but he was clever.

"Kate . . . ," chimed in Riley for the first time. "Be careful."

She snorted. Count on Riley to give useless advice. She scanned the warehouse, spotted the crates piled within reach of the steel rafters overhead, and started to climb, hauling herself the last of the way up just as the metal door rattled on its hinges. Kate froze in a crouch on the beam.

She held her breath as fingers—not flesh and bone, but something else—curled around the door, and slid it open.

Static sounded in her good ear.

"Status?" asked Liam nervously.

"*Busy*," she hissed, balancing on the rafters as the monster filled the doorway below.

For an instant, as it stood there, silhouetted by streetlights, she imagined Sloan's red eyes, his shining fangs, his black suit.

"Come out, little Katherine," he'd say. "Let's play a game."

But that was just her mind playing tricks on her.

The creature edging forward into the warehouse was something else entirely.

It had a Malchai's red eyes, yes, and a Corsai's sharp

claws, but its skin was the bluish black of a rotting corpse, interrupted only by the green dot of her tracking device embedded in its side. And judging by the bodies it left in its wake, this thing wasn't after flesh or blood.

It was after *hearts*.

Kate didn't know why she'd assumed the monsters here would be the same—this was a different city, after all, one with its own demons.

Verity boasted the highest crime rate in all ten territories—thanks in large part, she was sure, to her father—but Prosperity's sins were harder to place. On the books, they were the wealthiest territory by half, a robust economy rotting from the inside. If Verity's corruption was a knife, quick and vicious, then Prosperity's was poison—slow, insidious, but just as deadly. And somewhere, recently, the scales had tipped. Violence had begun to coalesce into something tangible, something monstrous; not in a wave, like Verity's, but a drip, slow enough that most of the city was still pretending the monsters weren't real.

The heart eater in the warehouse suggested otherwise.

The monster inhaled, as though trying to *smell* her, a chilling reminder of which of them was the predator and which, for the moment, was prey. Fear scraped along her spine as its attention panned side to side. And then up. To her.

Kate didn't wait.

She flicked a switch on her wrist, and UVR tracery lit up the edges of her jacket as she dropped down, catching herself on the steel rafter to ease the fall before landing in a crouch between the monster and the warehouse door.

She straightened, spikes flashing in her hands, each the length of her forearm and filed to a vicious point.

"Looking for me?"

The heart eater rounded, flashing two dozen blue-black teeth in a feral grimace. Each inhale was a shudder, each exhale a growl of *burntearhurt*.

The sweat on Kate's skin chilled.

"Kate?" pressed Teo. "You see it?"

"Yeah," she said dryly. "I see it."

Bea and Liam both started talking, but Kate tapped her ear, and the voices dropped away, replaced by the steady bass of music. It filled her head, drowning out her fear and her doubt and her pulse and every other useless thing.

The monster curled its long fingers, readying for a strike, and she braced herself—the first one had tried to punch right through her chest (she'd have the bruises to prove it).

"What's the matter?" she chided, her own voice lost

beneath the beat. "Afraid of getting burned? Or is my heart not good enough?"

She had wondered, briefly, in the beginning, if the crimes written on her soul would somehow make her less appetizing.

Apparently not.

The UVR tracery glitched, guttering for an instant, and in that instant, the monster lunged.

Kate was always surprised to discover that monsters were *fast*.

No matter how big.

No matter how ugly.

She dodged back, quick on her feet.

Five years and six private schools' worth of self-defense had given her a head start. But the last six months hunting down things that went bump in Prosperity—*that* had been the true education.

She danced between blows, trying to get under the monster's guard.

Nails raked the air above her head as she ducked and slashed the iron spike across the creature's outstretched hand.

It snarled and swung at her, recoiling only after its claws hit the UVR tracery on her sleeve and then the copper mesh beneath. The armor absorbed most of the damage, but Kate still hissed as somewhere on her arm the skin parted and blood welled up.

She let out a curse and drove her boot into the creature's chest.

It was twice her size, made of hunger and gore and god knew what else, but the sole of her shoe was plated with iron and the creature went staggering backward, clawing at itself as the pure metal burned away a stretch of blue-black flesh, exposing the thick membrane that shielded its heart.

Bullseye.

Kate launched herself forward, aiming for the still-sizzling mark. The spike punched through cartilage and muscle before sinking easily into that vital core.

Funny, she thought, that even monsters had fragile hearts.

They went down together, Kate on top and the creature below, its body collapsing beneath her into viscera and ash. She surged to her feet, holding her breath against the noxious cloud until she reached the warehouse door and slumped against it.

The song was ending in her ear, and she switched the feed back to Control.

"How long has it been?"

"We have to do something."

"Shut up," she said. "I'm here."

A string of profanity.

A few stock lines of relief.

"Status?" asked Bea.

Kate pulled the cell from her pocket and snapped a photo of the gory slick on the warehouse floor and hit SEND.

"Jesus," answered Bea.

"Wicked," said Liam.

"Looks fake," offered Teo.

Riley sounded queasy. "Do they always . . . fall apart?"

The litany in her ear was just another reminder that these people had no business being on *this* side of the fight. They served a purpose, yes, but they weren't like her. Weren't hunters.

"How about you, Kate?" asked Riley. "You okay?"

Blood dripped from her fingers, and sweat chilled on her skin, and she felt like shit, but Riley was human—she didn't owe him the truth.

"Peachy," she said, killing the call before any of them could hear the catch in her breath. The glowstick was fading, the warehouse plunged back into shadow, and when she switched off the UVR lights on her jacket, Kate was left in the dark.

But she didn't care.

The dark was empty now.